DRAGONFLY ILLUSION

Peter Bond

Dragonfly Illusion

ISBN 978-0-6487713-8-8

Copyright 2025 Peter Bond

www.pjbond.com

Cover design: Crayon & Maggot

DRAGONFLY ILLUSION

Peter Bond

PETER JAMES BOND, PUBLISHER

Also by Peter Bond

As author/creator:

Twenty-five Years (a memoir) * 978-0-9873470-5-3
Australian Commemorative Postmarks (4th ed.). 978-0-6487713-6-4
The Postage Stamps of Aden 1937–1968 (2nd ed.) ..978-0-6487713-4-0

As author/editor:

Irene Emily Louise Mutton ** 978-0-6487713-0-2
Bob – The Short Life of Robert John Mutton ** 978-0-6487713-5-7
Le Lion Rampant 1987–1990 ***

As editor:

The Spice of Life – by Eric Mutton ** 978-0-6487713-3-3

   *   out of print
  **   co-authored/edited by Graham Himmelhoch-Mutton
***   private edition: no commercial sales

For Bob

Prologue

An Unheard Silence 1996

The peculiar silence of a car after it crashes can be disturbing. Only the ticking of metal settling into its new form, or perhaps the dripping of unconfined fluid intrudes. Emergency vehicles' sirens eventually mask that silence, so it reigns only briefly. First responders never know it. Such was the case when a nondescript sedan skidded sideways off a wet Hampden Road and slammed into a large River Red Gum tree.

The first police officer on the scene quickly assessed the situation and mentally added two to the tally of car crash deaths he'd witnessed. He knew lifeless bodies when he saw them, but thought better of telling the medics not to bother hurrying. It wouldn't look good. More interested in the peculiar device hanging from the car's petrol tank, he pressed the call button on his radio.

'443 to base,' there was a momentary pause, 'get someone from E Section here, fast. Junction Victoria and Hampden. And backup. Area needs to be cordoned off.'

E Section had no permanent staff, but any officer with explosives training could be assigned to that group, and two were always on call. Officer 443 had correctly surmised that the curious apparatus was what they called a vehicle-borne explosive device. Regular officers would secure the area to keep curious onlookers, already gathering, at a safe distance.

Before the car crash that killed them, Roger and Jan Sugarman appeared to be a regular, middle-class couple. Comfortably installed in their conventional home in an ordinary suburb, even their friends matched the public persona that Roger wanted to project.

After the crash, those friends in particular, and the public more widely, weren't sure what to make of it. A local newspaper published a report in which a police spokesman made the mistake of calling the accident 'bizarre'. He revealed that had the impact with the tree not taken their lives instantly, the explosive charge fixed to the petrol tank of their 20-year-old Ford Cortina would have done the job only four minutes later. At least, it would have if the collision hadn't jammed the timer. A nameless bureaucrat reprimanded the public relations officer for releasing this information.

There was much speculation as to why two 'ordinary citizens' should be targeted in such a way. By the time the joint funeral was held, many were convinced that the Sugarmans were Russian spies or homegrown revolutionaries. Others insisted they were master criminals. The Victorian Police issued a press release saying that the Australian Federal Police, ASIO and the Department of Immigration and Ethnic Affairs had confirmed that Roger and Jan Sugarman were not persons of interest. No editor chose to publish that statement.

Newspaper interest eventually died away with the lack of new material. The press replaced the story with the softer subject of what would happen to the Sugarmans' eight-year-old son and only child, Jack. A close family friend organised a series of fundraising events. Jack's godparents adopted the young boy as soon as they could arrange it, but Jim and Angela Walker were not in a solid financial position. The community rallied around them, and within weeks – they were told public sympathy wouldn't have lasted much longer – a trust fund boasted a balance sufficient to ensure Jack's safe upbringing until he was 18.

The police determined the accident was just that, an accident. They ruled out suicide, putting it down to inattention, poor judgment or just plain bad luck. Official conjecture faded when an investigation into the explosive charge led offshore. An explosives specialist identified the material as RDX, also known as cyclonite. The expert reported that the Australian Army used a version known as RS-RDX, the prefix indicating, perversely, reduced sensitivity. When analysed, a sample of residue from the Sugarmans' car displayed a different chemical profile and 'wasn't manufactured in Australia.' To pad out the report, he added that Germany had patented RDX in 1898. Britain, the USA and Germany used it with striking effect during the Second World War.

The police found it difficult to find background material on Roger Sugarman. They could compile a picture of his work only with high-level clearance and assurance of strict secrecy. Roger himself had maintained confidentiality within the bureaucracy and in his private life. His official biography was a short one.

To anyone who asked, he worked in administration, which, for most, was sufficiently vague and dull to avert any further enquiry. If anyone persisted, he was a conflict archaeologist and 'you don't want to know' ended the conversation. Roger worked in a shady world of government investigation, answered to no minister and worked in no particular department. A committee directed his activities, or more accurately, the committee's chair. They rarely met, which suited Roger. He hated meetings. Written reports and the occasional phone call were his preference.

Officially, he was a special events coordinator with a team put together by a task force jointly managed by the offices of the Premier and the Governor. Occasionally, genuine events were attributed to his management skills. Roger insisted that such attribution was verbal only. He didn't want to steal other people's thunder.

His latest investigation was into what started as a routine cross-jurisdictional irregularity. His targets were often described as irregularities. It always meant illegal. This one involved four departments, three ministers, two government business enterprises and several contracts. Roger had identified 14 contracts having been awarded well outside Treasury directions. Many millions of dollars were involved, much of which the accountants couldn't trace. He had already delivered an executive summary of his findings but wanted a few more days to complete the full report. On the draft of that report, he'd scribbled 'Tears before bedtime.'

The crash investigation ceased after a month, and the case was suspended but not closed. Jim and Angela took to their new role as Jack's foster parents with dedication. Several sessions with a child psychologist seemed to help the youngster recover from the death of his parents. She suggested that a complete change of scenery might help even more. The Walkers agreed and moved from their Melbourne suburb to the more temperate climate of Tasmania. Jack quickly adapted to his new surroundings and school and easily made new friends, although he was just as happy spending hours alone with his books and stamp collection.

A few months later, the Walkers were surprised to receive a package in the mail from Stan Wright, a name they didn't recognise. It contained a letter and two heavily sealed envelopes boldly marked 'Jack Sugarman. DO NOT OPEN TILL AGE 18.' The letter identified the sender as a police officer who had been involved in a small way in the investigation of Jack's parents' accident. Stan was the officer who removed and catalogued the personal items from the wrecked car.

The letter read: 'It was mostly the usual stuff you'd find in a car, a street atlas, service logbook, a few receipts, box of tissues and such like. A few coins under the seats! But there was a briefcase as well. Inside was a folder with a long document but nothing to say who it was intended for, so we couldn't pass it on. I made a photocopy for head office to look at, but that never got sent on either. The original went to our secure evidence room.

'When the case was shut down, I read the report myself to help fill in a quiet night shift. It was probably his father's last piece of work, and I figured Jack might want to have it, but it's not the sort of stuff for a young boy. Actually, that's making rather light of it. Jack's father was investigating corruption in government and the public service.

'This might sound like a spy novel plot or loony conspiracy theory, but the more I read, the more I was convinced that someone wanted Mr Sugarman silenced. I can't take this any further myself, but maybe Jack will want to when he's old enough. The smaller envelope is a letter explaining what I'm telling you now but with more detail. You'll see I've marked it OPEN FIRST. The papers I copied are in the larger one.'

The letter ended by expressing the hope that the Walkers would keep the envelopes unopened for Jack and not simply destroy them. Angela was full of curiosity and wanted to open them there and then. Jim was more receptive to Stan's wishes, and after a lengthy discussion, the Walkers decided to honour the strange request. So it was that they secured the two envelopes in their deed box with their legal documents and sundry other papers. A short letter of reply to Stan confirmed they would indeed hold the documents and give them to Jack in 2006. It seemed so far away. They heard no more from Stan Wright.

Thirty years later, the unheard silence of the Sugarman's crash would become all too loud.

◆

Chapter 1

The Asquith Documents

An expected phone call never came, and his friend was late. His friend was often late.

'Always on a Monday,' Jack thought as he waited impatiently in the Blue Café. Only a good coffee helped alleviate his irritation.

Before his friend finally arrived, a nondescript chap wearing a Harris tweed jacket and flat cap and carrying a polished briefcase arrived precisely at eight o'clock. Jack had never seen him before and tried to determine his age but could only come up with 40-ish. Flat Cap paused momentarily to assess the geography of the place, spotted his quarry and shuffled, somewhat uneasily it seemed, to Jack's table near the window.

He ordered an espresso on the way. With the briefest pleasantries, he moved a chair to afford a view of the café interior, particularly the front door, and sat down. Uncomfortable not being in command of his surroundings, he had already established an escape route should that be necessary. It wasn't required this time, but he'd been caught out before. He produced a large envelope and slid it across the table, placing the briefcase on the floor to his left side, out of reach of passersby.

'Mr Sugarman, this contains some documents and photos and a USB drive. There's little point in a detailed briefing until you've reviewed this material, but I had to deliver it in person.'

'Very nice. Do you have a name?'

'I needed to see you to warn you.'

'Warn me? About what?'

Flat Cap shifted nervously and glanced out the window. The rain hadn't let up.

'There's nothing as specific as a vague threat, is there? Truth is, this material, this information,' he tapped the envelope and paused, 'is likely pretty dangerous to anyone who has it.'

'Wonderful, and you kindly thought I might enjoy that, did you?'

Jack tried to guess what the subject matter might be but almost immediately decided it would be a futile exercise. His orderly mind demanded more information, but he was pleased that there seemed to be plenty of reading. He liked a visual reference, even if it was primarily documentary.

Flat Cap's espresso arrived.

'Please accept my apologies for landing you with this. You're probably of interest to people you've never met and may never know. See that black SUV over the road? There are two men in that car. They may be watching me, looking for you, or maybe both. I haven't come across this pair before, but I know I've been under surveillance for a while.'

Jack eyed the SUV but couldn't make out either of its occupants.

'Is that why you're giving me this stuff?'

'I'm compromised. And this is too big for me now. I've lost the edge, but it's not a game we can afford to lose.'

The switch from 'I' to 'we' was intentional.

'We?'

'It's all in there.' He tapped the envelope again. 'Someone will contact you, probably tomorrow.'

'Come on, give me something here. What and who on earth are you talking about? The government? The police? I'd like to know where I'm starting from. How many letters?'

Flat Cap sipped his coffee, replaced the cup in its saucer and took up the crossword analogy, ignoring the 'what' half of the question.

'I don't know for sure, but I'll tell you this. It must be a group. I doubt it has any initials we've ever heard before, and I can guarantee it's not in your database, across or down.'

'My database is quite extensive. Maybe you know that.' Jack was fishing but suspected he wouldn't get anywhere.

'Extensive is rarely enough. Maybe you know that.' Flat Cap displayed a hint of a smile. 'It's all here, and my time is up.'

'All right, we'll play it your way. But tell me your name.'

'Oh, sorry, no secret there. Asquith, Derek Asquith, very pleased to finally have made your acquaintance, Commander Sugarman.'

Jack winced at the use of Commander, an honorary rank. He recognised his visitor's name and nodded. They'd had dealings before but hadn't previously met. Until today, Asquith had been content to provide information by email and post.

'Ah, so you're the secretive Mr Asquith.'

Asquith nodded, leaned sideways slightly and looked intently out the window again. The hint of a smile faded.

'Indeed, but,' still studying something of interest outside, 'I must away.'

With that, he downed his coffee and left the café, leaving a handful of coins on the counter.

Jack tried to take in what he'd just heard and realised it was pretty well nothing other than that he was now in some unspecified danger from someone unknown, for reasons unidentified. So, the usual. He also tried to assess the peculiar man, but gave up after determining his age, vaguely, as 50-ish. The contents of the envelope invited and menaced at the same time. He didn't notice his visitor cross the road, nor see him being bundled unceremoniously into the back seat of a second black SUV that neither had spotted. Mr Asquith's prediction that Jack's next contact probably wouldn't be himself may have been chillingly accurate.

The waitress, a young law student in her other life, smiled broadly as she delivered Jack's breakfast.

'Your usual Mr Sugarman, French toast, crispy bacon, banana and plenty of real maple syrup.'

'Thanks, Angie. I'd better have another coffee, too.'

'Sure, one double shot decaf almond cappuccino with butterscotch and easy on the chocolate sprinkles coming right up.'

It was a standing joke between them. Angie went to make his strong long black, and as usual, he spent a few pleasant seconds watching her alluring figure weave gracefully between the tables. Jack Sugarman's day brightened a little, even though the rain still showed no sign of letting up.

'It's settled in for the day, I reckon.'

This was the visitor he'd been expecting. The bearer of vague warnings and large envelopes was momentarily forgotten.

'Leon, mate, I didn't see you walk in.'

'I know, you were too busy perving on the waitress.'

'I wasn't perving. I was admiring her shoes.'

'Yeah, right. God hates liars, you know.'

'Never mind. Such is my fate. Anyway, have some breakfast. It's always good here.'

Angie returned with Jack's second coffee.

'What can I get you this morning, sir? I wouldn't have the raisin toast. They must have been standing on the mountain when they threw in the fruit today.'

'Raisin toast without raisins, eh. OK, I'll have a toasted brioche and some tea. Irish Breakfast. No, wait, Prince of Wales. Nice shoes, by the way.'

With a quizzical smile, Angie nodded and oozed back to the counter. This time, two pairs of eyes followed her on her short journey.

Leon Trapman and Jack had been friends since high school. He was sometimes called Leon Leon, a reference to his penchant for the music of Duran Duran.

'Heavy sigh, Mr T.?' Jack asked.

'Heavy sigh indeed, Mr S. Is this your briefcase?'

'What, ah, no, my first appointment must have left it.'

While devouring breakfast, Jack described his previous encounter, admitting to not knowing much about his caller. Derek Asquith might be his real name, but Jack called him Mr Nutter on the sound basis that he may be one. In his emails, he appeared confident and displayed considerable knowledge about subjects of which most people knew nothing. From this single meeting, though, Jack thought him somewhat awkward despite the obviously rehearsed presentation.

'He fancies himself as some kind of investigative whistleblower, always looking for a Watergate or something. He's really just a bit of a conspiracy theorist, but he has given me some useful stuff, as much by accident as design. So for that alone, I was glad to meet him.'

'Well, if he was the bloke wearing a flat cap, his friends didn't seem to have much time for him, judging by how he was shoved in that car.'

Jack dropped his fork with a clatter and sat up, alert. The envelope suddenly seemed far more interesting. Perhaps his Mr Nutter had stumbled onto something after all. He made an educated guess.

'Black SUV?'

'That's the one. Range Rover, I think.'

'Pass me that briefcase, will you.'

A quick inventory revealed another large envelope, another USB drive, a few personal documents, and a newspaper.

'That's odd.'

'What's odd?'

'This paper is two weeks old. Why would someone carry around a newspaper for two weeks?'

Leon ignored the rhetorical question. Angie brought his brioche and Prince of Wales. This time, Jack and Leon let the waitress retreat without a visual interrogation as they enjoyed their breakfast, and both hid their concern for Derek.

'So, what did you want to see me for?' Leon asked.

'Thought you might like a walk in the rain. No, it was about a case I'm about to take up. Do you still have your contact in IT? The hacker.'

Leon grimaced at the word hacker. 'If you mean Trousers, yes, I see him all the time. Why?'

'I'm looking into a tasty little share trading thing. Just need an expert technical opinion. That can wait a bit, though. No hurry. I'm only on it because of Sayer. It won't hurt him to practice a bit of patience for once.'

'Sayer?' Leon asked.

'You remember. The famous Detective Inspector Terry Sayer, Tasmania's finest. Finest according to him anyway. People call him D.I. Doom. We have a certain understanding that I don't quite understand. You know I get a pension, don't you?'

'Yup.'

'Well, it's not really a pension. Sort of a retainer. Sort of. See, technically, I took early retirement – very early – but technically, Sayer has some dirt on me. That's something you don't know. Anyway, it behoves me to take the odd case he can't handle. Or won't.'

'What dirt?'

Angie walked past. Jack paused.

'Damn fine shoes those, don't you reckon?'

'OK, you're not saying. But why do they call him Doom?'

'Partly because it's never good news when you see him, and partly because he hates it. Why Trousers anyway?'

Leon explained that Trousers' real name was Henry Ford, which he didn't like, and happily adopted the nickname when it emerged as a youngster. He was the first to wear long trousers in his group of friends. That those trousers were his older brother's cast-offs mattered not. He had other names, but Leon usually called him Trousers.

Investigating odd cases was something Jack liked to do, though. He called them varieties in deference to his stamp-collecting interest. They were often cases that regular authorities didn't much care about or wouldn't touch but couldn't let go. Some situations called for activities the police couldn't officially undertake or those a government didn't want to know about, formally or otherwise.

Commander Jack Sugarman was uniquely qualified – experienced, efficient, discrete and tenacious. He'd worked for the Navy, National Security, CIB, Serious Crime and at least one authority that didn't officially exist. He'd also taken on more than a few private cases.

His rank was entirely honorary, bestowed by the grateful president of a country with more admirals than capital ships. Telling the story of this particular adventure invariably resulted in a free drink or two, which adequately compensated for the hollowness of being called Commander by the few people who knew he held the rank.

In his field, information was a valuable commodity, and it paid to maintain a network of friends in the corridors of power and the back streets of commerce. Most of his friends weren't directors or highly placed officials, though he knew many. They were clerks, messengers, drivers, secretaries, IT people, and cleaners. In other words, the heart and soul of any organisation. Jack's friends were seen more often in the corridors than in the offices those corridors led to.

It was also helpful that he had accidentally become wealthy. Having decided to make a small share investment, he'd phoned an order to his broker only to have it, as he described it, 'stuffed up something chronic.' Rather than buying 20,000 shares in a mineral explorer called Blackaby, he received a contract note for 20,000 shares in Black Bay, a minor oil producer. He was the proud owner of a tranche of shares costing $1.50 each rather than 15 cents.

Before he could phone his broker to correct the mistake, he was involved in a road accident when a van, appropriately a black van, ran a red light and rammed his car. The car was a write-off, and for the only time in his life, Jack enjoyed the facilities of the nearest hospital and the benefits of private health insurance. The pain and discomfort were somewhat forgotten when, the following day, Black Bay announced a significant oil find that promptly tripled the share price. Within hours, a takeover bid had moved Black Bay to six dollars a share. So, an intended $3,000 punt on a penny dreadful had resulted in a $120,000 windfall and, courtesy of a carefully chosen insurance policy, a new car. It wasn't black. He told Leon an abbreviated version of the story as they finished breakfast.

'What did you do with the cash then?' Leon asked.

Jack enjoyed this part of the story.

'My broker phoned when I was in hospital, but I'd gone off Blackaby and told him to put my money into Southern Iron, you'd know it as the Big Sir, just for the dividends. Nice and safe. I think I said after the previous experience that it was the best option. When the order got to whoever was supposed to process orders, what I intended to be my original three grand in Southern became the whole lot, 120 large, in what they thought was the best option. That turned out to be a call option, deeply out of the money.'

'No idea what that means, Jack. Do I need more tea?'

'You need more tea. By the end of the day, I was down 20 thousand, and I thought I was set up to lose it all very quickly.'

'I think the Irish Breakfast.'

'By chance, commodities had a good day that night – does that make sense? – the company announced a profit upgrade, and there was talk of an exploration report showing significant results. Over the next several days, the shares rose very nicely. The options went up heaps, and then they went up heaps more. I chickened out when I was looking at $800,000 and sold half. The rest kept on going up and made me comfortably well off. Haven't touched the share market since. Of course, I have forgiven the bloke who stuffed up my orders. I've told you all this before, haven't I?'

Jack wasn't telling the whole story. He'd left a sizable sum in a discretionary account on the proviso that the broker who made his profits was to have sole responsibility for his investments. He was officially Operator 5, but he called himself Midas, and he continued to make serious money for over two years. Operator 5 then retired, sold up and moved to Barbados, or Bermuda, a week before the world's share markets started a lengthy decline. His timing was outstanding. By then, Jack Sugarman was a millionaire, having taken his profits safely out of the market. As far as his past employers were concerned, he was retired, but for purposes of the census and any casual enquiry, he admitted to being a master smoke grinder. If anyone ever asked what that was, he was ready to explain it was an acid etching process for printing detailed line drawings. But no one ever asked.

Angie returned with Leon's tea.

In government and public service circles, Jack's preference for dealing with his friends in low places was at first inspired by his dislike and mistrust of the alternative. He had worked closely with people in the higher echelons of power and found them to be, at best, only moderately competent and usually no more than occasionally reliable. The lowly clerk and humble receptionist carried out the business of government, if not with passion, then certainly with a higher degree of efficiency. Their bosses demanded more competence from staff than they could deliver themselves. Members of Parliament and very senior government officials, in his experience, were on the wrong side of that blurred line that divided the necessary business of government and the generally deplorable affairs of politics. Jack was often accused of being cynical. He preferred to think of it as a 'highly refined scepticism, carefully developed after years of objective assessment.'

Jack explained to Leon as he nursed his Irish Breakfast.

'The more senior the person, the less creative they are. They just rearrange what already exists or rehash an already failed program. No imagination, you see. I left every job I had because I kept seeing people coming in, full of the enthusiasm of youth, educated above their intelligence and promoted beyond their abilities. Time and time again, I was introduced to so-and-so, eager to please, robotically adopting a positive attitude towards any old crap dumped in front of them…'

'There's nothing wrong with being positive,' Leon chipped in.

'There is when you're presented with some "innovation", a bright idea that's failed already, sometimes twice. If at first you don't succeed, give up and don't be a Wally, I reckon. There are too many people in this business with too little experience. They're passionate, all right – how I hate passionate people – but they haven't got many clues. Take away their project templates, and they're utterly lost. Some of the drongos I had to work with. Honestly, you wouldn't feed them.'

'Not on the same page then?'

'Same page? Half of them couldn't find the library if you drew a picture and drove them to the front door. Anyway, set up a Trousers meeting, would you?' Jack grimaced slightly and added, 'That didn't quite sound right.'

Leon made a call. Trousers answered immediately, which meant he wasn't working on anything important. If he had been occupied, he was likely not to answer at all, and Leon would have to leave a message, which, just as likely, wouldn't be dealt with for hours or even days. After a preliminary exchange, he told his friend that Jack wanted to meet to discuss his share trading question. Trousers regarded discussions as consultations and offered noon at the usual rate, which was a free lunch. Leon passed on the offer to Jack, who nodded in agreement. They wrapped up the call with the further agreement that they would meet at the New London Arms, where could be found the finest selection of beers on tap in Hobart.

During the phone call, Jack scanned one of the Asquith documents. He handed Leon four neatly hand-written pages headed *The Evacuation of Skara Brae – 2,500 BC*.

'Here, read this. I'm going to add it to my *Dark History* files. Have to get in touch with this Asquith bloke, too. He'll want his briefcase back and I'd like to make sure he's OK. But first, I must visit what Americans insist on calling the bathroom.'

◆

This text is from an unidentified university magazine published by a campus literary group. It appeared as a contribution to an '800 words or fewer' short story competition under the title *The Evacuation of Skara Brae – 2,500 BC*. The copy I have is a badly faded photocopy. I later found an expanded version reading more like non-fiction. It was undated, so I can't tell whether it preceded the short story.

'Schama knew there was too much power. He knew, too, that he wasn't in control. Some elders doubted their understanding even before they realised their influence was ineffective. Warnings had been dismissed. They were the elders, after all, and would not be swayed by mere novices.

This was different, though. The dull vibrations were more noticeable; no one had heard the deep rumbling sounds before. It seemed disturbingly ominous. There was nothing more personally threatening than a general threat. Several nervous observers had already moved a prudent distance from the circle. One or two of the novices, eyeing an escape route, spotted a black dog observing them from a rocky outcrop nearby.

Schama reverently held the holy icon he always carried before him and walked into the circle. At the fifth step, he stopped. His knees buckled. Briefly, he knelt, dropped the relic to his side and fell forward without a murmur. No one realised that he was dead before he hit the ground. The sounds grew louder, and the younger men ran away. The remaining elders glanced at each other, shaken, then stared at their fallen companion.

The hard ground shook. Dust rose. Pebbles danced across the dirt, and larger stones moved aimlessly through a thickening mist. Schama's body writhed. As one shoulder sank, his head turned, and lifeless eyes stared at a darkening sky. Slowly, his body was enveloped into what was now a pulsing, eerily dry morass. Torn between comprehension and fear, the tallest elder threw his own holy cross into the seething ground. It disappeared instantly. Encouraged by this act of devotion, the others followed suit.

As the ground settled and stopped moving, the vibrations ceased, and the sounds faded. Mere minutes had passed, but it seemed time had stood still for the observers. An angry growl coming from the rocks broke the silence. Few noticed the dog until its anger was replaced by a persistent yelping as it ran off in pain, or fear, perhaps both.

The council had been intrigued, even mesmerised by their visitors' new knowledge, but now only feared what they could not understand. Some thought the gods were displeased and that this must be a sign of their anger. Several knelt in fervent prayer. Others silently followed the younger devotees who had fled earlier. Should they ever return, the visitors would not be welcome.

In the coming weeks, the elders placed a huge stone over the spot where Schama had been taken to Cob's underworld. Twelve smaller stones represented the remaining council members and marked the perimeter of the sacred circle. For years, the tale of the Taking was enough to persuade most to avoid the standing stones. Only the very curious, brave or the inebriated would venture into the circle of stones, and then only briefly.

In time, the younger children would treat the Tarken Stones as a play area. It was no more frightening than the nearby Glowing Tor, which provided a spectacular and harmless display of waving curtains of light every 11 or 12 years. Some years later, there was a second occurrence at the same place. This time, no one died, but the elders, recalling the first occurrence, decided that somehow, they had again offended the gods. It was time for the Skerra people to leave their ancient homeland. They moved to Big Island.

Imperceptibly, the tale passed into the half history of folklore, changing from time to time as storytellers modified details to suit their own prejudice for science, magic or sensational fiction.'

The dating of this story at 2,500 BC coincides with the generally accepted time that settlements on Orkney were abandoned possibly due to climate changes.

◆

Jack's *Dark History* was a collection of articles and stories concerning occurrences that neither science nor any other conventional rationale could explain. These were some of his *varieties,* and he relished them. While presented as fiction, the *Skara Brae* story earned its entry in his files because of the reference to a non-fiction version and particular elements in the tale that intrigued him. He wondered if it had won the short story competition.

◆

Somewhere outside the city, Derek Asquith was fielding questions. Some questions bordered on the bizarre and didn't warrant his free if unwanted, ride. He sat somewhat uncomfortably in a sparsely furnished office in a near-empty warehouse. The two heavily built men throwing questions at him displayed little patience. Based on their build and demeanour, Derek anticipated they would not be disinclined to use physically persuasive techniques in their interrogation. His answers were constructed to suggest to whoever these interrogators were that they had the wrong man.

He effected a graceless awkwardness that matched his appearance. He suspected that he'd been taken by the wrong side and could only hope they weren't convinced he was the right man. He'd handed over most of his information to Jack. Incomplete as it was, there was enough for someone with Jack's connections to reach what he suspected the conclusion must be. Leaving the briefcase behind, which he hadn't planned to do, might have been a happy accident.

'Who's your controller?'

Derek wondered if his captors had been watching reruns of *Callan*, but the word controller was a giveaway.

'Controller? What are you talking about? I'm a freelance journalist.'

'Bullshit. Controller. Name.'

'I have no controller. I work with editors. You must be confusing me with someone else.'

The larger man leaned forward. He adopted a tone of mock refinement.

'Ooh, confused am I? Do I look confused? I don't think so, Mr Asquith. Mr Derek Asquith, recently of Sydney by way of Melbourne.'

The aggression returned.

'What's your real name?'

'It's Asquith. Really. Derek Charles Asquith. Really. My parents preferred old-fashioned names. My brother is Eric John, and my sister Irene Emily. What chance did I have? Even their cat's called Graham. Our family is famous for it.'

The interrogator loomed even larger as he moved menacingly closer.

'OK, Mr Famous Family with a cat called Graham, tell me this. Who did you pass your famous files to? Other than famous Mr Sugarman, that is.'

Derek didn't show his surprise that they knew about Jack. He wondered if Jack was now in immediate danger from his kidnappers or whoever they worked for.

'What files?' was all he could think of to say.

Number two took over. The back-handed slap hurt like blazes but was quickly forgotten when he saw the second man open a smart-looking case.

'This is getting us nowhere. I'm using the drugs. Can't stand the smell of burning flesh.'

Derek's mind raced, and he guessed the equipment he'd seen under a tarp as his assailants dragged him to his seat was an oxyacetylene blow torch and gas tank. He also imagined a neat, clinically clean syringe. He decided drugs might be better than the burning flesh option. He needed to know which side was paying these two sadists.

'Look, you really have the wrong man. I haven't been to Sydney since the Olympics. I was a volunteer. Got a certificate somewhere.'

His tormentors appeared not to be listening. The syringe looked particularly threatening close up. He tried a long shot and pulled a name from the papers he hoped Jack would be studying.

'OK, OK, Southwood. His name's Southwood.'

'Go on,' the syringe thug demanded with more mock politeness.

'I don't know. Mr Southwood. He was always just Mr Southwood.'

Derek had encountered the name before. The first time led to an unpleasant experience, and it looked like today would be no different. It was a calculated guess that Southwood might be behind this interrogation. He hoped the two hired thugs would wonder if they might have taken one of their own people. Secrecy within their organisation sometimes worked against them.

All three exchanged glances.

The heavy with the syringe carefully replaced it in its little case and pulled out his mobile phone. Derek watched as he speed-dialled a number. There were no pleasantries when the call was answered.

'Mr Asquith,' he used the name with some respect, 'says he's working for Mr Southwood. What the bleedin' hell's going on here?'

Derek could hear a voice but not make out what was said. He thought it was an English accent, matching that of his interrogators. The conversation was virtually one-sided and lasted only a minute.

Syringe Thug put the phone back in his pocket, almost imperceptibly touched the side of his neck and nodded to his associate, who promptly and painfully secured Derek to his chair. Without the preliminaries of a sterile alcohol swab, he was injected in the side of the neck with a second syringe and rendered unconscious in a matter of seconds.

With frightening efficiency, the strange little man in the flat cap was removed from his familiar world. Both thugs knew there would be no lasting effects, but weren't about to let their victim know that.

◆

Chapter 2

The Dragonfly Blog

Back in his apartment, Jack dropped Derek's briefcase beside a chair and spent the rest of the morning going through his newly acquired material. Shortly before midday, he left for the 10-minute stroll to the New London Arms and his meeting with Trousers. The rain had stopped. The roads and footpaths were steaming themselves dry. He usually walked quickly, weaving between the slower pedestrians, intent on reaching his destination. Today, though, the improving weather dictated a more sedate journey. Jack's training and experience paid off within a minute, and he decided at least one man was shadowing him.

He could take a few routes to the pub and decided to go via the post office, where he rented a private box. Twice crossing roads unnecessarily and watching reflections in shop windows, Jack confirmed that just one man was following him at a constant distance. A black SUV also followed slowly but was beaten by traffic lights and then a one-way street. Jack made little effort to avoid him, figuring it might be better that his pursuer thought he hadn't been spotted.

Had anyone been asked to describe his pursuer, they would be hard-pressed not to say 'average'. Height, weight, appearance and dress were all unremarkable, ideal for a man wanting to follow another discreetly. Arriving at the New London Arms, Jack stopped at the bar close to the door. He had named his follower Trevor for no good reason and wanted to determine how good Trevor was in his shadowing role.

The New London Arms was popular with locals and tourists alike. Named after one of Hobart's oldest inns, now long gone, it was still one of the city's older licensed establishments. The building dated back to 1861 and was old enough to have stables, now used as a garage with disgracefully non-period roller doors. The current proprietor had to convince the licensing authority that, despite what the registered document dictated, they didn't need to employ an ostler and stable boy to tend to their guests' horses. There was no accommodation anyway, so there were no overnight guests. Some regulars called the hotel The Post Office, the bar was universally known as Moderation, and the little bistro enjoyed the nickname Gracie's. Grace was a cook there many years ago, affectionately referred to as Poison Grace, a punned allusion to her old-time elegance and reference to an unfortunate food poisoning incident involving some organic produce that turned out more organic than intended. Jack was always amused at the *Free Lunch: $20* sign on which someone had scribbled *+GST*.

He knew the girl behind the bar from many previous visits and asked for a pint of Guinness after a few words of greeting. The time it took for his drink to be poured provided an excuse to stay at the bar. As planned, Trevor entered while the stout performed its black magic, and Jack was able to study him while pretending to peruse the lunch menu. Jack concluded that he was about 25 years old, fit but not especially well-built, and took some pride in his dress and appearance, but not excessively so. 'European,' Jack thought. His clothes weren't quite typically Australian.

The Guinness settled into its familiar welcoming blackness, and Jack made his way to the rear of the pub where he preferred to eat. The girl behind the bar, unknowingly committing an act of secret revenge for Angie at the Blue Café, watched his departure, thinking, 'Hmm, nice bum.' Jack had no idea. While he regarded himself as ordinary, most women found him attractive. Men considered him good-looking too, in that any man might consider it at all, but not so much that they saw him as competition in social situations. He also had no idea what Trousers looked like but guessed the untidy man sitting alone at a table set for two was probably his target. He was in his late twenties, scruffy, well-built and looked more like an outdoors man than an IT expert. Jack surmised he could look after himself in a tangle. He didn't look like a typical nerd.

'You must be Mr Ford, I'm Jack Sugarman.' Jack thought he looked the worse for wear but made no comment.

'I guess I must be, not that I get called that very often.'

'Better known as Trousers, I understand.'

'Only by a few. It's Henry, but Harry to my family. My girlfriend calls me Steve, and others call me John. I don't know how all that happened.'

Jack was amused. 'I'm so pleased. There's no way I was going to call you Trousers, so Henry, you shall henceforth be Harry Steve John. Or Harry, for short. You don't have a drink. What's your preference?'

'I'll have one of those, cheers,' said Harry, indicating the Guinness. Jack caught the eye of a barman and pointed to his drink. The barman understood and nodded. Meanwhile, Trevor had settled himself at the bar with a light beer, and while pretending to occupy himself with his mobile phone, he closely watched Jack and his companion. He managed to take a few photos without being obvious about it. Jack noticed, though. He'd been trained to see such things.

Partway through briefing Harry on the share trading question, the second Guinness was presented with a degree of ceremony. The barman was a fan. Harry promptly pulled his glass closer and scribed the letter H into the foam with his index finger. He looked up, 'Sorry, I always do that.'

'No worries, won't change my life.'

Jack continued with his story just as the admirer of his posterior asked if they were ready to order. Neither had looked at the menu, but it wasn't an expansive document. After a quick scan, they almost simultaneously ordered the fish and chips with mushy peas. Jack asked if his follower at the bar had ordered any food. He hadn't. A toasted ham and cheese sandwich was added to the order.

Harry tried to come to grips with the issue.

'Let me see if I have this clear in my mind. The chronology might be important. First, we get a report of some stolen money. Then a report of stolen shares.'

'The shares were stolen first, then the money, only it wasn't really stolen,' Jack corrected him.

'OK, but the sequence of reporting wasn't the same as the sequence of events. Maybe that's not important. In any case, you say the shares weren't really stolen, just borrowed. How does that work? Sounds more like an irregularity than a crime.'

'It does, doesn't it.'

Jack had considered this, too. The case had been passed from one police unit to another and back again. Each had tried to liaise with the police of two or three other countries, found it too complicated, too big, or not in their jurisdiction, and finally handballed it to Tasmania for no apparent reason. Jack had seen the file in his capacity as a consultant, a title he relished as it covered everything but said nothing. His role in this enquiry was neither recognised nor acknowledged by any department of any government. He explained why he had the case.

'It's actually two cases, but I reckon they're linked – cause and effect sort of deal. I have a theory. Not quite sure which is which yet.'

'I like theories. Theories are good. Life gets interesting when you have theories. So give me the goss, and I'll let you buy me lunch.'

'One Thursday, the stock exchange computer system was hacked. After the close of trading, every sale of shares in the top 20 traded companies was redirected to the wrong client.'

'Buyers or sellers?' Harry asked.

'That's the odd thing. Every trade was registered to the wrong buyer. Just the one buyer, mind you, and if you think about it logically, a hacker would want the proceeds, not the shares.'

'But that couldn't work,' Harry suggested, 'The buyers would know when they didn't get their share certificates.'

'You don't get certificates these days. Both sides of a trade get a contract electronically and a statement from the share registry at the end of the month. The transfer of money and shares is computerised and automatic. Here's the clever bit, though. This all happened the day before Good Friday. First, pre-Easter trading is usually pretty hectic, and volumes are high. Second, the two working day settlement period is pushed out by the four-day weekend.

So, for nearly a week, someone had something like $6 billion worth of shares to their name. Now, this was never going unnoticed and the shares couldn't be on-sold anyway, but they could be used as collateral for a loan on the short-term money market. We don't have the actual numbers, but imagine that kind of money borrowed from a zero interest rate country like Japan and deposited with a higher rate country…'

'Like Australia?' suggested Harry.

'Like Australia, yes, interest rates are higher here. You're maybe looking at an easy profit of three to four million. Useful, eh?'

The fish and chips arrived. Jack noticed the toasted sandwich being presented to his follower, still at the bar, with the waitress saying, 'With Mr Sugarman's compliments.' Trevor adjusted himself on his stool slightly, annoyed that he'd been spotted. He nodded vaguely in Jack's direction. Harry didn't doubt the story's accuracy but wondered how such large sums could be transferred between countries without being tripped up on currency restrictions.

Neither Jack nor the local police knew the same thing had been pulled off simultaneously in several other countries. Commercial embarrassment, political humiliation, and national pride served to bring down a veil of silence around the world. Official information was as good as non-existent, and the little talk that circulated was either ignored or casually denied without explanation. No one ever found out exactly how much money had been made by this operation. It was in the tens of millions. Why Tasmania seemed to be ground zero was also unknown.

Jack was comfortable talking with Harry as both of them were inclined to activities that, put politely, were 'legally inconsistent'. Both considered the situation while demolishing fish and chips and enjoying their drink. Jack took the conversation to the next level.

'I believe you're one of the best hackers in the country. Can I say hacker? No offence meant.'

'None took. I also know others in the "best" category and some of the worst. Some of them are pretty good, but some of *them* are, shall we say, presently paying their debt to society.'

'In a disappointingly analogue way, no doubt,' Jack sardonically replied while checking a text message.

The two finished their meal while Jack filled in some details of his story.

'That was Leon. We're meeting again at my apartment. If you're still free, we can talk about this some more.'

They left the New London Arms, Jack settling the bill with a generous tip, enamouring himself even further to the girl behind the bar. As they passed Trevor, Jack couldn't resist a parting comment.

'We'll be back at my apartment soon. No need to be discrete about following me this time. Hope you enjoyed the toastie.'

Before Trevor had any chance to respond, they were out the door. They would never see Trevor again. He had already made a phone call, taking himself off the job, and would be replaced with someone who, he hoped, was better than he had been at discrete surveillance. Jack asked Harry to walk on slowly, saying he'd catch up with him in a few minutes. Ducking into a café bakery, he bought three pastries while watching for Trevor, who didn't appear.

Jack caught up with Harry, explaining his mission to buy some tasty comestibles and watch for his unsuccessful follower.

'No idea who he was or who he works for. He was German, though, I think. Spotted a Bayern Munchen badge on his jacket lapel. Bit of a giveaway.'

'Buy earn what?' Harry asked, puzzled.

'In English, Bavaria Munich, but usually called Bayern Munich in some half-arsed nod to the language. Bavaria is a state of Germany, Munich is the capital. Bayern Munich is a football team – soccer to you probably – in the Bundesliga.'

'Very observant of you,' suggested Harry, showing only slight concern.

The rain held off, and they walked casually towards the waterfront and Jack's apartment. He kept an eye out for another follower but saw no one. At Wellington Walk, a couple of tourists stopped them and asked for directions, saying this was their first visit to Hobart, but somehow, this part of town seemed familiar, as if they had been here before. Jack pointed them in the direction they needed, then enlightened Harry on this part of the mall sometimes being called Déjà Vu Lane or Boulevard, though the latter hardly applied for those obsessed with definitions. Many visitors experienced the same thing as Jack's disoriented travellers. That they were German tourists was not lost on Jack, who wondered about the coincidence.

Jack's apartment was a luxury penthouse, bought with the proceeds of his accidental millions. Despite its location on Davey Street, which was often busy with trucks and buses, double glazing effectively kept out the traffic noise, not to mention the sometimes icy winds blowing in from Antarctica. Jack bought the apartment after just a few minutes' inspection. The view over the waterfront was enough motivation to make the decision. When there was little activity on the water, it was relaxing and when busy, like today with much of the fishing fleet in port, that was relaxing too. Jack's father suggested he didn't know what hard work was. He responded that he knew only too well, which is why he chose not to do any but could sit and look at it for hours. This was taken in the right spirit, and the matter was never mentioned again.

They arrived at the door to find Leon waiting, and Jack ushered them into his private lift.

Leon spoke first. 'Hey, Trousers. You look like shit.'

'Yeah, well, I should. I've been up all hours trying to fix some moron's software cock-up. I don't know how these banks survive. I really don't.'

'Jack briefed you, I guess. Any ideas?'

After a cursory 'This is my place' tour, Jack made a large plunger of coffee and placed his pastries on three plates.

Harry adopted a thoughtful look.

'I have to tell you I already knew about this, but around the traps, it was thought to be just an urban legend in the making. You just confirmed it. I'd say it's doable. Not quite sure how you'd get around all the money transfer crap, but yes, technically, it's a piece of cake for the right bloke.'

'Piece of cake, you say?'

'Well, a nice pastry then.' He reached for an éclair. 'But a bloody complicated recipe. You'd need ingredients you've never heard of, but the short answer is yes, it can be done. Your next question will be, "Do I know who'd have the resources and contacts to do it."'

He paused, coaxing an indication of interest.

'Go on.'

'Well, I can give you three possibilities. One's supposed to be dead, the second found Jesus OS, and number three,' he paused again, 'number three is me. But it wasn't me. Too sloppy for me.'

Harry shared a similar personality to Jack. He was meticulous in his work and sometimes considered the process as important as the result. From what Jack had told him, executing this particular scheme would have needed too many people and too much precision for him to be happy with any plan he could devise.

'What about Jesus?'

'Last I heard, he was saving souls in Kenya or Uganda or possibly Florida. It's not him anyway. You don't want it to be him. He's a dirty player. Makes Vlad the Impaler look like a school bully. Take my word for it. It's got to be number one.'

'The dead guy?' Leon asked.

'He's been dead before, and he'll be dead again, eventually permanently, but till then, it's just a convenient way of avoiding unwanted attention. Being considered dead has advantages, provided you're not dead, that is.'

Jack repeated Leon's question.

'And the dead guy is?'

Harry and his hacker colleagues shared a loyalty. It was never defined but generally regarded as between the officer and gentlemen creed of the better regiments and honour among the better class of thieves. Most hackers were just larrikins out to cause mischief for no other reason than to see if they could. Some even managed to earn good money as IT security consultants. Others, though, were guided by that other great motivator, greed. This group gave the rest a bad name, or rather, a worse name. Generally scorned by the public, they weren't highly regarded amongst mainstream hackers either. Harry's loyalty was dictated by the hackers' peculiar version of ethics.

'The man you want,' he paused, 'I can give you an identity, but not a name. If you can ever find it, he puts out a blog under the name Dragonfly. And a number, which he changes all the time. The latest is 618, but they're random.'

'What did you mean by if you can find it?'

'Just that. You can hide a website from search engines if you want to by alternating servers, changing providers and using the Stealth Net Protocol. There's the dark web to deal with, too. So unless you have the latest URL and a password, you've got Buckley's. I've managed to get in a few times, but only a few. And I'm good,' he added modestly.

Harry detailed how he'd tried to out-hack Dragonfly but with minimal success. His blogs were cleverly written and gave few indicators to the person behind the name. No one could tell whether the clues were calculated red herrings or genuine, if unintentional, hints.

'As best as I can work out, your man is a heterosexual male in his twenties, well educated, English is his first language, lives in the southern hemisphere, likes good food and fine wine and is probably pretty well off.'

Jack took all this in but wondered how to start searching.

'Very Sherlock Holmes. Anything else?'

Harry explained how several clues if taken at face value, suggested that this mysterious hacker followed English soccer and Formula 1 motor racing. References to various names matched actual players and drivers. There was a cryptic reference to driving a Senna pod, which Harry took as a nod to Ayrton Senna. Chances are such a car wouldn't be a cheap sit-up-and-beg hatch but something worthy of the name.

'Anything more precise than southern hemisphere?'

'Well, yes and no. I'm fairly sure he lives in Australia. Don't think he's Australian, though. OK, I'm looking at yesterday's blog now… what?… ah… that's interesting. Give me a few minutes, will you.'

He took a bite of his pastry as Jack presented three coffees, neglecting to ask if anyone wanted milk or sugar. No one did. One of Harry's colleagues had managed to open the Dragonfly blog and copied the entries from the last few days for him. While he read, Jack and Leon took their coffee and pastry to the balcony and admired the view.

Jack indicated the fishermen hosing down their boats, cleaning up the week's worth of mess and making minor repairs.

'Those blokes could tell you how they know when the weather's going to be good for fishing. When there's almost no cloud cover, you'll sometimes see a wisp in front of the organ pipes early in the morning. Just a wisp. That's their cue. It'll be a nice day. Don't ask me how that works. I don't understand it at all. Not in Hobart.'

The organ pipes are collectively an impressive geological feature that dominate the high face of Mount Wellington, the otherwise modest 1,269-metre mountain behind Hobart. Tourists are often advised to ride the cable car or take the half-hour drive to the summit and enjoy one of the most spectacular views in Australia. Anyone visiting Jack was treated to this low-cost indulgence, snow and cloud permitting.

Jack knew, too, that some fishermen avoided certain areas of the estuary. They'll tell you there are no fish there. They won't say *why* there are no fish, but only because they don't know. If pressed – and encouraged with whiskey – one or two will relate half-true stories of deep holes and cold water sites. The Derwent is generally a cold river anyway. Even on warm summer days, a little depth provides enough chill to sufficiently cool the beer essential to engage in that popular pastime, recreational fishing. But this cold water is something else.

After two whiskeys, a talkative fisherman might tell you the 'deeps' get clogged with silt and weed and can't be found. Three whiskeys will tell you the tale of a foreign aircraft carrier that visited in the nineties. In trying to raise the anchor, the captain found it so firmly stuck in mud that it had to be abandoned, the chain cut and left behind. Divers sent to investigate reported it so deeply embedded in mud that it was 'not economically salvageable.' They also noted that the water was extraordinarily cold. The anchor was never recovered and is contentedly rusting away under a significant volume of the Derwent's finest mud. Anything after four whiskeys it just gets silly. The better fishermen will never let the constraints of fact stand in the way of a good story or a free whiskey.

Jack had heard many such stories. He trusted one fisherman in particular, Mick, who fancied himself something of an amateur astronomer. Mick told the aircraft carrier story many times, embellishing it occasionally with something 'just remembered'. On the last occasion, he 'just remembered' that this event occurred during a period of high sunspot activity. A week later, Mick was temporarily lost at sea; his boat capsized by a freak wave. He and his crew survived but spent a few days in hospital. His fishing boat *Hermes* was found a fortnight later where it should never have been, the hull curiously distorted. It was still afloat but overturned. *Hermes* was written off and sold by the insurance company for scrap.

Harry appeared on the balcony. 'Hey Jack, you got a tablet or laptop? I can't do this on my phone.'

Jack pointed to a drawer. 'In there. You'll need the power cord. The battery's buggered and won't hold any charge.'

Harry returned to his research, and Jack noticed a black SUV parked nearby. He couldn't be sure it was the same car that appeared twice in the morning but made a note of the number plate. Jack muttered 'Black Range Rover' to himself but let it go and returned to the kitchen. He asked Leon what he thought of the *Skara Brae* story.

'Yeah, not a bad little read. Not really my thing, though. Set back a bit too far. Why?'

Jack told him of similar stories in his *Dark History* collection.

'It looks like Harry's settled himself in for a while. I'll show you another one, more recent. Hang on.'

He delved into a drawer set into the base of a ceiling-high bookcase and returned with a sheaf of papers.

'This one isn't quite so old. Only a century ago. Have you heard of the Tunguska Event? 1908.'

'Sounds familiar,' Leon replied. 'Remind me.'

'This is one of the earliest stories I held on to just because it was interesting. At the time, I wasn't collecting and didn't record the name of the bloke who gave it to me. He was a Russian sailor visiting Hobart for one of the Wooden Boat Festivals. I wish I knew his name. It's one of my favourites and since going through the papers I got this morning, I see it in a new light. You might see why when you read it. Won't take long.'

Leon settled in an armchair, coffee in hand, and read.

◆

Only a few witnesses of the Tunguska Event of 30 June 1908 were ever interviewed. One such witness was Mikhail Krutovsky, who was 14 years old at the time. Little is known of Krutovsky apart from what he revealed in his interview, and that he was briefly a minor official in the Provisional Siberian Government and later the Provisional All-Russian Government.

That chaotic period in Russia's history is reflected in the jumbled accumulation of archives scattered around what is now the Russian Federation. There are suggestions that Krutovsky was involved in the White Movement until 1921. Apart from his interview, in about 1958, there are few references to Krutovsky in official archives.

No English language record of the full interview seems to exist, but fragments have survived. Only modern reprints appear. Krutovsky may have spoken Russian, although Evenki was undoubtedly his first language. With the discrepancies of twice translated documents, this is part of his story.

'My people are Evenks, from eastern Siberia. My family kept reindeer for milk, about 30, more than most in our community, but we were a large family. And horses, of course, we had horses. Everyone had horses. We hunted and fished and traded furs. Me and my brothers cared for the young reindeer in our encampments. They trusted us, not so much the others, but they trusted my family. No one knows why.'

Mikhail continued this preliminary to his story for a few paragraphs, clearly proud of his traditional way of life and the community spirit enjoyed in their semi-nomadic lifestyle.

'In the early spring of 1908, we had moved to an area west of Lake Cheko – the lake wasn't there then, of course – for the reindeer calving time. We always went there. Very nice land. On the last day in June, I was tending our herd and looking after the calves. They were very young, and some were still suckling.

The day before, the herd had been very unsettled, so I slept outside with them. They seemed to like me being there, but at sunrise, it was hard to keep them together. I remember the ground was very cold, colder than usual, I mean. I was sitting down eating – it was after eight o'clock – and I noticed many small animals running towards the south. Birds, too, all flying south.

A very bright light appeared in the sky, not the sun, but it created its own shadows. There were no clouds. I could see the birds very clearly.'

There are a few paragraphs about the reindeer's behaviour at this point.

'The light stayed there for 10 minutes but didn't move. It was like a tall jar (Probably meaning cylindrical. – ed.), but I couldn't see it very well. It was too bright. As I watched, the jar exploded, and there was a terrific bang, many bangs, like artillery going off. More than 10 times, 20, more. Bang, bang, bang. I thought the army must be nearby. The soldiers sometimes camped near Karelinski village.

'Then it got hot, very quickly it got hot. Cold ground, hot air. It didn't make sense, but so very hot. I took off my coat and went to the stream to drink. There was ice forming at the edges. Nothing made sense. Some of the reindeer ran off, but the new mothers wouldn't leave the young who couldn't walk well yet.'

Another gap in the story here.

'I was sheltering by the steep creek bank when the wind came. It blew harder than the winter winds but hot, so very hot. I couldn't hear the reindeer over the noise and later saw they had all been killed, blown away like the trees. All the trees were knocked over, all in the same direction – fallen away from the light. After this, my memory is not so good. 50 years ago.

'All my family was killed. All of them. My friends too. The whole encampment, all gone. They say no one was killed, but they don't care about Evenki. No one cared. I don't remember what I did next. I was 14 then. Don't remember much after that.'

There is another gap in the translated interview, and the story continues for later years.

'I was working with the Duma then when I met Leonid.'

The Duma likely referred to the Siberian Regional Duma and Leonid was almost certainly Leonid Kulik, a mineralogist who undertook a survey mission for the Soviet Academy of Sciences. This was the first known expedition to the site of the Tunguska Event. It was 1921. The event was commonly thought to be a meteorite strike, and the survey was primarily a search for a large crater. No such depression could be found, though many smaller ones were identified and thought to be caused by meteorite fragments.

Mikhail's story continued.

'He (Leonid) needed guides, and some Evenki hunters took him most of the way. They wouldn't take him all the way. They said it was an unlucky place, but it was because they were scared of the Valleymen. I found two new guides for him and joined the group. I hadn't been back since 1908, but still knew the way.'

'We found the trees still standing at the centre but with no branches, and the trunks burned. All dead. They were all dead. About eight kilometres across, it was like that. All dead. I took them to Lake Cheko after that. They didn't know about Lake Cheko. It wasn't on their maps. They only had old maps. It was a new lake. Something had fallen from the sky to make it, I think, something very big. There were no fish in it, though. No fish in Lake Cheko in those days. Plenty now.

'When Leonid finished his survey, I led him back to their camp and said goodbye. Then I tried to find where my family had been. I found the creek where I had sheltered, but everything else was all gone. No tents. Nothing there anymore. All gone. I never saw poor Leonid again, either. He died in the war.'

Mikhail told the interviewer – we don't know who that was – the rest of his life story, up to the late fifties anyway. He stayed in the general area but moved from village to village, never staying anywhere very long. His time in the civil service lasted only a few years. It is known that he never married and died in 1980, aged 86. Mikhail Krutovsky was possibly the last surviving witness to the Tunguska Event of 1908.

◆

When he'd finished reading, Leon realised he'd been so engrossed that he'd forgotten his coffee, which sat patiently beside him.

'Nice story, Jack. Bit sad. I'll tell you this for nothing. Lyn would want to read that. She loves that sort of stuff, and she's Russian too, I think. Or Hungarian. Something like that.'

Leon liked to think Lyn was his girlfriend, but she didn't know about that. Jack did. He photocopied the five pages and handed them to Leon.

'There you go. For Lyn. Good excuse for you to see her again. I want to meet her sometime, too. You mention her often enough.'

'I will if I can get hold of her, she's hardly ever at home. You know, you can see her place from here, up Mount Nelson on the bends. You'd need binoculars.' Leon gazed out the window. The road up the northeast side of Mount Nelson, which was hardly a mountain at all, was a narrow, winding affair called Nelson Road. Most locals call it the bends.

Jack doubted she was Russian or anything like it. Her surname was McKellyer, and Leon had never mentioned a husband, current or ex. He changed the subject.

'Harry, old son, what are you up to there? I don't have to delete my browser history, do I?'

Harry had been busy reading and, for the last few minutes busily working on the keyboard.

'Ah, yes, no, I mean. First, I've updated your operating system and some other software. It was about ready for a museum. No charge for that, by the way, unless you've got any more pastries.' Jack shook his head.

'Right then. The interesting bit. Seems the Dragonfly thing has blown wide open. It's been shut down, but not before my mate downloaded loads of stuff. I've copied some of it to your laptop – I see you call it Doctor Watson, think I know why – but the rest is encrypted. Encrypted bloody well, too. Might take me a day or two, but I'll get the rest to you sometime. Now your share scam thing. That was mentioned a dozen times, but a name kept cropping up. Southwood, sometimes South Wood, two words. Mean anything?'

Jack shook his head. 'No, nothing.'

Harry continued.

'So it could be a person, a place, an organisation, or a code word for something. Might even be a school. Doesn't help much, does it? Look, thanks for the lunch and stuff, but I have to nick off and see a man about a dog.'

Jack said he was about to kick both of them out anyway, as he had an appointment with Detective Inspector Sayer about the case he was on. He didn't know whether to mention the Southwood reference. Leon took his cue.

'OK, I know when I'm not wanted. See you around, eh.'

Jack showed them out, having first checked to see if the black Range Rover was still there. It was. He told Harry and Leon about it.

'When you get downstairs, take the back door through the guest car park.'

They did.

◆

Chapter 3

'What's the Joke, Terry?'

Before leaving for his appointment, Jack made a call.

'Billy, hi. It's Jack. I need you to check… yeah, another one. Fox Sierra 9866, black Rangie. I think I know what the answer is.' He waited for only seconds and heard what he expected.

'Cheers Billy, you're a champion. How's Sally? Good, good. I owe you a beer. Take care, mate.'

Jack knew that this series of Tasmanian car number plates ended in 2008 with the FS prefix and, thanks to Billy, also knew that several fake sets were circulating.

His appointment with Sayer was three o'clock and he arrived a few minutes early but knew he'd be kept waiting. Sayer kept everyone waiting. Jack thought he should have been a doctor for that reason alone. The opening riff from *Smoke On The Water* alerted him to a call. It was Leon, but 'Detective Inspector Sayer will see you now' intervened, precisely at three o'clock, before he could answer. He'd have to call back. The P.C. knocked and opened the door. 'Mr Sugarman to see you, sir,' she said and left, closing the door again. Jack liked the office. On the fourth floor, it had a view over the city towards Mount Wellington which Sayer enjoyed when on phone calls, which was often. A bookcase was full of titles on policing and detective theory, as well as many neatly labelled ring binders. One shelf held a small bronze bust of Sherlock Holmes, complete with the famous calabash pipe.

Jack sat down, uninvited. Sayer placed a file in his desk drawer and looked at him glumly.

'What's the joke, Terry?' asked Jack.

'Joke, Sugarman?'

'You never see me on time. It must be a joke. Or is it something serious? Go on, surprise me. You know how I like surprises.'

'This *is* something serious, very serious.' He paused as if carefully considering his next words. 'Look, I know we don't exactly get on, but it looks like we're going to work together on this, and it will be a lot easier if we both drop the hostility and try to, well, work together. Neither of us sees us as allies, but perhaps, in this case, we can at least agree to be co-belligerents. For the duration, as it were.'

Jack was amused at the 'co-belligerent' reference as he'd heard it used recently in a Winston Churchill documentary on TV. He suspected D.I. Sayer had watched the same show. Terry Sayer was considered a consummate professional by his superiors, based on his record for achieving a result practically on demand. He could seemingly meet any deadline within any budget but was as interested in looking good as achieving a good result. As far as Sayer was concerned, an arrest and a charge were all that mattered. A conviction was down to someone else. However, the high regard he was held in by the upper echelon of the force was not shared in the other direction. Some of the lower ranks thought him aloof and uncooperative.

Jack had worked with Sayer before and found his methods irregular. He knew he didn't want the share market case. He had no time for it, thinking it was outside his jurisdiction, but having failed to pass it on to any other agency, had been advised – which meant ordered – 'to get on with it, bring in a consultant if you have to.' Jack was that consultant.

If only for a more peaceful life, Jack was prepared to bury the hatchet.

'OK, it's a deal. No more fighting in the quadrangle, but no more of your infamous shortcuts, eh. We'll be the best of friends. Now, what's the goss? Sounds like you have some more intel.'

Sayer continued. 'Until yesterday, you had…' he cleared his throat, 'all the goss that I had. But that was yesterday.' He retrieved the file from the drawer but didn't open it.

'This isn't one case. It's many cases. The same thing happened in the UK, Ireland, Italy, Hong Kong, Germany, France, South Africa,

New Zealand, fourteen exchanges that we know of. Probably anywhere they have public holidays at Easter. Some countries aren't talking. Must be – no - *is* a global embarrassment. None of my guys can even guess how it was done. I'm thinking it's a one-off. The exchange tech blokes are working overtime to figure it out. Problem is they're not talking to each other. I guess some of them can't, anyway. Language barriers and that. We've never had to work with Italy before, and we don't have an Italian-speaking liaison.

'My commissioner wants you in because – these are his words – you're like a toothbrush that reaches parts others can't. Funny man, my commissioner.'

Jack raised his eyebrows, indicating he thought he wasn't funny at all.

'You can get away with stuff that we can't. Now, I'm not giving you a free hand, but we need a result, and we need it fast. I've been authorised to release certain documents to you.' He tapped the file. 'This is a copy. The originals are being scanned now for you. Remember, you've signed our confidentiality agreement. But there's something else.

'Our finance guys reckon this little exercise would have netted hundreds of millions. Australia is small fry. They've been trying to find unusual movements of money, big money I mean, but nothing. Whoever designed this did a good job hiding the cash. It's probably in God knows how many accounts. You have to wonder what's going to happen to it all. Maybe it's going to finance something even bigger.'

Jack hadn't known about the worldwide extent of the scam but wasn't surprised to hear of it. If it worked in Australia, there was no reason it couldn't work anywhere else. There were no clues about the size of the organisation. Their conversation was interrupted by Sayer's phone ringing. Annoyed, he answered it brusquely and swung his chair around, as he always did, and again admired the view over Hobart.

'Sayer. Yes, yes, go on, briefly, please.'

Sayer listened, saying very little. Jack took the opportunity to assess his co-belligerent's library and determined that he either read very little or very carefully. He maintained his own books in as-new condition and charitably decided that Sayer was a similarly inclined bibliophile. The phone call concluded as Jack was adjusting Sherlock's pipe, which wasn't sitting quite right.

'It always does that. A bit loose,' Sayer apologised.

Jack couldn't resist telling him that the calabash pipe was something of a furphy.

'You know that it was William Gillette who created the Calabash connection with Holmes? Doyle never mentioned it.'

'I did. It seems we have an interest in common, apart from detective work,' Sayer suggested. 'That call was some background stuff. It'll be in the material I'm getting for you. Have you got anything for us?'

Jack told him of Harry's thoughts generally, without mentioning his name, and said he was still reviewing it. He decided to share two things.

'One tip. In two parts. Have someone check your records. See if you have anything on Southwood, one word or two, and Dragonfly. I'm dead-ended on them for now.'

'Where'd you get those names from,' Sayer demanded, ever the policeman.

'Found 'em at the bus stop, Terry,' Jack replied, a standard response when he wanted to protect someone's identity. 'By the way, you'd have a contact in Traffic. Get them to keep an eye out for a black Range Rover, rego FS9866. It's a fake plate. I checked. Anyone in it might be handy with their size 10s, so tell your boys to watch out.'

Sayer raised a quizzical eyebrow.

'Been following me about,' Jack continued. 'They could be German. If I'm right, they'll probably have diplomatic passports, but they'll be fake too, I reckon.'

Jack left the building, having been handed a USB drive by the same constable who had shown him into Sayer's office. He noted her ID tag, P.C. Blackman, and decided the easiest way to remember her name would be by association. Honor Blackman of *The Avengers* TV show would achieve that. He also tried to imagine what she would look like out of uniform and with her hair down. Walking back to his apartment, Jack remembered Leon's phone call. He would call back later. On the way back to his apartment, Jack spotted the two German tourists he had assisted earlier. The man was taking photos and appeared to recognise Jack from their brief encounter. He waved. Jack waved back. 'Germans', he said to himself and again wondered about the coincidence. There couldn't be many German tourists in Hobart on any given day. He contrived to walk by them as they hovered around the docks, photographing the fishing boats.

'Good afternoon, again. Did you find what you were looking for? I directed you to the Botanical Gardens earlier.'

'Yes, we did, thank you, I have many lovely photographs', he said, patting the Nikon hanging from his neck.

'Your accent. Berlin?'

'Berlin? Nein. Meine Frau, she is from Munchen, Munich. I am Austrian.'

Jack was happy with that. 'Ah, Austria, I have never been to Austria. I must visit one day,' he replied. 'Well, enjoy the rest of your visit.'

From this brief exchange, Jack determined the couple were each about 35 years old and possibly not married as neither wore a wedding ring. 'No football club badge,' Jack thought, 'how uncooperative.' He wasn't convinced they were bona fide tourists. There was a camera but he saw no maps or local shopping bags. At this time of day, most visitors would have succumbed to the temptation of a souvenir or two. He decided, until proven otherwise, that they had been following him. For the time being, they were New Trevor and Mrs New Trevor. Jack smiled at his thought process. He wouldn't forget *their* names and recalled P.C. Blackman, pleased that he'd remembered hers. At the door to his apartment, he looked back in the direction of his German and Austrian followers. They had disappeared.

Without trying, Jack had amassed a volume of documents and decided to devote the evening to going through it all, starting with the Dragonfly documents that Harry had unearthed. His original case had expanded considerably, and now he knew it was global. He wondered whether it might be even more significant than anyone realised. Despite the size of the haul, the massive level of organisation required most likely wouldn't be wasted on a single enterprise. Derek's unwelcome departure still irritated, and Jack decided to follow it up tomorrow.

He switched on the laptop Harry had upgraded for him, probably illegally. Some new icons appeared briefly before his familiar display opened. In the Dragonfly folder on the desktop, 112 documents appeared in the Name column. 'This is going to require music and wine,' Jack said aloud to himself. He checked his watch. 'Wine first, it's gone four.'

With a glass of red wine poured and *Groovy Laid Back Jazz Volume 1* playing softly, he settled down to read. A minute later, the intercom buzzed. It was P.C. Blackman. Jack was surprised but pleased.

'Take the lift. I'll let you up.'

Jack's apartment occupied almost the entire floor so he had security access to the lift, a luxury he relished. The doors opened with no alerting sound. He'd had that deactivated.

'Welcome. Come in, come in.'

Blackman was dressed in civvies, clearly no longer on duty, and had brought more documents and some photos that hadn't been ready when Jack left Sayer's office.

'D.I. Sayer keeps on about how big this case is,' she said, 'so I thought I'd bring this lot around, rather than wait till tomorrow. I pass this way anyhow.' She handed him another USB drive.

'Thanks, I think. I thought I had enough to read as it was. Glass of wine? You're off duty, obviously.'

'Don't mind if I do. But just a half, I can't stay long. Got a cat to feed.' She wandered to the balcony window and admired the view. 'I like your place, Mr Sugarman. I'm Sarah, by the way. Don't want you calling me P.C. Blackman when I'm undressed. Out of uniform, I mean. Sorry, a private joke amongst the girls at work.'

Jack handed her a glass. 'Then I shall laugh only privately. Cheers, clink and all that. And call me Jack.'

Wine was another of Jack's passions, especially Tasmanian wine.

'Oh, that's nice,' Sarah said, 'I like a cabernet.' Jack was pleased she could tell the grape variety and thought he might have accidentally found a new friend, or perhaps more than a friend. Sarah was more attractive than any uniform could display, a fact not lost on Jack, who approved entirely. She wore her hair down, a rich auburn, just shoulder length.

Jack plugged in the USB drive, copied the documents to his desktop – he would organise them later – and returned the device to Sarah. He noticed his new reading matter was in two directories, one named SMS and the other Dragonfly. Sarah explained that she wasn't part of the team that had initially worked on the case but was instrumental, as D.I. Sayer's assistant, in compiling the data that had been accumulated. SMS stood for Share Market Scam. The police had yet to allocate a code word to the case. She sat down, nursing her glass of wine.

'Now then,' she sounded more serious, 'the Dragonfly folder is a collection of random documents that aren't from the police database. These are extras, with my compliments. Sayer doesn't know about these, and I'm not sure they're directly relevant anyway.'

Jack was intrigued.

'Not Sayer's? Whose then?'

'Most are from Derek. You might have some of them already. I know you met this morning. I'm a bit worried, Jack. He seems to have disappeared.'

Jack leaned forward in his chair. 'Derek Asquith, you mean?' Sarah nodded.

'Derek said someone else would contact me. I didn't think it would be so soon. But how do you come to be working with him anyway?'

Jack had a dozen questions but stopped there. Sarah enlightened him.

'We met years ago at a UFO convention in Sydney. He was obsessed with flying saucers and such like. I was dragged along by my boyfriend,' she added and stressed '*ex*-boyfriend now. I wasn't much interested in UFOs, but Derek intrigued me, so we met up from time to time. He had some wonderful stories, all factually accurate, supposedly. We just got on famously. What Derek didn't know about UFOs, ley lines, knowledge of the ancients, clairvoyance, resurrection, levitation, race memory, well, he could have written a book – several books probably. Maybe that was his plan. A very private man, though, so I can't tell you much about him. I moved to Hobart a few years ago, but he did only recently, so mostly we communicated by email. He liked to use the post, don't know why, so I got a lot of actual documents. I'll go through them for you and scan anything that might be useful.'

She interrupted herself, 'Oh, Euge Groove, I love his work. I think this is from one of his earlier albums. I can't think which one.'

Jack said he didn't know; it was a playlist a mate put together for him, but he agreed it was an excellent track. Sarah continued.

'I was able to feed him a couple of local cases, all very unofficial, of course, but they weren't sensitive matters. You may have heard of a local fisherman, Michael Something, and his boat, *Hermes*. Caused quite a stir in certain circles, but wasn't really a police matter. We got a report from the search people, though, so it's all on file. One of the papers kept calling the boat *Herpes,* which amused everyone at the station. I think it was a deliberate mistake.'

Jack was still amazed at the coincidence, if it was a coincidence, that Derek's forecast contact was a policewoman who worked with D.I. Sayer. He accepted it at face value and also realised that, somehow, the share market scam was connected with Dragonfly, whatever that turned out to be.

'I have a lot of reading to do,' Jack said, adding, 'More wine?'

'Thanks, but no, I have to meet a girlfriend at the gym later. I shouldn't have had this one, really, but it was very nice.'

She put down her glass and, to Jack's surprise, added, 'Perhaps you'll offer me the other half sometime.' There was the slightest sparkle in her eyes, and Jack suspected she was flirting a little. He didn't mind at all and took the hint.

'Of course, though I doubt this bottle will outlive the evening's research.' He pointed to the laptop. 'I have an older vintage, but that one is better with food. Maybe a meal sometime?'

'Yes, maybe,' she teased, heading to the lift, 'Sometime. I'll see you again soon. Sayer wants to be kept up to speed on this. His bosses are applying pressure. Good luck with the reading.'

'Have fun at the gym, and don't forget to feed your cat.'

The lift door closed quietly, and Jack was alone again.

◆

Earlier that afternoon, Leon had driven up the bends to call on his would-be girlfriend, Lyn, planning to give her the *Tunguska* story Jack had copied. Despite neglecting the courtesy of a phone call first, he was warmly welcomed, and conversation flowed easily when he handed over the document. Any hopes for a coffee and, therefore, an excuse to stay a little longer were dashed, though, when Lyn asked for a lift into town. He gallantly agreed and tore himself away from her window where she had an expansive view over Sandy Bay, Battery Point and the River Derwent.

'Shopping?' he asked.

'No, hairdresser, just a trim.'

'Oh right, I have a few things to do in town as well. I can give you a lift back home if you like. I'll be free after an hour.'

They agreed to meet at about two o'clock. Lyn never kept that appointment. After some unanswered calls to her home phone and mobile number, Leon drove back to Lyn's apartment to see if she had made her own way home. The doorbell went unanswered, and Leon looked through a curtained window. He didn't like what he saw. He made another call. It was three o'clock. That was the call that Jack didn't answer.

While Lyn had been receiving the expert attention of her hairdresser, the two men who had been watching the Blue Café that morning were systematically searching her apartment with no consideration for orderliness. Drawers were upended, bookcases emptied, and clothing scattered around. Thoroughly and quietly, they went about their task without speaking. They ignored the phone when it rang twice. After the 30-minute search, what had been Lyn's neat little home was reduced to chaos, undamaged but a mess. The search revealed a few letters and a computer hard drive, the former of interest only because of their length and that they weren't written in English. Someone else would assess their value. Nothing of any monetary value was taken. The men looked at each other.

'Done?' one asked.

'Done, this is it,' the other replied, indicating the modest haul. They left Lyn's apartment, carefully closing the door, the lock of which they had easily picked. Without undue haste, the two housebreakers drove their black Range Rover back to base to report to their boss. They spoke little. Thirty minutes later they pulled off the sealed road heading to Richmond and continued along an unsealed road boldly signposted PRIVATE PROPERTY PRIVATE ROAD. The road eventually led to a secluded establishment of no apparent function. A small cottage was in poor repair and unoccupied, while a collection of sheds appeared to have been built randomly wherever was deemed appropriate.

Pulling up at the largest shed, the driver reverse-parked next to another black Range Rover with similar fake number plates, FS9886. Ignoring the high roller door, they entered by a side door and paused briefly to let their eyes adjust to the dim light. It was a windowless construction lit only by a few clear roof panels. The shed seemed bigger than it was, being substantially empty. Only a few pieces of equipment and two cars were stored there, everything neatly covered by dusty tarpaulins. Opposite the side door was a small office where a man worked on a computer. He looked up distractedly through the dirty window and waved the two men in. A second internal room was securely padlocked. Derek Asquith rested uncomfortably and still sedated in this room.

The small office looked even smaller with the two men standing at the desk, waiting for instructions. The third man was younger, wore a suit, and steel-rimmed glasses, and carried an air of superiority. He finished what he was doing and leaned back in his chair.

'Excellent timing, gentlemen, what have you got for me?'

The larger of the two placed the proceeds of their search on the desk.

'Papers and a hard drive, Mr Hall. Nothing else, the place was clean apart from this. Not very clean now, though,' he laughed. His companion grinned broadly.

'Save the humour. This is too serious for humour right now. We have a situation no one is happy with.'

Mr Hall inspected the goods just delivered.

'I'm guessing you have no idea what these documents are.'

'Nuh. Just thought you better have them, being foreign.'

Mr Hall was pleased with that.

'Good thinking, well done. It looks like Serbian. That makes it harder.' He explained, 'Serbian is a synchronic digraphia language. That means more than one writing system. In this case, Cyrillic and Latin alphabets. Most of this is handwritten, and it's all over the shop. I'll have to send it to our people in Sydney.'

Mr Hall paused and looked carefully at each page.

'Oh, sit down, won't you? Grab a coffee if you want.' A steaming kettle and jar of instant coffee sat on a bench. Both declined.

'A straight translation is easy enough, but interpretation may take a while. Too easy to slip coded messages into Serbian. It's a real prick like that. We got nothing from Asquith. He either knows nothing or is a shit hot actor. Hard to tell. You gave him too much stuff.' Mr Hall motioned with his hand, indicating an injection in the side of the neck. 'I'd say he'll be out till tomorrow.'

'Sorry, Mr Hall,' said the syringe wielder.

'Not important. If he's one of us, it won't matter, though I reckon he'll have a word with you two about it. If not,' he paused, 'he'll be dealt with. Right, anything else?'

Both men shook their heads.

'OK, we're watching Sugarman, so you two can call it a day and do whatever it is you do in your free time. Something alcoholic, I'd guess. We'll need you tomorrow, so try to be sober, eh.'

Both men nodded and left. In their Range Rover, they looked at each other.

'New London, Mr Johnston?' one asked.

'New London, Mr Boucher.' Mr Johnston replied, adding, 'Damn that synchronic digraphia, eh.'

'Right, it's a real prick, isn't it?'

Both laughed, and they headed to their favourite pub.

◆

Jack had been sorting, indexing, and reading his many documents for three hours when he decided it was time for a break. He ordered a pizza.

'Large meat lovers, deep-pan, extra chorizo. Yes, that's it. No, no garlic bread. No drinks, nothing else. It's Jack Sugarman. Is Jim working tonight? OK, get Jim to deliver, will you? He knows where I am. Cheers.'

Jack hated being asked if he wanted garlic bread or drinks. He never ordered extras but knew the staff were only doing what they were told, so he kept it polite despite wanting to suggest that had he wanted garlic bread and drinks, he would have asked for them. Besides, the girl who always seemed to take his order sounded very pleasant and called him sir. The documents so intrigued Jack that his wine had sat virtually untouched for at least an hour. He topped up the glass and wondered whether he would see Sarah again and get to cook her the meal he half promised. Smiling at the thought, he was about to return to his studies when he remembered the call he'd ignored from Leon and picked up his phone. Leon answered promptly.

'Leon. Sorry I couldn't take your call this afternoon. Been a crazy day all round. What's occurring?'

Leon related his excuse for visiting Lyn and her not showing up later in the day.

'I went back to her place. She's not there. The door's locked, and the windows seem OK. She's probably just decided to stay with a friend. I was a bit worried but it's probably nothing. I'll try calling again tomorrow. What are you up to tonight anyway?'

'Just stopped researching. Right now I'm wondering why I ordered myself a large pizza. You eaten? Come round if you want. There's some fascinating stuff here. I'd like to know what you think.'

In 20 minutes, Leon announced his arrival over the intercom. A few minutes later Jim did the same with a piping hot meat lovers' pizza and, 'with compliments of the management' garlic bread. That meant 'with Jim's compliments' and that some other customer didn't get their garlic bread that night. Jim knew Jack always tipped well, so the occasional freebie seemed appropriate. Jack offered Leon a drink.

'Wine?'

'I'd rather have a beer. Can I help myself?' Leon asked. Knowing there was always beer in Jack's fridge, he relieved it of one stubbie.

'Yes, help yourself. Oh, you already have,' Jack responded with mock indignation. Now, wrap yourself around some of this tucker.' He pushed a plate over. In a very short time, most of the pizza and all the garlic bread had gone, and Leon twisted the top off another beer.

'You're getting a bit low on beer,' he advised helpfully, 'thought you should know.'

'Very remiss of me, I shall rectify that with all haste. Here, sit in the comfy chair and read this. It's more recent, slightly, than the Tunguska story and a bit closer to home. It's not long.'

Jack's expanded collection of documents included an unpublished and untitled article. With only the initials PDM to indicate its author, it was as intriguing as it was brief, and he cursed the lack of detail. It was now safely saved in his database as *The Sunken Church of Linda – 1912*. Leon settled into an armchair, put his beer on the side table and started reading.

◆

Ask anyone in Tasmania if they know Linda, and you'll probably not be told about the town of that name. Driving to Queenstown on the A10, you will pass a sign identifying a town no longer there. Once a sizable settlement, it was populated mainly by workers at the North Mount Lyell mine. In 1903, the mine was taken over, and a slow decline began, a not-unusual story for mining towns. The residents gradually moved their families to nearby Gormanston.

In October 1912, a fire broke out in the North Mount Lyell mine. On that fateful day, 170 men were working underground and 42 were not to return to the surface alive. Many had lived in Linda just a few years before. The disaster rates as one of the worst in Australian mining history, and despite the passage of time, debate continues as to what caused the fire. A Royal Commission report was inconclusive, leaving survivors and bereaved family members with little satisfaction.

Any two-paragraph description of Linda will tell you little more than that, perhaps adding that the small town survived for a few decades and the post office closed down in 1966.

Now beyond the realm of living memory and with scant written references, the other mystery of Linda is all but forgotten.

The fire broke out on Saturday, 12 October 1912, consuming the interest and activities of all mineworkers and hundreds of nearby residents. What no one seems to have noticed until the following day was that the solitary church of Linda had been 'taken to the depths of Hell', as one contemporary writer reported.

Stories of sunken churches abound, particularly in Europe, and they usually, but far from always, have a conventional explanation based on geology. Churches were built on land selected for a strategic, imposing or otherwise convenient position. Little consideration was given to the security of foundations. Many churches were positioned on land ill-suited for the construction of anything significant. Subsidence, flooding and sinkholes have taken a fair share of churches, sometimes centuries after their construction.

Predictably, though, not all such events can be so conveniently dismissed. The church at Linda is one such event. Solidly positioned on a mountain range nearly 300 metres above sea level, finding a building site at Linda that wouldn't provide a secure foundation is almost impossible.

The dozens of locals who found their local church in ruins and half-sunken into what was thought to be solid rock were already distressed, and this only added to their anguish. With the tragedy of the mine fire still being played out, though, it proved to be but a minor chapter in the area's history. The church was never rebuilt, and few people could now say where it was. The stone was salvaged for other projects but was found to be strangely brittle. It was primarily used for fencing.

The mystery of Linda's sunken church is found only in the works of those left-field historians who like to chronicle the unusual, the unexplained and the bizarre. Few of those writers have managed to uncover the single record of another enigma of the day. Also on that 12 October night, all the dogs of Linda disappeared.

A few lines in the diary of an elderly resident described how her faithful Max, having been unusually quiet for about a week, suddenly became agitated, ran into the hills and never returned. Several dogs were found over the next week, all dead but with no apparent injuries. – PDM

◆

To that story, someone had appended an observation that the sunspot cycle was ebbing and due to bottom less than a year later, in August 1913. Whoever wrote that also noted, with a string of question marks, 'Is the level of sunspot activity a guide to the timing of such events.' Jack knew that sunspot activity was measured in large cycles and smaller cycles within those. The present Modern Maximum has been in play since 1900, a period of *Dark History* reporting.

Leon put down the papers and reached for his beer. 'Do you see any connection between that and Tunguska?' Jack asked. Leon thought carefully before answering, staring at his stubbie label for inspiration.

'You obviously do, or you wouldn't ask. Apart from the fact that both involve disturbances of the ground, no, I don't. There's no geographic link. They're four years apart, in Olympic Games years, but I doubt that's relevant. Both mention animals. No, that's it. What do you make of them?'

Jack was pleased with Leon's observations.

'You got the two biggies, ground disturbances and animals. I've read a lot of those kinds of stories, and they have common themes. Much older stories often mention a black dog or more than one. Even in Australia, Aboriginal stories mention black dingoes…'

'Black dingoes?' Leon interrupted, 'I thought they were all sandy-coloured. Or tan, whatever you call it.'

'Most are. You get white ones as well, and cream. Most people know that animals can sense danger better than we can. They seem to be more attuned to their surroundings. As for ground disturbances, that includes ocean events. Plenty of weird stuff is happening on the oceans, and under. I must write that book one day.'

Jack and Leon discussed a few more cases and theorised on links, trying to find a common denominator, but they kept coming back to ground disturbances and animals. However, aerial phenomena were regular components of the stories. The Tunguska event was an extreme example. Eventually, the wine ran out, as did Jack's beer, and his friend decided to call it an evening.

'Do I have to leave by the back door this time?'

'Hang on, better let me check,' Jack said as he scanned the road outside. 'No, it should be OK. There's not much happening out there. I'd say my limpet friends have packed it in for the night. But watch yourself, eh.'

With his friend gone, Jack returned to his research. It was well after midnight before he realised he was absorbing only half of what he read. A final inspection of the street revealed no late-night surveillance. Only beeping traffic signals and a solitary jogger disturbed the serenity. He waited until the jogger ran out of sight.

'Idiot,' he said to no one and went to bed.

◆

Chapter 4

Cirrhosis of the River

Awake, showered, dressed, and breakfasted, Jack decided an instant coffee wouldn't be good enough this morning. He grabbed his wallet, keys, phone and laptop and headed to the Blue Café. It was quiet, almost empty. The breakfast crowd had come and gone, and mid-morning coffee addicts were yet to start trickling in. Angie busied herself cleaning tabletops, straightening newspapers left askew by hurried patrons, and rearranging cakes and pastries yet to find grumbling stomachs. She smiled as Jack walked in.

'Morning, Mr Sugarman. It looks like we're in for more rain today. Breakfast is it?'

'Hi, Angie. No, just one of your most excellent long blacks, please. When you're ready, no hurry.'

Despite the 'no hurry' qualification, she immediately selected a cup from the warming tray, studied it carefully, frowned, and removed a mark no one else would have noticed. She nodded, satisfied that the cup was worthy of her customer, and proceeded to prepare her 'most excellent long black'. Jack chose the table he used the previous day but sat where Derek Asquith had been. A view of the door might be a prudent move. He idly leafed through a newspaper, wondering about Derek and the documents he'd left behind. Angie brought his coffee.

'Coffee, black, long, double shot,' she said smiling.

'I thank you from the bottom of my spleen. Hey, do you remember that bloke I met here briefly yesterday? The queer little chap in a flat cap.' Angie indicated that she did. 'Right, did he call back looking for his briefcase?'

'Not while I was here, but I knocked off at three. No one mentioned it anyway, sorry. Anything else for you?'

'No, thanks,' Jack said and returned to his newspaper, too distracted this time to admire the waitress's captivating retreat.

He thought it strange that losing something so significant, the contents of the briefcase, if not the case itself, hadn't inspired contact with himself or the café. Jack started to worry about Derek, especially given the warning he'd received. He remembered the chilling caution that the material was 'likely pretty dangerous to anyone who has it.' He thought it rather theatrical at the time. Now he wondered if the danger might be real. A glance out the window across a now drizzle-dampened street revealed no black Range Rover or any loitering German tourists. Jack frowned. He needed to collect his thoughts and try to distil the previous day's events into something definitive. There was much to consider. He pushed his coffee aside and switched on the laptop.

He created a new document, named it *Derek* and started a chronological list headed 'Day 1'.

- Met Derek A., gave me some documents, left a briefcase behind
- Met Leon
- Lunch with Ford, tailed by 'Trevor' (lost him); German tourists – following me? More docs?
- Meeting with D.I. Sayer re share market scam; more documents
- Dragonfly blog
- P.C. Sarah Blackman called in (v nice); more documents; references to Dragonfly; Sarah knows Derek!
- Pizza with Leon, drank all my beer – buy more.

Jack stared at his list deep in thought until the screen saver kicked in. He'd read dozens of documents, and they swam in his head. Some were stories that would find a home in his *Dark History* collection, though most would need to be rewritten as they read like lifeless reports rather than the findings of an inspired researcher. Other documents were transcripts of conversations and interviews or outlines of scientific processes with complex mathematical formulae that Jack didn't understand. Some didn't seem to fit into any category. Two words kept appearing, Dragonfly and Southwood. After re-reading a few of the longer documents, Jack changed the name of his document from Derek to Dragonfly Files. It would be a much larger file by the time he finished it.

'You've let that one get cold. Try this.' Angie had been watching Jack and noticed he had hardly touched her most excellent long black. She replaced the first with a second and added a small plate. 'You look like you need a kiss,' she paused and cleared her throat softly, 'biscuit.'

'Too kind, thanks. I'm a bit occupied – lost track of time. You've made a happy man very old. Or something.'

Jack tried to decide if she was only being nice to a regular customer or flirting with him. Yesterday Sarah, now Angie. By his own admission, he had always been poor at recognising amorous signs from women. As a younger man, he missed real signs and misinterpreted others that were entirely innocent. He'd got it wrong so often that he didn't bother much anymore and relied on unsophisticated, obvious approaches to the women he fancied and preferred them to respond the same way. Most did. The subtlety game he left for others.

Mulling over recent events, Jack sipped his coffee, took a bite of biscuit and hit the space bar, bringing his list back to the screen. 'OK, Jack,' he said to himself, 'try to make sense of this, eh.' He started typing anything that came to his mind. Stream of consciousness, he called it, no structure, no logic, just anything he thought of. He'd put it all together later. This was almost automatic writing. He let his subconscious mind lead his conscious one and became intuitive instead of analytical. In 40 minutes, he had several pages of thoughts, an empty coffee cup and a few biscuit crumbs. He now knew what he needed to concentrate on and that a few favours might be called in. The following 24 hours would be a busy time.

Jack decided he'd typed enough for one session and closed the lid on Doctor Watson, his laptop, just as his phone rang. It was Leon.

'Leon Leon, how's it going?' Jack greeted his friend.

'A bit ordinary Jack Jack. Just how strong is that beer I was into last night? I got a bit trolleyed.'

'Oh, a modest eight per cent. Good, isn't it? I'd stick with just a couple in future. Not that I have any left now. Those 500 mil bottles sneak up on you, typically German.'

'Racism, Jack?' suggested Leon.

'No, I, ah…' Jack was going to defend the remark, but his thought process stuck on something else. He'd deduced that Trevor was German. The two tourists were German, one of them anyway, and he thought the two in the Range Rover might be German but now couldn't think why.

Leon continued. 'Just a quick one. Trousers emailed me more documents, the encrypted ones. He didn't have your email address, and I'm just forwarding his email now. See you around, eh? Don't forget, you need more beer.'

'I'll try to remember, mate, see you.'

There was now no one in the café except Jack and Angie. He asked her what today's Wi-Fi password was. She looked at a sticky note in the till.

'Kiss biscuit, one word,' she replied.

He fired up the upgraded Doctor Watson again. Software opened faster than he had been accustomed to, and 'kissbiscuit' quickly provided online access. He found Harry's email. 'More documents', he thought and scanned each one. The decryption process produced some errors, but they were still readable. Most were similar to the ones Harry had already provided, but he focussed on one called DA. It was a description of Derek Asquith, age, address, family, and a record of several days' movements. Derek was right. He had been under surveillance. Several photos hadn't succumbed to Harry's decryption, and each was represented by a red cross inside a white square. 'Even Trousers has limits,' Jack thought.

With a frown, he returned to his dot points and, after 'Met Leon', added 'Derek abducted'. It was Leon who noticed the odd little man being bundled into the back seat of a black SUV. Jack suddenly felt somewhat responsible for that. The pang of guilt motivated action, but first, he would have to lose the two men he'd just spotted sitting in the Range Rover in the car park across the road. He dialled a number.

'It's Jack Sugarman. Is D.I. Sayer able to take a call?'

P.C. Blackman answered with an official-sounding 'One moment, Mr Sugarman, I'll check for you.' After just a few seconds on hold, she added in a more friendly voice, 'Putting you through now.' Jack guessed that Sayer had been in the room, and Sarah was following a standing instruction to check before putting calls through.

'Jack, hello, have you got something for me?'

'I've got plenty, but if I gave it all to you now, you'd get confused. Have to put it together first. Remember I told you about that Range Rover with the fake plates? Well, it's over the road from my place. Same two blokes inside watching me with more interest than I care to enjoy.'

D.I. Sayer responded enthusiastically, 'Right, I'll get my boys on to it. Traffic can sort out the car; I'll deal with the guys inside. Ten minutes, and they'll be watching someone completely different, helping us with our enquiries.'

Jack reminded Sayer that his two tails might be disinclined to 'come quietly'.

He paid for his coffee, telling Angie, 'I may have to get away for a couple of days. If anyone asks, tell them I went to Zurich, yeah?'

'Zurich, right, got it.' Angie smiled and returned to her counter.

With the laptop safely under his arm, he left the Blue Café and strolled back to his apartment, being careful not to indicate he was aware of anyone watching his movements. He grabbed an overnight bag, always ready for an unscheduled departure, and waited for the police to arrive. True to his word, four of Sayer's plain-clothed men soon came in two unmarked cars, blocked any escape route, and had the two heavies surrounded. Jack saw the men protesting vehemently and waving what he imagined were passports, probably also fake. In a short time, all that was left was an empty Range Rover. He would check in with Sayer. On a hunch that the car would be impounded, he called a friend and asked him to watch for it. He asked him to give it the most tender loving care, a code for something only they knew about.

Jack's apartment had parking for two cars, and he rented another from a tenant who needed only one. He briefly considered which car he should take, something fast and fun with personality, or sensible and anonymous. Grabbing the relevant keys, he took his few necessities to the garage and carefully removed the tarp from his white Commodore sedan. 'Now then, Jack, old son,' he said aloud. 'Music. Drivey thinky music. What's it to be?' He decided on a lyrics-free Vangelis CD, eased it into the slot, punched a few buttons, adjusted the volume and headed out. He was amused to see the now-vacated Range Rover had already been treated to a parking infringement notice.

The drive to Opossum Bay took only 40 minutes. Here he owned a small, comfortable bungalow he'd named *Zurich*. Only when turning into the driveway did Jack recognise he'd been listening to the same track play several times. He also realised he'd distilled the essence of the Dragonfly Files into three themes. Leon had spotted two just by reading the *Linda* and *Tunguska* stories. To animals and ground disturbances, he added a topic he couldn't yet describe in a single word. In 24 hours, he promised himself, he would have the Dragonfly thing clear in his mind and be able to report to D.I. Sayer.

Like the previous day, the rain had failed to dominate the weather, beaten by an insistent sun and now cloudless sky. Hobart's citizens often told visitors that if they didn't like the weather, they should come back in 10 minutes. Hobart could deliver four seasons before lunch and then something combining any two for the afternoon. Jack settled at a table on the deck of what he liked to call his country residence and scanned the view. Set back only slightly from a seven-metre cliff, he admired the uninterrupted westerly scene over the Derwent Estuary and Storm Bay to the south, which today was calm and peaceful, belying its tempestuous name.

For hours, Jack sorted, categorised and indexed his collection of documents, interrupting the task only to make coffee. It was a multi-coffee day. Trying to make sense of the curious accumulation of papers led him away from what had initially prompted his research. Jack decided the share market event would be called Dragonfly for now. It was undoubtedly linked to Southwood, but it seemed now to have been nothing more than a complex fundraising exercise for the benefit of whatever Southwood was. A late sea breeze finally countered the sun's warmth, and Jack reluctantly moved indoors. Doctor Watson's battery demanded recharging anyway and was duly plugged in. As the laptop gratefully received more power, its owner's waterfront apartment in town was being raided.

Several cars pulled up outside and a dozen men emerged, one wearing a suit, the others in matching coveralls of military appearance. They had their instructions and rushed into the building. Two remained outside the front door, and the rest took the four flights of stairs to Jack's floor. One of them held a battering ram and waited for a nod from the suit. Assured that his men were ready, the suit nodded. A single precise blow from the 16-kilogram enforcer shattered the lock surround. The door flew open, then bounced back, trembling in protest as the door-breaching expert stood aside, satisfied with his work. With firearms poised, his colleagues rushed in, variously and simultaneously shouting, 'Police, no one move, stay where you are, on your knees, hands behind your head.' The empty apartment made the instructions pointless, embarrassing, and contradictory. Each room was declared 'clear', and the shouting stopped.

'Gone, sir, no one here,' the senior officer confirmed to the suit.

'Blast, he must have been tipped off. Thorough search, Williams, find that briefcase.'

The search didn't need to be thorough as the briefcase was in plain sight, still containing Derek's documents. Williams handed it over.

'No computer. Curious, Mr Southwood, leaving the briefcase lying about like that. Maybe he doesn't know…' A withering look stopped further speculation.

'He knows, Williams, he knows more than is good for him. It's not healthy to know too much about this.' Mr Southwood sounded ominous. 'But we know an awful lot about Jack Sugarman, and that's not good for him.'

Whatever it was that Mr Southwood knew about Jack, he didn't know that his apartment was discretely fitted with six security cameras. They had been activated by a motion sensor that couldn't fail to sense the partial destruction of his stairwell door. Each camera was now silently uploading footage online. A security company was immediately alerted to the intrusion. As arranged, Jack was called.

'Mr Sugarman, sir, this is Sally from Wapping Security. Your alarm has been activated. Would you like us to send a guard along to check?'

Jack was only slightly irritated. False alarms were common enough.

'Thanks, Sally, give me a minute, I'm just outside.' He opened his video footage website and six screens promptly appeared. On selecting live streaming, the screens showed all too clearly his apartment crowded with – he counted – eight military-looking men milling about. He also spotted the man in the suit and Derek's commandeered briefcase. This would need some thinking.

'You still there, Sally. Sorry, it's all OK, it's the neighbour's cat destroying my curtains again. What?' She had asked the name of his cat. 'Oh, Leon, he's called Leon,' he lied, wondering why he made up the cat excuse. 'No need to send anybody. Thanks for the call. Oh, password, yes, "fish milkshake."'

Jack continued watching his screens until the motley group left his apartment. If his system had audio as well as video, he would have heard Southwood's name and that he curtly ordered Williams to 'Get that door replaced. Fast. Chances are he won't notice the switch.'

'The loss of the briefcase was of no importance unless,' Jack thought, 'Derek ever returned for it.' All the documents were duplicates except the newspaper and personal papers, so their loss didn't matter. The newspaper couldn't be replaced, but it was a recent edition and could be found at the State Library, and was probably online. He remembered its date and that the lead article was an insignificant local political drama.

With the raiding party gone, Jack realised he'd been watching the drama unfold as a disinterested onlooker rather than the owner of the now-defiled apartment. 'Bastards,' he muttered, 'What was that all about?'

It seemed evident that the briefcase was the goal, and Jack was thankful it hadn't been necessary to tear his place apart to find it. Along with a broken door, he'd also been the victim of a 'collector' in the group who helped himself to a scale model Bentley, a favourite of his small collection. However, Derek's briefcase was the article du jour and a clear giveaway. The raid itself was suggestive, but the seizure of the briefcase was conclusive evidence that what Jack had been trying to fathom was important. He was onto something. Unfortunately, someone knew he knew something, and Jack decided they probably knew more than he did.

The entire raid, from the cars pulling up to their departure, was over in under 15 minutes. It had been well planned and effectively, if not expertly implemented. Jack saw most of it live and then carefully reviewed each camera's footage, concentrating on the man in the suit, though the Bentley enthusiast was scrutinised in some detail too. He would recognise both if ever their paths crossed again. Years of training and experience suggested to Jack that only two of the men were likely to be professionals. The others behaved like hired muscle, briefed to undertake a specific task. When that task was done, they were unsure what to do next. The coveralls provided no clue to identity, typical of any police and military outfits, but there was no badging.

Jack switched off his laptop and, realising he hadn't eaten lunch, put a frozen lamb korma in the microwave. Convinced that wine would help the thinking process, or at least not hinder it, he poured himself a generous glass of Shiraz just as *Smoke on the Water* played again. It was Leon.

'Hey, Leon, what's happening?'

Leon sounded troubled.

'Jack, bad news. Your place has been raided by the cops. I called round. Couldn't get near the place, no one was allowed in. What have you been up to? Look, wherever you are, you better stay there. I'm with Trousers, and he's got more documents for you. Our network put together more stuff from the Dragonfly blog. I'll email them to you.'

Jack was a step ahead.

'No, don't do that. Did you find Lyn?'

Leon said that he had phoned several times and been back to her place once. He'd even tried a couple of friends. Neither had seen her, but one said she often disappeared for days on end and that he shouldn't worry. Jack was unconvinced.

'OK, look, after this police raid,' he stressed the word police, hinting it may not have been the police, 'I'm working on the basis that Derek and your girlfriend Lyn have been abducted. If I'm right, you and Harry could be at risk. You need to pack a few things and drive to that slip yard I told you about a while ago. Do you remember where that is?'

Leon indicated that he did.

'I'll arrange for a mate of mine, his name's Keith, to get you to my country place. You don't know about that. Very few people do. Try not to be followed, especially lookout for a black Range Rover. Got it?'

'Got it,' Leon replied and hung up.

Jack's mate Keith was one of his many friends in low places and known to many as Keith the Milkman for no reason anyone could fathom. He was a driver, sometimes cabs, but mostly under contract to drive politicians and senior public servants around. Drivers hear a lot of conversations they shouldn't. Keith the Milkman made a tidy sum, feeding snippets to the news media and occasionally to Jack. He underestimated his source once, though, and would have faced prosecution had Jack not convinced some people in high places that the information in question had already been leaked and was common knowledge in certain areas. Keith was appropriately grateful and ready to provide his driving prowess at a moment's notice. Jack called.

'Keith, it's Jack. I need you and your boat for an hour or so.'

'G'day, Jack, any time, you know that.'

'Any time is the correct response because it'll be in about 10 minutes. What's the name of your boat again?' Jack asked.

'No sweat, Jack, *Cirrhosis of the River* is always fuelled and ready to rock and roll. Where do you want to go?' Keith asked.

'It's not for me. Not directly. Two friends, Leon and Harry. They're on their way to you now. Introduce yourself and take them to Opossum Bay, will you? Can you look after their car for a bit too? I'll meet you at the jetty when you get here. Oh, and not too much of the rock and roll, eh? I don't know how well these guys travel on water.'

With the travel arrangements made, Jack settled down to his curry and shiraz and reread one of the documents Derek had provided. It encompassed the three themes he'd identified. An introductory note to the article indicated it had been put together based on documents from several sources, none of which were cited. It was titled *Lord Howe Island: 38,000 BC*.

◆

The Pallia were an ancient people who lived on what is now Lord Howe Island. They called their home Woy Woy Pallia. During the closing stage of the last ice age, the dry land area of the island was considerably more extensive, as ocean levels were at least 120 metres lower than today. What remains above sea level now is the millennia-weathered peak of an ancient shield volcano.

In the 18th century, the French writer Charles de Brosses theorised that an 'old black race' existed somewhere in the Pacific Ocean. He couldn't have known that this race was the Pallia, nor that they had left their island home 38,000 years ago.

Pallia technology was minimal by modern standards, but their understanding of nature was very advanced. Today, we might call them mystics, and a few European historians of the 19th century even referred to the high Pallia as holy men. As often as not, they were attributed with the ability to perform magick – that's magick with a 'k' to differentiate it from illusionary stage magic. Those historians were little more than storytellers, though; their work mainly exists as unpublished papers and diaries.

The Pallia were excellent mariners and expert navigators like their many Melanesian and Polynesian neighbours. So much so that the (then) 500km distance to mainland Australia – to an area they called Daingatti – presented little difficulty. The journey was undertaken from time to time for trading purposes. Western history doesn't record the reason for the Great Pallia Migration, though it is commonly thought they were driven away from their homeland by Polynesian aggression.

However, at least one notable diarised record of folk history mentions another possibility. Story songs tell of them being forced from their home by 'angry ground spirits', suggesting that volcanic or seismic activity had made life there impossible.

At the time of the migration, the high elder was Mandu Pallia, although he was named Mandu Mandu at birth. His father was also Mandu Pallia. The first-born son was always so named after his father. By tradition, the high elder relinquished his status when his eldest son reached 25. A year after the father's death, the son's name would revert to the single given name. A strict and complex hierarchy of lesser elders ensured a continuous male line. There was never a female high elder, though Pallia women held a special status because of their extraordinary healing powers.

In his seventh year as high elder, Mandu convened a council of elders at the December full moon. Important decisions were made only during a full moon. They called the moon Ngalindi (man moon) during daylight hours and Vena (woman moon) at night. The bright light of Vena at full moon was created when she burned evil spirits; this light increased the Pallia's insight.

Mandu told the elders that the ground spirits were angry and could not be appeased. Strange lights appeared at night and danced around ponds and lakes. These were the Min Min and caused great fear, especially amongst the children. He tried to explain the dull, inaudible rumblings he'd experienced when fishing at one of the larger lakes. No fish had been caught that day. Nor the next. Other elders nodded knowingly. This was hardly news. Three days before, two young boys had been found close to the lake. They were dead. The women could not explain why.

The decision to leave their home and travel west to Daingatti was traumatic but inevitable. Their largest boats carried only 14 people, and many voyages were necessary to take the 3,000 Pallia away from Woy Woy Pallia. None would see their traditional home again.

Intrigued by the new lands, the Pallia explored their larger surroundings in extended family groups. For no apparent reason, their explorations became a steady, if disjointed, migration southwards. Over many years, the Pallia were welcomed and then farewelled by other peoples, some more warmly than others. The southerly trek continued until they reached the Great Southern Ocean, which they called Nyitting Wardan. The land they found they named Trowenna. The climate was cooler than they were used to, but the land was rich in fauna and vegetation and otherwise unpopulated.

The migration took a generation to complete and Mandu had joined his ancestors long before reaching Trowenna. By the time they had travelled as far south as what Europeans now call Cox Bight, the high elder was Parlevar, as the younger Mandu had no sons to continue the name. It was at this remote but beautiful place that Parlevar saw a star fall into the sea. He called the star Moinee. It fell with a great roar and much smoke and was followed by many smaller stars, which he thought to be devils. This part of the coast was avoided for a long time.

Parlevar was the first high elder of the Pallia in Trowenna. Later high elders and their families enjoy no record in modern history but live on in the hearts and minds of thousands of descendants who now call their people Palawa.

Imperceptibly, over thousands of years, sea levels rose, and the land bridge that afforded the Pallia the route to their new home was flooded. Trowenna became an island. The same rise of the oceans drowned what the Pallia left behind on Woy Woy Pallia. No one visiting Lord Howe Island now could realise they might find remnants of ancient and proud people a mere 120 metres below the surface.

Today the world knows Trowenna as Tasmania.

An English historian, Professor Samuel St. John Gordon-Bennett, investigated the intriguing story of the Pallia. Developing a thesis from the works of his contemporary, Charles de Brosses, he advocated the possibility that Woy Woy Pallia was 'one of the Atlantis civilisations.' His thesis was never completed. The Professor disappeared, although an investigation in the 1960s suggested he changed his name and emigrated to Australia.

That later investigator was John Lake, an American journalist who also vanished without explanation. Most of Lake's records disappeared with him, but a few tantalising pages surfaced years later. His work expanded on Gordon-Bennett's conclusions and concentrated on the theory that Atlantis wasn't a single island or lost continent but a civilisation spread over multiple sites. That there may have been an Atlantis in the Pacific Ocean is curious, to say the least.

None of these researchers realised that the Pallia people's history and that of their original home, Woy Woy Pallia, while linked, were also very different stories. Woy Woy is an Aboriginal term and means 'deep water'. The island would have been surrounded by very deep water when the Pallia lived there 40,000 years ago.

The people and their island home enjoy only a tenuous presence in the recorded accounts of our times. The definitive history will never be written, but many people believe that the inheritance left by ancient people is not limited to their written stories or physical relics. In particular, the healing powers of the women of Pallia were extraordinarily advanced. Modern medicine relies heavily on physical diagnosis and intervention for its remedies. By contrast, the Pallia placed their faith in what we would now call spiritual healing. Even physical injuries were treated in a manner we would not contemplate today.

The Pallia's knowledge of the night sky is equally remarkable. Their rock carvings – nearly all of which are now under 120 metres of the Pacific Ocean – accurately depict constellations that we would recognise today. Some show star patterns familiar only to those with access to telescopes or the more esoteric star charts. How the Pallia knew of such stars is an enigma.

An affinity with nature extended to the animal kingdom. During their long migration, the Pallia learned much about species they hadn't known in their old home. Some of these species were regarded as a food source. Others were simply animals they shared the land with. One learned to follow Pallia hunters, aware that they were efficient trackers and killers of prey. Today, we call them black dingos.

The concept of inherited, genetic, or race memory is generally regarded with scepticism. But for every voice discrediting the theory, another might assure us that it exists in our spiritual DNA. Modern scientific life has little place for the elemental inheritance of our existence. People who claim ancestry of the ancients – who we insultingly call primitives – may have this primaeval knowledge without realising it.

Such is the brief story of the Pallia people and their forced migration from a now-flooded land to a southern outpost today called Tasmania.

[A footnote referenced the journalist, John Lake.]

John Lake was last seen in Manhattan, walking with a female friend towards the subway. A missing person report was filed, and his disappearance investigated. Years later, Lake's son was shown a photo of a corpse that bore a resemblance to his father. However, no definitive identification could be made, and the case remains unsolved. The disappearance of Professor Gordon-Bennett also remains a mystery.

◆

The coincidence of two missing people was not lost on Jack. The *Lord Howe Island* story was hardly a definitive work of non-fiction, but Professor Gordon-Bennett and John Lake were both reported as having vanished. Jack found no reference to the professor online, but John Lake was a verifiable missing person case over 50 years ago. He was pondering the disappearances when the sound of a motorboat disturbed his train of thought. The jetty was a two-minute walk from his back door, and by the time he arrived, Keith was tying up, with the engine burbling.

'Keith, you're a champion, coming in?' Jack asked.

'No thanks, Jacko, I want to get back before I lose the light. It's nice and calm, and hardly anything on the water, so I can let *Cirrhosis* fly. Be good to blow the cobwebs out I reckon. Leon's car's in the back shed. You know where I hide the key if I'm not around. See you both.'

Leon threw the ropes back and shouted his farewells and thanks over the sudden din. He then described his boat ride. The word maniacal was used.

'What happened to Harry,' Jack asked as they walked back to *Zurich*. 'Jump overboard?'

'I reckon he might have if he'd been on board, but he went bush. Trousers likes the bush as much as his computers and your call was all he needed to pack a few things, jump in his Land Rover and scarper. Said he'd be a week, but that could mean a month. Don't worry; he's a bushy from way back, and if he doesn't want to be found, he won't be. Got any beer? Hey, I didn't even know about this place. What's the deal?'

Jack maintained his little cottage by the sea as a quiet escape from everyone and everything, even though it was less than an hour's drive from the city. Very few people knew about it. His neighbours knew him as Simon Jackman. Only the shopkeeper, who was also the sub-post office manager, was in on the secret and he understood the concept of confidentiality. The cottages on either side were weekend retreats, except in the summer months, and presently empty. He enjoyed the solitude. The shopkeeper's daughter maintained the small garden, and his son looked after the cleaning and ensured the kitchen and bathroom were always stocked with necessities. They were well paid for their services.

'No beer, sorry, down here I never have visitors. Hardly ever, anyway, so I only cater for myself. It's wine or whisky. Your choice. Hungry?'

Leon said he might eat something once his stomach settled down, but for now, a glass of red would be good. One shiraz was duly poured. Leon was curious.

'Um, the "hardly ever" visitors. They wouldn't be young ladies by any chance? Would they?'

'Um, they might be Leon, they might be. The last one was.'

They clinked their glasses and toasted 'hardly ever having visitors'.

Jack became very serious.

'Now then, old friend, sit yourself there,' he pointed to a comfortable armchair. 'Help yourself to wine. There's plenty more, and you don't have to drive home. I have something of a story to tell you. It's all theory and pretty far-fetched. I'm not even sure of it myself. It's good you're here. I need someone to bounce ideas off. One more thing, that police raid. I'm pretty sure it wasn't the police, not our lot anyway. I have it all on video, I'll show you tomorrow. But first, I believe you have something for me.'

'I do. Almost forgot. That's why I'm here, one reason anyway,' Leon replied and handed over the flash drive.

'Ta, I'll look at all that tomorrow too.'

Jack had read more documents than he cared to count, some more than once and a couple several times. He'd copied them all to a single folder, in chronological order as far as possible. They were classified, indexed, cross-referenced and footnoted. With dozens of comments added, his *Dark History* had evolved into the makings of the book he'd often promised to write. Given any keyword, he could locate and extract information most people had never heard of, though much of it was unproven.

Leon would prove to be a useful foil when Jack described his hypotheses, as much for his benefit as for his friend. Writing was one thing. Putting voice to theories sometimes made what appeared to be entirely reasonable on paper sound preposterous. Jack knew that if he could half convince Leon, he was onto something and on to something very, very big.

◆

Chapter 5

Older Than Science

Jack told Leon his conclusions were still amorphous and then explained what amorphous meant. The evidence supporting his conclusions was sourced from several individuals in several countries over several centuries. In a court of law, he'd be laughed at, but he was convinced the nature of the documents he'd collected pointed to converging deductions.

His *Dark History* files were a good starting point but, in themselves, didn't reveal anything sinister. The Asquith papers increased his collection very neatly. Derek was a kindred spirit when it came to left-field information. It was only with the addition of files from D.I. Sayer and the Dragonfly blog that Jack had identified two clues simply because certain words were repeated more often than random chance would generate. Dragonfly and Southwood, or South Wood as was sometimes found, were significant. Initially, Jack had no idea what they meant or how important they were.

By the time he'd secured the second set of documents from Sayer, he was convinced he was privy to something not only unusual but unusually crucial. His investigation revealed a case measured in hundreds of millions of dollars, which only made later conclusions all the more impressive. A fundraising exercise the size of what he called *Dragonfly* suggested a massive second part to the story. Part two, whatever it turned out to be, was still conjecture in Jack's mind, but it was possibly a scary story for anyone to write themselves into. Derek had said as much, and that seemed more likely to be accurate as each hour passed.

Having moved beyond the initial enthusiasm of accumulating material for his long-planned book in little more than 24 hours, he realised the knowledge that started to coalesce was much bigger than his ambition. Had Derek not been abducted, it might all have seemed like a bizarre conspiracy theory, but his kidnapping and the possible disappearance of his friend's friend Lyn removed any doubt. There was a link between Dragonfly and Southwood. He just needed to work out precisely what that link was and, more importantly, what Southwood was.

As Jack moved from one train of thought to the next, Leon listened intently, trying to make sense of it all.

'Jack,' he interrupted, 'a question.'

'Go on.'

'Why is my glass empty, and what can I eat?'

Jack grinned as he reached for his friend's glass. 'That's two questions, the first of which,' he paused while refilling the glass, 'is now no longer operationally valid in that the glass to which you refer is patently not empty.'

'Smart arse. Anyway, it's one question in two parts if you want to get technical.'

'But grub-wise,' Jack continued, 'look in the freezer and microwave, grab anything you fancy. If you like lamb korma, bad luck, I had that.'

Leon raised his glass in mock salute, took a sip, and proceeded to select something he fancied. In four minutes, he was tucking into what he would later describe as 'some shit Jack made me cook myself.' Jack continued his discourse.

'Listen carefully. This is important. It might be anyway. We've been through a bit of this before. I've decided there are four clear themes in these documents. You spotted two, and I must say I was impressed. Ground disturbances and animals, remember?'

Leon nodded.

'And Olympic Games. Remember that?'

Leon nodded again and repeated, 'Olympic Games,' with glass poised.

'Well, forget that. But to ground disturbances, add oceanic disturbances, on and under. And for animals, think dogs primarily.

Dogs figure heavily in unusual folk tales, but they are man's favourite and possibly earliest pets, particularly black dogs. I haven't quite figured that out yet. Then there's something I can't put into one or two words. Would you understand what I meant if I said "knowledge of the ancients"?'

Leon nodded again, 'Well, yes and no, in that, yes I don't.'

Jack continued.

'This is pretty obscure stuff and a bit mind-bending. I'm talking about inherited memory, race memory, mystics, magicians, alchemists, holy men, faith healers, clairvoyants, fortune tellers, the afterlife, reincarnation, the list goes on. Anything that our Western brand of science can't accept and won't consider. It's an odd thing that something we don't understand we decide can't exist. Some of us anyway, but these concepts are all centuries older than most of our science. It existed long before any language developed to describe it.'

'Older than science, nice turn of phrase that,' Leon interjected.

'Thanks. Now then, to refine it a bit. It's often that "primitive" people – sorry, but that's the best word – display these qualities better than us mere "moderns". Indigenous peoples whose minds are untainted with the 21st or even 18th-century way of thinking are more likely to have the abilities that we dismiss. Not dismiss, ignore. So Australian Aboriginal people, North American and African natives, as well as individuals who have close links to the likes of Celtic and Saxon cultures – they're the ones most likely to have certain abilities. Mostly that's just being able to read nature better than we can. Is this making any sense at all?'

Leon put his glass down.

'It is – a bit. I'm not sure how it helps us, though. You're saying that modern European culture has lost those abilities.'

'Yep. Not just modern Europeans of course, though much of the world has been influenced by Europe. The people we conveniently call the ancients still exist, nominally anyway. The Egyptian civilisation of the pharaohs isn't much like modern Egypt. The same with other old civilisations, Persians, Aztecs, Mayans, Mesopotamians; they understood nature better than we do now. Some descendants of all those people would have some abilities to some extent. Have you ever been to a place for the first time and thought it seemed familiar?'

'Yep.'

'That's something. Something odd. It could be an inherited memory or a kind of mental stimulation we can't even guess at. Everyone has experienced déjà vu. Everyone. And have you ever taken an umbrella out even though the forecast was for fine weather?'

Leon nodded again. 'You're just making me say "yes" all the time, aren't you?'

'That's because we still have some degraded vestige of an ability to read nature, even though we don't do it consciously. It's all subconscious, automatic. We just *know*. Over a hundred years ago, people could read the seasons and read the weather better than they could read a book. Actually, that's a given. A couple of hundred years ago, a lot of people couldn't read much anyway. But if you talked about isobars, low-pressure systems and approaching fronts in 1577, you'd likely be thought a lunatic.'

Leon leaned forward, '1577, Jack?'

'Ah, sorry, I could have picked any year over a couple of centuries ago. 1577 happens to be a particular favourite of mine. Fascinating year is 1577.'

Jack admitted to three main hobbies: stamp collecting, reading and the year 1577. Stamp collecting developed his expansive general knowledge, particularly of history and geography. Reading was an obsession, again with a penchant for history and geography, but he also devoured biographies. It was his fascination with 1577 that intrigued friends, though. The question was always the same, 'Why 1577?' The answer was generally 'Why not?' but if anyone persisted, he was happy to recount the better-known events.

The most celebrated for anyone of British descent was Francis Drake's circumnavigation of the world, only the second time this had been achieved in a single expedition. That voyage started in 1577. He delighted in researching the Treason of Don Juan, the Peace of Bergerac and even Pope Gregory XIII's instigation of the renewal of ecclesiastical hymns. At this point, most people he spoke to lost any trace of interest they may have had in the year 1577.

Jack had the money to indulge his curious interest and commissioned much private research. At one point, four academics were delving into various archives across Europe. One day, he would write the definitive history of 1577. 'It might sell as many as 10 copies,' he would tell his friends. Till that happened, though, and until a couple of days ago, the result of his historical compilation was little more than a crudely indexed accumulation of documents, not all of which had yet been satisfactorily translated into English. For what he called a teaser introduction to 1577, he wrote a short article that was published in *One Thing After Another,* a low-circulation semi-professional magazine for amateur historians. He mischievously concentrated on the more esoteric happenings of the year.

In a later edition of the magazine, a letter to the editor proved as rewarding as frustrating. Some additional details were provided which had eluded Jack's researchers. By the time he attempted to contact the writer, identified only as 'Bob de Slob', the magazine had ceased publication. That in itself was something of a mystery as Jack was unable to locate the editor or anyone who knew his whereabouts.

◆

This is an abbreviated version of his article, which appeared as *Some Funny Things Happened in 1577.*

Samuel Muton was the eldest son of a wealthy Essex landowner. During the brutal winter of 1576/77, he decided to undertake what would later be called the Grand Tour of Europe. He crossed the English Channel in February 1577, leaving from Harwich. Well-educated and with a passable knowledge of what is now called Middle French and Early New High German, Samuel could travel as freely as a purse full of gold and silver allowed. Letters of introduction were usually well-received but more for their appearance than content. Lowly border officials typically boasted only minimal literacy and rarely any English.

Their low wages were occasionally supplemented courtesy of the Muton purse. Such were the protocols of travel in the 16th century.

Late in February, Samuel found himself in the province of Luxembourg (now part of modern Belgium), not to be confused with the smaller but better-known Grand Duchy of Luxembourg. His visit to Marche-en-Famenne coincided with the signing of an edict that formalised the departure of Spanish forces from the Netherlands. This significant event, known today as the Edict of 1577, would have been lost on Samuel had it not been for a 'dark happening' in the town square.

Though not a witness, Samuel found a locally published pamphlet that recorded the event. It was written in Luxembourgish, a German dialect he had no difficulty translating. A sinkhole had appeared with little warning. The warning was evident to the many people nearby who heard 'demonic voices' emanating from the ground immediately before the hole appeared. It was of only modest depth but very wide, though no measurements were quoted. An icy mist quickly developed and pulsed slowly in the base. It dissipated within a day after a local priest was induced to 'drive away the evil one' with his prayers.

The pamphleteer – also the town crier – suggested the pit was a sign of the devil's approval of the signing of the edict. There was no explanation why the devil might be interested in such political events. Samuel left the area and intended to travel to France, his French language skills being somewhat better than his German. However, news of the outbreak of the Sixth War of the French Wars of Religion persuaded him that a leisurely journey to Brussels would be more agreeable and possibly safer. Samuel carried the pamphlet on his journeys, which has survived in the family archives. When he returned to his Essex estate, he delighted in relating the story of the devil's pit and that he had seen Don John of Austria, the Spanish governor-general of the Habsburg Netherlands, who signed the proclamation.

Again, not a witness, Samuel was near a similar event late in April. Don John was travelling to Brussels when progress was hampered by a 'cold and eerie mist' just outside Namur, 60km from their destination. One of his entourage told of the horses refusing to walk into the mist even though they were all familiar with that sort of low country weather. John dismounted and led his reluctant steed through the worsening haze. His travelling companions stayed back and waited. Very soon, sounds of terror were heard from the now unseen horse, and this was immediately followed by John's rapid but unsteady footfalls as he scrambled back into the clear light.

John was visibly shaken and clearly in pain. He fell to the ground and with difficulty and aided by his valet, struggled to his feet again. Resting for an hour and taking a restorative draught of wine, John and his party watched amazed as the mist dissipated, seemingly being drawn into the ground. On a spare horse, he again led the group on the road to Brussels. His white stallion, called Marengo – many years later, Napoleon Bonaparte also rode a horse named Marengo – was found a few hundred metres along the road. He had stumbled into what looked like soft ground and was partially buried dead. Saying a private farewell to his old friend, the son of Charles V noticed that the earth wasn't soft at all. How the horse came to be partially buried puzzled him, but more important matters lay ahead, and he continued to Brussels.

Don John died the following year, reputedly of gaol fever, better known now as typhus. He had endured fevers and headaches ever since his encounter with what he referred to as the Mist of Namur. Samuel heard John's story in a Brussels tavern and, despite the storyteller's inebriation was satisfied as to the truth of the tale.

He was later to hear of the Black Assize in Oxford, which in July and August of 1577 resulted in what was called, with some understatement, an 'unhappy history'. During the court hearings, a foul air, thought to have 'arisen out of the bowels of the Earth', caused much discomfort to all those present. The Lord High Sheriff and Lord Chief Baron of the Exchequer died. In what one record describes as 'those fearful 40 days,' some 300 people perished. It was pointed out that more people were dying during their incarceration than those who ever wore a hangman's noose.

Samuel had been keeping a diary on his travels, and this is also still in the family archives in Essex. On returning to England, he compared his account of Don John's experience on the road to Brussels with the Black Assize at Oxford. The stories were very different, but Samuel made a note in the margin that read, 'disturb. of ground again'. It appeared he had made the connection that later researchers also deduced. Many of these dark events were accompanied by disturbances of the ground or under it.

The frustrations of travel through Europe bettered Samuel's perseverance, and within a few months, he decided it was prudent to abandon the tour. A more leisurely exploration of England might be more amenable. So it was that on 21 June, the summer solstice, he found himself again on English soil and enjoying familiar food, English ale and his own language. After a week or two of sharing his experiences with family and friends, Samuel set off to explore his immediate surroundings intensively rather than the rest of the country extensively. He spent some days exploring Cambridge and its nearby countryside. In Cambridge, he visited Trinity and Magdalene Colleges, and some of the older colleges.

A desire to be closer to the sea found him travelling east. By way of the village of Newmarket, Samuel stayed for two days in Bury-St-Edmunds. Intending to reach Yarmouth, unseasonal weather forced a stay in the village of Bungay, where he was to witness first-hand the town's most extraordinary claim to fame, other than its near destruction by fire many years later in 1688. During a storm on 4 August, St Mary's Church was struck by lightning. Samuel recorded, 'The parishioners were much afraid when a black Hell Hound did appear in their midst.' Accounts state that members of the congregation were attacked before the apparition vanished, reappearing '12 miles distant in the Holy Trinity Church at Blythburgh.'

Samuel transcribed part of the account into his diary. He wrote of 'darkness, rain, hail, thunder and lightning as was never seen the like. The hound ran about the church, killing two men instantly and causing another to shrivel up, burned so severely that he would likely die.' A later margin note indicated that, happily, the man did survive the ordeal.

At this point in the article, Jack departs from the story of Samuel Muton's travels and reports on a few other significant events of 1577. The signing of the Treaty of Bergerac was one such event. Well before that September, though, Samuel was back in England and did not refer to it in his diary. The article continued with two of the better-known incidents.

In 1577, a great comet appeared, visible in all of western Europe. With disgracefully limited imagination, even today, it is known as the Great Comet of 1577. In the 16th century, comets were misunderstood. Even Galileo insisted they were an optical phenomenon. Most of the population would have been superstitious peasants (let's call them that), and typically, comets were seen as omens of misfortune. The Danish astronomer Tycho Brahe made detailed observations from 13 November 1577 till late January 1578. His first observation nearly coincided with Francis Drake's departure from Plymouth on his voyage to circumnavigate the world.

Anyone connecting the comet's appearance with Drake's attempt may have decided the voyage was doomed. Such views soon appeared well-founded as inclement weather proved to be such an impediment as to force Drake to seek shelter in Falmouth and then to return to Plymouth, where repairs were made. Crossing the Atlantic proved to be a laborious exercise, and two ships had to be scuttled. Upon reaching Puerto San Julian in Patagonia (Argentina), the comet's portent seemed to be validated when Drake's men saw the bleached skeletons of executed Spanish seamen. They were the victims of Drake's predecessor, Ferdinand Magellan, who had put them to death for mutiny.

A recently rediscovered account of the early stages of Drake's voyage described a curious incident that occurred on Christmas Eve, 11 days out of Plymouth. It described a favourable wind but poor progress. A pod of dolphins, which had followed the fleet for three days, disappeared suddenly. One of Drake's officers described their progress as 'valiantly attempting to sail uphill.'

◆

Jack concluded his article with some general observations of life in England under Queen Elizabeth I, particularly in the mid to late part of her reign, which ended in 1603.

'Number four?' Leon asked.

'Eh?'

'You said there were four themes in all this stuff.'

'Well spotted,' Jack replied. 'Number four is really a subset of ground disturbances, but it appears often enough, mostly as a mathematical construct. There isn't much actual story. Ever heard of Axel Furst?'

'Not recently, Jack.'

'When did you last hear of Axel Furst, Leon?'

'Never, Jack. Never heard of the man.'

'As I thought. He was a Norwegian geologist, way ahead of his time. Developed a theory of Earth's formation and naturally occurring geomagnetic hot spots. According to Furst, there are fluctuating gravitational pressure points that occur in magma right around the planet. They move around like giant oceanic currents. He likened them to two massive Gulf Streams, one in the northern hemisphere, another in the south. He speculated that there were also pockets of "tung magma", or heavy magma, that more or less stayed put. But he couldn't convince his colleagues or the scientific community generally. He wrote a thesis – never published, as far as I can tell – but published a short novel in 1895 using his theory as background to the story. I've read it. It seems to have been inspired by H.G. Wells and the earlier works of Jules Verne. It was never published in English and is very rare. It's called *Dyp Strøm*, Deep Current. I managed to find a copy years ago and had it translated. Looks like it was privately published, and not very professionally at that. It's a bit cryptic. You need to accept his hypothesis for it to make any sense at all. Maybe the translation is a bit dodgy.'

Leon said he thought it sounded more like science fiction than science fact but that it was an intriguing thought. 'It could account for some ground disturbances, I suppose.'

Jack agreed, 'Quite right, though it's still a very vague concept. No one has done any serious research into it.' He thought for a moment. 'Except that I now have quite a few references to it in my files, so who knows. My files are incomplete, I've decided.'

It was time for a break.

'Good gracious, it appears your glass is empty again. It appears mine is too. It appears the bottle is also devoid of content. Hang on, I'll get the other half.'

There was no protest at the mock surprise. Never short of a few bottles of wine, Jack retrieved an older vintage of the cabernet that P.C. Sarah Blackman had enjoyed the day before. He would have to find something else for her if they ever shared the meal he'd half promised. Jack thought his friend's appreciation of fine wine needed some guidance, but he kept only better bottles at *Zurich*, as they were mainly drunk when he was alone, which was most of the time.

'You'll like this,' he said, with more hope than anticipation. 'It's Tasmanian, east coast. You won't find much better out of Australia for the price. I hope it doesn't get "discovered". The price will double overnight. But back to business and changing the subject completely. I'm still trying to work out what's beyond Dragonfly. I'm working on making it a starting point for Southwood. If I can figure out Dragonfly, *we might learn* more about Southwood. Conversely, when we find out what Southwood is, we'll know everything we need to know about Dragonfly. Working backwards sometimes works. That would keep Sayer off my back anyway. He wants this share market thing sorted. But I'm now almost convinced that Dragonfly was nothing more than an elaborate fundraising scheme, though it could have been simple theft. The money is to finance something else, and as best as I can make out, that's a project to control some energy scheme. Priority one, though, is Derek. We have to find him, if he's anywhere to be found, that is. I'm not ruling out anything. And your friend Lyn. I'll have to leave that to you, but I'll help if I can. Tomorrow, I have some calls to make and some post to post. But now my head's just about done in.'

To put some white space between his mental exertions and sleep, Jack settled into an armchair with his wine and picked up a remote control. He'd left a disc in his DVD player and it was three episodes of one of his favourite TV shows.

'Leon.'

'What?'

'No talking now. We have to watch this.'

'If it's a quiz show, I'm leaving,' Leon said.

It wasn't.

◆

Chapter 6

A Frozen Bentley

By the time Leon forced himself out of bed the next day, Jack had been up for two hours and had his first coffee on the deck. He had slept only intermittently, unable to switch off his mind. Just before six, the not-unusual rumbling of a container ship disturbed what little rest remained as it made its way upriver to Hobart. The day had dawned almost cloud-free with no apparent prospect of rain.

'Jack,' Leon said in greeting, stifling a yawn.

'Leon,' Jack replied, 'you want coffee? I'm one ahead of you. Been up before sparrow-fart. Breakfast will be eggs and bacon, or bacon and eggs, as you prefer. I do a mean poached egg, by which I mean a very average poached egg. I can't poach eggs for toffee, so fried is your best option.'

Leon yawned again.

'Fried's good. I'm easy pleased. Eggs is eggs to me.'

Jack's restless night had at least resulted in further clarification of his thoughts, and he knew what the next few steps would be. As he'd said to Leon the previous evening, finding Derek and Lyn were priorities, though he was uneasy about whether either was still around to be found. As soon as office hours rolled around, he could call another friend to take the first step on what he hoped would be a rescue mission. If that call didn't yield anything, he'd have to come up with a Plan B, though he had no idea what that might look like. Something else occurred to Jack.

'Hey, Leon, how are you for time? Do you have to get to work or anything?'

'No mate, free as a bird for a while. Between contracts, as they say.'

'Good, you won't have to rush your breakfast then. Don't make any plans for the next few days, eh.'

Leon assured Jack that his time was Jack's time, and anyway, he wanted to find Lyn and realised that working together was the surest way of doing that. They sat on the deck with their eggs, bacon and coffee and gazed at the river. A cruise ship sailed serenely towards Hobart, a little late in the day, Jack noted aloud, they usually arrived very early.

'It's because they have to sail uphill,' Leon suggested helpfully, 'and they are very, very big ships, you know.'

Jack changed the subject. 'Can we contact Harry Steve John?'

'Trousers? Technically, yes, but probably not. Why.'

'We need to know who was running this blog thing. It would be useful to know why he called it Dragonfly. It's either very random or very specific. Got me bugged. Harry told me this bloke is well educated, in his twenties and might live in Australia. Oh yeah, and he likes Formula 1 motor racing. And something else. Not a lot to go on, is it? If you can get in touch with Harry, let him know I want to meet again, will you.'

Leon said he would try but reminded Jack that when Trousers went bush, he did the thing properly. Breakfast over, Jack outlined their first steps. It would all start with a phone call, which he hoped would lead to something useful. Another visit to D.I. Sayer was called for, too, but that could wait a little. Significantly, though, he needed to find out if it was safe to go back to his apartment. Somewhere between Opossum Bay and Hobart, he would post several large envelopes he'd prepared at about three in the morning. He didn't explain what they contained.

Smoke on the Water played again. It was Wapping Security with another alert that Jack's security system had been activated. He immediately checked online and was surprised to see two tradesmen installing a new door to replace the one broken the previous day. This time, he made no excuses about the neighbour's cat, assuring the caller that it was a known visitor who wouldn't know how to turn off the alarm and that the alert could be ignored for an hour or so. The call terminated; Jack selected a number and touched the ironically old-fashioned green telephone icon.

'Jimi, it's Jack. How's it going? Listen, did you get that black Range Rover in? Great, and you looked after it for me? Better still. I'm going to guess it's been collected. Fantastic.'

Jimi worked for a company contracted to tow vehicles and hold them securely until the police told them otherwise. Jack gave Jimi more instructions, promised him a beer – which more accurately meant a slab and a bottle of scotch – said his farewells and turned to Leon.

'That's a break. I'm betting that the blokes in the Range Rover who were watching me were the two who nabbed Derek. I'm also betting that if we find that car, we'll be able to find him. When it was impounded, I had a mate install a tracker. GPS is a wonderful thing. OK, you done? Let's get going.'

Jack's Commodore was fitted with a GPS screen that looked like any other car navigation aid. His version was modified, though and had a remote control. Sitting comfortably in his after-market Recaro bucket seats, he carefully entered a code. The display cleared, and the screen remained blank for several seconds, save for a 'loading' icon, which pulsed annoyingly. Jack frowned. Presently, a new window opened, and the frown passed.

'Good old Jimi. Check it out, that Rangie isn't far away, just off the road between Cambridge and Richmond.' He thought for a few moments. 'We're going to need a drone, a nice quiet drone. Luckily, I know a man who knows all about drones.'

Jack sent a lengthy text. There was little traffic on the single-lane road back to town, so it was with some annoyance that Jack spotted an old ute tailgating him with headlights flashing.

'Being followed?' Leon asked unnecessarily.

'Possibly, or just some bogan from nowhere. Watch this.'

Jack hit a switch hidden under the dash. Within moments, the ute had dropped back to a more respectful distance, and the driver soon turned onto a side road.

'You can't see it until it's activated,' Jack explained, 'but the central brake light in the rear window flashes a rather brilliant blue when I throw a certain switch. Very useful.'

Leon was impressed. 'Let me guess, you had a mate in the police put it in for you?'

He was partly right. One of Jack's friends in low places who had briefly been employed in the police garage before it was outsourced had 'inherited' some surplus equipment. Jack enjoyed a few options not available from regular sources. Having persuaded the impatient ute driver he wasn't wanted, Jack was further annoyed to see another car, this time a recent model sedan, similarly following with headlights flashing. The frown returned.

'Bugger, another one. Can you make out the rego number,' he asked Leon.

Leon turned to look out the rear window.

'I can't read it all. It looks like L-something, and the last numbers are one-one. Why, does it matter?'

'Maybe. If I'm right, it's an unmarked police car. I've been discovered. No one should know where I was last night. Hang on.'

Jack pulled up when a straight section of road permitted, and waited with the engine still running. The police car pulled up, but not before its own discretely installed blue lights were set to flash mode. The uniformed driver approached while another officer – also in uniform, as Jack could now see – waited in the car. The driver carried neither a notebook nor a breathalyser. It was P.C. Blackman. Jack switched off the engine and opened the door.

'No, stay in the car. I'll get in the back if that's OK.'

After introducing Leon, Jack waited for whatever was to follow, hoping his many questions would be answered. The P.C. outlined her mission.

'You know your apartment was burgled yesterday,' she stated. It wasn't a question. 'It looked like an official exercise but wasn't us, and our liaison people haven't been able to identify any authority prepared to admit it was them. A member of the public reported it, actually complaining about the traffic disruption, and we made enquiries. Seems your local barista reckons you went to Zurich.'

Jack confessed that was just the name of his Opossum Bay cottage, though he had been to Zurich in Switzerland on two occasions. Blackman continued.

'Technically, you're a grade two missing person. Or you were. Luckily, we were able to locate your car. I'm afraid we took the liberty of putting a tracker in it, standard procedure for staff and contractors on certain assignments. Your understanding would be appreciated. Much easier to beg forgiveness after than ask permission before, if you get me. We've been monitoring movements to and around your place, but nothing until this morning when some tradies came in to replace your stairwell door. Did a good job; you'd never know the difference. Oh yes, and they left a model car on your coffee table. Don't ask how we know. We have our methods. By the way, here are some more documents you might find interesting.' She handed Jack another USB drive.

'Anyway, now that we've found you, D.I. Sayer wants a meeting. Can you make it this morning?'

Jack was slightly annoyed that he'd been played at his own game with the tracking device but let it go. He was pleased that his door had been replaced and intrigued about the return of his model Bentley. That told him something about the professionalism of the organisation and the discipline of some of its employees. He would need to tread carefully. Blackman's radio clicked to life.

'382 come in.'

'382, go ahead.'

'We're wanted back at base. Are you nearly done?'

'Stand by.'

Blackman muted her radio.

'Jack, are you going into town now? It would be good if you could see D.I. Sayer ASAP.'

'I can be there in 30. Less probably, but I have to do one thing first.'

P.C. Blackman checked her watch and agreed that would be OK; said to Leon she was pleased to meet him and farewelled them both. Without responding to the radio further, she returned to the police car, and the flashing blue lights were switched off. She waited a minute till Jack and Leon drove off before rejoining the traffic.

On the road again, Leon suggested that P.C. Blackman was a 'bit of all right'. Jack agreed but said nothing more about her. His immediate plan was to visit a post office to send his letters. They were large envelopes addressed to various contacts. Inside was another slightly smaller one, stamped and addressed. Like Russian dolls, the envelopes were similarly treated, and would be posted on. The final envelopes were addressed to himself at a post office box address or D.I. Sayer, the latter boldly marked PRIVATE AND CONFIDENTIAL. Each contact knew they were to hold these for three days before posting the contents. Jack wanted the final envelopes to take some time to reach their ultimate addresses. He described the process to Leon.

'It's low-tech. I've copied all my *Dark History* files, the Dragonfly documents, and more to a memory card. I could copy it all to the cloud, but I don't trust it. Clouds have a habit of dissipating. Can't rely on the security of my own place either, it seems.'

The rest of the trip back to Hobart was uneventful. Jack posted his letters and logged into his security site. He activated the cameras and scrutinised the interior of his apartment. As expected, no one was inside, but he couldn't tell if his uninvited visitors had installed their own surveillance equipment. He would have to take the risk. Logging in to the Hobart traffic cam site and selecting the Davey Street camera revealed no lurking black Range Rover. It was probably safe to return to the comfort of his own home. Jack surmised that the raid to secure the briefcase and its contents had satisfied whoever was responsible, for the time being anyway. If these people were any good, they would be aware of the post-raid interest shown by the local police. Jack was comfortable, presuming his safety was assured, at least for today, but he wasn't prepared to extend that presumption to his friend.

'Leon, your car is safe with Keith, and unless you can't live without it, I'd prefer you leave it there and stay with me. In fact, it might be useful if you met Sayer. OK?'

'Sure. Like I said, my time is your time.'

When they returned to the city, Jack took a circuitous route to his apartment, keeping a lookout for any car following them. There was none. Having parked the Commodore, Jack had an idea. He took the stairs rather than the lift and told Leon to wait in the stairwell while he quietly unlocked his new door. The surreptitiously replaced door had the same lock in it. Stepping inside, Jack scanned his familiar surroundings and satisfied himself that nothing was amiss. Only the model Bentley was out of place; otherwise, his home seemed undisturbed. Very carefully, he picked up the Bentley. As expected, a small electronic device had been fixed to the underside. It was a microphone and transmitter.

'Clever,' Jack thought to himself as he gently wrapped the model in a tea towel and, equally gently, placed it in his freezer.

He motioned to Leon to come and held a silencing finger to his lips. On the balcony, he called another friend in low places, this time the security expert who had installed his camera equipment.

'Sam, Jack. Got a small job for you. I need my cars scanned for bugs. Trackers, anything. I'll leave the keys on the kitchen bench. The flat, too, sweep that. I found one already. It's on a model car in my freezer. Leave anything you find in the freezer. You know how to get in. I haven't changed the code. Cheers.'

He duly left his car keys on the bench with four $50 notes.

'Some friends have families to support,' he said to Leon, who had given him a quizzical look. 'I don't expect anything for nothing. Let's get this meeting with Sayer out of the way. But first, I have to finish writing something for him. I was working on that last night. It's very draft but has loads of attachments. Sayer loves reports with loads of attachments. Give me eight and a half minutes.'

Leon spent the next few minutes gazing at the view. Jack returned to the balcony. 'Come on, let's nick off. I've finished this.'

◆

The atmosphere in the city police station was chilly until they reached D.I. Sayer's office, where they were met by P.C. Blackman. She half-smiled when Jack and Leon approached, escorted by a young police officer.

'That's OK, Wilson, I'll look after these gentlemen,' she said to the bored officer.

'Mr Sugarman, and,' she paused to remember the name, 'Leon. I didn't get your surname in the car earlier.'

'Trapman, Leon Trapman,' Leon filled in the blank.

'Right. Detective Inspector Sayer is occupied just now but should be free in a few minutes. Have you made any progress with Dragonfly?'

Jack saw no reason to be secretive about his findings but admitted he had more to offer about Southwood than the share market scam. He started to describe what he'd found out, but the intercom buzzed. It was Sayer instructing Blackman to show Jack in when he arrived.

'They're here now, sir,' Blackman responded.

'They? Oh, never mind, show them in. No calls, please.'

Jack introduced Sayer to Leon, explaining he was a strategy and tactics consultant he used occasionally. Leon tried not to smile at the grandiose description. The detective inspector didn't look happy and avoided eye contact for a few moments. Jack wondered if their co-belligerent status had been dissolved for some reason. They all sat. Sayer rearranged some papers and dropped them into a tray.

'There's a thing, Jack. Let me tell you what that thing is. The two blokes in that car you put me on to. They were Feds, not the Federal Police, but part of that new international security mob, you know, police, armed services, border security, the whole works. They have a long name I can't remember; even the initials are a mile long. We call them The Hague because it's all double Dutch. Anyway, we looked like a bunch of idiots. Tried to anyway. Tried to look very embarrassed about it.'

Jack was amused at The Hague reference and surprised about the rest. He wondered where it was leading.

'We tried to check their credentials, but these blokes won't tell us much about much. They admitted to placing a couple of agents here, and that's about it. But that car. Why did it have bogus plates? We didn't let on that we knew about that – thanks for the tip-off, by the way – and sent them on their way with our best wishes. I even offered to liaise, but they said they'd go up-line and let others make that decision. A bit odd for field operatives. They usually have that sort of discretion. I reckon they're part of the Dragonfly thing. Thought you should know.'

Jack had reached that conclusion already.

'Now, the raid on your place. Blackman has already briefed you on that. We now think it was down to The Hague, but we can't confirm it. Bloody annoying, I can tell you, we're used to collaboration, not competition. But all that's just a bit of distraction. What can you tell me about…'

Sayer's phone rang.

'Blast, I said no calls… what… who… oh, you better put him through then.'

There was the briefest delay.

'Good morning, commissioner, it's… very well…'

As usual, Sayer turned his chair and gazed out the window, but Jack could see he wasn't comfortable with the call, his left hand firmly gripping the arm of the chair. Sayer said very little and finished the call by looking at the handset, as people do when their caller hangs up abruptly.

'Not good news, I take it?' Jack suggested.

'Strange news,' Sayer responded, 'the commissioner has pulled me off this case. Said it's been taken over by the Fed's, The Hague mob probably. Reckons we're "bungling incompetents", and we've come up with nothing so far. Your name was mentioned, Jack, not very complimentary, I'm afraid. So that's an end to it.'

While relaying the news, Sayer scribbled a note and pushed it to Jack. Both he and Leon leaned forward.

It read, 'Say nothing. Office bugged. Agree to lunch.' He continued.

'So, my apologies for the time you've spent on this. The least I can do is offer you both lunch at my club. Hang on.'

With that, he dialled a number and asked if the private dining room was available. It was, and he reserved it for 12:30.

'Jack, do you know White's in Davey Street?'

He nodded.

'Meet me there at a little after 12. We can have a drink in the bar before we eat. I hope you like seafood; it's a fixed menu. The chef does a terrific chowder, and the wine list is more than adequate. Blackman can join us, too. She's spent quite a bit of time on this. It's jacket and tie, I'm afraid.' The last comment was for Leon's benefit.

White's was one of the city's few gentlemen's clubs, named after a similar club in London, the oldest and possibly most exclusive of such establishments in England. It wasn't the most exclusive club in Hobart, nor was it strictly a gentlemen's club, as women had been permitted membership since 1977. That had been a tribute to Queen Elizabeth on the occasion of her silver jubilee, but it went largely unnoticed, much to the gratification of many long-standing members. The club maintained high standards of tradition, decorum and discretion. Members had been known to have their membership suspended or even terminated over immoderate behaviour, even outside the club's confines. Members were always called Mister, even the few women members. Professional titles were 'left in the car park' although knights, lords and the like were accorded their appropriate titles, as were officers of the armed forces. Such was the imposition of tradition at White's.

The main premises comprised a single large building, formerly a private home, built in the late 1850s using – so the club prospectus claims – stone left over from the construction of Government House on the Queen's Domain. Lesser buildings behind the two-storey mansion were originally stables, servants' quarters and two sheds but were now used as garages and a gardener's shed.

Jack found himself and Leon a suitable jacket and tie at his apartment and decided to drive to White's for their appointment. Sam had already been in and left a scribbled note that read, 'Tracker in each car. Three other bugs inside. All in freezer. Cheers.' It was initialled simply S. Under the now debugged model Bentley, Jack's $50 notes were still there, next to the neatly folded tea towel. Jack smiled.

'Come on then, we'll take the Jag.'

In the car park, he carefully removed and folded a tarp to reveal his pride and joy, a Jaguar XKR convertible. He turned to Leon.

'2013, five-litre supercharged V8, six-speed automatic. I bought it in the UK and had it shipped over. It arrived last month. Beautiful car. Like it?'

Leon nodded as he walked around it.

'Nice. Very nice indeed. I like the number plate, JAMJAR. Bet that cost you.'

'A bit over a thousand.'

'How much?'

'For the plate, not the car. It was JAMJAR or NUMBER.'

Jack took a very roundabout route to White's, partly to watch for and lose any following vehicles but mostly because he just liked driving the Jag, especially with the top down. Leon relished the journey, too, looking at home in his borrowed Harris tweed jacket and Gordon tartan tie.

'I should be wearing a flat cap with this jacket,' he said.

'There's one in the glove box if you want it.' Jack suggested, but by then, they had arrived at White's.

Two wide iron gates provided entry to and exit from a considerable gravel circular drive where several cars were parked. Two large Mercedes Benz sedans sat side by side and, looking somewhat out of place, an enormous Cadillac Escalade. Jack parked next to that, which made the Jaguar look even lower and sleeker than it was. At that point, his host arrived in the same car Blackman had used that morning on the road from Opossum Bay. Neither Sayer nor Blackman were in uniform. Uniforms were discouraged at White's.

Initial greetings out of the way, Sayer pulled the old-fashioned doorbell. At White's, you had to be admitted. There was no boorish walking in unannounced. The on-duty secretary would admit members, having first identified them thanks to a discretely installed surveillance camera and hidden monitor at the reception desk. Today's secretary was Roy Graham, a Yorkshireman with Scottish ancestry who disliked beer, preferring lowland or Speyside single malt whisky. 'Mr Sayer, welcome to White's,' he discounted the detective inspector title, 'and Commander Sugarman, so very nice to have you back, sir. It's been some weeks since we've seen you. Gentlemen, if you would care to sign in your guests, the bar is at your disposal. Your dining room is being prepared.'

Sayer turned to Jack.

'You're a member too? I didn't realise. Seems we have more in common than either of us suspected.'

Jack explained to his companions that White's membership list is a closely guarded secret. Members knew of others only if each divulged it or happened to meet on the premises. He had been a member for several years, longer than his host, and a regular visitor, though he had never coincided any visit with the detective inspector. The bar was at the rear of the ground floor and extended to a sizable tiled balcony where, on fine days, comfortable furniture was provided. Today was such a day, and the four settled at a table as the barman approached. They had this area to themselves.

'Good afternoon, gentlemen,' he added 'miss' in deference to Sarah's presence, 'may I suggest our selection for today, DOM Benedictine et tonique. Very refreshing on a sunny day.'

Both members knew it was bad form not to accept a White's barman's suggestion, though Jack at least knew the liqueur was more generally taken as an after-dinner drink. It was traditional for club staff to wear a badge displaying only their surname, and members were expected not to use given names if they knew them. Jack observed this rule.

'Thank you, Richardson, that sounds perfect. Four please.'

Richardson returned to what he called his spiritual home and prepared the drinks. Leon spoke first.

'I'd rather have a beer, Jack.'

'No, you wouldn't. Maybe later. Now then, Terry, I think I can use your first name, yes? Social occasion and all that. What's going on with this Dragonfly business? And your office, bugged? Really?'

The detective inspector looked less imposing out of uniform. Despite this, he still considered himself in charge of the case, even though he had been officially relieved of it.

'I'll have to come clean, Jack. I've been indiscreet with some of my own enquiries and managed to annoy some people it's best not to annoy – corridors of power and all that. It seems a certain government minister has been approached by a certain...' he chose his phrase carefully, 'captain of industry after I asked the wrong questions. I can wear that. Trouble is, Commissioner Baker is a bit of a wuss and collapsed under the pressure of pressure. Does that make sense?'

Jack nodded. He'd come across this situation before.

'This morning, my office looked like it had been cleaned, and I don't mean dusted and vacuumed. Some of my files have been rearranged; you've seen how orderly I keep them. I noticed it straight away. As for being bugged, that's only a suspicion, but it's better to be safe than sorry. I'd guess you've come to at least one conclusion that I have, that the share market thing is a symptom of something else. Something bigger. Much bigger.'

'You told me as much, didn't you,' Leon chipped in, looking at Jack.

Richardson returned with the drinks on a silver tray, deftly placing them before his customers, starting with Sarah. It was ladies first at White's. Leon couldn't resist.

'Thanks, mate. You couldn't recommend a beer, I suppose. Something dark.'

'Indeed, sir,' Richardson replied, with an eyebrow slightly raised at being called mate. 'We have a very fine porter from one of the local breweries. It has proven very popular with our more discerning members.'

Leon succumbed to the implied compliment.

'OK, one of those, thanks.' Richardson bowed almost imperceptibly and left the table, having first determined that no one else required further refreshment. Terry continued.

'I'm a copper through and through, and I can't let this go just like that, but my activities must be very guarded from now on. I'll have to rely on you two mostly. Blackman here will be reassigned to other cases but still attached to my office. Sorry, Blackman, I know you've taken a particular interest in this.' He sipped his drink before continuing.

'Hmm, nice. I could get used to these. But Dragonfly. Let's forget about that for the moment. The organisation behind it and what they're up to is more important. Any ideas, Jack?'

'Plenty of ideas. All supposition and theory, really, but it makes sense in my mind. You might think it's a bit science fiction, but I'd say there's more science than fiction. I've compiled plenty of evidence – I think I can call it that – with my own documents and others. Derek gave me some, and you gave me some, and I managed to get more from Harry. You probably don't know about Harry, but he's made himself scarce. Leon, did you manage to get hold of him?'

Leon retrieved his phone and checked.

'Not yet. I tried phoning, but it went to voicemail, so I sent a text. Two, actually. No reply. He may have switched his phone off, but it'd be unusual. He loves his phone.'

Richardson returned with another tray. 'One Crayon and Maggot porter, sir.' He retrieved Leon's already empty square-based Old Fashioned glass. This time, Leon thanked him by name and not by 'mate'. Richardson looked pleased and again bowed slightly before leaving the table. Jack continued.

'And I hope I can say this. Sarah gave me some other stuff.' He looked at Sarah, who shifted slightly in her chair.

'I know about that too,' Terry admitted, 'I would have done the same. Go on.'

'Harry busted a secure blog site and got me a mountain of stuff. Some of it was encrypted. Some of it still is unless he's managed to decode that as well. That site was called Dragonfly, which is what I call this share market thing. Through all that, though, I came across Southwood. I told you about that. Did you have anything official?'

'Just an occasional reference. Nothing useful.'

'I'm not surprised.'

Jack outlined some of his general thoughts on Southwood. At 12:30 precisely, Graham approached and announced that their dining room was ready.

'You're in for a treat today, gentlemen, miss. Anton has surpassed himself. The seafood chowder is superb as always, and the lemon-crusted ocean perch quite outstanding.'

Their private dining room was originally 'the front room' of the house, where the less welcome guests might be entertained briefly before being sent on their way. This in no way reflected on the members using its facilities today, nor any other day. It was opulent without being vulgar and featured some of the club's better paintings, including a George Phoenix landscape that Jack had presented to the club on permanent loan. He maintained that a man who loved art loved life. If anyone seemed prepared to listen, he further claimed that where an artist recorded life, the collector preserved it. Today, though, no one else seemed to notice the artwork.

Comfortably seated, Graham presented 'Mister Sayer' with the wine list, who promptly handed it to Jack. 'Your domain, I think.'

Jack glanced at the extensive list of white wines. 'I see what you mean. It's a very nice selection.'

'Whatever Anton suggests would best complement our meal, Graham.'

'Excellent, sir. I have already ascertained. We have an outstanding 2012 Pouilly-Fumé, which I am sure would satisfy.'

Without waiting for confirmation, Graham left the table, which was soon set with the appropriate glasses.

Jack had a thought. 'You two aren't drinking on duty, are you?'

Sarah chipped in, the first time she had spoken since arriving.

'As of 12 o'clock, we're both off duty. Time off in lieu. No overtime budget, you see. And D.I. Sayer sets his own timetable, don't you, sir.'

A nod confirmed. 'RHIP,' he confessed, 'rank has its privileges.'

Lunches at White's tended to be relaxed affairs with little regard for timing. Members understood this and were content that their midday meal would take two hours or longer. Today was no exception, and when coffee was served, it was after 2:30 p.m. By then, Jack had explained his theory over a satisfying lunch. He realised later that he seemed to have done more explaining directly to Sarah, rather than the group generally. He wondered why, but only briefly.

◆

Chapter 7

Sailing Uphill

Jack knew that what he knew wasn't the whole story. He was also canny enough to realise he didn't know what he didn't know; the unknown unknowns. His collection of documents might technically be evidence but they were only suggestive of his antagonist's activities at this stage. Either way, he knew enough to deduce what he was up against. During their excellent lunch at White's, he told his colleagues probably more than they needed to hear about the situation. But they listened politely.

Southwood is an organisation. It has existed for many years by many names. Some researchers think it goes back to the Knights Templar of the 12th century, but it has been corrupted since then.

The Club of Berlin, a legitimate and respected group established in 1964, inadvertently adopted the name of a highly secretive organisation founded decades earlier in the days of the German Empire. That earlier incarnation was originally a group of researchers whose aim was purely financial. As the founding members retired or died, though, new recruits degraded its aims into something sinister. It secured ready allies within less reputable governments and shadier elements from the world of commerce and organised crime. Without any ambition to become so, it turned into one of the world's largest semi-secret organisations. Most people have never heard of it.

Its secrecy is maintained partly by its structure. With a unit in overall control, it otherwise exists as many groups of various sizes. Groups are unaware of the others' operations unless Berlin deems it necessary. The controlling unit calls itself Berlin, or sometimes the Berlin Desk, for no other reason than it's a contraction of the full name. As far as anyone knows, they now have no presence in Berlin.

Why and when the Club of Berlin changed its name to Southwood is unrecorded. What is known is that it is a progressive organisation that, for the past couple of decades, has used technology as a basis for its activities.

The Dragonfly scheme, to generate considerable profit in several countries, was a Southwood project that was planned two years ago. Many programmers were engaged in developing it, most of whom innocently thought their contribution was for legitimate purposes. Others harboured suspicions. Some of these died in unusual circumstances. Had Southwood's structure been more formal, it would have been able to use open communication to ensure external security, but with its secrecy a priority, it suffered one significant failure. The Dragonfly blog was created by a Southwood contractor who worked out what the organisation was up to. His cryptic postings were designed to suggest rather than inform. His logic was that blatant advertising of the scheme would drive the organisation further underground than it already was. Using secrecy against a secret organisation seemed appropriate, as well as ironic. The hope was that someone like Jack Sugarman would see the big picture and do something about it.

However, the blog was taken down, and the blogger vanished. It was anyone's guess as to whether they were still alive. Jack's Dragonfly files were now a substantial volume of work and might in themselves identify not only the Southwood organisation hierarchy but precisely what they were planning. By his own admission, most conclusions were inconclusive, but he had to run with what he had. From Southwood's documents, he deduced the organisation's aim, global control of clean, inexhaustible energy. He only surmised the source but knew nothing of its distribution.

The bizarre theory of Axel Furst was central to this energy supply. It was ultimately presented as a 19th-century science fiction novel and almost immediately faded into obscurity. However, his idea that energy could be extracted or captured from gravitational pressure points finally found favour in some scientific circles. Southwood scientists had confirmed Furst's theory that the upper levels of the

Earth's mantle included magma that flowed like giant oceanic currents. These currents had been described in *Dyp Strøm* as being like massive Gulf Streams. Jack didn't know whether Southwood knew of the Furst theory, had developed it from other sources, or even their own investigations. Whichever it was, he was grateful for the starting point provided by the little-known Norwegian and promised him a fitting epitaph when this thing was over.

Jack could only speculate about how massive flows of magma could generate energy. He thought it might involve variations in gravity strength but would leave the science to others. Other documents in his collection pointed to a natural grid around the planet. His mind baulked at the mathematics of the thing. Independent of Furst's proposition, researchers with more mathematically inclined minds had already speculated on such an energy grid. Their theories ranged from a propulsion or navigation system installed by aliens millennia ago to a condition of all rocky planets. The latter might explain how birds and other animals could migrate vast distances with incredible precision. They could detect slight variations in gravitational fields and use them as direction finders. Most theories threw up more questions than they answered.

Changes in gravitational fields might not always be subtle or constant. Jack's 'ground disturbance' index heading pointed to many events that could have been caused by such a phenomenon, even if there was no definitive evidence of it. Obvious seismic activity did not always coincide with the strange incidents he recorded. Earth's atmosphere and oceans were affected by the Earth's gravity and that of the sun and moon. Extreme anomalies were often reported by ships' crews. Several of Jack's reports described vessels sailing much slower than should have been as dictated by tides, wind and their own power. One interviewee said, 'It was like we were sailing uphill.' Another insisted he saw a depression in the ocean 'like a mile wide man, and 10 feet deep in the middle, and circling like a slow whirlpool.' Jack recalled his earliest record of the 'sailing uphill' claim during Francis Drake's voyage in 1577.

Land-based events were usually more dramatic, causing damage to buildings and other structures and changes to the landscape. Jack recalled the many stories of sunken churches and at least one of a complete village that all but disappeared with much loss of life. The lost village story was three hundred years old and the sole report of the event, but neglected to state its name or exactly where it was, despite being otherwise thorough. The account referred to Borisov's village. Borisov may have been the mayor or equivalent administrator of a Bulgarian or Russian township. It was this story that prompted him Jack to create what he called his 'Double I' classification, his code for Intensity and Impact. The Borisov village event rated 55 on his scale, the highest. He had yet to classify his entire catalogue.

The intensity rating of a disturbance was established by several factors. Duration was the first, with most events lasting only minutes. Some were lengthy, and others appeared to be a series of events that lasted for a few days. Whether the disturbance occurred under sandy soil or rocky terrain also influenced the rating. Rocky terrain events were rare, and Linda's story was an extreme example. For a disturbance to be noticeable, let alone destructive, under even modestly mountainous terrain suggested the energy release was significant. Intensity ratings were subjective, given the often limited data available. Event reports usually concentrated on the impact, especially where loss of life was concerned. Older stories, of which there were many, often provided details of the behaviour of animals and birds.

Jack tried to understand the nature of the energy grid and its relationship to the magma flowing under the Earth's crust. How kinetic energy translated to electrical energy remained a mystery to him. He tried one of his 'stream of consciousness' exercises, but after two hours, he had only a page of dot points and a vague scientific premise he later dismissed. He would work on the presumption that the thing existed. The understanding of it would have to wait until greater minds could be persuaded to describe the science behind it and distil the concept into pure numbers. One thing he was sure of, though. The mathematics would be far more complex than he could ever imagine. To wait till all the answers presented themselves was to lose traction as well as time.

One dot point in the failed stream of consciousness read 'Animals/Birds' while another, with no precision at all, read 'Mind Stuff.' The behaviour of animals and birds during, and notably before, disturbances convinced Jack that they could detect anomalies that humans could not. More attuned to their environment than humans, the 'flight' part of their survival matrix kicked in. This was often witnessed and recorded as mass departures. Sometimes, a single animal, usually a horse or dog, figured prominently in stories. As domesticated animals, they were frequently reluctant to flee and leave their owners in dangerous situations. It is well known that horses and dogs could sense danger long before people recognised it.

Jack had scribbled a box around the two dot points in a printed copy of his thoughts. His 'mind stuff' included all the attributes he had spoken to Sarah about, but he had yet to come up with an acceptable word to describe the grouping. Some people have 'the cunning of a fox' or some such animal-world characteristic. He was sure that the brain, operating on electrical impulses, was somehow influenced by natural variations in electrical fields. The degree to which those variations were received and interpreted was one of the questions Jack chose to leave alone.

A related question he would also leave alone was, what created those variations in the first place? Furst's proposed tung magma might affect his magma Gulf Streams, as would our distance from the sun, solar activity at any given time, the moon, and planetary alignment. At least one document in Jack's *Dark History* collection referenced sunspot activity and, obliquely, the effect on the rate of occurrence of the events recorded. That one form of energy could affect another was a logical conclusion. Since 1945, the detonation of nuclear weapons has inspired many researchers to consider the higher mathematics of such things. At least one academic developed a formula for predicting when and where test detonations would occur. Jack was particularly puzzled by this. Were detonations timed and sited to maximise energy release? Were Hiroshima and Nagasaki simply in the right place at the right time?

Nuclear testing after the Second World War was prolific. The USA alone conducted over 1,000 tests from 1945. This activity declined from a high point in 1962 to low levels in the late 1980s. Ufologists point to a correlation between atomic tests and UFO sightings. Conspiracy theorists in UFO groups point to the United States Airforce *Sign* and *Grudge* projects established in the late 1940s to study the subject. The much longer-lived *Project Blue Book* commenced in 1952 with a brief to investigate UFO sightings and determine if there was any threat to national security. It took 17 years to determine there was not, and theorists suggested that reaching that conclusion took a long time. They maintain that *Blue Book* was a cover for a much darker project to research the flying saucer phenomenon and its relationship to the energy grid. The director of *Project Sign* concluded that flying saucers were real craft and probably extraterrestrial. The Pentagon ordered the report that included this conclusion to be destroyed. A copy might have survived.

Jack made one definitive decision before shelving further consideration of the mathematics. There were so many variables in the equation that to be able to manage the energy grid at all, it would be essential to constantly collect massive amounts of data. This would be done globally, and the only way to monitor everything would be by a satellite that communicates with at least two ground stations boasting enormous computing power. A *Dark History* document had described such a satellite.

Black Knight, it claimed, was in a high and rapid polar orbit. There was no indication as to when it was launched. A popular urban myth insisted the object has been circling Earth for 13,000 years and was the work of aliens. NASA reportedly photographed space debris, which debunked that theory. With this story, Jack identified a common thread in his studies, the circular conspiracy. What better way to discredit a myth than with another myth? He called it seclusion by confusion. It also occurred to him that too much effort had been put into discrediting Black Knight.

Several countries have taken the trouble to deny the satellite was theirs, implying there was something to deny ownership of. For convenience, Jack named the theoretical satellite Dragonfly, a name he thought appropriate. He knew, too, that Black Knight was the name of a British rocket launched many times from Woomera, South Australia, in the fifties and sixties. The name of that rocket, he concluded, was pure coincidence.

Dragonfly is now identified as a satellite, the share market scheme and a collection of documents. Jack wanted to concentrate on Southwood. He was sure that references to South Wood as two words were just errors of reporting. The 'Mr Southwood' he constantly saw references to was possibly only a code name for whoever was in charge of the organisation or perhaps each group. Annoyingly, at least one mention of 'MR Southwood' and 'magnetic resonance' in the same document suggested that the former might be a division of the organisation or a project name.

Jack decided that for the time being, he would stick to what he had evidence for. First, Derek Asquith had been abducted, and Lyn McKellyer had possibly suffered the same treatment, despite her involvement being minimal. Second, his apartment had been raided and searched. He had video evidence of that. Finally, there was a volume of documents, though some were pretty enigmatic. He also had allies in Leon, D.I. Sayer and P.C. Sarah Blackman. The elusive Henry 'Trousers' Ford, aka Harry Steve John, would be helpful to have onside, too, but there was no telling when he might reappear. That the case had been taken from Sayer was a blow, but Jack thought some unofficial assistance might be forthcoming anyway, especially from Sarah. The Hague was a new entity, and no one seemed to know much about it. That even Sayer couldn't recall its real name was indicative of something approaching sinister.

The Hague presented little information online; what was available was vague. Officially it was the Internationaal Coöperatief Strategisch Defensie- en Veiligheidsalliantiebureau. That was the 'home' name in Dutch, which translated to International Co-operative Strategic Defence and Security Alliance Bureau. More encompassing than NATO, it was a multi-government organisation that seemed as secretive as Southwood. Sayer suggested that despite its government backing, it appeared to operate outside political influence. Secretive organisations were just as annoying as secret ones, more so when they were government bodies. The Hague qualified for further research. It remained to be seen whose side they were on.

Jack had a hundred ideas coalescing. He knew most would lead nowhere and hoped some would be useful. Inspired by one random idea, he read again one of his favourite *Dark History* documents, *The Flying Saucers of Brady Station,* which seemed particularly relevant to his inconclusive conclusions.

◆

There was a small school in outback South Australia which, in 1966, had one teacher, an occasional teacher aide (purely voluntary and the mother of an ex-pupil) and 16 pupils aged 12 to 16. The teacher theoretically taught the entire range of high school subjects but, in practice, restricted the curriculum to English, maths, science, social studies and, for the boys, woodwork. The teacher aide, Mrs Le Fevre, taught the girls cookery.

The teacher was Colin Hunter, a single man of 28 years who had accepted a posting to Brady Station with stoic grace. It was a teacher's lot to revenue remote postings to 'qualify' for more agreeable locations. As a keen fisherman, he was assured that nearby lakes would provide ample distraction for the otherwise bland lifestyle he would endure. Brady Station was a small township with a population almost entirely dedicated to local copper mines.

Colin found his pupils' age range a challenge at first. He was nothing if not dedicated, though, and he convinced himself that 24 months was not too much of a burden for a man with plenty of time on his hands. His enthusiasm was not lost on his charges; they responded well to his teaching style. They enjoyed outdoor activities, particularly as they were able to teach Mr Hunter, Sir, almost as much as he was able to teach them. There was much amusement when they enlightened him as to the fishing prospects. The many so-called lakes in the vicinity had been dry beds for years. Some of the younger pupils had never seen them with water and were hard-pressed to be convinced that such a thing was possible. On his arrival, Colin was assured by the shopkeeper-cum-postmaster that no significant rain had fallen since 1958. His fishing gear was put away.

On 25 May 1966, Flight 4 of a *Europa* rocket was news of the day and caused much excitement amongst his pupils, particularly the older boys. Mr Hunter, too, was fascinated by the new technology and pleased to be able to share what he knew about the event. Within an hour, though, his knowledge of the European Launcher Development Organisation, *Europa*, rocketry and space flight in general had been exhausted. To close the lesson, he made a promise he was to later regret. His class was delighted to hear that another launch was scheduled for later in the year and that when the date was known, Sir would take them to the highest accessible vantage point to witness Flight 5 take off. The Woomera launch site was not too far distant.

On launch day, Tuesday, 15 November, Mr Hunter, Mrs Le Fevre and 14 pupils – two were ill and stayed home – were joined by four parents. A small convoy of dusty four-wheel drives carried the group, somewhat uncomfortably, to 'the mountain', an hour's drive away. The mountain was insignificant so far as height went and had no official name. The local indigenous people considered the general area sacred and, with due respect, were asked permission for the group to visit. Auntie Annie, an elder, approved of the visit for the benefit of 'the little ones' but advised them not to stay after dark. She warned them not to follow the Min Min lights, which Colin Hunter had never heard of. He was sure the excursion would be over well before nightfall anyway.

With binoculars and telescopes on hand, the observers were thrilled, first by a billowing cloud of red dust, then by a lengthening streak of white smoke that hung undisturbed for many minutes before it slowly dissipated and finally disappeared. The oldest boy impressed his teacher by calculating their distance from the launch site through the delay between the red dust appearing and the sound reaching them. He won a gold star that day. The observations were over in minutes, but Colin had the children write about their experiences or draw or paint a picture. He had the foresight to bring plenty of materials for such activities.

When leaving, one vehicle refused to start, and not wanting to leave it behind, two of the accompanying fathers sent the others back while they rectified what they insisted to everyone was a common problem and easily fixed. So it was that most of the group ventured back in five vehicles while the sixth was repaired. The common problem was fixed in an hour, and everyone made it back home safely, but not before the two would-be mechanics had a most uncommon experience. Having completed the repair and packed away their tools, they took a final look at the vista towards Woomera.

'See those planes. Did you see them when the rocket took off?' one asked.

The other indicated that he had not but suggested they were probably helicopters, 'the way they change direction like that.'

As they watched, the helicopters – they counted five – seemed to be flying in formation in straight lines 'as if mapping out an area between Woomera and us.' One man decided they were looking for something that had fallen from the rocket when it was in flight.

'Yeah, that's it. Silly buggers have lost something. Let's get going.'

Their return journey was 10 minutes in when the passenger noticed the helicopters again. He alerted his companion. The moment he did so, the engine cut out, and their four-wheel drive drifted to a stop.

'Vapour lock?'

'Yeah, give it a minute. She'll be right.'

They got out to watch the odd manoeuvres and realised they were unlike any helicopters they had ever seen. They later described their movements as silent and jerky, coming to sudden stops and changing direction at right angles. At one point, they formed a circle, or rather a pentagon, and remained stationary over what the men knew to be a dusty lake bed. Each machine was 'like a flying saucer'. They apologised for the description but said they were the traditional disk-like shape and added that they believed they were 'something the rocket people had.' Neither had any time for flying saucer theorists. While over the dry lake, a bright light was generated so that they couldn't observe directly without it hurting their eyes. This lasted a minute or two until the light went out, and the disks shot up vertically. They disappeared before either of the men could focus properly on the retreating craft.

Both were astonished to see that the previously dry lake now seemed to be full of water. Curiosity got the better of them, and they walked, unspeaking, towards the lake. In a few minutes, they were at the water's edge and stunned to find the 'water' was, in fact, solid ice.

'No, get out of here,' one said in disbelief.

The other tossed a small rock onto the surface. It bounced once and slid several yards along the surface. In patches, the lifeless ice had started to melt, the dry surface turning wet and glossy. Neither man had brought a camera with them, and they cursed their lack of planning. After scanning the sky to ensure their mysterious aircraft had gone, they trudged back to their vehicle. The engine started immediately, and they drove back, not knowing whether to mention their experience to anyone. By the time they reached home, they had agreed to stay silent unless anyone else mentioned the incident, though they thought it unlikely.

'It's agreed then, we were just delayed with the repair, yeah?'

'Right. Anyway, I don't want to get into any talks now. Got a bit of a headache.'

'Me too, a touch of sun, I reckon.'

The next day, the school was excitedly comparing the pupils' stories and drawings. They all wanted to watch the next launch, whenever that was. Mr Hunter awarded a gold star for the best story and another for the best drawing, which pleased the two children immensely. Another picture made by the only Aboriginal child at the school intrigued Colin.

'Charlie, what's this you've drawn in the sky near the hills?'

Charlie appeared nonplussed. 'The flying saucers, Sir. Didn't you see them?'

◆

The text ended with Charlie's simple question. Jack discovered the article had been written by the teacher, Colin Hunter, despite referring to himself in the third person. The author seemed to fancy himself as a writer and presented his article as a narrative by someone who had undertaken some research. The title, *The Flying Saucers of Brady Station*, suggested he selected a sensational header in hopes of publication. Still, Jack wondered why he had chosen to end the story where he did, as it was obviously unfinished.

Further research revealed that there is plenty of subsurface water in the area, but why or how it was drawn to ground level and then frozen has never been identified. Jack tracked down the son of the shopkeeper-cum-postmaster, now retired and living in Adelaide. He could answer a few questions, though what he knew was second-hand knowledge. Mr Hunter had asked the Woomera Test Range management about the odd flight characteristics of their aircraft. Initially, they inferred the aircraft were theirs, but later denied all knowledge and recanted the previous admission, claiming they had confused the description with another event altogether. After that, he was denied access to any base personnel and a visit to his home soon after by two military-looking men was quite alarming. His visitors were particularly interested in any photographs taken on the day. Mr Hunter had taken half a dozen shots of the launch and handed over the film, which he had planned to have processed the next day. The two officials seemed satisfied to have his film and that he was the only one in the group with a camera. According to the shop-keeper's son, the luckless teacher never saw the men again, nor did he ever see his photos.

The shopkeeper's son also revealed that the two men who saw the lake briefly frozen did tell of their experience when similar observations were described over the following week. It was supposedly reported in a local newspaper, but Jack could not track down a copy. The two men suffered from recurring headaches after the event and, within weeks, had been transferred to the Royal Adelaide Hospital. Both died. Autopsies revealed they had suffered tissue damage and succumbed to a cerebral haemorrhage. They had been described as otherwise fit and healthy. Jack concluded that this was why Colin Hunter referred to the 'promise he was to later regret' and possibly why he never finished writing his story. Another possibility was that the two men who took away his photos had warned him not to go public with what he had seen.

Jack couldn't reconcile that the two men who died, having been declared fit and healthy, should suffer the same fate so soon after being close to whatever it was they saw. He also wondered why it had been thought necessary to declare a prohibited area of 122,000 square kilometres of land for a civilian rocket test base. In his documents, the establishment of the exclusion zone in 1947 was highlighted in orange, with a footnote to remind him that 1947 was a pivotal year for UFO sightings. As with many of his *Dark History* stories, this one, 21 years later, generated as many questions as it answered.

Chapter 8

The Cambridge Rescue

As Jack drove back to his apartment after lunch, he summarised the situation to Leon.

'It's you and me, Terry and Sarah. And Harry, if we can ever get hold of him. That's our team, such as it is. No offence, but we're a bit limited. Our opposition is pretty well unknown but there's the two blokes who follow me around, the mob that raided my place, and that Mr Southwood character. Then there's The Hague, which seems to be against us for some reason. My guess is they've been got at. Bloody oath, I sound like a spy movie. Who else?'

'All of Southwood, just a small thing,' Leon suggested.

'Right, a global organisation with as good as unlimited resources. Just a small thing. But I have some ideas about that. Their strength may also be their weakness. What I've read tells me they have a solid power base but are pretty well fragmented. It's run by rich people. I mean really rich people; and powerful. That's a problem. Most multi-millionaires are powerful, some of them dangerously powerful. There are others, too, the ones no one knows about. They're a bloody menace. On the plus side, Southwood is made up of small groups scattered about the world, none of which knows anything about the others, or much anyway. So we're possibly dealing with quite a small unit. It's like a book with most of the pages stuck together. It's all there, but you can only read part of it.'

Leon laughed, 'I know a bloke like that. He's the full six-pack but doesn't have the plastic wrap to hold it all together.'

'Yep, we all know someone with a driveway that doesn't quite reach the street. The point is we're only dealing with a small group, but we don't know what resources it can pull in. What we need to do now is find Derek and Lyn.'

'Right. I'm worried about Lyn. And your friend Derek,' Leon confessed.

The journey home was uneventful. There was no sign of any black SUV following, not that it mattered. If anyone wanted to find Jack, they knew where he lived. Maybe Southwood was satisfied that they'd recovered all their lost documents. The Jaguar was parked and treated to its tarpaulin cover. Leon sat silently by the window in his friend's apartment, again admiring the view. Jack looked at his watch.

'We've got some time to spare. We're meeting my mate with the drone at four. He's fussy about his toys, doesn't like sharing, but he'll fly it for me. We might need some muscle, too.'

Jack called yet another friend in low places, though, as usual, there was plenty of mutual respect. Known in his motorcycle club circles simply as Ric, the police database listed him as Eric Martin, age 32, and recorded a string of traffic infringements, mostly for speeding and a few minor 'public affray' incidents. Nothing resulted in anything more than a fine. One serious charge had been dropped when, as Ric liked to explain it, the 'Sugarman influence' was brought to bear. Jack provided a half-true alibi, half-convinced of his friend's innocence or fully convinced of his half-innocence. Neither can remember the situation with any accuracy. Alcohol was involved. Ric now devoted much of his spare time to helping out at youth clubs, motorcycle rider training and – unlikely as it seemed – playing in a harmonica band. He was also a skilled motor mechanic and part-time personal trainer. As an amateur bodybuilder with many years of training behind him, he was well-built and looked like someone to be avoided.

Upon hearing that a couple of minders might be needed to assist in Derek's rescue, and possibly Lyn's, Ric readily agreed to help. He would bring along his training partner who he just happened to be with. They would all meet at Cambridge and follow Jack to where he knew the Range Rover was, or at least had recently been. Whether Derek and Lyn were there as well was the big question. Plan A might come to nothing. Jack decided not to involve the police in this escapade, officially or otherwise, as he suspected some of their actions might not go down too well with representatives of the law. Besides, he still wasn't sure who he could trust.

'We're not taking the Jag I take it,' Leon asked, sounding disappointed.

'Not for this one. The Commodore will do; we might need the blue lights. In fact, we better head off.'

It was only a 15-minute drive to Cambridge, but Jack took the precaution of taking an indirect route out of the city. Both kept a lookout for any cars tailing them, but neither saw anything to be concerned about. Leon suggested their adversaries may have lost interest. The afternoon traffic was light, but progress was annoyingly delayed for a few minutes when they were stopped on the Tasman Bridge as an ore carrier sailed beneath it, heading upstream. This was a measure implemented following the *Lake Illawarra* disaster of 1975. Locals who cross the bridge regularly think the precaution is unnecessary. On arriving at Cambridge, Jack pulled into the Memorial Oval car park, having arranged to meet his friends there. As planned, he was the first to arrive.

'I'm glad they're not here yet. Just want to check something.'

Jack fiddled with some buttons on his non-standard GPS.

'I thought I spotted that Range Rover a few clicks back, heading into town.'

'Clicks?' Leon asked.

'Kilometres, sorry. Army-speak from my days with – never mind. Watch this.'

His high-resolution dashcams recorded forward and rear views.

'There. Two of the buggers. Two black Range Rovers, both with FS plates. Too much of a coincidence, don't you think? It's got to be our guys, and I don't think they're any less interested in us than they were before. Watch again. How many do you see?'

Leon watched both recordings. 'Three. Two in the first one, just the driver in the other. Right?'

'I concur, thank you, nurse. Three. I wonder who that third bloke is. Anyway, that could mean the coast is clear. Better play it safe, though and stick with the drone recce. Frank won't forgive me if he doesn't get to fly today, anyway.'

Jack was uneasy despite seeing that their known adversaries weren't at the site. There were too many unknowns for this to be a simple matter of search and rescue. Leon, too, was feeling anxious, though for more personal reasons.

At that point, Frank arrived with his drone secured in the tray of a truck amusingly oversized for its role that day. A minute later, Jack's temporary minders also drove in. After introductions, he unfolded a map and pointed out their destination. The entrance to the property they wanted was probably gated, but Jack knew that the field next door was easily accessible. He instructed his drivers to follow him and ensure their two vehicles shielded his car from the road when parked. The remainder of the journey was only a few minutes from Cambridge. As predicted, a securely padlocked gate barred access to the property they wanted. Their parking area was a large gently sloping field recently vacated by sheep.

Frank busied himself preparing the drone, which essentially meant attaching the video camera and testing that it was operating correctly.

'Flight plan?' he asked.

Jack unfolded his map again, marked their location with a cross, and drew circles around the buildings he wanted to see. He had sketched the group and numbered each one in the order he wanted them scanned. Frank knew he was supposed to fly his drone in line of sight but had little respect for such rules. He suggested that the group walk up the slight hill for better piloting, then handed Jack and Ric a tablet each so they could all see what the drone was recording. On the hilltop, a line of scrubby plants provided a helpful screen to hide behind and some shade so they could better make out what the tablet screens were displaying. Assured everyone was ready, Jack took a breath and asked Frank to fire up his toy.

'It's right behind us, Jack. Been following us up the hill. You did say you wanted a quiet one. OK, is everyone catching this live?'

Nodding heads indicated that they were, and Frank expertly directed the drone towards the first building. This was the dilapidated cottage. At slightly below roof level, the display showed that the building hadn't been used for many years. The back door was slightly ajar. It was not a practical prison. Frank ventured an opinion.

'You won't see anything through the windows, Jack. Not only is it too dark inside, they're too dirty anyway.'

'I wasn't expecting to. It's clearly empty, and there hasn't been any foot traffic near it for a while. Try the next four. They look like crappy old sheds, but we better make sure.'

The inquisitive drone circled each shed at Frank's practised command and confirmed they were neglected and unused. The first two showed broken windows and no padlocks on the doors. One had its door lying unceremoniously on the ground. The drone moved on. Jack provided a running commentary.

'Five is in better nick, but doesn't look like it's been used recently either. Huh, number six is only just still standing, but let's look at the back of it.' They were all amused to see that the rear wall of shed number six was utterly missing but with the door sitting defiantly in its frame. A curious wallaby eyed the drone from inside the shed and, apparently satisfied there was nothing to see, nonchalantly hopped away.

'OK, number seven. That's the one I'm most interested in. It looks more recent than the others. Take it easy, Frank. And up a bit. I want to see that one from a bit higher.'

From their vantage point, the group couldn't see the car parking area or the doors to the building. The drone's bird's-eye view rectified that. There were no cars or any sign of movement outside. Dropping lower and circling, they could see the large roller door and a smaller one secured with a hefty padlock.

'No windows. How close can you get to that side door?' Jack asked.

'Hang on. How's that?'

'Brilliant.'

Jack considered for a moment. He was sure there was no one at home. There were plenty of tyre tracks, but no cars, and the padlocked door meant anyone inside was there unwillingly. Otherwise, the place was deserted. Jack's unease abated, but Leon's increased.

'Frank, my thanks. Your work here is done. You can withdraw your troops.'

Frank nodded and, with a few deft movements of the controls, had the drone returning to their vehicles, where he landed it a metre from his truck. The group walked back down the hill, and Jack again thanked his drone pilot, suggesting he had better not stay for the rest of the operation as it was possibly dangerous and certainly illegal. After securing his equipment, Frank wished them luck and left.

One of the unofficial options in Jack's car was a set of 36-inch bolt cutters, as equipped in police cars around Tasmania. It made short work of the padlock on the gate, and the four invaders drove to the large shed. Leon held on to the cutters, thinking they might be a sound defensive weapon, though he handed them to Ric at the door of building number seven. The bodybuilder made even shorter work of the padlock that barred their entrance. Still secured with a standard door lock, the door readily surrendered to the solid impact of his right foot. Jack was impressed.

'You've done that before, haven't you?' he asked.

'Once or twice, Jack, once or twice.'

Inside, the four spread out slightly so as not to present an easy target, and their eyes adjusted to the dim light. There was no sign of any computer or communication equipment, but the kettle was warm. Jack indicated the door to the interior office. As expected, it was locked.

'Ric, your master key if you please,' Jack requested.

The size-10 boot did its job, and the door yielded to persuasion by simultaneously breaking and distorting, jamming in the frame only slightly ajar. Ric forced it open. Jack pushed through and saw Derek lying on his side on a folding bed. He was barely conscious. On another bed was Lyn, in the same condition. Leon was visibly distressed, something not lost on Jack.

'Mate, you need some fresh air. Get back to the car, will you. There's a medical kit in the boot. We'll get these two comfortable.'

Leon returned. 'This isn't a medical kit, Jack. It's more like a hospital in a box.'

'Yeah, I know, you won't find many of these outside an emergency services truck. I'm just glad we don't need the defibrillator. Get some cold water, will you. We better move fast. Those bastards could be back here any time.'

Leon gave Lyn a sympathetic look and entered the small office where a single tap over a sink served as a rudimentary kitchen. While he searched for clean glasses or mugs, Jack removed a small oxygen tank from the medical kit, fixed a hose and gently placed the mask over Derek's mouth and nose. He looked in worse shape than Lyn, who, now aware of her rescuers' presence, was trying to sit up. Derek regained his senses. Within a couple of minutes, he was also sitting up and sipping the water Leon had returned with.

Lyn was also treated to oxygen and water. She appeared confused and distressed and, spotting Leon, grabbed his hands. 'What's happened to me, Leon? How long have I been here?' Jack didn't let Leon explain.

'Time for all that later, Lyn. Right now, we have to get you both out of here. I don't know when those guys will be back. Can you stand?'

Lyn nodded, and Derek was already forcing himself up from the bed he'd spent too many hours tied to.

'We must leave this place, leave quickly,' Lyn blurted out. 'People coming back.'

Jack was worried their escape would be spoiled by the return of their captors, but they were able to drive away unimpeded. Their first priority was to get to a retired doctor that Jack just happened to know – 'What a surprise,' Leon said – where the unfortunate abductees would be checked over. Just minutes away, the two cars pulled into a driveway and stopped behind a line of trees that provided a welcome screen from the road. An untidy garden surrounded a weatherboard cottage with a corrugated steel roof, all needing paint. The front door opened. A man appeared with a quizzical look on his face. On spotting Jack, the man's curiosity was replaced with delight.

'Mr Sugarman, a delight to see you once again. And you have friends with you. Excellent, we don't get many visitors here. Not since… you know, the thing.'

The thing was left unexplained, and no one asked. Jack introduced everyone using only first names. Their host was Doctor Robert. A small bedroom served as a consulting room, though it was little used. Doctor Robert sympathetically examined his patients. He prescribed rest and gave them both what he called a 'mild restorative'. Jack knew well enough not to ask any questions about what it was. The doctor's wife, full of compassion, made them some chicken soup and thick buttered toast, which they gratefully received. They hadn't been fed well while in their tiny prison.

Jack explained the key points of Dragonfly and Southwood to his rescued accomplices. Derek already suspected much of what he was hearing and interjected Jack's narrative with 'Of course' and similar statements. When the conversation leaned towards *Dark History* stories, Lyn became more interested and, at specific points, nodded knowingly as if a fundamental explanation was being presented to her. Derek and Lyn were focussing on different elements of the stories. After much discussion and many cups of tea, Ric and his friend returned to their everyday life, having been assured their protective services would no longer be required, at least for today.

'What do you think, Leon, what's next?' Jack was thinking aloud.

'I think I could murder a beer. But what are we going to do with these two?' Leon indicated their rescued colleagues. 'And you really must change that ringtone.'

Jack's phone again played a bar of *Smoke on the Water*. He picked up and listened but said very little. All his friends heard was, 'Yep… right… OK… half an hour then.' He ended the call and sat in deep thought for longer than the others thought polite or necessary.

'Well?' Leon demanded.

'Sorry. That was Sarah. There's been a development. Seems she and Terry have been suspended. By the commissioner, no less, personally. It sounds very suspicious. I'm meeting Sarah in –' he looked at his watch, '– well, in 30 minutes. We better get a move on. Hey, doc, can I use your computer?'

The doctor switched on his ageing desktop computer. Jack took over the keyboard and opened his security camera website, carefully checking each image for any sign of unwelcome activity. There was none. Jack concluded that his trick with the bugs had worked, and whoever was monitoring his movements was confident that their electronic surveillance could be relied on.

'Good old Sam,' he said. 'We can use my place. Those Southwood boys are surveilling nothing more interesting than the inside of my fridge.'

'Surveilling?' Leon asked, 'and why don't you use your mobile for that?'

'Yeah, yeah, crap word, very American, but you know what I mean. I'll check the traffic cam. It's usually aimed at the car park opposite my place. Looks OK. And a mobile screen is just too bloody small.'

Derek was recovering from his experiences only slowly and Doctor Robert suggested that he stay overnight. Jack happily accepted the offer as he didn't quite know what to do with him. Lyn was much improved but still 'fragile' – her word – though she had many friends, and according to Leon, a temporary home could easily be found.

'Thanks, Doc, appreciate that. Derek, you take it easy. You know my number if you need me, eh. Oh, one last thing, why were you carrying around a two-week-old newspaper?'

'That old was it? I was trying to finish the crossword. Suppose I never will now,' Derek confessed.

◆

Jack was pleased to be back in his apartment, though now he had two guests instead of the usual none. They'd stopped at a bottle shop for more beer, for which Leon and, as it turned out, Lyn were grateful. Their host opened a bottle of red and poured himself a generous glass, leaving another empty for Sarah. After their afternoon's experience, a comfortable chair and beverage of choice were welcome to all three. The suspended police constable was true to her word and arrived on time.

'Wine?' Jack offered, ready to pour.

'Actually, I wouldn't mind one of those,' she replied, indicating Leon's stubbie. 'Hi, I'm Sarah, you're Lyn, yeah? So glad to see you're safe. You must tell me what happened. Hi Leon.'

There were clinks of bottles and glasses as the group wished each other cheers and good health.

'Bottoms,' Jack insisted, 'you have to clink the bottom of your glass as well as the top. It's a Tasmanian thing.'

'Bottoms then,' they chorused and clinked again with some bemusement.

Sarah told the story of how she and D.I. Sayer had been suspended. Despite being off duty, the commissioner had phoned them both in the afternoon and told them they were to report to his office immediately. The meeting was brief, unpleasant, and not a little mysterious as another man was present. The other man was not introduced, nor did he say a word during the largely one-sided conversation. Neither Terry nor Sarah knew this anonymous man, though his bearing and expensive suit suggested someone in authority. By the time they were curtly dismissed, Terry and Sarah had decided that whatever that authority was, it was higher than the local police force.

According to the commissioner, their handling of the share market investigation had been grossly inadequate. Engaging Jack Sugarman 'to the extent you did' was unacceptable. That Jack's engagement on the case was at the commissioner's near insistence was conveniently overlooked, and the detective inspector's reminder of the fact was not well received. The word insubordination was used at least three times. Sarah's sin was 'quite unofficially' passing on documents to Jack. How the commissioner knew about that wasn't revealed.

After some unnecessary statements about the image of the force, disgracing the uniform and questions in parliament, two officers escorted the pair off the premises. They were relieved of identity cards and ordered not to wear their uniforms until told otherwise, which would be for 'at least two weeks.' They were also instructed, rather too firmly both thought, not to discuss the case with anyone. The suspension was on full pay, so apart from a little professional embarrassment, it was little more than an involuntary leave of absence. Once outside the police building, Terry and Sarah looked at each other.

'What the hell was that all about?' Terry asked rhetorically. Sarah answered anyway.

'Curious thing, or rather things. The word over-reaction springs to mind, don't you think? And who was that other bloke?'

'A representative from The Hague, maybe,' Terry suggested.

When Sarah finished her story, she held up her empty stubbie.

'Jack, would another be possible?'

Jack replenished his guests' drinks and suggested the commissioner had made a tactical mistake or, more likely, had been forced into one. Justifying the suspension of two dedicated officers for their handling of the share market case was flimsy. The presence of the other man suggested something bigger, something ongoing.

'I don't know what *they* call it, but you were suspended because of Southwood, not Dragonfly.'

Lyn's interrogation had been rudimentary and amateurish, with a reliance on the drug she had been injected with. The dose she had been given was excessive, which only served to provide her captors with a subject on the wrong side of wakefulness. Lyn had spent much of the time semi-conscious at best, so not only would her captors have gleaned no helpful information, they couldn't even know for sure if she knew anything worthwhile.

The group's conversation drifted from subject to subject, with insights becoming more refined, or in some cases more bizarre, in line with their intake of beer and wine. Leon offered Lyn a semblance of an apology, telling her that it was probably his handing over Jack's Tunguska story that led to her abduction. Jack agreed there may have been a link but had another idea, still only half-baked, which he kept to himself. Derek had warned him that the material he delivered might be a health hazard. Lyn half-smiled.

'I knew something was about to happen already, Leon. I could feel it,' she confessed. 'I didn't know it would be all this, though.'

Leon was intrigued. 'Are you Russian? Not that that's relevant, I guess.'

'Not Russian. Serbian. I left during the war, a refugee I suppose. You know me as McKellyer. Some people think I'm Scottish, but it's spelled M.R.K.E.L.J.A. Pronounced the same, though. I was Keller for a while, too. Some of my close friends call me Scary Lyn because I have these feelings. Elemental things. I don't understand it. Things just come to me sometimes. Not all the time. Just sometimes. Sometimes, I see things very clearly. But only sometimes. I'm not really scary, am I?'

'Elemental! That's the word I was looking for,' Jack said excitedly.

Lyn sounded melancholic, and the others tried to cheer her up. Sarah had an idea.

'It's probably better you don't go back to your place tonight. Not alone. You can stay with me if you like. My flatmate moved out a week ago, so there's a spare room, and I can sort you out with a few things. We can walk from here in no time.'

Lyn agreed, and Jack said he would feel better about them having each other's company. Sarah could be a target too, but she was a police officer – suspended or not – and her training might discourage unwelcome attention. Leon would stay with Jack. As the two girls left, it was apparent they were fast becoming good friends.

'I suppose you want another beer,' Jack asked.

'I suppose I do,' Leon answered. 'You understand I only drink to be sociable?'

'You must have a lot of friends.'

'And I reckon you've got a new one,' Leon replied.

'Sarah?'

'It's pretty obvious, mate.'

Jack smiled. His conversation had been directed at Sarah more than the others.

Leon's phone announced the arrival of a text message.

'It's Harry. He says, "Decrypted everything. Tell J – that'd be you – Easter egg hatches mid-night. Back tomorrow. Will call." He's a sly one. I bet he didn't go bush at all. He's just been keeping himself to himself somewhere close by and working on your Dragonfly stuff. Have to wait till tomorrow, I guess. What's this Easter egg thing?'

Jack grinned.

'I think I know. I reckon he installed something on my laptop. We won't see it till midnight. Bugger. I don't want to stay up that late. Let me see that text. Curious.'

'What's curious?'

'Mid-night with a hyphen. Most people abbreviate text messages. They don't put in unnecessary stuff like hyphens. You'd think of midnight as 12 o'clock, but mid-night, with the hyphen, might mean solar midnight, literally the middle of the night. You know, midway between sunset and sunrise. So right now, in Hobart, it would be about 20 past one.'

'That's bonkers. Why bother?' Leon asked, not expecting a reply. He got one anyway.

'Hyphen midnight is mystical. Witches of old did their best work then. Or worst work, if they were black witches. But I admit it seems – what did you call it? – slightly bonkers. I've been looking at all this through a scientific lens. Maybe it's just Harry suggesting something else. Maybe it's a clue. Then again, maybe it's all science anyway. Hey, you know what?'

'Not at all.'

'I'm about done in. Bed for me. Stay up and watch tele if you want.'

Leon did stay up watching an old movie from Jack's collection that he'd seen a dozen times before. By the time 'mid-night' ticked over, neither was up to notice Jack's hibernating laptop come to life at 1:16 and quietly activate a Trousers special, a hidden program that accessed a stealth website and downloaded hundreds of compressed documents and images. They were saved in what Trousers would call a black folder. The download was completed in a little over three minutes. The program self-deleted, and Jack's laptop returned to its hibernation state.

The rest of the night passed without incident.

◆

At Sarah's apartment, she and Lyn shared a bottle of wine and chatted about everything and nothing till the early hours. Lyn kept mentioning someone named Bob.

'Who's Bob? Sarah finally asked.

'Bob? Bob would play outside when it was too dark to see properly. He'd race walnut shells down street gutters when it was raining, listen to the same song all day, read a book and then read it again. He'd stare at the stars and dream of infinity. That's who Bob is.'

'A younger brother?'

'No, I haven't met Bob yet, but he's part of everyone I ever knew. I'll meet him someday. We'll fall in love and be happy forever.'

Lyn was soon to meet her Bob. She hadn't yet realised that Leon was her Bob.

◆

Chapter 9

"There's a Bloke I Know"

Harry phoned the next morning while Leon and Jack enjoyed their first dose of caffeine. He was three minutes away. Jack made more coffee. The intercom buzzed, and Harry was admitted, somewhat breathless.

'Coffee?' Jack asked, handing it to him without waiting for an answer.

'Yeah, OK. I was followed, but I lost them. They don't know Hobart's one-way streets. Get in the wrong lane, and you're stuffed. Guess they're not locals.'

Jack nodded. 'I guessed that too. If they knew who you were, they probably knew you were heading here, anyway. What you got for us?'

'This blog thing bugged me, so I got some mates onto it – don't worry, they're all cool – and between us, we got this encryption sorted. It was a pretty damn clever blend of cypher and code.'

'There's a difference?' Leon asked. Jack jumped in.

'I can explain that. I was in cryptography for a while with the French – ah, well, I better not say who – just the French. A cypher is a complicated replacement of letters and numbers with other letters and numbers, often in groups to really confuse things. A code is usually a simple substitution of a word or phrase with another, like the Normandy invasion beaches being called Omaha, Gold or Juno. Even the invasion…'

Leon interrupted, 'Operation Overlord.'

'Quite right.'

Harry sipped his coffee. 'Yeah, yeah, enough history you two. We were getting nearly nowhere until we realised most of the source documents weren't in English. German some were. Couple in Serbian.

It looked like a pretty random set of papers. One of my mates does this sort of thing as a hobby. Bit of a nutter but bloody good at this stuff. His great-something-grandfather was in Room 40 during the First World War.'

Leon looked puzzled. 'Room 40?'

'You've heard of Bletchley Park? Second World War? Admiralty Room 40 was the First World War equivalent. Anyway, my mad mate knows as much as anyone about Bletchley and Enigma. He even built a replica, a small one,. Whatever process your Dragonfly stuff was encrypted with – or is it encrypted by? – was flawed by the same problem as Enigma. Sloppy usage. Just as well. Anyway, he took the lead and we cracked it in 20 hours. Not much sleep was had, I can tell you. I've never drunk so much coffee and eaten so little.'

'Much appreciated, Harry,' Jack proffered and took up the unsubtle hint. 'I expect you'd like to get your dinner manglers into some breakfast?'

Harry smiled broadly.

'Oh yes, breakfast would be great. Just some toast. And an egg. Maybe two. Bacon would be good if you've got it. And tomato. Got any sourdough? I like sourdough toast.'

Jack thought briefly and decided the three of them would be better served in the Blue Café, where they found themselves in short time. Angie welcomed them with a genuine smile. Selecting a table with a view but not too close to the window, Jack asked for a plunger of strong coffee and, following nods of agreement, three glasses of fresh orange juice. They sat silently for a moment, observing Angie's enticing departure first and then the menu. Harry spoke.

'I'm not used to making decisions before lunch. What do you guys think?'

'Full English?' Leon suggested, seeking confirmation. It was agreed. Small talk filled the gap between the decision and the waitress's return with orange juice and coffee.

'There you are, gents. Your special blend, Mr Sugarman. Anything to eat today?'

Jack did the honours. 'Three Full English, Angie, hold the hash browns on mine.'

Angie understood. 'Chef can do bubble and squeak instead if you like.'

'Perfect,' Leon chipped in, 'haven't had that for years. Full English with bubble and squeak times three. You'll like this, Harry, don't worry.'

After explaining to Harry what bubble and squeak was and that it used to be a dinner-time staple of Leon's family for a day or two after a Sunday roast, the conversation turned to the more important subjects of Dragonfly and Southwood.

Harry was itching to brief his friends on what he was able to uncover. He'd confirmed that the share market scheme was indeed called Project Dragonfly but that the word dragonfly seemed to apply to several events and endeavours. It was a generic code word reused from time to time. He thought that no two events of the name overlapped chronologically. Southwood was the organisation behind it all, just as Jack had suspected. The longest document they had to contend with, which provided several decryption clues because of its length, seemed to be part of an even more extensive work. Harry's team called it the Genesis paper. Parts of it had denied all efforts at decryption, but it was substantially now in plain English.

Project Dragonfly was implemented simultaneously in 22 countries. No Southwood team appeared to know of the others, which made the coordination all the more impressive. Each of the 22 groups was led by its own Mr Southwood. There was one reference to 'her' that raised the question of whether 'Mr' was a title or, as unlikely as it seemed, a nod to tradition. On hearing this, Jack asked Harry if he'd noticed the 'Mr' capitalised. That was a maybe, but some documents appeared in upper case only.

'Is it important?'

'Could be Harry. MR might mean magnetic resonance and that,' Jack stressed "that" with a meaningful compression of a thumb and forefinger, 'that might be important. MR Southwood could be something else, something bigger than just a team leader.'

Jack pondered whether MRS meant missus and whether an organisation like Southwood would concern itself with correct titles. MRS SOUTHWOOD might be an error of abbreviation, like calling a PIN a 'PIN number', something which annoyed him more than it should. Perhaps it was an odd plural. Something else that annoyed him was he now had confirmation that the Southwood he was dealing with was one of at least 22 groups, possibly there were dozens scattered around the world.

'But that's not the interesting bit, Jack. The interesting bit is about what I call New Dragonfly. The share market thing is done and dusted, and I think they've just reused the name. New Dragonfly is bigger than Ben Hur. When I borrowed your laptop, I have to confess I "accidentally" copied some of your own files. *Dark History*, is it? Sorry about that. I enjoyed the piece on Alex Furst.'

'Axel, Harry. It's Axel Furst,' Jack corrected him.

'Axel, right. Anyway, it seems Mr Furst was way ahead of his time and spot on with his theory of magma movements. That's according to this Southwood crowd anyway.'

Angie interrupted with three breakfasts. 'Bon appetite, chaps,' she offered with a vaguely English accent before weaving her way back to another customer at the counter.

'She fancies you, Jack. I'm sure I saw a wink there,' Leon suggested.

Jack countered. 'Now then, Leon, you know damn well you weren't looking at her eyes. But do you think? She's a bit nice, isn't she?'

For a couple of minutes, conversation lapsed into male-centric observations of what they found attractive in women. Shortly though, the lure of sausages, eggs, bacon, tomato, mushrooms, and bubble and squeak distracted them and talk reverted, via food, back to the matter at hand.

Harry explained that he was summarising only some of the documents he'd decrypted, all of which were now safely on the hard drive of Doctor Watson, Jack's laptop. He'd guessed Southwood's interest in recovering their lost property was primarily driven by their limited knowledge of which documents had fallen into the wrong hands. As Derek Asquith had managed to find already decrypted papers, they also wanted to know the source of those versions. The texts in Jack's collection weren't necessarily from Southwood, though the local Mr Southwood seemed to think they could be.

Harry tried to explain how Southwood developed a method by which the movement of magma could be converted into electrical energy.

'It's very simple, so of course, I don't understand it at all. I think I can remember it, some of it anyway. When amplified by a massive magnetic field, the energy of motion – that's kinetic energy – produces a phased long wave… something, no, it's gone. Bugger. It's all about converting kinetic energy into electrical energy, anyway. Those magma movements are the key. It's all in the papers. Oh yeah, and far-field radiative wireless energy transmission. Now, how did I remember that? They're big on that. That's in the papers, too. This bubbly squeak stuff's OK, isn't it.'

Harry's newly revealed data described the mathematics. Much of it was in diagram form, which was the hardest to recover.

'You'll be impressed with the projected power, Jack. Loads of big numbers in terawatts and a couple in petawatts. I had to look that up; never heard of petawatts. It's an energy thing. And something called Black Knight, whatever that is.'

'That's their satellite, Harry. I'm pretty sure about that; every conspiracy theory nut can tell you about Black Knight. I've already got that documented to death.'

Jack's mind was racing from document to document, trying to stitch together what was likely fact and discarding anything that wasn't. He'd already suspected that Black Knight was an artificial satellite, most likely in a polar orbit. Most of the stories he'd heard were pure disinformation created to discredit the real story. No one claimed ownership, and most countries denied its existence. A few made the mistake of affording it a degree of status by saying, 'It's not ours.' Southwood wouldn't go to the trouble of documenting Black Knight, let alone encrypting those documents if it wasn't legitimate.

'My coffee's gone cold.'

It was Leon's complaint. He'd been listening so intently that he'd forgotten his coffee was even there.

Jack held up the coffee plunger and caught Angie's eye. She nodded and prepared another, delivering it with three vanilla slices, one of Jack's favourites.

'On the house. Our supplier sent us an extra tray this morning.'

'Aw great, a snot box,' Harry said with obvious delight.

Ignoring the bogan renaming of Australia's favourite French pastry, the trio threw ideas around, trying to figure out how Southwood could harness the energy supposedly available from so deep under the Earth's surface and, more importantly, how they could profit from it. Jack had been thinking and listening at the same time.

'I may be talking up the left here – are you two familiar with the theoretical energy grid around the planet?'

Their silence suggested not, and he explained the theory that a complicated network of naturally occurring energy lines encircled the planet. Nikola Tesla recognised that what previous generations called ley lines was a genuine phenomenon. In more modern times, the New Zealand airline pilot Bruce Cathie was convinced of it and published several books on the subject. He contended that the energy lines were used to power flying saucers and were instrumental in siting nuclear detonations. Unfortunately, references to flying saucers placed the topic well below the already disparaging term 'pseudoscience'. Mainstream scientists have, until very recent times, not taken up the baton passed on by Tesla and Cathie.

The combination of a hearty breakfast and Jack's left-field discourse left the three in a mild state of stupor, and silence reigned for a good minute while they all nursed their remaining coffee and gazed out the window. Jack was looking for black SUVs while the other two were just looking. The sky promised at least comfortable weather, and pedestrians passed the café sedately. Two young women stopped briefly and chatted. A couple of youngsters nearly collided, heads bowed, engrossed in their mobile phones. Across the road, a steady stream of cruise ship passengers made their way into the city at the pace of those with all day to do everything. Jack interrupted the peace.

'Something occurred to me last night. I was wondering why this Southwood mob would be so interested in recovering the documents I had. And Derek's too. They would know that anything could be shared with anyone at any time. Look at the blog library. Heaps of stuff online for almost anyone to see.'

He paused.

'So?' Leon demanded.

'Well, thinking sideways again, I reckon it wasn't a recovery effort at all. I think they just wanted to know exactly what it was they'd lost.'

Harry caught on immediately.

'Of course. If they can figure out what we have and don't have, they can figure out if we know enough to be a risk to whatever they're up to. Right?'

'You got it,' Jack agreed, while Leon nodded and finished his coffee by dribbling it down his chin and onto his already unclean shirt.

'You're a scruffy article, aren't you,' Jack admonished.

'It's not my fault. I was born in a small room.'

Jack took up his line of reasoning and suggested that until now, they had been drawn into a situation and simply been reacting to events as they unfolded. It was time they took the initiative and started being proactive. He also suggested he wasn't quite sure what that initiative might look like, but as a start, they should assess their resources and analyse the opposition as best they could.

'Bloody dangerous, this Southwood crowd,' he said to Harry, 'we better remember that.'

Harry just nodded.

As to resources, they were a small group with, as yet, limited knowledge of the problem at hand. Potentially, they had the local police on side, but it was also possible the higher echelon was in Southwood's pocket. Jack decided they could at least rely on D.I. Sayer and P.C. Blackman, despite being suspended. Derek might be helpful for information, but was otherwise a non-combatant. Jack wasn't sure about Lyn – Scary Lyn – he smiled at the name. He suspected she would be a valuable player but didn't know how. He would think about that before he checked on her, still at Sarah's place he guessed, later in the day

The opposition was both easier and more challenging to work out. Easier because it had to be conceded that they were global in reach, had enormous resources, were probably ruthless, and had infiltrated high levels of government. What was difficult was that the organisation, while secretive, appeared to be respectable. That its respectability was an illusion based on an absence of the opposite didn't help.

'Absence of evidence isn't evidence of absence,' Jack said to himself.

'What's that?' Harry asked.

'Nothing. Thinking aloud.'

'Where'd you get that line from anyway?'

'Found it at the bus stop, Harry. Look. Southwood. Problem. Right. Sorry, still thinking. Too early. Everyone finished eating?'

Empty plates and coffee cups indicated that breakfast was indeed over. Back in his apartment, Jack intrigued Leon and Harry for a solid hour with selected stories from his *Dark History*. He read excerpts that usually unknowingly described evidence of the theory Southwood was somehow planning to control.

He was becoming increasingly convinced that Southwood aimed to harness and manage a worldwide energy grid. It would be expensive to put in place but theoretically cheap to maintain. Selling virtually free power at any price would be enormously profitable. Jack didn't think there was any likelihood of benevolence. Expert, professional, secretive and ruthless, Southwood was in it for the money. Their treatment of Derek and Lyn for what was, on the face of it, a minor matter proved that.

Conversation flowed freely with many ideas tossed around, some sensible, some bizarre. The subject moved gradually from Southwood's methods to its purpose. Eventually, the three settled on the organisation's goal. The rest was 'out there' speculation. In the lead-up to any announcement and demonstration, they would short-sell shares of the world's major energy companies and make a fortune on those profits.

The organisation's energy would be transmitted by microwave links, probably by geosynchronous satellites and ground stations. All conceded that they didn't know if the technology existed to do that, but they had to start with something. Technology aside, a more pressing question was how could Southwood launch satellites without them being detected? Again, every hypothesis raised at least one curly question.

'Anti-gravity. Or levitation,' Jack suggested.

Leon leaned back in his chair.

'What, are you mad? You haven't been drinking that German beer, have you?'

Jack leaned forward.

'German! Of course. Not beer, though. You know, sometimes you say the most profound things. I'm reminded of something… something politely called 'an incident' at the end of the Second World War. Our lot was advancing into Germany from the south when they came across what looked like a missile launching site, only not like any other. Most sites were further north anyway. But this one was weird. Their engineers had drained a lake and diverted two small rivers to build the thing. Why would they do that? When their missile program started, middle of 1944 I think, sites had to be close enough to Britain to be of any use. This one was too far away for it to be a standard military thing. Hang on. I've got some papers on it. I need to tidy up my cross-referencing.'

Jack located and went through the paper, one of his *Dark History* documents, reading aloud excerpts he thought were relevant. It was untitled and attributed to GRHM, which he thought might be an abbreviation of Graham, though not much of one. The initials might also refer to George Rex His Majesty, but that was just as unlikely.

◆

By the time the Americans arrived, it was deserted and had been methodically cleaned, meaning almost everything mobile had been taken away. All that was left was a row of filing cabinets and some furniture. There were no locals to be found, either. The barracks suggested only a few dozen men were there at any time. The first clue that this wasn't a standard missile site was that there was merely a small fuel dump, that looked like it only serviced a fleet of military vehicles. Some empty containers were marked Dieselkraftstoff – diesel fuel – and no missiles used diesel.

The first American engineer to reach the site decided in a minute that nothing had ever been launched. There was no evidence of scorch marks on the ground. Instead of the usual thick concrete launch platform, there were vegetable plots. The official record listed the site as just another German missile location that had been taken out of the war. A small 'hold and contain' group was left in charge as the military advance continued towards Berlin. All roads led to Berlin at that time.

In charge of that small group was a young officer named Sam Hipp – his rank was never identified – who fancied himself a bit of a scientist. Luckily, he was a diarist as well. Hipp had Piegan ancestry and was inordinately proud of his native heritage. Before volunteering for the United States Army, he had been a postman and part-time teacher, trying, with some success, to instil in his fellow Native Americans the value of their culture and ancient knowledge.

Hipp's awareness of his people's traditions was accompanied by uncanny insights into his surroundings. He had been nicknamed Owl Fox by his men because he displayed the supposed wisdom and cunning of those two animals. On more than one occasion, he avoided leading his men into hostile areas for reasons not apparent to anyone else.

It was as much his affinity with the land as his scientific knowledge that led him, one quiet evening, to write many pages in his diary after a thorough investigation of his surroundings.

There were several references to V4, which was taken to be a Nazi vengeance weapon.

Unsurprisingly, Jack had managed to secure a photocopy of several weeks of Sam Hipp's meticulous diary. Some of the content had been included in GRHM's article.

'Day 45. I knew this place wasn't a typical German military setup. Something about it wasn't quite right. There was something odd. One of my men, a farmer back in the States, worked out that we were camped in a dry lake bed. He'd recced the area and seen where two small rivers had been diverted into another. It was a heck of a job, he said. That didn't make any sense. Plenty of flat ground not far away for a missile site.

'Our first night there was peaceful enough. The guys pulling watch didn't even hear any animals, they said. That was queer, I thought. In the morning, though, an old black dog wandered in, it seemed to be looking for a feed. We gave him breakfast, but he didn't stay. Probably, his people had been moved away by the Germans. He looked very nervous and eager to leave after he ate. I felt sorry for him. Cats can survive better than dogs when they're removed from a domestic home. This one – the guys called him Buddy – might not last much longer without a regular handout.

'Day 49. Settled into a dull routine, wondering when we'll get orders to leave. Reported to HQ the documents we found – all in German – and sent back films for them to develop. Buddy visited again. Seems he likes our chow.

'Day 52. Radio message from HQ. Some English unit will collect the filing cabinets and take more photos. Ordered to assist and cooperate fully.

'Day 53. Three trucks arrived late in the morning. An English Captain in charge of a dozen men. They sealed each cabinet and loaded them onto their trucks. One man in Lieutenant uniform was clearly not military. I guessed he was a specialist – something to do with the site. Rockets maybe. They took measurements with gear I'd never seen, and more photos. We gave them lunch, and they gave us red wine they'd liberated from Wurttemburg. The guys made short work of it.

'Day 54. Ordered to leave site, head north and rejoin our division. Packed up. One of the men painted "Gone to Berlin" on a wall. Didn't see Buddy, but I heard a dog howling in the hills. Hope he survives the war.'

◆

In their haste to leave, the retreating Germans left several filing cabinets untouched. The contents had been shipped to England, where they were stored, undisturbed, for decades. The entire record series had been translated, classified as Ultra-secret Military and closed for 70 years. An amateur historian and friend of Jack's had been first in line to access those records when they became available. His four days of research revealed more than a few surprises.

Jack couldn't even guess why V4 would be developed in southern Bavaria. He remembered his shadow in the New London Arms bar with the Bayern Munchen badge on his lapel. Later, he decided V4 wasn't a vengeance weapon at all. It was the abbreviation of Vilin 4. There was a single reference to Vilin Prsten and a curious phrase, 'vilin vazka velmi vysoke', which had him stumped for a while.

'It's not German. I figured out that Vilin Prsten might mean dragonfly ring or circle. I sent a text to Lyn – excuse me if I don't say "texted", hate that word – and she agreed. It's not quite right, but in Serbian or Croatian, that's what it is. As for the other, note the alliteration of "V", four Vs. The translation is clumsy but quite clever and means something like "dragonfly very high." So there you have it, confirmation of sorts. V4 was a rocket but not a weapon.

'But, now pay attention, it means Southwood was big enough to, let's use the word, infiltrate German high command in the Second World War. That says a lot. It's just a bit scary, I reckon. There's no telling what this crowd is capable of. They can pull some serious muscle.'

Jack's mind was racing at the thought of a ring or group of Dragonfly units operating in Germany through the Second World War.

'If Southwood could infiltrate the Nazis in the forties, maybe even earlier, who knows what they're capable of now. On the other hand, maybe they all just joined the Nazi Party because it was convenient. Hitler may have seen them as something clever that he'd created.'

'Fascinating, Jack, but it doesn't really help us, does it?' Harry said.

Jack had to agree.

'True.'

He made the thumb and forefinger gesture again, then tapped the Hipp papers.

'I think these pages contain the key to the entire story of that missile site. That drained lake in Starnberg,' he paused, 'in Bavaria, is telling us something.'

Jack thought that, despite only limited scientific support, or perhaps because of it, Hipp's story took his speculation to a new level. The obscure German rocket launch site may have been located where it was simply because it needed to be in that place. The worldwide energy grid, which Jack was only beginning to understand, dictated such things.

'A river is where a river is. An energy line is where an energy line is.'

'Energy line, Jack?' Leon asked.

'Just a phrase I'm using. Like ley lines. If there is such a thing as an energy grid – let's presume there is – my guess is they run north-south primarily, but east-west as well, and maybe it's all a bit random. Points of intersection would be areas of stronger energy. I've read up on some of this. The maths is beyond me, but there would be fixed lines and others that move about. I don't know which would be stronger. In fact, there's lots I don't know.'

Hours passed, and the discussion developed into firm ideas about what Southwood was up to, even though the science baffled all three.

The bottom line was that Southwood planned to hold the entire world to ransom by controlling the production and distribution of electricity. Pricing would probably appear reasonable, initially low enough to make coal-fired power stations and even hydroelectric schemes uncompetitive. New solar and wind farms would cost too much to establish. Once these alternative sources of electricity were made redundant, Southwood's pricing would rise.

Leon reminded Jack that they'd decided they ought to take the initiative as, until then, they had only been reacting to events.

'I'm glad you brought that up,' Jack replied, 'I have an idea along those lines, two actually. But right now, I want some quiet time to read and think. Look, I'm convinced you two can go home safely. You're no less safe there than here, probably safer. I'll order an Uber – there's a bloke I know…'

'No, really?' Leon interjected.

'Yes, really. He'll see you right. Leon, you can pick up your car outside Keith's boat shed. I'll call you tomorrow. I have a feeling it's going to be an interesting day.'

Jack couldn't have known just how interesting it was going to be.

◆

Chapter 10

Brother Ringo

Only three men sat in the city boardroom, but it could easily accommodate more than 20 people. They sat comfortably and quietly in plush leather executive chairs, adjusting what little was presented at their chosen positions, two pens, a pad of paper, a crystal glass and bottles of chilled water, one still and one sparkling. With a valuable Gerhard Richter painting on each of the shorter walls, it was an image of luxury and subdued indulgence. Each man wore an expensive suit and presented themselves as what they were: successful businessmen. The man in the centre removed the jacket of his Hugo Boss suit, placed it neatly over the back of his chair and rolled up his shirt sleeves. He was heavily built and no stranger to the free weights of the gymnasium he owned. An ornate tattoo of Celtic design covered most of his tanned right forearm. The man to his left caught the chairman's attention and tapped his watch, effecting an expression that said, 'Well?'

'Patience, Keeper, patience. We're on schedule. Two minutes more. You'll be home before sunrise.' He rechecked his watch. Sunrise was two hours away.

Keeper was the man's title, Keeper of the Silence. The organisation had adopted but later discarded several ancient position titles. The older title was retained to present a menacing aspect. The modern equivalent might be Director of Security. To be silenced in Southwood was usually a permanent arrangement. Like the chairman, the current Keeper was solidly built but had more material means than muscle and martial arts skills to draw on. Out of his suit, he commanded respect borne of natural caution and would suffer no unwanted attention in a bar. In the boardroom, Keeper was equally imposing. As a security man, he disliked video conferences and was ready to disable any connection should he think it necessary.

The third man, the chairman's right-hand man, was a combination minder, fetcher and secretary. Less imposing than the other two, he still carried plenty of administrative weight and could be relied as an all-round fixer.

In front of the three men, a giant monitor had been set up, divided into 24. Each sector was blank, save for a steady red light in the bottom left corner. The red light of monitor four turned green. The others followed suit. For a few seconds, computer code scrolled quickly, a cursor blinked momentarily, and unseen hands keyed in a password, appearing only as a row of asterisks. One monitor showed three attempts at the password. A security protocol would be immediately activated on a third unsuccessful attempt, and the link severed. The dark displays lightened and showed single figures seated at a table. The face of each was blurred. The internal security of the organisation was as thorough as its external secrecy. Monitor 14 remained blank. The chairman rechecked his watch, a limited edition from an obscure Swiss maker. He frowned, picked up a mobile phone and pressed two digits.

'Fourteen,' was all he said, followed a few seconds later by, 'Understood.'

He pulled a microphone closer and threw the switch on the base.

'Gentlemen,' he commenced – despite the concealed faces, each person was clearly male – 'it appears some unseasonal weather event has prevented Bermuda from joining us today. He will be briefed later.'

To the chairman's right, the third man scribbled a note and said, 'Brief Bermuda.'

The chairman continued. 'There is only one item on the agenda for this meeting: a progress report on Dragonfly. As usual, I alone will speak. Should you have any questions or comments, you are to key them in. They will be translated, and I will determine whether a response is warranted. Limit your questions to 30 words. Also, this is an advanced security conference. You all know who I am; of course,

I know each of you. You do not know each other. Let's keep it that way.'

He looked at a printed list.

'For the six of you who are not fluent in English, this briefing will be translated and relayed in real-time. Before I commence, are there any questions?'

A separate monitor, number 25, remained blank, save for the cursor, which pulsed lazily.

'Very good,' the chairman continued, 'then I shall proceed. Black Knight is in orbit, and compliance testing has concluded. The Koreans were very helpful here, though I hardly need say, they are unaware of it.'

Monitor 25 displayed 'Clever' and was signed '9'.

The chairman frowned slightly. 'Thank you, Melbourne. Pertinent comments only, please. The urban myth surrounding Black Knight has been strengthened with additional misinformation. It has proven to be a simple process. Some people will believe anything, no matter how incredible. That aside, our orbiting framework is such that we need 10 auxiliary AST satellites. Eight have been put in place using our gravity-neutralising technology.'

His attention was again drawn to monitor 25. 'AST?' showed up twice.

'Advanced Stealth Technology, my apologies, developed by our Munich facility. This is an extension of a project the Americans think is a private game. The British product is superior, but the American version easier to acquire.' The Chairman allowed himself a smile, which no one could see. 'The American version will suit our needs, providing the British don't reverse engineer their technology for offensive purposes. We consider that unlikely. Critically, as you will know from earlier briefings, we consider traditional rocket launches clumsy and insecure. A side benefit of the entire project is what some people might call levitation.'

He ignored a single exclamation mark that appeared on monitor 25.

'Gravity neutralisation sounds more scientific, I'm sure you'll agree.'

The exclamation mark was deleted, but 'More info?' appeared, signed '4'.

The chairman collected his thoughts. 'This is not easy to describe briefly, Wellington, but it is appropriate that you should ask. New Zealand is active at the moment.'

He summarised the energy grid theory, which Southwood had proved to itself, but not the world, was far beyond being purely theoretical. Southwood scientists had undertaken considerable four-dimensional mapping of energy fluctuations, covering the entire globe and, as far as possible, back-tested for several decades. Less reliable data over three centuries had also been extrapolated. The chairman muted his transmission and pressed '1' on his microphone.

'Display grid globe number one for 30 seconds.'

For half a minute, each of the conference parties saw a computer-generated globe rotating slowly. Lines roughly parallel to the equator, and longitudinal lines crossed at several points around the planet. Named areas were labelled as the world knew them: Tasman Sea, South China Sea, Bermuda Triangle, Lake Anjikuni, Lake Cheko, and Lake Michigan. Others were marked with their latitude and longitude coordinates. Thin dotted lines appeared between the primary thicker lines in complex five-sided patterns, fluctuating gently. The chairman clarified that the primary grid was essentially static. Those lines didn't move much. The secondary grid was more volatile. Counter-intuitively the energy variations from the secondary intersections were the target of Dragonfly. Southwood had coined the term 'Dragonfly Feed-In', but that had been corrupted to Dragonfly Feeding and had stuck.

The chairman continued with a critical element of Southwood's early interest in the project. For 20 minutes, he outlined the work of Axel Furst, the first man to speculate that gravitational pressure points occurred and fluctuated around the planet. He also proposed that magma flowed like ocean currents, creating a giant electromagnet. This, in turn, was a simple source of energy. Anyone with the knowledge, science and resources to capture and distribute this energy could dominate the world's electricity supply.

Monitor 25 came to life. 'Aren't you just describing gravity?' It was Southwood Wellington again.

'We all think of gravity as a force, but it can't exist without certain conditions. Stars and planets exhibit gravity. But – and I don't pretend to understand it thoroughly, gentlemen – gravity is simply a consequence of the unbalanced distribution of mass. Einstein called it the curvature of space-time, and that's where I'll leave the science, unless anyone has any questions. If not, we'll break for five minutes.'

The three men at Southwood turned their gaze from the bank of screens and glanced momentarily at monitor 25. The cursor continued blinking as the chairman poured himself a glass of sparkling water. There were no questions. Satisfied that his audience was still in place, he continued after the prescribed five minutes.

'We now have the technology and resources to monitor and forecast the movement of energy grid lines, to capture and store that energy. We are confident we can transmit electricity by microwave link to whoever is prepared to pay our price. Of course, everyone will be prepared to pay that price because we will undercut all countries' prevailing rates. Within months, coal-fired power stations, hydroelectric systems, and wind farms will appear to be as expensive and archaic as they actually are. Our only real competition will be tidal power. Luckily for us, the world can't see how easy that energy infrastructure is to build, but another team is dealing with that.

'Our testing is at stage 8, that is, at 80% completion. The final two auxiliary satellites will allow full-force testing. Simulations indicate we have allowed for every variable. Solar activity is forecast to be favourable for the next 18 months. Mapping the moon and planetary alignments is a simple process. By then, we will have secured global control of energy distribution.'

The chairman spoke for another 15 minutes, describing the roll-out of Southwood's plans, the timetable, and the profits they were likely to draw from this, its most audacious enterprise.

Monitor 25 came to life. 'Qué acerca de la Sugarman ameaça?' It was instantly translated. 'What about the Sugarman threat?'

The chairman frowned again, glanced at Keeper, and wondered how Portugal could have known about Jack Sugarman.

'Threat is too strong a word, Lisbon. Commander Sugarman and his ally Asquith stumbled onto some documents – the source has been dealt with – but we concluded that what he has could only allude to Dragonfly in the vaguest terms. Indeed, our agent has provided him with more material – all pure fiction, of course – to confuse the issue. Sugarman is no threat to our program. But we continue to watch him. His friends are just stumbling in the dark and are even less of a concern. Our local team,' he paused to recall a name, 'Mr Hall and his associates have been instructed to watch only Sugarman.

'To return to your briefing. Those of you with ground stations to manage have already been briefed on your requirements. Your regular reports have been encouraging. All Southwood units will soon be instructed on which energy companies to short-sell. Funding will be through the usual accounts. You all…'

The Chairman was about to wrap up the conference with his usual 'well done, everyone' speech when Keeper suddenly reached over to the microphone console and violently punched a large red button.

'Shit,' was all he said as each monitor blacked out and the little green lights turned red. The Chairman sat back in his chair, arms outstretched and rigid. He looked at Keeper, who held two fingers on the earpiece in his left ear. For half a minute, no one spoke. Keeper finally lowered his left hand.

'That was Comms. Lisbon just called in.'

'But we had Lisbon online, right?' asked the third man.

'Lisbon couldn't connect. Whoever asked about Sugarman wasn't our man. Security has been compromised.'

Keeper picked up his mobile phone and punched two numbers. 'Get me a full diagnostic for this conference – links, IPs, routes, everything. Lisbon first, anything out of Portugal. Tell Facilities to dismantle Lisbon and relocate to the Tagus building. Do it now. I want a report in 30 minutes, and anything critical or unusual, immediately.'

He listened briefly, pressed END CALL and threw his phone down. It slid half a metre, and the screen flickered as if protesting its rough treatment. The Chairman knew Keeper would explain momentarily.

'Right. We've been hacked. At the Lisbon end, not here, so the damage is limited. Easily fixed, but someone heard the entire conference. That…' he paused, 'that isn't so easily fixed. I should have checked when the password was attempted three times. The question is, who is that hacker?'

'Sugarman?' the chairman asked.

'No, not a chance. He doesn't have the skills. We think only a handful of people are capable of getting through our controls. If I was a betting man, my money would be on our old friend, Brother Ringo.'

'Can we trace it?' asked the third man.

'Not now. Hackers this good would have their security to prevent tracing.'

The chairman stood up, rolled down his sleeves and put on his jacket again. The conference was over. The others stood as well.

'Gentlemen, I'm disappointed. Keeper, I want an update on Sugarman. Known associates, recent movements, you know the script. Get it from Hall. And I want a recommendation on Hall as well. One hour.'

Keeper nodded. He already suspected what his recommendation on Mr Hall would be.

◆

Well away from the comfortable boardroom, the late-afternoon vista down the valley was a delight to anyone who had the time to admire it. The entire facility staff were indoors, with no windows to distract them from their work. They were too busy and too engrossed in their jobs to take any interest anyway. The Bavarian countryside could, they realised, be enjoyed some other time. For the present, their life was a large building that, from the outside, looked like what it was supposed to look like, a storage shed.

It was one of two identical buildings, both boldly emblazoned Südbayern Speicher Firma – South Bavarian Storage Company – an innocuous cover. The operation was legitimate. Shed two housed motor cars, mobile homes, yachts, agricultural machinery, and even a few Second World War tanks. On the other hand, the company's wealthy clients never saw the interior of shed number one.

The local Mr Southwood pulled a microphone closer. 'Attention, all personnel,' he said. 'We are about to commence compliance testing of tonight's activities. Your full attention, please.'

He perused a printed list.

'Launch hardware. Testing and readiness?'

A technician's response was immediate. 'Primary and beta testing complete. Ongoing inspections continuing till T minus 15.'

'Thank you. Fixed facilities condition and readiness?'

The same voice responded in a methodical, almost bored tone. 'Fixed facilities have been fully reviewed and renovated as per your instructions. Additional works were completed one hour ago. All ready.'

Mr Southwood nodded.

'Excellent. I want a full report on those modifications post-launch.' He continued.

'Satellite?'

The satellite man was a woman, one of only two on the base. Her report was delivered with more enthusiasm.

'Satellite nine has been reprogrammed, sir. Twice. It was very satisfying. Your idea to provide quantum processor backup has been put in place. Brilliant thinking, if I may say. Should we include that in number 10 as well?'

'Yes, continue.'

'OK, integration is being examined now and will be completed in…' there was a pause, 'completed in 31 minutes. I expect no issues. Should be a blast.'

Mr Southwood let the last unprofessional remark go.

'Ground systems. Has the lateral convergence problem been dealt with?'

The ground systems team of three technicians was led by an Englishman who had amyotrophic lateral sclerosis and was confined to a wheelchair. The resultant loss of his speech forced him to communicate through a speech-generating device.

A metallic voice, slightly modulated, reported, 'Suitable filters have been designed and installed. The convergence delays suffered previously will not recur. Applications to patent the filter are ready to be submitted. Your instructions?'

Mr Southwood frowned and responded with some intensity. 'Not yet. It's a fix for a problem no one else has and probably never will. Any longitudinal wave interference detected?'

After a brief pause, the metallic voice said, 'Wait, please.'

Another of the ground systems technicians reported that none had been detected but that scalar waves were unlikely to be monitored externally during the daytime. Southwood had determined that monitoring this kind of technology had been more or less abandoned by officialdom, including the military, as storm frequencies confused the issue. Only a few oddball amateurs were the least bit curious now. Keeper maintained a list of the individuals within the area, about 400 square kilometres. They only operated at night as all seemed to have daytime jobs, family commitments, or both. Senior personnel were nevertheless concerned that any such detection might stimulate unwanted interest and that it should be discouraged if it occurred.

The compliance test reports continued. Another disembodied voice came through the speaker and reported that primary line movement was as anticipated with no divergence from mapped expectations. Secondary and tertiary line movement had been fluctuating, but tertiary lines had been pulsing around regular phase activity. Computer modelling suggested that optimum positioning would be achieved that evening at 9:11 p.m.

Mr Southwood wanted more detail and asked for data on parameter divergence. With only a moment's delay, he was advised of a 0.07% divergence. Mr Southwood frowned.

'That's acceptable. I want any early warning on geomagnetic field polarity movement. Our Melbourne team thinks an incomplete shift could occur in the next 12 months,' he said.

During this process, the local Mr Southwood and Keeper observed the task force from a mezzanine-level office, the only section of the building with a window. Banks of computers and other apparatus, the function of which neither could fathom, indicated considerable activity. Technicians compared notes and fine-tuned their respective equipment.

The reports kept coming, and it was clear that preparations were not only on schedule but also at or near optimal tolerances. There seemed to be no cause for concern.

'What about that new thing?' Keeper asked. His boss leaned forward slightly and pressed a button on the microphone.

'Supervisor, any sign of diamagnetic vortex fluctuations?'

A technician quickly returned to his post, having been in discussion with a colleague.

'Southern hemisphere stations have reported some activity there, notably New Zealand and Australia, but nothing noted in our radius. It is being monitored.'

After an hour, Southwood was satisfied with the proceedings and decided that little more could be achieved until launch. Just two more things concerned him. He could see that the weather looked benign and shouldn't interfere with their program, but it was better to be sure. The microphone was pushed away in favour of a mobile phone.

'Southwood here. What's the weather forecast for 9 o'clock?'

The organisation's meteorological expert had anticipated the request.

'Much as it has been today. By 2100, the temperature will be 12 degrees Celsius, no precipitation, air movement from the west, 10 knots. Any changes, I'll text you.'

'What about security, Keeper?'

As a legitimate high-value storage facility, security was as expected, though perhaps a little overdone. High fencing, barbed wire, lighting and many obvious cameras were sufficient to dissuade all the curious and most criminal elements in the area. The facility's remote location helped as well. Keeper reported that no activity had been observed that day, except for two young people on a cycling holiday, who had become hopelessly lost and were seeking directions.

'It looked like they might set up camp nearby, so we took them, and their bikes, to the village they had been looking for, 40 kilometres away. It has a youth hostel or some such. It appeared to be genuine.'

Late afternoon turned into early evening, and in shifts, the white coats wandered into their modest dining room for a quick meal. Most were in and out in 15 minutes, not wanting to be away from their stations for too long. A couple went outside for a cigarette and noticed the clear afternoon light had run its course. A light ground mist was developing, drifting slowly down the valley, though from their slightly higher vantage point, the sky was still clear. 'Good night for a lift,' one said to a colleague.

◆

In a beer hall some forty minutes away, the two cycling tourists met with a small group of Germans, mostly students, planning their evening activities. The band had come together accidentally, having common interests. They would visit the South Bavarian Storage area, where a hidden observation point had been found. On a hillside, a well-hidden cave could comfortably shelter three or four adults. From this unseen vantage point, they could watch over most of the high-fenced grounds. One of that group was Sean, a radio technician who, with a student physicist, Emma, had stumbled upon unusual activity that they thought might be military. It was to be a stealthy exercise, partly because it might be fun but primarily because if it was military, their curiosity undoubtedly would not be welcome.

After a round of beers and much discussion, the group decided that three would use the cave as an 'Alpha site' – they all agreed on the scientific terminology – and the others split themselves between two other observation points. The Beta and Gamma sites were less advantageous, being on lower ground and more distant. The three teams had sound recording and video equipment as well as devices of a more technical nature. They were sure evidence of some activity would be recorded, though they had little idea what that activity would be. They would communicate by text messages but only when something notable happened.

The strategy was settled, such as it was, and the group decided to encourage the beerhall's chef with orders for eight servings of the day's special. Onion tart as a first was followed by generous helpings of crispy pork loin with wild mushroom sauce and what they all decided was 'some kind of red onion thing.' This was accompanied by another Weizenbier, wheat beer. They would be at their respective sites by 7:30, stay till at least 2:00 a.m. and meet again at the village's largest café at 11:00 a.m. the next day.

Alpha group comprised the two lost cyclists and the would-be physicist, Emma. The latter didn't know that her companions for the evening were members of a largely unknown group whose interest lay in identifying subversive government activity. Their goal was infiltration and destabilisation of any mechanisms that, they were convinced, existed in most of the world's governments. On the way to their hidden cave, they told their new friend what they suspected without giving the entire story. They had evidence – 'Perhaps too strong a word,' one added – that a government organisation was developing an energy platform that could be provided across the globe. Once in place, countries could be held to ransom and forced to pay whatever was demanded of them by what would then be a power monopoly. Observations tonight might provide more data for their research and help explain the energy model.

By the time the three reached their cave, it was twilight. The failing light meant that only the keenest of observers would have seen them trekking up the hill, though they made the most of the trees and shrubs screening their route, just to be sure. The hollow afforded a good view over their objective, but a couple of taller trees blocked part of the grounds. They hoped their companions would be able to cover those sections. Previous cave users had set up a makeshift table with large stones and logs providing somewhere to sit. Having set their equipment to standby mode, they looked at each other, waiting for one to give the word.

'Might as well start the party,' one finally said, and within a couple of minutes, their little boxes' lights were glowing or blinking, and meters settled at zero, waiting for something to record. Minor fluctuations indicated background noise.

A pair of binoculars was handed around, and each scanned the complex before them.

'Apart from a couple of guys having a smoke, not much happening,' one said. 'That's a bit odd though.'

'What's odd?'

'Why would guys working in a warehouse wear white coats? Lab coats by the look of them.'

The others looked again and agreed it was a clue that this was technical and had little to do with storage. They were familiar with this type of worker and they usually wore hi-vis vests. Two text messages within a few minutes revealed that the Beta and Gamma groups were in place. One added that a ground mist threatened to obscure their view, and they hoped it would dissipate. From the cave's higher vantage point, the mist was noticeable but not a hindrance.

Alpha group settled down with their equipment and decided to drink the two bottles of beer they'd brought. There was an apology for the plastic beakers. Comfortably nestled in their hiding place, the three speculated on the timing of any activity from the so-called storage facility. The older cyclist, an Australian called Conway, decided to share some intelligence he had received by email the previous night.

'News flash, guys,' he announced with mock excitement. 'We're waiting for an alignment of conditions that we think are critical to this mob's MO. Mostly, it's geographic but with some astronomical positioning chucked in as well. The weather might play a part. Our blokes don't have all the data, but they reckon definitely tonight and probably after 10 p.m., less likely a bit before.' He looked at his watch.

'It's now 8:30, so we can relax for a while, but keep your gear running and keep an eye on that site.' He scanned the area with the binoculars and grunted.

'That bloody mist is getting thicker. It wasn't forecast. Might be a technical watch tonight. Better get a polarising lens on the video camera. Not sure if that'll help much, but we have a full moon at the right angle. At least they've kept their security lights on, so far anyway. They switch to red lights at midnight. No idea why.'

A text from Beta group said they couldn't see anything now because of the mist and were 'flying on instruments.' Conway told the others and suggested, intentionally mixing a metaphor, that the third group was probably in the same boat.

'Right, let's finish that beer and see what happens.'

All three were startled by movement behind some bushes.

'What was that?' Conway asked.

His cycling companion, Tony, spotted it. 'Just a dog, wandered away from a campsite probably.'

'Black dog?'

'I think so. At night, most dogs look black.'

The evening was serene, and the amateur sleuths were pleased that the full moon provided sufficient light to add visual observations to their technical recordings. Only the mist threatened to interfere. Tony had temporary custody of the binoculars and seemed reluctant to surrender them. He held on to them for several minutes, finally venturing a comment.

'That's just odd.'

The mist, still only at ground level, hadn't penetrated the so-called storage facility perimeter despite its fencing being a regular wire style, albeit a thick wire. He told the others and handed the binoculars to Conway.

'Yes, I see. Odd is about right. Makes no sense. Hang on. It's starting to move, to rotate around the grounds. Slowly, but that mist is definitely rotating, and there's no wind. Anything odd on the instruments?'

Everyone checked their equipment. Nothing was untoward, and the group decided it must be an unusual micro-climate phenomenon. Anyway, it wasn't what they were there for. Conway then made a confession.

'I couldn't tell you this before. Our little venture tonight isn't unique. I work for a group looking into precisely what we hope to see tonight. We aren't sure about anything right now other than it's probably not a benign exercise. We've seen enough to know that.

'But,' he paused to collect his thoughts, 'our understanding isn't sufficiently advanced. I like that phrase. We're trying to fathom function and application. Knowing what something does isn't the same as knowing what it's for.'

Tony interrupted.

'Two questions. What group and what is it you don't sufficiently understand?'

Conway continued.

'OK. We are the International Co-operative Strategic Defence and Security Alliance Bureau. I wouldn't be surprised if you've never heard of us...'

'You mean The Hague?' Emma asked with some glee.

'Oh, you have heard of us. So much for secrecy. Anyway, it's lucky we found you, though I admit my colleagues have been watching you for a while. Nothing ominous, you understand.'

Tony revealed that in their research forays, they encountered many government and civilian groups that weren't mainstream general knowledge. They had heard of The Hague but not its full name – 'So thanks for that update.' – and had few ideas about its function.

'Anyway, we don't use The Hague name, though it seems to have been well established by common usage. I'm allowed to tell you this much; we're like NATO or MI40, only bigger, so definitely one of the good guys.'

'Wait,' Emma interjected, 'MI40?'

'Right, a short history lesson. You'll know about MI5 and MI6. Five is the UK domestic counter-intelligence and security agency. MI6 is the overseas equivalent. MI40 started in the Great War as Admiralty Room 40, a code-breaking unit. It's the most recent of the trio, created six years later. The modern version is way beyond MI5 and MI6. It doesn't work with either, but has high-level connections with the armed forces.

'My Bureau – OK, we'll call it The Hague – also works with MI40. Right now, the project du jour is to monitor certain things in space, underground and under the sea. This is pretty much common knowledge, but the details are the stuff of the Official Secrets Act. I don't know any of those details, so don't ask. The British Prime Minister, Chancellor of the Exchequer, two other Whitehall officials and possibly the king. They know. It's financed covertly by the Treasury, like, ah, better not let on.

'The bottom line is that potentially, you two are greatly assisting MI40 and The Hague in a matter of global importance. So are Beta and Gamma Group, but it's probably better they don't know about it.

'As to the "what", at the risk of introducing yet another organisation, have you heard of Southwood?'

Blank expressions indicated a 'no' from Emma and Tony.

'Southwood is every security group's worst nightmare. You just need to know they are definitely the bad guys in this tale. As I said, we know little about what they're doing and even less about why. Tonight's surveillance might help change that.'

Emma noticed it was getting colder during this surprising disclosure and retrieved a jacket from her backpack. The others followed suit. One of their instruments monitored the ambient temperature and recorded a six-degree drop in only 12 minutes. Conway confessed they had encountered this phenomenon on other surveillance exercises but that the swirling mist was new to him.

It was 9:00 p.m. The mist continued to rotate but wasn't getting deeper, so visibility was largely unimpaired. Any thoughts that this would be a long, possibly fruitless night were dispelled when the facility's security lights changed. The stark, cool white LEDs were replaced by red, turning the mist into an eerie, pulsating mass.

Conway chuckled slightly. The others looked at him with expressions, asking the obvious question.

'My first flat was a cheap, crummy bed-sit, and when I moved in, the only lighting was equally cheap 40-watt bulbs. When I turned them on at night, the rooms seemed to get darker instead of lighter. All the bulbs did was throw shadows. That's what these red lights are doing, sort of, providing illumination but less light, if you get what I mean. It's a bit ominous, don't you think? I'm guessing they have infra-red in the mix, too. Whatever, they don't usually switch to red till midnight, so something is about to happen, I reckon. Is that video camera recording?'

'Recording and uploading in real-time. Our people can see what we see, subject to buffering,' Tony replied, 'but pretty well as we see it.'

The 'something' about to happen started at 9:07. As the Alpha trio watched their instruments and the scene before them, the curious red mist disappeared. It faded in seconds, seemingly replaced by an equally mysterious-looking frost, still coloured red by the security lights. Emma unzipped her jacket.

'So much for cold,' she said, 'now I'm hot. What's the thermometer say?'

Conway checked. 'Bloody oath, 22, 23, and rising fast, 26. How is that possible, and where did that wind come from? Make a note, 9:08; rapid temperature increase and sudden wind from,' he paused, 'the west.'

The weather was suddenly forgotten when Tony, with the binoculars to his eyes, described something they weren't expecting. The roof of the larger storage warehouse began to slide open from the western end. They could hear a klaxon sound, not unlike a Second World War air raid siren. He described the roof action. It was smooth but not slow and revealed a heavy-duty construction. He suspected it was more substantial than was strictly necessary for a regular roof. However, this was no regular roof, nor was what occurred next a regular event.

'If that camera has a zoom, get in as close as you can.'

The westerly wind developed into a broad whirlwind, circling the warehouse facility but not affecting anything within the grounds, the eye of the storm. Several small trees were barely moving. The roof was fully open, slightly overhanging the eastern end, and the klaxon stopped its mournful cry. From their high vantage point, The Hague's agent and two unwitting colleagues could see the inside of the warehouse was bathed in the same red light as outside.

'We'll have to think of a new name for this place. It ain't no warehouse,' Tony said.

Conway knew that The Hague referred to it as SLF9, Satellite Launch Facility 9, but decided against passing on unnecessary information. They were too far from the facility to hear that the klaxon had been replaced by a repeating digital tone of four beeps followed by a longer sound. It was a count-up rather than a count-down, as the launch personnel didn't know precisely when the lift-off would occur. Another counterintuitive element of this event was that, within the peculiar circle of Southwood technicians, the event was called a push-off, not a lift-off.

Also unknown to Conway, Emma and Tony, 250 kilometres underground, a vast flow of magma was disrupting their comfortably accepted nature of gravity. Axel Furst's theory was more than a theory. It was a reality that few knew about. Of those people, fewer still understood its ramifications. Southwood's scientists knew, understood and believed they could manage the fluctuating gravitational pressure points for their own ends. With seismic observations recorded and mapped by a new generation of quantum computers, they could forecast the location, timing and magnitude of any gravitational anomaly. Today was just such a time.

The magma flow was as rapid as such dense material can be. In a very short time, millions of tonnes of the stuff would impact a mass of virtually stationary heavy magma. This was Furst's tung magma interfering with his northern Gulf Stream. What was an orderly underground flow became a vortex of, as the Southwood scientists called it, mass into energy. It couldn't be seen or heard, but its effects were about to become extremely apparent.

Its influence on air temperature and movement had already occurred. Once warm, then cold, the wind again became a hot sirocco-like airstream, while the ground was icy cold. The weather was behaving in a way most people would regard as irrational. Conway and his friends moved their equipment inside the cave to avoid the worst wind. The noise level increased so that conversation was difficult without shouting, and sound recording was as good as impossible, though they kept it running, just in case. Later, reviewing the footage, one suggested the soundtrack wasn't the prettiest noise but better than some so-called music he'd heard.

The integrity of their equipment was forgotten at 9:11 p.m. From the open roof of the warehouse, the dull red light was replaced by an incandescent white glare as a cylindrical object of about 12 metres in length appeared. The brightness of the light made observation difficult, but all three later agreed it had the appearance of a small rocket with a pointed nose and fins at the base. Despite the noise of the wind, they also decided that the missile – they called it that – made no sound of its own.

There was no on-board propulsion, though stabilising jets were automatically activated and controlled by computers within the missile or, if needed, from the ground facility. Launch speed was rapid, though casual observers' expectations couldn't have been quantified with any accuracy. It disappeared within seconds, partly due to its speed but mainly because of the sky's now murky appearance.

This was the first launch Conway had observed, and he now knew why the first eight had not been seen. The three set about checking their equipment and comparing notes. They couldn't know that, within the facility, several men and women in their white lab coats were doing the same thing. Their job was done, objective achieved. Schnapps was handed around in celebration.

Text messages from Beta and Gamma groups revealed they had also seen the missile launch, but much of their equipment had failed to record anything. The gravitational activity had treated it with disdain and temporarily rendered much of it ineffective.

At their elevated post, Alpha group's gear worked well, though as expected, sound recordings were useless. The digital recordings of all other machines would provide, they hoped, valuable data for later analysis. The video of the event had already been streamed to the world, or at least to those who knew where to find it.

Conway took control of the operation.

'OK, that was worth seeing, right?'

Emma and Tony agreed.

'I'm not entirely sure what we did see, but my colleagues will be well pleased with the video and everything else we recorded. Have you noticed? The wind has died down, and the sky is clearing. Whatever was going on has passed, I'd say. Hey, look. The warehouse roof is closing again. It's probably best we don't hang around. Better pack up and get going. We can transmit the other data later.'

He contacted the other groups and suggested the same thing, with a reminder to meet at the agreed rendezvous point at 11:00 a.m.

With their equipment again packed up and secured, the three made their way back down the hill.

Tony asked Conway, 'Hey, does this Southwood crowd know about The Hague?'

'They shouldn't, but I reckon it's as likely as not.'

Emma suddenly stopped, startled and looked behind her.

'What's up?' Tony asked.

'Nothing. I saw that black dog again. Must have been watching the fun.'

◆

Chapter 11

'I'm From The Hague'

In Dr Robert's comfortable little cottage, he and Derek talked about UFOs and other left-field phenomena all night. The doctor's wife went to bed as early as possible without appearing rude and contented herself with a romance novel. Despite his formal medical training and a grounding in fundamental science, the doctor showed great interest in Derek's research. Eventually, the subject changed, and the visitor revealed he had been a successful stockbroker before retiring. Asked why he quit, Derek told how his employer discovered he was what the press loved to call a 'rogue trader.'

'At the risk of prying, what sort of money are we talking about?' the doctor asked.

Derek paused.

'Not sure about that. I should know, but I ran several accounts. About seven million dollars, I think, and...'

'That's not too bad, surely.'

'... and 45 million pounds, and 80 million US dollars, and six billion yen. I think the total was over 500 million dollars equivalent. Or 600. I lost count on the last day.'

Doctor Robert leaned back and let out a long whistle.

'That's a lot of money to lose.'

'I suppose it is, but I didn't lose it. That was profit, but you never hear about rogue traders who make money,' Derek corrected him, 'and there have been plenty.'

Another long whistle followed, and a brief silence gave his guest the hint to continue.

'My firm was old money, and the partners, well, they were just plain old. Their methods were stuck in the past. I ignored their protocols and used my own systems. Technical analysis; charting. The company was all about fundamentals, but that's just following old news. There's no point buying a share because of a $20 valuation when it trades at 10 but might fall to seven or eight. The charts tell you everything if you know how to read them. Anyway, they sacked me. Said I'd just been lucky. Can you believe it? A 500 million dollar lucky streak. I told them as long as my arse pointed to the ground, I would use my own systems; thanks very much. Anyway, I moved my private accounts to other brokers before I left. I didn't want anyone to lose what I'd made for them.'

Derek had little opportunity to talk to anyone about this aspect of his career. Most understood very little and cared even less. Under the influence of his host's tawny port, he confided that one of his private clients was their mutual friend, Jack Sugarman.

'I set him up, modified some of his orders, and it looked like the company had got them wrong. Funny how it worked out, really, but it ended up a joke that I could never share. I don't think Mr Sugarman ever cottoned on to what I did. I gather he never queried why his account had been moved to a different firm. I think he was in hospital at the time; probably thought it was just a name change or something. His new broker was a genius with charts, too. Of course, he was using some of my techniques, Elliott Waves, Fibonacci retracements, reversal zones, trend and countertrend swings. All that 'lucky' stuff. Excellent port this,' he added, holding up an empty glass.

It was duly topped up, and the all-night discussion continued. Derek admitted that trading in his own account was as successful as Jack's but that his tastes were far more modest. Most of his profits were donated to various grateful charities.

The doctor's side of the conversation also referenced Jack. A decision made in college to study medicine led to several years as a general practitioner. That part of his life was cut short, though, thanks to an event he referred to only as 'the thing'. Jack had come to the rescue and saved him from disgrace and a threatened prison sentence, though it cost him his licence to practice medicine. He was happy now to live quietly with his wife in their little country cottage, grow rhubarb and gooseberries, and keep a few chickens. The latest incident was a welcome distraction.

◆

Jack woke early that Friday morning, something he hated doing. He ate a light breakfast, and, at what he thought was a decent time, phoned Derek to ask how anyone might profit from share trading if Southwood's plans were put in place. He had been considering this already.

'Ah, well, yes, I think they'd short energy companies, coal mining companies, shipping and index futures. Gold will go up, no doubt about that. Resource-dominant countries like Australia will fall. The A-dollar will drop against most currencies. It'll be mass confusion for a few months, or maybe only weeks. In any case, the world's markets are looking a bit toppy right now, so that won't help. When is all this going to happen? Timing is everything.'

'Don't know that, Derek. We need to find out how advanced they are, and I don't even know who to ask. It might be days, might be months. We'll have to get a line inside, and I have some leads. Two individuals, three if Trevor is still about. Haven't spotted him, though. I'll get back to you. Tell the good doctor I said hi.'

Jack sat on his balcony with the ubiquitous coffee and watched Hobart come to life. The peak-hour traffic was dissipating, and the gentler pace was returning. He pondered the excitement of the last few days and took a mental inventory of where everyone was. Sarah was at her place with Lyn. Leon was at his place with Harry. 'Trousers,' Jack said aloud to himself, for no reason, then added, 'Where's Sayer? I don't even know where he lives.' He supposed he was also at home, wherever that was.

A text message arrived, announced by a single, desultory ping. It was from D.I. Sayer, though Jack had him listed simply as Doom.

'Aha, right,' Jack said, 'must be a day of talking to myself. Now, Leon.' He replied to the message 'OK thanks,' and was about to hit send, but added 'Useful' first.

He called Leon. 'Mate, it's Jack. Do you fancy lunch at Gracie's after you pick up your car? Midday? Come to my place. Parking's easier, and we'll have a coffee first.'

The invitation was accepted, and Jack made another call, this time to Ric, his harmonica-playing, bodybuilding friend. The same invitation was offered.

'Bring your mate if he's free. Great. See you.'

Jack was following two leads. One was the tip he'd got from Sayer by text message earlier. The other was more an educated guess.

When Leon arrived, Jack was working on another story for his *Dark History* book but couldn't decide whether to use it in case it caused offence. Lifting a story from the Bible and applying science is bound to upset those who take their scriptures literally. However, he was fascinated by the account of Moses crossing the Red Sea from the Book of Exodus. He wanted to run it past Leon but first had to remind him of the text, as he was largely ignorant of such things.

'Right, you heathen, you must have heard the story of Moses parting the Red Sea so the Israelites could escape some nasty Egyptian blokes chasing them in chariots. Now, here's the first revelation – if you'll excuse the word – it wasn't the Red Sea anyway. It was the Sea of Reeds. Close, but no cigar. Translators got it wrong. In any case, the Book of Exodus wasn't written by Moses. It ended up as a compilation of writings and didn't reach the form we know today until perhaps 900 years after the event.

'Here, Matthew recorded: Shortly before dawn Jesus went out to them, walking on the lake. When the disciples saw him walking on the lake, they were terrified. "It's a ghost," they said and cried out in fear. But Jesus immediately said to them: 'Take courage! It is I. Don't be afraid."

'Here's an important point. The King James Version of the Bible was the third translation into English. You need to be careful when you're dealing with versions – I'd wiggle my fingers in the air for quotation marks, but you'd think I was a wanker – but you have to work with something. So, are you following this, Sea of Reeds, not the Red Sea? One is quite shallow. The other, well, isn't. The Red

Sea is very deep in parts. The story is that Moses and the Israelites were being chased by Egyptian soldiers in chariots. At some point, supposedly, Moses stretched out his hand over the sea, and all that night, God drove the sea back. He turned the sea into dry land.'

Leon interrupted. 'Is there a test after this? I might need that coffee.'

'No to the test, yes to the coffee. Kettle's on. I'd get an espresso machine, but I like my café visits. Where was I? OK, so the Israelites crossed the riverbed, the water flowed back, and the Egyptians drowned. That's the story. Presuming there's some truth to it and further presuming you don't believe in divine intervention, what happened? There are things called wind setdown and wave setdown, when strong winds contrive to lower water levels, often in conjunction with tidal movements. The Exodus story tells us of a strong east wind. That could be the answer.

'Right, this was all in about 1,445 BC, on a Tuesday. Here's something else. Halley's comet comes around every 75 years – 75.27 if you want to be precise – and we know it was seen in 12 BC by Chinese astronomers. They were right into astronomy then, the Chinese. Earlier appearances were in 240 and 467 BC. If we take the 75¼-year orbit as historically stable, it means it would have neared the sun in 1,446 BC. The orbit might fluctuate slightly. I'm no astronomer. That's pretty damn close to the 1,445 BC Moses Red Sea story, isn't it.'

Leon's eyes were glazed over. 'Close, yes, closer than my coffee anyway. How near is that in astronomical units.'

Jack plunged the Bodum and poured two black coffees.

'Remember those odd seismological events of 1986?' Jack asked.

'Nuh.'

'No, I'm not surprised. It never got much coverage. But Halley's comet was just enough to tip some balances, especially around the Pacific Rim. New Zealand geysers were pretty active in '86. Never mind. We can't know the alignment of the sun and moon when Moses did his thing, but if it was enough, with Halley's help, to create a very low tide, those east winds might have been enough to create a wave setdown situation and leave a dry, well dry-ish, river bed you could walk on. Heavy chariots would sink to buggery in the mud, though.'

'Is that a biblical text?' Leon asked.

'Only in the Gospel according to Jack, chapter something, verse whatever. Last thing, 1,445 BC was in the late Bronze Age when the climate was getting colder and drier after a warm period. Sea levels were probably not what we'd recognise today. The Sea of Reeds was likely shallower then.'

'What, climate change even then?' Leon chipped in.

'Mate, there's never been a time when the climate wasn't changing. Is that coffee all right? And then there's sunspot activity. If my calculations are right, the sun was getting more active about that time after the 90-year cyclic low. And if that activity coincides with fluctuations in the coronal magnetic field – I don't know what that is – you could get a very interesting scenario.'

'Coffee's fine. Yeah, I wondered about the 90-year cycle,' Leon quipped, 'Hey, you're not going to rewrite the whole Bible, are you?'

Jack said he'd thought about it but decided he didn't want to deal with the backlash. He was still contemplating whether to include the Moses story in *Dark History*. He added two more points.

'I'm not sure how long it took to finish this crossing. The writings say, "All that night, the Lord drove the sea back." Supposedly, 600,000 Israelite men, plus their wives, children and livestock, crossed the sea bed in a matter of hours. It's pretty unlikely, I reckon. Maybe there was a miracle. But here's what interests me. There's a reference to "a pillar of fire" – hang on.'

Jack put down his coffee and retrieved his Holy Bible, bookmarked at Exodus.

'Here it is. "And the Lord went before them by day in a pillar of cloud to lead the way, and by night in a pillar of fire to give them light, so as to go by day and night." I've got so many references to pillars of fire or light; it's not funny. More than a coincidence. This story used to be seen as metaphorical, but I'm leaning towards it being historical.'

After much discussion, mainly on Jack's part, he looked at his watch.

'Come on, we'll go to Gracie's for lunch. I've booked a table, and we're meeting some people.'

'Excellent idea, and you're not allowed to change your mind.'

The walk into town was uneventful, though Jack kept an eye out for anyone following them. Once, they stopped briefly to look at a bookshop window display to see what a potential shadow would do. The shadow also stopped but hopped on a bus. 'False alarm,' Jack said. 'Maybe I'm getting paranoid.'

'Maybe you're getting hungry,' Leon replied.

The hotel was already busy, as it usually was on Fridays. Jack and Leon manoeuvred their way to the bar, where Ali, the licensee, busied himself with customers. Two drinks were secured, and Jack asked Ali if the back room was ready for them. This was a private dining room on busy days and, otherwise, a short-term storage area. He was told, 'If you'd like to sit at the bar for a few minutes, I'll make sure it's prepared.'

This suited Jack as he wanted to welcome Ric and his friend when they arrived, which was almost immediately. With handshakes and a proper introduction of Scott, Ric's mate, the four chatted amiably until two other heavily built men walked past them and settled into a booth near the back of the dining area. Jack recognised them immediately.

'We have unexpected company today. Those two guys are the bastards who did the dirty on Derek and Lyn. I very much want to return the favour, and maybe I will, but not right now. They might redeem themselves with some information.'

Ali indicated their table was ready, and Jack asked if he could 'set up another two places, sorry, late notice.' Ali nodded to another barman who scuttled off to do the deed. 'Just a couple of minutes, Commander.' Here was another ex-serviceman who liked to refer to ranks, even if they were honorary.

'Sayer tipped me off earlier that these two might be here today. They're hard nuts, but I don't want to cause any trouble in the hotel. We'll play it easy. Ric, Scott, stand close and look menacing but don't say anything. I have a feeling that pair are going to be useful, as much as it pains me to say.'

The group presented themselves at the booth, and the heavies stopped talking. Seeing their adversary accompanied by two muscular sidekicks – Leon stood behind, almost unseen – they knew their position was one of entrapment. There was no escape from the bench seats. Their expressions of frustration and surrender were easily read. There was no fight in them. One said something about 'missing that bloody plane.'

Jack held back his true feelings and didn't bother introducing his friends.

'I believe you are Mr Johnston and Mr Boucher, on holiday from Melbourne. We have some unfortunate history between us, and there are elements of that history I'd like to discuss with you. If you'd care to step into this room, we can avoid any unpleasantness.'

Leon opened the door, trying to appear useful.

Jack and his friends stepped back a little, and the pair made an ungracious exit from the booth.

'Bring your drinks,' Jack advised, 'it will be a civilised discussion, I assure you.'

There was a single circular table in the dining room, with six chairs and appropriate cutlery set out. Jack placed his two adversaries at the back setting, with Ric and Scott on either side. They moved their chairs slightly to be a little further away. He and Leon sat opposite.

'Now. You have a menu each, but I can recommend the New York steak. Is medium-rare alright?'

There was no objection from anyone. Ali appeared at the table and proffered a bottle of wine.

'Domaine A Cabernet Sauvignon, one of the older vintages from our cellar. You've had it before. Would you care to taste?'

Jack indicated that wouldn't be necessary and that he'd serve. Ali removed the cork and quietly left. Jack poured six glasses, though he baulked at serving fine wine to the men opposite. He held up his glass and proposed a toast.

'Friends and villains,' he said. There was no clinking of glasses, but everyone took a sip and reverently placed their drink on a New London Arms coaster.

There was a moment's silence. Jack wanted to see who spoke first. Whoever did was likely the senior partner of the two villains. The taller of the men was Mr Johnston.

'That's a bloody nice wine. Have to say that. Also have to ask why.'

Jack responded. 'I'm glad you appreciate it. I expected less of a couple of thugs. You don't mind if I call you that? But it's reassuring to know you have at least one redeeming quality.'

He went on to describe, in detail, the kidnapping and interrogation of his friends Derek and Lyn.

'I hope you'll be pleased to know that Lyn is recovering nicely, but (a lie) Derek isn't doing so well. He's with a doctor full-time (the truth, although out of context), and you two could be facing serious charges if he doesn't pull through. However, your MO looks like it was drawn from the College of Ineptitude rather than anything more sinister, so you have that in your favour.'

Boucher and Johnston looked at each other blankly. Jack continued.

'Speaking of favours, you could do yourselves one by providing us with some information. Number one, who were you working for?'

After a short silence and a nod to his colleague, which was returned, Johnston spoke.

'OK, you've got us over a barrel, and I'm as sure as shit we're not going to get any help from our side, so… yeah, we did the girl's place and took your friends and did everything you said. It was just a job. Understand, nothing personal in it. Just a job. Our contact was Hall. Don't know his first name, just Mr Hall. His contact was Southwood, Mr Southwood. Never heard a first name. Not once, and that's the truth.

'Hall was scared of Southwood. We could tell that. It was a hard business. We were sacked, though. Services no longer required, he said. Didn't get paid either, not the second half anyway. The money was supposed to go into an account, but nothing. Not a razoo. I tried to phone but the number, how does it go, is no longer in service. I reckon Hall is no longer in service as well. Good luck finding him, if that's what you want. Tell him we expect our money. No, don't bother with that. We've written it off. Didn't even get to keep the Range Rovers. We should be back in Melbourne by now, but we missed the flight. Your stupid bridge was closed, so some ship could go under it.'

After some minutes of discussion, two waitresses delivered their steaks. One of the bartenders brought in six steak knives and removed the regular blades. Jack noticed the wine had been enjoyed during their discussion and asked for another bottle.

Jack was skilful in interrogation, so adept that the two in question weren't aware that this was anything more than a question-and-answer session over a pleasant lunch. That was the plan. He had cleverly secured a lot of detail about things he knew only from first-hand experience and basic information he would otherwise remain ignorant of.

'One last thing,' he asked them both. 'What do you know of The Hague? Where do they come into it?'

'It's a scotch, right?

'That's Haig, H.A.I.G., I'm talking about H.A.G.U.E., the organisation. What's your link?'

Johnston and Boucher looked at each other and shrugged. They obviously knew nothing. Jack's phone pinged. A text message. He read it and returned the phone to his pocket.

'Right, you two can go. I don't particularly want to see you again. Ever. Understand?'

They left.

'You're just going to let them go?' Leon almost demanded.

'Not quite, look out the window.'

Outside, Messrs Boucher and Johnston were in the process of being arrested. Within a few minutes they were handcuffed, cautioned and bundled into a police van. Resigned to their fate, they didn't even bother to look back towards the hotel.

'Nice one, Jack. I like a happy ending,' Leon said, briefly placing a grateful hand on his shoulder.

◆

Jack was feeling modestly pleased with himself that evening. His soft interrogation of the Southwood heavies provided more information than would have otherwise resulted. The cost of the lunch was a good investment, and his friends also appreciated their free meal. He thumbed through the small notebook he'd used. At the very least, the mobile number for the mysterious Mr Hall might lead somewhere. He'd hand that over to Harry tomorrow. In a curious case of synchronicity, Harry phoned at that moment. He sounded downcast.

'Jack, good news and not good news. I've managed to decrypt more of those documents. Mostly it's pretty old stuff, minutes of meetings, technical reports, some operational records,' he paused, 'and something from 1996.' He paused again. Jack prompted him.

'OK, I'm sitting down. What is it?'

'There's a report of a car bombing. It was linked to Southwood, somehow. I'm hoping it's just a horrible coincidence, but two people were killed, Roger and Jan Sugarman. Tell me you don't know them.'

Jack hadn't been sitting down, but he flopped into a lounge chair and collected his thoughts. A long pause ensued. Finally, he spoke.

'Sorry, Harry, still there? They were my parents. I don't remember it very well. I was only eight. I don't remember them very well either; probably a coping mechanism. Someone could throw some pyschobabble at it, anyway. But you don't want to hear about all that. Anything else?'

'Yeah, a lot of this stuff looks like pure fiction to me. Your *Dark History* stories all make sense – sort of – but there are texts here that don't gel with me. They sound made up, and there are inconsistencies: dates, places, people. You might have a different view, but I've uploaded everything to the cloud, and I'll email the link to you.'

He changed tack.

'Hey, I'm sorry to bring you that stuff about your parents. Do you need some company? I'm free if you…'

'No, that's cool, but thanks. I'll be OK. Got some thinking to do. It's a universal remote situation.'

'How's that?'

'It changes everything. Now that I know what happened, I feel more like an orphan than ever, even as an 8-year-old boy. This Southwood thing is different now. It's personal. I'll be in touch.'

Jack sat, his head spinning. He looked around his apartment, and the comfortable accoutrements of his successful life seemed a little less important. The bookcase, groaning with stamp albums, stock books and heavy Stanley Gibbons catalogues, brought a smile to his face. Unrealised until a few minutes ago, that was a legacy of his father, who was also a collector. His eyes fell on the drinks trolley – an old-fashioned piece that looked out of place – and he poured himself a scotch without thinking about it.

Standing at the window, scotch in hand, Jack watched people coming and going. All these people, he thought, were oblivious to an event in 1996 that changed his life forever. And why should they know? They had their own lives to deal with. He placed his glass on a side table, the whisky untouched, put on a jacket and went for a walk.

The jacket was a good idea as the evening was cool. Turning left, Jack headed towards the King's Domain, cursing the traffic lights. Most shops had closed for the day, but a late-night licensed café encouraged the few people passing with a garish 'OPEN TILL LATE' flashing sign. Soon, he'd passed the last shop and reached the Intercity Cycleway, which served as many walkers as cyclists. At this time of day, it was virtually deserted, and Jack was alone with his thoughts: thoughts of his parents, their untimely deaths, being lovingly raised by Jim and Angela Walker.

There was little activity. Nearby road traffic offended the ears, but the electric light rail service was now running its limited evening 'stealth' timetable. Beyond the Tasman Bridge ('your stupid bridge' as one of the Southwood thugs called it), Hobart was quieter and a little darker, with the street lights more widely spaced. His thoughts matched his surroundings, bleak and sombre.

Ahead was a brighter area. The Norton Halt light rail station was brand new, fresh, modern, and well-lit. It was also little used, being a request-stop and effectively a private station, though open to the public in practice. Financed by the tech billionaire Norton Chase, it primarily served employees of his underground data centre built deep within the hill of the Domain. Apart from the unobtrusive train station, the data centre was noticeable only by an antenna array in a fenced area shared by a mobile phone tower and a radio relay-station repeater.

As Jack approached, a northbound railcar pulled up. It was the first time he had seen the station in use. A dozen passengers alighted, men and women, all clad in identical neat blue-grey uniforms. None were chatting, and they looked like they were heading to a place they didn't want to be, to do a job they didn't want to do, with people they didn't want to be with. Such was the joy of working night shifts.

Motion-sensor lighting activated as they neared the facility's main entrance, and a sliding door opened. Another 12 employees, similarly dressed, exited. Some boarded the waiting railcar while the rest waited for a southbound service. Jack concluded these were NCDC workers changing shifts. He wondered why the security camera was positioned so prominently. Passing the facility entrance, he noticed not-so-discrete signage extolling Private Property status, which appeared under a logo Jack thought read 'VIV'.

When the railcar left Norton Halt, Jack was again alone with his thoughts. The walk took him to Cornelian Bay, New Town East, Moonah and further north. By the time he reached the station at the Museum of Old and New Art, Hobart's famous MONA, he had been walking for two and a half hours and done enough thinking for a lifetime.

Inspired by the sighting of the railcar at Norton Halt, Jack decided to return that way. Expecting to see several people at the MONA Station, he was surprised to find only one solitary would-be passenger waiting for the next train. While not in any mood to be sociable, his amiable response to a 'good evening' didn't discourage conversation. The young man waiting said the next service would be in eight minutes, but he wouldn't take it.

'I'm homeless tonight. Going to sleep right here. The benches are comfortable enough and sheltered from wind and rain. I'm not really homeless, though. I'm a writer and need the experience, so I don't make a hash of it in my novel.'

Jack nodded. The writer continued.

'My view is that sometimes you just have to get into something deeper. Get some solid experience. Look at things from another angle, or what I'm doing now, from the inside. That way, you understand it rather than know it. There's a big difference. Knowledge is just seeing how something works, or simplistically, that it happens at all. Understanding means you see why a thing is panning out the way it is. That's our point of control.'

Again, Jack nodded and said something appropriate but, later, couldn't recall what that was.

The railcar back home was a pleasant 20-minute journey, particularly the picturesque riverside section from Cornelian Bay into the city. Jack was nearing his apartment building five minutes later when he noticed a tall, slim man waiting outside. The man took a step closer and spoke.

'You must be Commander Sugarman. I've been waiting for an hour, but uninvited, so it's all cool. I couldn't reach you on the phone. Can we talk? It's rather important. I'm from The Hague.'

◆

Chapter 12

Unusual Activity

The Hague man presented his credentials; a small folding leather wallet displayed an unsmiling photo on one side with his name beneath it. On the other side, there was no mention of The Hague. Instead, it nominated the International Co-operative Strategic Defence and Security Alliance Bureau as his employer.

'Bit of a mouthful, all that. Management doesn't like The Hague title, but it's so well established now that they accept it. Anyway, Steven Andrews, but I also answer to Andrew Stevens. People are always getting it mixed up. Useful sometimes, actually. No rank. We're not military, but I'm an A.F., which means Field Agent. It's the wrong way round because, essentially, we didn't want to be called F.A.'

Jack smiled at that and had already decided he liked A.F. Andrews. He invited him to his apartment, where, spotting his untouched scotch, he grabbed the glass and offered one to his new friend, sizing him up as he did. Andrews was fit and athletic, not just slim, well dressed with stylish, but not flashy clothes. He wore a Burberry blazer, dark blue with a discreet check, over dark trousers and 'sensible' shoes. 'Something you could run in,' Jack thought. The deep red socks implied a degree of 'sod convention' that Jack approved of.

'Yes, thanks, a scotch would be great. It was a bit cold waiting outside for you actually, and it's not like we can't drink on duty.'

Another large scotch was duly poured.

'Ah, Speyside. My region of choice. Cheers. I like your place. High enough to get a great view without being too far up. But to business. Essentially, my superiors know something about you, what you do, and what you've achieved. We have our methods. Sorry if that sounds menacing, but information is our business. Don't worry, though. We're on the same side.

'About your parents. I dislike the expression, but I'm sorry for your loss. I really am. I was briefed about this only a little while ago and, until then, didn't realise all this was personal for you.'

Jack explained he learned only a few hours ago that Southwood was responsible for his parents' deaths.

'It was a shock, I can tell you, and I tried to walk it off. Been away a few hours. Left in a hurry and forgot to grab my phone. That's why you couldn't reach me. It was a long time ago, and I expect the individuals responsible are no longer in the picture, but I'm after some sort of reckoning.'

Andrews sympathised and expressed his hope that Southwood's day of reckoning was near. However, that single event wasn't their primary consideration, and he told Jack that The Hague was investigating Southwood at a broader, not to say higher, level.

'The crowd's criminal activity goes back decades, if not centuries. I suppose you've guessed that already. Not guessed. Sorry, how insulting. Worked it out. My briefing was necessarily, well, brief, but I know the story goes back to the sixties with something called the Club of Berlin. They were legitimate, as far as we can work out, but were infiltrated and taken over by Southwood.'

Jack was thrilled that he'd met someone aware of this brutal organisation, doubly excited that he'd found an ally.

'Back in the seventies – way before my time – we did have a big win. Well, we thought it was big. Turns out we were only dealing with a single cell of the organisation, and it essentially made nothing but a small dent in their overall plans, whatever they were. We learned one thing, though. When their people are compromised, they don't want to know about them anymore. No loyalty in Southwood, none at all.

'Briefly, we were pretty pleased with ourselves but fell into that trap of the victor, thinking we were right and very clever. But we only had part of an answer to part of a question, which didn't get us any further than we were before. The organisation went into stealth mode, even stealthier than usual, I mean, and our sources of information dried up. I mean completely. I'm told we had a couple or three informants, but they vanished. No one said so, but I reckon they were, what's the word, liquidated. Now look what you've made me do. Talking so much I've actually finished my scotch.'

Jack grinned at both the unsubtle hint and because he realised The Hague man often added 'actually' and 'essentially' to his speech. He replenished both glasses. Andrews asked if he knew anything about the Europa program.

'Quite a bit, if you mean the European Conference of Postal and Telecommunications Administrations. But I'm guessing you don't unless you're a stamp collector. It's also one of Jupiter's moons, but as far as a program goes, there were the Europa rockets. Is that what you had in mind?'

'Exactly. I didn't know about the Conference of Postal thingies, but yes, Southwood took a very close interest in the rocket program. Run out of Woomera, actually. We had a bloke looking into it unofficially. He was a teacher and agreed to watch what went on and get back to us. Trouble was, he was a teacher first and an agent, well, hardly second, barely at all. The poor guy had no idea what was really going on.'

Jack put down his glass.

'You're talking about Colin Hunter, right? Flight 5, late in 1966?

Andrews put down his glass, too.

'Bloody hell, Jack, no one is supposed to know about this stuff, apart from the actual launch, that is. I thought it was later than '66, shows you how limited my briefing was. It's just as well I'm authorised to bring you up to speed; otherwise, I might have to arrest you. But we won't go down that little rabbit warren. Hunter wrote a report, but I gather he had plans other than sharing it with us. He had to be persuaded to drop it. Scary men in black. You understand? We got a few photos from him anyway.'

The evening turned into night. Jack and his new friend finally realised they hadn't eaten, and Jack ordered more pizza (with extra anchovies). Jim wasn't working, so there would be no freebies.

'I don't think it's done to drink scotch with pizza. I can offer you beer or wine,' Jack said.

Andrews was a beer lover and opted for a Crayon and Maggot porter, which he instantly took a liking to. So it was over scotch, pizza, and beer; for another two hours, the pair shared their knowledge, suspicions, and theories of Southwood and Dragonfly. While Jack had a considerable volume of material, much of it was, as he liked to put it, historical. Andrews referred to them as 'legacy issues' and apologised for the expression, putting it down to a previous life as a Treasury employee. Jack offered to make his entire archive available to The Hague, but with the understanding that they wouldn't publish any of it.

'We're not in the publishing business, so no worries there. We try to avoid publicity of any sort. From what you've shared with me already, I'd say Shoelaces could analyse your data, given time, and come up with something useful. No, not useful. Practical.'

'Shoelaces?' Jack asked.

'I don't know where the name came from. Probably a contraction of some long title, misheard and poorly remembered. It's our quantum computer – not my field – but a computer that holds data in qubits, not just bits, so 0, 1 and 0&1. I don't even know how I remembered that, actually. Anyway, our tech-heads are using it with AI and making good progress, though the damn thing seems to have developed an attitude and plays up a bit. Work in progress, as they say.'

Andrews' mood then appeared to change. He became grim as he outlined the latest Southwood satellite launch in Bavaria. There were two things no one other than Southwood knew. One was how many such satellites had been made operational. The Hague had monitored 14 launches, some of which had failed. They thought onboard malfunctions destroyed the missiles, though it may have been control system destruct imperatives or self-destruct deployment. The other thing was how many more satellites were planned.

'The team watching this last launch was able to stream footage and upload data in real-time. It makes for interesting viewing, and we're analysing the data now. But here's the thing. Eight people were watching it, including a couple of Aussies. They've all disappeared. We suspect the worst.

'Now, we assign a contact risk assessment to Southwood cells. All its European cells have been upgraded to Critical. Our A.F.s are to avoid personal contact unless armed and preferably operating in pairs.'

Jack started to worry.

'What about here, in Australia?'

'Each country usually has its own assessment. The Aussie outfit seems to be run less aggressively, but I know your two friends were badly treated. I'm told the guys responsible were more clumsy than malicious, and we haven't found their handler. What's his name? Wall?'

'Hall. First name unknown, but as to malice, those blokes suggested he may no longer be of this earth. Not their words, of course.'

'OK. Essentially, Southwood Australia has a risk assessment of Caution, but we may need to advance that. Perhaps Extreme Caution. Sounds like a bushfire risk, doesn't it?'

Jack asked if they had any contractors or outside advisers connected to their Shoelaces computer. The answer was yes, one, 'a genius from Amsterdam. I've never met her, though.'

The thought that it might be Harry, aka Trousers, was dismissed from Jack's mind. He realised it must be getting late, and a tired mind tends to wander down strange paths. He would ask Harry to set up a secure cloud depository for his *Dark History* material, with access for Andrews. The Hague may even be able to tie it all together 'with Shoelaces'. Jack smiled at his little joke.

Andrews' grim countenance cleared slightly with his next announcement.

'Now I'm going to let you into something I bet you don't know. We learned of it yesterday. Only a few of us know so far. Essentially, there's a Southwood facility in Hobart, right under our noses. Sneaky bastards, these people. It's a case of a cover story being the real thing and then some. There's an underground data centre on your Domain.

Well, under your Domain. As far as we can determine, it's a legitimate operation, but we've looked at their site plans. Even Southwood had to get council approval to build the thing. It's a subsidiary of a larger facility and not directly accessible to the public. Clouds ain't clouds, Jack.

'Our experts reckon the size of the excavation was more extensive, and I mean much more than would be necessary for their stated operational parameters. I sound like a government report. Anyway, their power consumption far exceeds what they'd need for the data centre alone. They can't hide that. There's something else going on there. We don't know exactly what. Everything transmitted from it is encrypted, and they use frequencies no one else does. Pretty strange.

'They even have their own train station. You've probably seen it. It's just before Cornelian Bay, and most people prefer that stop. We've been watching the workers come and go. Most of them we don't know but a few are on our radar. Specialists in stuff unrelated to mere data storage. It's a work in progress, this one. Oh yeah, it has a name I can't remember just now. It's too late in the evening to think straight. But we've come across a few instances where it is referred to as Viv, whoever she is. Some trading name, perhaps.'

Jack was quietly taking all this in and offered no interruption. He stood up.

'Mr Andrews, you deserve another scotch.'

He retrieved a bottle from a cupboard and poured two generous measures into fresh glasses.

'If you liked the Speyside we already had, you'll love this one. Same distillery, but a 21-year-old. I save it for special. And what you've told me is special, if not remarkable. I passed that station tonight and saw what I thought must be a shift change. It's only just hit me. That name Viv isn't Viv. It's VIV, all capitals. I saw it. It must be V, space, IV. Or V4. Let me enlighten you.

'It's a nice case of synchronicity that we've just had that launch in Bavaria. In the Second World War, the Americans came across a missile launch site that didn't make sense. It was too far from anywhere to be useful, and there was no evidence of any launches. However…'

Jack paused for effect and stressed his next statement with his meaningful compression of a thumb and forefinger.

'However, there was evidence, documentary anyway, of a V4. At first, we thought, or they thought, it was a new vengeance weapon. But no. It was the abbreviation of Vilin 4. Hang on.'

Jack retrieved a document.

'Here we go. There was a reference to Vilin Prsten. My friend Lyn told me it's Serbian or Croatian for "dragonfly ring" or "dragonfly circle". The translation is loose, but there was also something – I'll get the pronunciation wrong – "vilin vazka velmi vysoke." Lyn said that could mean "dragonfly very high." Note the alliteration, four Vs, or V4. Or Vilin 4 or VIV when you use Roman numerals. How's that scotch?'

Andrews mimicked Jack's thumb and forefinger gesture and said the scotch was excellent, worthy of the information they'd exchanged and vice versa. He also suggested they continue their discussion tomorrow.

'Look, it's near midnight, and my head is too full of stuff to work properly. I don't think your scotch is helping, either. My hotel is an easy walk from here. The air will help clear my brain. They do a good breakfast. Join me, say 8-ish, and I'll treat you to whatever kind you prefer. There's one more thing you need to know. Rather interesting it is. I'll explain then.'

◆

Alone again with his thoughts, Jack made a long-delayed decision. He retrieved two envelopes from his safe. They were old and bore the patina of much-handled documents. Having remained unopened for many years, he placed them on a table, side by side, hesitated, and picked up the smaller of the two. It was heavily sealed once, but a letter opener made short work of the inch-wide sticky tape, which was now brittle and yellowed with age. Having complied with the insistent OPEN FIRST instruction, Jack read a letter from a police officer.

'Dear Jack,' it read in neat cursive handwriting, 'if my wishes have been honoured, you are reading this later than 2006 and are at least 18 years old.'

'At least,' Jack said aloud. He continued reading.

'My name is Stan Wright. You probably have never heard of me. I was a police officer at the time of your parents' deaths, and I say "was" because I expect to be retired by the time you open my envelopes.'

Stan went on to record what he'd told Jack's foster parents many years ago. He related the same story Jim and Angela Walker heard, that it had been his grim task to catalogue the items found in Roger and Jan Sugarman's crashed car. He listed the banal ephemera one might find in any vehicle at the time, street atlas, service logbook, a box of tissues, etc., even down to the 35 cents under the seats.

However, there was a significant difference with one discovery. Stan said a lengthy document in Jack's father's briefcase appeared far more critical than its official treatment in 1996 suggested. Having photocopied the document for head office, the now-retired police officer was surprised to learn that the original, presumed to be safely held in the locked Evidence Room, had gone missing. His photocopy was only semi-official as it never made it to head office or Records and was never enquired after. After P.C. Wright read the document, he was torn between his official duty and fear of what might happen to him if he fulfilled that obligation.

His letter to Jack continued:

'I told Jim and Angela as little as I thought it safe to. What your father was investigating was corruption in government and the public service. I said it could have brought down the government. That's true enough, but it's not the whole story. I don't want to quote from your father's work as I reckon you'll be reading that soon enough, but corruption is possibly the least of what he'd uncovered. As I write this, I'm a little ashamed that I didn't have the courage to take his work further. The truth is I didn't know who to trust among my superiors. The more I thought about it, the more confused I became.'

Stan concluded his letter by wishing Jack success in whatever course of action he took and that he hoped to live long enough to perhaps hear from him one day.

Jack wondered if his strange benefactor was still alive. He concluded that as he'd spoken of retirement by 2006, it was likely that P.C. Wright had ended his working life long ago. Hopefully, he was still enjoying the benefits of a healthy superannuation balance.

Placing Stan's letter aside, Jack tapped the bulky, large envelope with the letter opener and looked at his watch. The contents promised to be revealing, and dismissing the time, he emptied the manilla envelope to find over a hundred pages of closely typed documents. A cursory examination showed that his father's report comprised only the first eight pages, with the balance being attachments. It was the first time he'd seen his father's signature, which, like his own, was illegible, acknowledging authorship but not providing identification.

Jack skimmed the report. It referred to information and data in the various attachments and would take a concerted effort to read properly. The summary included a statement that made Jack sit up straight.

'The head of this organisation – whatever it's called – is one Mr Southwood. His first name is unknown. On no account is this individual to be considered anything but dangerous. He has been linked directly or indirectly with the deaths of several people. This man is ruthless and not averse to extremes.'

◆

Jack didn't like appointments like '8-ish', and next morning, he arrived at Andrews' hotel reception at precisely 8:00 a.m. It was a new establishment, one of Hobart's many new hotels that seemed to open every second month. This one was typical of the modern concept of what a hotel should look like: steel and glass, with plush but hard-wearing carpet throughout, interspersed with areas of granite tiles. An abundance of potted plants subdued its otherwise clinical aspect.

'Jack Sugarman for Steven Andrews, he's a guest of yours, expecting me,' Jack told the receptionist.

'Certainly, Mr Sugarman,' she replied, picking up her phone. 'I'll let him know. You can wait over there if you like.' She indicated an area furnished with oversized chairs and lounges. Jack sauntered off and didn't notice the receptionist nudge her colleague, smiling slightly and raising her eyebrows. Her companion agreed with the unspoken message.

Andrews appeared momentarily.

'Hi, Jack, you like to be on time, I see. I've booked a table by the window, not that there's much to see apart from traffic.'

The dining area on the ground floor doubled as a bar in the evenings. Jack eyed the top shelf offerings.

'You can judge a bar by the top shelf,' he said. 'This one looks great. Have you tried Mandarine Napoléon? Not with breakfast, but check it out sometime.'

They perused the menu. Both decided on the Full English, Jack first ensuring it included black pudding and Cumberland pork sausages. The waiter insisted they 'do it proper here, sir' and they would love it.

Waiting for their meal, Andrews immediately launched into his 'rather interesting' one more thing.

'We've been working with MI40…'

'MI-what?' Jack interjected.

'I'm glad there are one or two things you don't know. I might be out of a job otherwise. MI40 is the great-grandson of Admiralty Room 40, essentially the First World War version of Bletchley Park. But it's bigger than a code and cipher operation. These days, they're into broad-brush security things from a scientific perspective, not overseas as such, but outer space, underground and oceanic. It doesn't work with MI5 or 6, but does liaise with us. For now, anyway, I don't think they're very enthusiastic. Very insular is MI40. Like us, I suppose.

'I saw a report the other day. They're looking at odd things happening in oceans. "On" oceans, too. It seems to be one of the climate change topics, sea levels. I could never understand how some islanders claim the sea levels are rising but that it's not noticed in other places. You'd think there'd be a uniform rise. They've been monitoring deep-ocean detection buoys – not just deep-ocean, some shallower waters as well – looking at sea level changes.

'That's pretty exciting stuff, but it gets better – some of the buoys don't float. They're submersible and at controlled depths. 5,000 feet seems to be popular for some reason'

Two Full English breakfasts were presented to them by the same waiter who had taken their order. 'Extra black pudding today, gentlemen. Some of our guests aren't keen. Can't understand why.'

Jack spotted the waiter's name tag.

'Thanks, Nick, appreciate that. Could we have a couple of coffees? Long black?' The question was to Andrews, who assented with a nod. 'Yep, two long blacks, thanks.'

Andrews continued.

'These buoys were intended to detect and report tsunamis before they hit land. Well, they still do that, but they've been reporting other stuff as well. Onboard programming is supposed to hold the depth at whatever, and a separate instrument records that depth. Sometimes, though, it just doesn't work. They've been rising to lower depths. That sounds backwards, eh, lower depths. This black pudding is OK.

'The boffins reckon it's something to do with higher salinity, but it would have to be much higher, you'd think. One bloke claims it's because of heavy water, but the others say he's essentially talking up the left. But think, heavy water is over 10 per cent denser than the regular stuff. We can't guess how it's going to behave, and yes, before you ask, it does occur naturally, but not – we think – in vast quantities. Not ocean-like amounts, anyway.

'I've been researching this. Well, I looked it up on the internet. The stuff freezes but at about four degrees Celsius, not zero. It will sink, too. This "talking up the left bloke" reckons the polar ice caps aren't melting. Somehow, the molecular structure of the ice has been spontaneously changing and sinking. Bit of a shipping hazard there, maybe.'

Jack agreed the black pudding was superb. He asked what all this had to do with Southwood.

'Getting to that. A long way around, but getting there. These buoys have also recorded depressions in oceans. Smallish ones, but some huge mothers, too. Many miles across. If we're seeing regions of heavy water mixing with regular seawater, you're going to have all sorts of weird stuff happening. Point is, if this is a natural state of affairs, it's probably been happening since the year dot.'

Jack offered an observation. He had recently seen the aftermath of a ship struggling out of a vast depression. The late arrival of a vessel watched from *Zurich* was suddenly revealed. In an early *Dark History* entry, he had the story of prolonged sailing times during the 1952 Sydney to Hobart Yacht Race. When a five-day journey was typical, the winner, *Nocturne,* took six days and two hours. Jack speculated about ocean depressions and included the Tasman Sea in that conjecture. He compared that area of ocean to the Bermuda Triangle and called it Abel's Lozenge, after the Dutch explorer Abel Tasman. He told Andrews this and offered another thought.

'This all sounds like science fiction, but I'm thinking the technology of our life in the 21st century was all once the realm of science fiction. Look at mobile phones. They didn't exist before 1973. But I want to expand your ocean thing. Let's presume what you say is fact. Let's also say that it's all a byproduct of Axel Furst's magma Gulf Streams. Now, let me think. Finish your breakfast. I've beaten you.

'Got it. Those detection buoys could give us early warning of the kind of events that Southwood is mapping. And that…'

Jack made the same gesture with his thumb and forefinger again.

'… well, that might, just might give us the jump on them. It makes sense. The Earth's crust is thinnest under the oceans, only about five kilometres thick, so oceans are going to be sensitive to energy pressure points. Is MI40 the kind of organisation that could be persuaded to share this data? Not that I can do anything with it, but I know someone who could.'

Andrews said he doubted MI40 would play nicely. On the other hand, they might be enticed to follow Jack's line of reasoning and made to think it was their idea all along. The previous evening, Jack had asked Harry to set up a secure cloud depository, and a text message reported that he'd done just that. The URL and password were included, and Jack forwarded the details to Andrews.

'"FreeLunch!618"?' he asked.

'Yep, that's Harry's standard fee. You owe him lunch.'

'Sounds like one of the good guys. Known him long?'

'A while, found him at a bus stop. You should meet. In fact, you should meet several of my people. It's time we had a bit of a conflab. Not at my place, though. Anything available here at the hotel this afternoon, you think?'

Andrews went back to reception and booked a meeting room. The conversation wandered off-topic at their table until they'd decided breakfast was over. Andrews steered it back.

'I've booked a small conference room for three o'clock. Catering for eight enough?'

'That should do. I need to see if I can get everyone. Are you working alone here?'

'I usually work solo but happy to have you onside for this. I got a text when I was at reception. My Coordinator has some intel for me. Seems there's some unusual activity I need to know about. "Unusual activity" generally means high-level stuff, so I better hang around here. Phone call imminent.'

Jack thought that 'unusual activity' encompassed everything he'd dealt with over the past few days. He wondered if The Hague had a descriptive hierarchy of activity. He'd have to wait and see. They parted with a firm, friendly handshake, and Jack strolled back to his apartment, spying a black Range Rover outside the hotel. Interstate number plates and a youngish couple with two small children suggested it was pretty innocuous. But Jack crossed the road anyway. Half a minute later, he looked back. The black SUV had disappeared.

◆

At his apartment, Jack scribbled the names of 'several people' in a notebook. With a coffee, he moved to the balcony, made himself comfortable, admired the view for a minute and turned his attention to the list of people he thought should meet his new contact.

A bold tick was placed against the first four: Leon, Harry, D.I. Sayer and Sarah. 'Definitely,' he said aloud. 'Now then, stop talking to yourself.' Derek's name was crossed out. 'No need to involve you,' he thought. Dr Robert wasn't on the list. He wondered if the pair were still discussing their experiences, then considered Lyn. Given her close contact with Southwood's heavies, she may have some insights others didn't. She got a tick as well.

Thirty minutes and several phone calls later, the list had two ticks against Leon, Harry, Sayer and Lyn. Harry even scored an exclamation mark, as Jack hadn't expected him to be available or even in town. Lyn was unsure but 'would try'. He couldn't reach Sarah but left a message. The meeting might be over-catered, which, from his experience of meetings, was the usual state of affairs. 'Still,' he thought, 'if something is worth doing, it's worth overdoing.' With that last thought in mind, Jack added Ric Martin to the list and phoned. He was available, but his friend was interstate. Two ticks were appended to his name.

The most important meeting of Jack's life was coming together.

◆

Chapter 13

A Most Important Meeting

The meeting attendees arrived separately at the hotel, some before three o'clock, some later. Jack was there at precisely 3:00 p.m., as was Field Agent Andrews. Leon was late. He was often late. According to Leon, his attitude towards punctuality reflected his laissez-faire approach to life in general. Unexpectedly, Lyn did show up, though she appeared distracted, and Jack wondered whether her attendance was more out of politeness than anything else.

The supposedly small conference room was large enough for a much bigger population than the modest group in it today. A highly polished table was set with 20 chairs. Eight comfortable chairs surrounded a food-laden coffee table by the expansive window overlooking Mount Wellington. Introductions were made as each person arrived. Sayer helped himself to coffee and sat by the window, admiring the view.

'Just like my own office, only higher up. When I have an office, that is. Still suspended. So is Blackman. Is she coming today?'

Jack tried phoning Sarah, but again, there was no answer. 'I guess not. Haven't been able to reach her. I've left a message. While we're waiting for Leon, help yourself to coffee, tea, whatever, and please eat some of this stuff; otherwise, the staff will.'

At that moment, Leon arrived with a perfunctory apology, saying he'd been working on something important and had lost track of time. 'Ah, great, nosh, I'm starving.' He promptly filled a plate with party pies and sausage rolls and another plate with biscuits. 'Are we sitting here? I'm not a fan of big tables.'

Jack took control.

'Yeah, we may as well be comfortable. Thanks for coming, everyone. Sarah might join us later. Let me formally introduce a new member of the group, Steven Andrews, a field agent for what we'll call The Hague, as its full name is just too damn long. The Hague, if I may be concise, concerns itself with international security. Its brief includes inner and outer space, that is, on and under the oceans, and any altitude higher than 45,000 feet. That's a bit under 14 kilometres, as high as any commercial plane can safely manage. Is that right, Steve?'

'Correct. Our mandate covers more than that, but I won't go into it.'

Jack continued. 'OK, you've all had some experience with an organisation called Southwood, including individuals called Mr Southwood and a project called Dragonfly. That last title seems to cover many operations, but the first one we came across was a share market scheme. That's what led us to Southwood.

'To be very serious for a moment, this mob is bad news, unhealthy to be around. Lyn here can attest to that, as can Derek, who I decided needn't be here today. On top of that, there was recently an incident in Germany. Steve?'

'Yep, incident makes it sound a bit innocuous, though. Jack knows most of this. Southwood runs a facility in Bavaria. Essentially, its cover is high-end storage for posh cars, artworks and stuff. Expensive. But it was just used to launch a missile. We had an agent watching the whole exercise, with seven others roped in. Now, this bit Jack doesn't know. The local police found them all dead the following day. We're supposed to believe they were in a minibus accident, but it's all too convenient for Southwood. Also, the warehouses now look like, well, warehouses. There's no launch pad, no technical equipment, no scientists, no clue at all that it's anything other than a storage facility. Beyond suss, I think. Our European team is still looking into it, but I'm not hopeful.'

Jack stood up.

'Dead? All of them?'

'Afraid so. I was told only an hour ago.'

Jack sat back down, then stood up again.

'This coffee isn't doing it for me. Any booze here?'

The conference room boasted a small bar behind sliding doors. Jack explored, found a bottle of decent scotch and poured a measure into a wholly inappropriate glass.

'Anyone else? There's gin, tonic, scotch, soda, wine – red and white – real beer, light beer, and some strange stuff called zero alcohol beer.'

The meeting was adjourned briefly while drinks were provided. Lyn satisfied herself with a soda water.

'This is no way to serve decent whisky, Steve.'

'What's up? Out of mugs?'

Jack smirked and continued.

'This puts an entirely new light on things. If anyone wants nothing more to do with it, say so now. I won't be surprised.'

No one spoke for several seconds. Lyn broke the ice.

'Nagyon szomorú.'

Leon put a hand on her shoulder.

'In English?'

'Very sad. If I can be useful…'

She didn't finish the sentence, but everyone understood and agreed. They were in this to the end.

Jack suggested they take a break, finish their 'afternoon tea', and then move on. Steve agreed and told the group he had something else to share, something local. At that point, the phone on the conference room table rang. Jack answered and listened for a few seconds. 'Ask her to come up, thanks.'

Shortly after, a polite knock announced Sarah's arrival. She immediately rushed to Jack and embraced him affectionately.

'Well, that was unexpected. Welcome, but unexpected. Glad you could join us. Drink?'

'Yeah. I need something. It's not too early for a scotch, is it?'

'It's six o'clock in New Zealand, so, no. Scotch it is.'

Sarah was introduced to Steve and took a chair at the coffee table. She apologised for her late arrival and told a story wrapped around more apologies.

'Everyone, I have a confession. It's important. Jack, those documents I gave you…' she glanced at Sayer, who smiled and nodded, '…most of them aren't legit. Some are. Most not. I was forced to give them to you. I have a sister, a younger sister, she's a nurse. Someone claiming to be from Southwood contacted me and said they 'had her', and I knew what that meant. I tried her phone, but there was no answer. There was never an answer. It was pretty clear what they wanted. I had to feed you fake documents to confuse the issue.

'But Ann is OK now. My colleagues found her. She's all right, just a bit shaken up. Not the sort of thing she's used to. I don't suppose anyone is. I've just left her, and she's in good hands. Sleeping it off now. No sign of her captors, though.

'But, those fake documents. You can work out which are which. From what I saw, they were written in a bit of a rush and pretty amateurish. The dodgy ones I modified slightly, putting in the word 'driving' twice towards the end of each one. I don't know whether Southwood is as clever as it wants us to think. Anyway, that's my story of betrayal and redemption. If you still want me in, I'm in.'

Everyone took this in and was pleased that Ann was safe and sound. Sarah said her sister just wanted to get back to her regular life, looking after her patients. There seemed to be no long-term harm done.

Jack took the initiative.

'I think I speak for us all when I say: yes, we still need you on our team.'

He waited for any dissent, but there was none.

'One thing this proves is that Southwood puts a lot of store in these documents. We've worked out the science behind the technology they're using, not that I pretend to understand it. Getting there, though. We know what it does and we're figuring out what it's for.'

Jack spent some time detailing his understanding of the gravitational pressure points and the energy grid caused by magma movements and how Southwood seemed to be able to manage the resultant energy production. Despite insisting he was 'not a scientist', by the end of his briefing, everyone agreed they had a decent idea of what it was all about.

Leon was scanning a room service menu and caught Jack's eye, who looked at his watch.

'We may be here for a while yet, so if The Hague has a catering budget...' Steve nodded, '...we should order some food. Only Leon seemed to be especially hungry, but Steve hit '4' on the phone provided and ordered pizza, sandwiches and what he was assured were 'tasty comestibles'. He also asked that some proper whisky glasses be brought up.

Jack remembered that Steve had something else to report to the group.

'Yes, thanks, Jack. Two things. First, I want to reiterate that Southwood, despite its global reach, seems to operate entirely with local groups, sometimes relatively small ones at that. This supports their penchant for secrecy but leaves a point of weakness as it provides no firm lines of control. Our guess is that they depend more on directions and reporting by encrypted transmissions than by face-to-face or other voice contact. There must be a central control somewhere, but it could be pretty mobile. Our monitoring suggests they deliberately maintain an open network. "A" will direct "B", who will direct "C", but "A" and "C" will hardly ever contact each other, except through "B". How they deal with the loss of "B" escapes us. There must be a contingency.

'OK, part two of "first" is that their Tasmanian operation has managed to achieve some pretty high-level infiltration of your government and public service. It's been going on for years and isn't just here. Other states are in their clutches, too. Some of my colleagues are working on that. But here, a couple of your ministers have, shall we say, an "understanding" with Southwood. Of course, they'd tell us it's all in the public interest. Of more immediate concern is your police commissioner. He's in deep. I gather our police friends here – he indicated Sayer and Blackman – have experienced that.'

Sayer intervened and told the group about the brief meeting with the commissioner when he and Sarah were suspended.

'One thing makes sense now. There was some other bloke there. No idea who he was. He wasn't introduced, and he said nothing. That must have been someone connected with Southwood. Bloody commissioner.'

Steve nodded. 'Ah, you've had the privilege of meeting one of them. At least you were only dismissed and not kidnapped. Or worse. I used the word infiltration before. I should have been blunt. It's corruption, pure and simple.'

'Only here?' Sarah asked.

'No. In Australia, five states. Four are definite, and one probable. But that leads me to the second part. We've identified a Southwood data facility in Hobart. Jack kind of stumbled onto it yesterday, too. Like their Bavarian warehouse business, it seems to be a legitimate operation, but it's got to be more than that. Our tech guys looked into their transmission gear, and apart from the above-ground stuff, there's a huge array a half-metre underground. Let me get my notes. This is all way beyond me.

'Let's see. Something about a subsurface phased array. According to the Internet of Underground Things…'

Leon interrupted, 'The Internet of Underground Things? Seriously?'

Harry spoke, delighted to be able to add his peculiar expertise to the proceedings, 'Oh yeah, that's a thing. A mate of mine is trying to map it all, but I think he's trying to nail jelly to a wall. It ain't easy.'

'Thanks, Harry,' Steve continued, 'such things are basically used for seismic mapping and getting precise spatial resolution measurements. I hope you're as lost as me. But our guys have been monitoring transmissions from there. They use frequencies no one else does. Not even the military. Well, not that we know about officially if you get my drift. We need to tread carefully. But anyway, these antennas filter out noise for pure reception, and no one can trip over them.

'Now, here's a thing. The Domain is Crown land, and building or installing anything on it is a practical impossibility. So, how did Southwood manage it?'

'Just a small matter of government corruption, I'd hazard a guess,' Sarah suggested.

Steve continued with his briefing. Southwood had sweetened whatever deal they made by undertaking remedial groundwork and producing a veritable park on the otherwise dry bushland above its facility. The additional light rail train station was the icing on the cake. Quite incorrectly, this was all attributed to the billionaire benefactor Norton Chase. As far as the citizens of Hobart were concerned, it was a great deal. Finally, some thought, here was a practical use of the otherwise little-used 190-hectare King's Domain. Mr Chase had provided a pleasant parkland and an additional train station, completely free. Even the local block-all-progress environmentalists were assuaged.

Jack asked no one in particular if they'd heard of the Hickman Crater.

'Where's that? On the moon?' responded Leon.

'Western Australia. Identified by Google Earth. You'd be surprised what you can see on Google Earth. The latest images of the Domain were taken soon after the so-called data centre was finished. That underground antenna array, well, you can't see that, naturally, but you can see where it is. The land restoration, horticultural enhancement program, whatever you want to call it, left a pretty clear map of the whole setup. In a year, it won't show at all. But it's more than an OOPART. We have to presume it's entirely functional and pretty sinister.'

'Google Earth, eh? And here's me thinking you found it at the bus stop. Anyway, what's an OOPART?' Leon asked.

Jack identified the acronym as a contraction of Out of Place Artifact. He decided against launching into an outline of the writings of Charles Fort, one of his favourite authors. No one asked.

There was a firm knock on the door. Jack opened it to find Nick, their breakfast waiter, delivering their room service order.

'Piping hot, sir,' he said. 'With extra anchovies on the pizza, as requested.'

Jack thanked him and slipped a $20 note into Nick's hand.

'A short break, I think, so this stuff doesn't go cold.' The expansive boardroom table became an informal dining table as the group dived in, having decided they were hungry after all.

Conscious that the meeting was getting on, Jack felt it necessary to wrap it up with something positive and asked Steve if there was anything else.

'Yes, very important. Our Response Team is planning a raid on the Domain facility. Find out exactly what's going on. I should have said "was" planning, past tense. We need to do it by the book, and that means high-level clearance.

'It's a Catch-22 situation. To get that clearance, we need to involve the police and state government. Given that they're both in Southwood's pocket, we won't be getting any clearance. Essentially, they'd be tipped off, and we wouldn't get anywhere. All we've achieved so far is getting a copy of the facility plans. Even Southwood had to submit a development application. Back to square one. But my people are considering options. Sometimes, you need to colour outside the lines.'

'In the wrong colour,' Jack added.

A lot of information had been shared that afternoon. However, Jack and his friends were a little disheartened. There seemed to be no plan that might advance their cause. Without having said as much, they all wanted Southwood stopped.

'Oh, wait up, there is one more thing,' Steve said. 'I think you'll all appreciate this. I'm authorised to make a presentation, though it's unofficial, virtual and deniable. That's just the way we work. Some years ago, Commander Sugarman here – sorry if I use your rank, I know you avoid it – was instrumental in saving the lives of possibly dozens of people. No one knows about it. Or rather, no one was supposed to know.

'Here's the story. Briefly anyway. Jack was reviewing the sudden deaths of four records clerks in a government business enterprise somewhere. I don't know which one or where. The cause of death was a strain of sarin gas, but no one could figure out how it was administered. Jack here worked it out when he looked at some packages the clerks were dealing with. The gas was in bubble wrap, which was otherwise quite ordinary.

'Most people will pop a few bubbles, won't they, with bubble wrap? Small doses but in close proximity, it did its job. We were able to intercept more parcels and safely dispose of the packaging. We dealt with the source, too. So, Jack Sugarman, on behalf of a grateful government, I thank you and present you with a digital medal with no name. I did say it was virtual. Well done, nice work.'

Jack was appropriately grateful, though he hated these things. But he was pleased it was in front of friends rather than a hall full of suits and uniforms. He closed the meeting, leaving one item on the agenda for the next, if there was to be one. The raid on Southwood's Domain facility was a no-go for now, but Steve promised to inform everyone of any further developments.

The strange group of individuals said their farewells and went their separate ways. Jack noted that Leon and Lyn left together. Ric appeared to be occupied on his phone and, by the time everyone but Jack and Steve had been 'seen off the premises' – as Jack delicately put it – was the last to leave. He replaced the phone in his jacket pocket, walked to the door and closed it. He addressed them both.

'This raid that isn't going to happen. I might be able to help. I have some friends who don't mind a bit of fun, legal or otherwise. But they'll need some encouragement.' He rubbed a thumb and forefinger together, the universal symbol for money.

Ric's friends were all members of what the press loved to call a 'motorcycle gang', and the front was helpful. It intimidated and kept away most people, drawing attention only from the law. Adherence to legal activities, when in the public eye, meant they were hardly ever 'persons of interest' to the police. The core membership participated in charity events often enough to convince authorities that the club was harmless. Jack had known Ric long enough to know that his biker mates were better to have as friends than as enemies.

'I didn't want to say this with your cop friends here. From what you told us today, I reckon eight of my guys and the two of you should be enough. My blokes are ex-military, and they all have their own...' he paused momentarily, '...let's call it equipment. There's no point doing this and not expecting a lot of resistance. These bastards are already down for kidnapping and murder. What do you think? Any use?'

Steve was nodding, then spoke.

'You know what? Officially, I have to say no. But officialdom is the problem here, so it's a maybe. I didn't tell you that, though. I'm not telling you this either, that The Hague sometimes resorts to what Hollywood likes to call Black Ops. We call such things DGAs, Dark Grey Actions. You need a sense of humour in this business. That's not official either, the grey actions, I mean, not the humour. But someone's got to approve that shit too.

'Anyway, basically, a job worth doing is a job worth putting off till tomorrow, as my father used to say. But then, he said a lot of crap, my father. He told me he had an uncle who was an only child. I believed him till I was eight.'

Jack also nodded but said nothing until suggesting the three of them check the quality of the ground floor bar. Ric had 'things to do' and declined. As they left the boardroom, hotel staff arrived to clear up. The booking had expired, so their timing was perfect. Steve noticed the bar was called Moderation.

'We better drink in moderation then, my shout', he nudged Jack. 'What's it to be?'

'A cleansing ale, I think. I see they have the whole Crayon & Maggot range here. The lager is good.'

Steve opted for another porter, and Jack selected the lager. Two beers and an hour later, the pair decided they'd done enough talking for one day and parted. But not before Steve shared a text he'd just received.

It read, 'SW launch 10 imminent. NZ. Tele-conf 2200 your time.'

'Seems our hand may be forced. Talk to you tomorrow.'

◆

Jack sat on the deck of his apartment and absently watched the city end its day. He liked doing this. Retirement had its privileges. People were going home late or going out early. They were oblivious to the systemic upheaval of everyday life being instigated by an organisation they'd never heard of.

'Ignorance is bliss,' Jack thought as he realised he wanted neither food nor drink. The afternoon meeting had been well catered, something he'd neglected to thank Steve for. Tomorrow would have to do for that. Right now, again, he needed to take stock of the events of the past few days. He went inside, found a writing pad and pen – he'd do this the old-fashioned way – and wrote SITUATION ANALYSIS at the top of a fresh page.

Under the title Bad Guys, he wrote Southwood and police commissioner. After the second entry, he added a '+?' as there was no telling who else was involved.

The title Good Guys was longer, and Jack produced a bullet-point list:

- Me (obviously)
- Leon
- Harry Steve John 'Trousers'
- Steven Andrews + The <u>Hague</u>
- Terry Sayer
- Sarah Blackman
- Lyn Mrkelja
- Ric Martin +?

Derek Asquith's and Dr Robert's names were added but crossed out. Jack realised they were on the side of the 'good and fair', but their participation was over. His friends in low places would remain undocumented. He didn't envisage using their peculiar talents again anyway. 'But you never know,' he said aloud.

Jack was still confused about why Southwood was so eager to secure his documents, and those of Derek and Lyn. The suggestion they needed to know what he didn't have rather than what he did, seemed logical. But was it as simple as that? Was their operation so delicately balanced that the mere knowledge of it put it at risk? It seemed unlikely. It was time for some lateral thinking. Perhaps it wasn't the information itself, but who had it.

Mild-mannered Derek appeared to be an improbable candidate as a threat to Southwood. How could Lyn Mrkelja fill that role? Jack realised he didn't know very much about Leon's would-be girlfriend. Still comfortably ensconced on his deck and watching the city, he grabbed his phone and hit Leon's number. He answered almost immediately.

'Leon, mate. It's Jack. I'm pondering, not to say reflecting. Tell me about Lyn. I know almost nothing about her, apart from what's happened in the past few days.'

'Oh, inquisition time, is it? OK. As it happens, she told me a lot about herself after we left that meeting of yours. I'll start from the beginning. I always thought her first name was Lynette, but it's Kalynda. Everyone calls her Lyn. And the surname, well, she lets people think it's like the Scottish name McKellyer, you know, M.C.K. et cetera. Close friends sometimes call her Scary Lyn, but she doesn't much like it. She's Serbian; left after the war in the nineties. Very unhappy story there. Parents didn't make it, I gather. They were scientists or science teachers, not sure which.

'I reckon I know what you're after here. I've been wondering why Southwood was so interested in her. It couldn't have been the papers those blokes nicked. It must have been what she knew. She knows loads of stuff that we don't. I couldn't stop her talking once she got going. The details – wrong word, not much detail really – it's all feelings, intuition. Scary about sums it up. She shouldn't know what she does. I don't know how we can use it, though. That Hall character would have got more out of her if they hadn't botched the drugs they used. Could have been nasty. There's one important thing you should know. As of this evening, we're officially an item, Lyn and me. You can buy us a drink sometime.'

Jack was delighted.

'I bet Lyn knew before you did, mate. Congratulations. It's great to hear some good news for a change. And yes to that drink. Sometime. But I've got something for you too. Steve has a team phone call happening later tonight, pretty soon, about Southwood launching another satellite. He'll fill me in tomorrow.'

'Yeah, I know,' Leon said, 'Lyn told me as much. Spooky, eh? There's no way she could have known that. She didn't say satellite but kept getting the number 10 in her mind and seeing a dark sky. Tell me it's satellite number 10. Go on. It'll be the last one.'

'It is satellite number 10, Leon,' Jack replied. 'Whether it's the last one is an unknown for us. I'll let Steve know what Lyn told you.'

◆

Jack would have been either pleased or annoyed that Southwood's New Zealand management was entertaining the newly arrived Munich group with good Marlborough wines. He was partial to the pinot noirs from that region. The three men who hosted the recent videoconference were on the South Island to oversee the launch of the tenth and final auxiliary satellite. They were joined by their technical supervisor, Merlin – another legacy title – who would rather have been with his team already at the Awatere Valley centre. Despite this, he enjoyed an excellent meal and, as an after-dinner speech, delivered a briefing mostly devoid of technicalities.

Told only what they needed to know, Southwood New Zealand had been instrumental in securing and refurbishing an abandoned national park facility. With some thinly disguised bribery and an offer of returning an improved establishment, a new launch site had been constructed and fitted out in only a few months. It was ready for service, and the bulk of the launch team was nearing their temporary workspace. Some had already been there for a few weeks, installing and testing equipment. Security wasn't as apparent as the Bavarian forest setup. High fencing was thought to be out of keeping with the national park image, but a boom gate kept unwanted visitors away. Dozens of signs alerted bushwalkers to a fictional Hydatids Research Area, a disease New Zealand had eradicated over 20 years ago. Other signs bordered an area hosting newly identified delicate ground cover plants and warned people not to enter.

Early the following morning, the senior Southwood personnel left their Christchurch accommodation for one of the smaller airports, where a Bell 429 helicopter waited for them. The sleek machine, appropriately in anonymous black livery, efficiently took the group to the Awatere Valley, 200 kilometres north-north-east of Christchurch in just over an hour. The pilot was 'tipped' $10,000 for his efforts. He would immediately continue to Picton and modify the flight records to remove any reference to his passengers and the intermediate stop.

On arrival, Merlin immediately sought a briefing from his 2IC – locally known as Little Merlin – and was assured that phase one arrangements had been implemented satisfactorily. There was just one element bothering him. That element was subject to ongoing monitoring and would be raised later if necessary. He then reported to New Zealand's Mr Southwood, who had found his temporary office and sourced an acceptable coffee from a small windowless room that passed as a staff canteen.

Merlin joined Mr Southwood, who managed to look fresh and surprisingly uncrumpled after their cramped helicopter ride. He pointed this out, comparing his own dishevelled appearance.

'Hugo Boss,' was the two-word reply.

Merlin nodded.

'I'll just grab one of those,' he indicated the coffee, 'and be right with you.'

At that moment, Keeper joined them with two more coffees.

'Ah, ahead of me as usual,' Merlin continued. 'Then I'll proceed. Launch hardware and facilities are in place. Installation was faster than expected, and I've initiated beta testing, but it looks good. The satellite has a quantum processor backup installed. Testing is underway now.

The ground systems lateral convergence issue was rectified from L9. No problems there. Primary, secondary and tertiary line movement is more significant than anticipated but within acceptable parameters. We're watching that closely.

'Now, I'm concerned about geomagnetic field polarity movement. You wanted that monitored. The Melbourne team has been mapping diamagnetic vortex fluctuations for a possible polarity reversal – an incomplete one, anyway – and they've brought forward their 12-month timeframe. It's now "imminent" but they won't be drawn into any precise forecast.'

Mr Southwood put down his coffee.

'This isn't the positive report I was hoping for. Recommendation?'

Merlin frowned slightly.

'We have to continue as scheduled. Either that or wait 13 days. In any case, complete reversals occur rarely, once every half million years, and take centuries to complete. We're interested in harmonics. Very common, very brief and barely noticeable. Partials are regular. Only a few labs in the world have the equipment to monitor it. We do, of course.'

He checked a small device.

'Bottom line is our schedule remains. 1609 hours.'

'Splendid work, Merlin,' Mr Southwood said, almost mechanically. 'Keeper, security issues?'

Keeper hadn't spoken during the briefing and now leaned forward with his left forearm resting on the desk.

'We had to forgo our preferred security, as you know, but increased surveillance indicates zero incursions into the exclusion zone. The birds and animals are leaving, as usual. Drones haven't sighted anyone for three days, but we can't monitor the western hills. Heat signature cameras haven't picked up human profiles. I have no concerns. The Bavarian issue was dealt with.'

The last sentence was delivered with a gesture. Merlin couldn't tell if Keeper was only scratching an itch or passing a finger across his throat. Mr Southwood nodded but made no comment.

Almost as an afterthought, Merlin reported that the weather forecast called for 17 degrees, no rain, and no wind.

Southwood was ready for the launch of auxiliary satellite number 10. What the organisation didn't know was that The Hague was also prepared. From a large white van boldly marked with a non-existent communications and logistics company, three agents watched a bank of monitors. These displayed live feeds from five fixed cameras, with two blank screens dedicated to drones waiting to be deployed. As yet, there was nothing to see, apart from the occasional sighting of Southwood personnel moving outside the main building.

'There's our chain smoker,' one of the observers said. 'On the hour, every hour. Must cost him a fortune.' He recorded the sighting in a log, entering '1500h. CS hourly smoke.'

All transmissions to the van were routed to a fixed ground station via satellite. The Hague had assembled an analysis team but had little to analyse so far. That was about to change. Nearly an hour passed.

Another log entry recorded a curious mist developing around Southwood's facility. The senior Hague agent checked data received from sensors connected to their fixed cameras.

'That's weird,' he said to no one in particular, 'the temperature just increased by 13 degrees. Localised. Just on the valley floor. That might explain the mist, hot air mixing with cold.'

Another agent leaned back in his chair, 'But the mist doesn't explain the temperature, does it?' Can't see a damned thing now. Switching to infrared and polarising.'

He threw the relevant switches, and the monitors changed from their familiar display of lush greenery to monochrome, the abundant foliage appearing ghostly white. Southwood's main building appeared in sharp relief. The senior agent threw another switch.

'Orange filter on camera two,' he said, 'log it will you. 1602 hours. Where's our chain smoker? He should be outside by now, filling his lungs with poison.'

The agent wasn't to know that their cigarette smoker was busy at his station, readying the satellite for departure.

'Zoom out camera three. Stop. That's bizarre.'

What attracted his attention was again the mist. It was now rotating slowly clockwise and being drawn upwards, centred on the large building. Before being completely hidden from view, a section of the roof slid back, revealing an intense glow. The camera angles were too shallow for anything inside to be visible. The observers' log was now filled with minute-by-minute notations. At 1608, they recorded strong winds and high temperatures (neither of which had been forecast), and poor visibility. A minute later, the sky, by now a murky dark grey, was briefly illuminated by an amorphous bright light that rose vertically, rapidly, and silently. It was out of sight within seconds, though the cameras couldn't be adjusted quickly enough to capture the point of disappearance.

'Well, you don't see much of that these days, do you?' one of the agents joked.

The senior agent shook his head. 'Did we get any sound with that? I got nothing.'

He was talking to himself while reviewing a replay and checking calibrations.

'No, all good. No sound to record, just background stuff. Maybe our tech guys can work it out, but I've no clue what that was. But you missed something.'

'Go on, I'll bite,' the other agent replied.

'That mist was rotating clockwise. In the video of the Bavarian thing, it was anti-clockwise. The Coriolis effect. Cyclones and hurricanes show the same behaviour.'

◆

At the satellite launch site, amid a brief period of self-congratulation, one of Southwood's scientists tried to explain optimised electromagnetic levitation and electrostatic levitation. He was talking to a programmer and communications expert who nodded politely but held up his hands in surrender when the subject turned to the mapping and focusing of Earth's natural energy grid. The programmer said he would stick to what he knew and leave the mystical stuff to the mystics.

The launch of number 10 completed Southwood's auxiliary satellite encirclement of Earth. Compliance testing would take more than 24 hours, after which a full data transmission test to ground receivers would be undertaken. Fine-tuning, technicians estimated, might take minutes or hours.

Mr Southwood permitted his team the luxury of celebratory drinks, though a couple of the more dedicated operators returned to their posts after a single glass of sparkling wine. Primarily, however, their job was done. At 1500 hours, the chain smoker left the building for his hourly smoke. Most staff would leave the site in a day or two, never to see it again. It would soon be dismantled and 'cleaned'. In a few days, no trace of anything Southwood-related would be evident.

The launch went according to plan, with only minor adjustments to trajectory made automatically by the onboard navigation computer. Merlin reported on 'the tiniest incomplete polarity reversal causing a short-lived vortex fluctuation.' He further reported that no one would have noticed unless they were looking for it.

Mr Southwood received this information dispassionately. It would be passed on appropriately, as would Keeper's report that there had been no security issues. The organisation's measures had failed to locate The Hague's cameras or drones, equipment protected, ironically, by the same stealth technology that Southwood employed.

Keeper also delivered a briefing on further investigations into Jack's interest in Dragonfly.

'This Sugarman is an enigma. He supposedly retired from service some years ago, despite being young. However, he's been very active for a retired person. We conclude his retirement is a front. He has contacts with the local police, though our man circumvented that to a degree. We didn't want to make it too obvious. Our monitoring suggests he has three tech experts working for him. We only have first names, Harry, Steve and John, though one of them has the surname Tresizes or something similar. They must be deep undercover as we can't find any details. We consider them a risk, those three.

'His agent, Asquith, is a blundering fool but did secure some of our minor documents. He's vanished and appears to be out of the loop. The cop, Sayer, has been suspended and has no access to police resources. Same with Blackman. We managed her very prettily and had her feed fake evidence to Sugarman. Disinformation is a powerful tool. The documents Sugarman has were RSA encrypted. They won't be able to hack them. He was spotted near our Hobart facility recently, but our front is well-established, and he likely thinks it's just a data centre. We consider the site secure.

'The local controller Hall has been retired. His two goons proved to be incompetent. We won't be using them again.'

Mr Southwood received Keeper's report without emotion but nodded when told of Hall's 'retirement'. He understood what that meant.

'What Sugarman knows and doesn't know is becoming increasingly irrelevant, but maintain surveillance. He might be little more than a nuisance, but I don't want to see him become more than a "little" nuisance if you see what I mean.'

The two men were about to discover just how much of a nuisance Jack could become. Before that happened, though, nature intervened.

◆

Chapter 14

Auxiliary Satellite 10

One of Southwood's technicians had christened the tenth satellite ASatX, claiming with limited conviction that it had the 'X' factor, being their final orbiter. However, his attempt at nominative adroitness was soon forgotten when a colleague announced that test transmissions from Satellite 10 had ceased. He immediately tried the secondary frequencies but, with one hand on the left side of his headphones, announced, 'All transmissions failed. Attempting a reboot.'

The reboot function had never been needed before, except in trials on the ground. No one spoke, waiting for news.

Mr Southwood instructed the technician to stream his monitor to a larger one on the wall so everyone could watch the progress. The multi-element display showed rapidly scrolling code with plain English appearing below.

'Phase one of eight implemented,' it said. That was transmission of the reboot code to the satellite.

Several seconds passed, and the scrolling code stopped.

'Phase one completed. Phase two in progress; installation.'

Someone said, 'So far, so good.'

The computer had other ideas, and the wall monitor displayed 'Phase two failed. Awaiting instructions.'

They all knew what that meant. There was little point in trying again, but Mr Southwood told the technician to attempt another reboot on a slower cycle. The technician complied, knowing it was almost certainly a futile exercise. The monitor still held a captive audience.

'Executing phase one of eight, cycle B,' it said, 'duration three minutes, 40 seconds.'

While the team waited the prescribed time, Satellite 10 continued its orbit in space. Southwood couldn't know its transmission failure was due to a neat two-centimetre hole drilled through it. A tiny fragment of the solar system, silently circling the sun for uncountable millennia, had challenged the satellite and won. ASatX would not participate in Southwood's scheme. It was now just another piece of expensive space junk.

Mr Southwood wasn't a patient man, and by the time the three minutes and 40 seconds had elapsed, he was severely irritated.

He watched the big screen, which resolutely displayed 'Phase two failed. Awaiting instructions.'

Mr Southwood spoke with as much self-control as he could muster.

'Supervisor, Merlin, my office.'

At that moment, two banks of overhead lights switched off as if to rub salt into the wound. The facility was reduced to a dim half-light.

'And get those fucking lights fixed.' The self-control failed.

The office in question was a small room barely meeting any office-like criteria. The three men sat, somewhat uncomfortably, around a coffee table devoid of embellishment.

'Contingency?' Mr Southwood demanded.

The supervisor looked at Merlin, who delivered only tolerably good news.

'Plan A is a waiting game. Possibly, comms has suffered some internal drama and is self-diagnosing. If the issue can be rectified automatically, we'll receive a transmission as soon as it's done. I consider that unlikely. Plan B is to launch another satellite. We have spares, of course, two anyway. But not here. It would take three days to get one here, or we could launch sooner, from Bavaria.'

The news did little to improve the senior man's mood. He brooded for some time.

'OK, have a spare prepared. But I don't like two launches from the same site, and the conditions might not be right anyway. Check for the earliest… no, I'll do that.'

He turned to Supervisor.

'Two things. Have this place decommissioned. Move everyone out to wherever they came from and lose the hardware. Somewhere safe, and I do mean safe. Second, the Oceania region is to be put into Deep Sleep. Get it? All activities are suspended, no routine communication, no web activity, you know the drill.'

Supervisor made a few notes on a notepad.

'Duration?' he asked.

'Three days, minimum. But check with me first before going back online. Now, get that chopper back. Same pilot, I liked him, never said a word. Book me a flight to Hobart, too.'

He looked at his watch.

'It'll have to be tomorrow.'

Neither Merlin nor Supervisor was game to point out that the two things were really three.

◆

Jack had many bizarre reports in his *Dark History* files that he neatly grouped into a sub-history of UFOs. He disliked the term Unidentified Flying Objects, preferring the more accurate Unidentified Aerial Phenomena. However, UFO – not UAP – had been long established by common usage as the accepted norm. Many of his papers detailed old reports long since satisfactorily described. But not all.

While modern learning and understanding have relegated some 'unidentified' to the 'probably explained' category, many remain firmly impenetrable. Luckily, the UFO phenomenon has equally firmly captured the popular imagination. Hardly a week went by without Jack receiving an email or, occasionally, an old-fashioned letter outlining some new mystery.

As he told anyone who would listen, 'The old ones are the best.' An unfinished article he intended for a now-defunct magazine outlined some of his tales of ancient times.

◆

UFOs – Nothing New to See Here

Technology be damned. Sometimes, science doesn't know, or want to know, or claims 'insufficient data' to present a lucid explanation. As an amorphous group, scientists are prone to glossing over inconvenient data, awkward documents, and incomplete anecdotal evidence, and moving on to more profitable research.

What we now call UFO sightings are often dismissed as the science fiction imaginings of witnesses. Before science fiction, sightings were just as readily scorned as alcohol-induced hallucinations, at least from the 1600s when the word hallucination first appeared. Earlier sightings were variously interpreted as mystical or religious omens of misfortune.

Whatever casual, unscientific method of rejection was employed, the fact remains that sightings of UFOs – I prefer UAPs, Unidentified Aerial Phenomena – cannot entirely be written off.

The modern era of UFOs – I'll stick with that popular term – is considered to have started in 1947. Pilot Kenneth Arnold reported seeing nine shiny objects travelling at an estimated 1,200mph near Mount Rainier, Washington State. That story is well documented and need not concern us here other than to reiterate that the sighting still has no satisfactory explanation.

But 1947 is very recent. 300 BC is another story altogether. Reports from ancient China of a luminous pearl-shaped object flying erratically suggest UFO observations are hardly new. Similarly, from Ireland, dating to the year 966, a written report of 'fire and a horrible dragon' evidences the difficulties experienced by diarists of the time. Such unknown things were described in terms of superstition with, perhaps, the merest hint of science.

Ancient Egyptian hieroglyphs depict what could be construed as aerial objects in flight. Through the ages of man, observations of airborne phenomena, whether apparently solid objects or only lights, have challenged science. Refining scientific methods, especially from the 15th century, led enquiring minds to consider alternative explanations.

Limited, however, by the framework of knowledge prevailing at any given time, those explanations were often lacking in what 21st-century observers would call 'science'. Especially before powered flight, non-atmospheric anomalous light displays baffled our predecessors. Similarly, conventional rationalisations usually fail to take into account bizarre flight characteristics. Pelicans do not fly at 1,200mph (as Kenneth Arnold pointed out), nor do meteors change direction at right angles.

A favourite report of mine is the Great Airship Mystery of 1896 and 1897. Sightings of cigar-shaped airships, usually described as dirigibles, were widely reported. Encounters with the occupants were also claimed; classic UFO stuff. While usable airships had been around since the 1850s, they were far from common but sufficiently 'known' for irregular aerial phenomena to be thus described.

Here lies a curious example of otherwise inexplicable circumstances being woven into a narrative describing technology that was more or less conventional for the time. Contemporary newspaper reports suggested that the number of witnesses was more than 100,000. This particular chapter of UFO history has been variously concluded as being hoaxes and the misidentification of stars and planets. However, a modern historian has stated that 'a small residuum (of sightings) remains perplexing.'

◆

Jack's article stopped at this point, though another half-dozen examples of ancient UFO reports were bullet-pointed. As an occasional contributor of articles to various magazines, he aimed for 800 words. This one fell short at nearly 500. In a footnote, Jack wrote of the demise of the magazine he had intended this article for. He would finish it later.

Scribbling down notes against each story, he noted that many were of bright lights during daytime or at night. He also observed that some light displays were accompanied by ground disturbances. 'That again,' he thought. A theory he'd been toying with for some time was that the substance of such observations was not necessarily the most crucial aspect. They may be evidence of something else, different but not unrelated. His unfinished article may be another element of *Dark History* rather than a magazine article. He believed in the adage that perfection is the enemy of completion. Sometimes, it's better to reimagine something rather than persist with its original form.

His phone rang. It was Harry.

'G'day, Harry, what's occurring?'

'Wondered if you want some company. Also, there's been a development you'll want to know about.' Harry said.

'Well, I can tolerate your company if you can put up with mine. Come around.'

'I'm glad you said that because I'm in your carpark. You eaten?'

Jack had forgotten about food, and the pair met outside his apartment. A new fish and chip shop had recently opened nearby. Jack liked its name, The Fry Brigade, and they supported the owners with 'a family-size fisherman's basket and large chips, to go.'

Back at his apartment, with dinner unskilfully plated, Jack offered beer and white wine. Harry, as usual, opted for a beer. Jack suggested they first deal with their late dinner and the development afterwards, but Harry was keen to talk.

'Me and my mates have been monitoring the web and scanning certain radio frequencies. Probably best you don't ask which ones. It was all plodding along nicely, lots of data, mostly encrypted, but at 10 last night, it all stopped. And I mean exactly at 10. Websites we were watching shut down, data transmissions stopped, VOIP messaging stopped. Anyone looking for Southwood or Dragonfly now couldn't find a thing. You know anything?'

Jack finished a succulent mouthful of the chip butty he'd made.

'Yes and no, and maybe. Steve called me earlier about a teleconference he'd been on. Seems The Hague cottoned onto Southwood's New Zealand launch yesterday. It went well. I mean well for them, not for us. We were monitoring the thing pretty closely, and some banal transmissions suggested, what did he say, "pre-operational compliance testing".

'They couldn't physically find the thing, though. Too small for visual, no heat signature and it must have some advanced stealth material. Radar and whatnot couldn't find it either. But here's the thing. At some point, transmissions stopped. Dead in the water, seemingly.'

'Or dead in the sky,' Harry suggested.

'Yep, dead in the sky', Jack agreed. 'How's this for a hypothesis?'

'Now look, if you're going to hit me with a hypothecary or whatever, I'm going to need another beer.'

Jack motioned at the fridge for Harry to help himself, and suggested that Auxiliary Satellite 10 had 'become operationally unviable' – another of Steve's phrases – and either abandoned or allowed to self-destruct. The next logical step was to launch another satellite, but to protect any such planning, temporarily, nothing was communicated to Southwood's broader world.

'It's as good a theory as anything,' Harry offered. 'My guys wondered about some internal drama, a leadership coup or something.'

Jack hadn't considered this.

'And that, my dear Harry, is as good a theory as mine. We're both being rational, but we may both be misguided. I'll get Steve to check on Southwood's known associates. I wouldn't mind betting they've gone to ground. But first, I'll make a call.'

Jack selected a number, hit the green icon, and waited only briefly before a disinterested voice identified itself.

'Sayer. That you, Jack?'

'Indeed, 'tis I. How's suspended life treating you? Fed up yet?'

Disinterest changed to concern.

'Oh, yes. There's only so much gardening I can put up with. Hate gardening. I'm not hearing much from anyone at HQ. You got something for me?'

'Possibly, we should catch up again. But I have a question for you. Has your commissioner suddenly gone on leave or otherwise vanished? Might be nothing, might be plenty.'

D.I. Sayer revealed he had heard nothing from any senior officers since he was suspended but would make discreet enquiries about the commissioner and report back the next day.

'Anything else? I'm itching to get back to work.'

'No, that's it. As I said, might be nothing. See you.'

Jack told Harry that Southwood's sudden silence might be revealing, as well as concealing. 'If that commissioner has vanished, it's 90% certain he's part of it.'

Harry looked at his empty plate, beer glass, and watch.

'I want to get back with the team. Better be off. Thanks for dinner, et cetera. Those beers are pretty strong. I think I'll leave my car here and grab a cab.'

Jack walked with him to the front door. He had just finished tidying up the dinner things when his phone rang again. It was Sarah.

'Hi, Jack, are you home? Good. I'm stuck with a rather fine red wine that needs sharing, can I come round?' she asked, almost sheepishly.

Jack thought it must be a good evening for visitations. He looked around his living room and decided if it was tidy enough for Harry, it was good enough for Sarah, though Harry was hardly a good litmus paper test for presentability. In 20 minutes, she was at his door.

Jack hadn't seen her wearing anything but trousers or jeans and was pleased to see her in a skirt. It was short, without being mini, and showed off her athletic legs. A light v-neck jumper – 'A little tight,' Jack thought – complemented the skirt's colour and texture, with a boldly patterned scarf finishing the ensemble. She dropped a small handbag on the couch.

'I was planning a meal with Lyn, but she's out with Leon – yeah, I know – and I can't drink this on my own.' She held up a bottle.

'Southern Rhone, shiraz, or syrah rather. The bottle shop bloke said it would go well with cheese. So, I brought cheese. You got any crackers?'

Jack smiled, 'I think I can manage some crackers. Give me a minute. Oh, look, Sarah's Crackers crackers. How appropriate.'

'Cheeky sod,' Sarah said, retrieving two Burgundy glasses and pouring wine to the widest point. 'Good health.'

'To us all. May your path be straight and in front of you,' Jack returned, effecting a passable Irish accent.

Conversation was initially about Leon and Lyn getting together. Sarah said Lyn seemed so much more relaxed and happy now. Lyn had suggested to her that everyone was in for a quiet few days, but she didn't know why.

Jack shared Leon's visit earlier in the evening and that Southwood seemed to have gone to ground, but no one knew how long that would last. As if on cue, Jack's phone rang again. He looked at the screen.

'Oh, your boss,' he said to Sarah. 'Terry, I didn't expect you to get back to me so soon.'

It was a brief conversation, mostly one-sided.

'Well?' Sarah demanded.

'Your D.I. Sayer still has some friends in the force apparently, suspended or not. Seems the commissioner has vanished, gone to ground. Plus, a government minister has suddenly announced a leave of absence "to spend more time with his family" – that old cliché – and a departmental secretary went on leave without notice. It's suggestive, if not conclusive. But I reckon they're Southwood cronies we didn't know about.'

Sarah took up the logic, 'It looks like Southwood's silence has been shouted to their upline people. And their behaviour has shown their hand. Pretty dumb mistake if that's the case.'

Jack agreed. The conversation switched to more technical matters and Jack's UFO article. He outlined a theory, not fully developed, that observations were of manifestations of unrelated activity within the energy grid. He said he planned to map solar activity against his *Dark History* events, but that was a job for another day.

'Or another year,' he added, 'it'll take a while. I've just reread an article I wrote about UFOs – never finished it, actually – and how the modern era started in 1947. Sunspots and solar flares were extraordinary about then. Maybe it's not a coincidence. And there was a 70-year period from 1645 when hardly anything was recorded. It's called the Maunder Minimum. That time was the coldest part of the Little Ice Age in the northern hemisphere. I have no entries in my files during this time. I wonder if the level of solar activity is related to the stability of Earth's energy grid. Sorry, digressing there. Anyway, it's effect but not cause. It's all rather complicated. My brain has done quite enough thinking for one day. Any more of that fabulous wine?'

Sarah poured two more glasses, suggestively walking behind Jack and placing a hand on his shoulder, somewhat longer than he thought was necessary.

'Of course. Your wish, as they say.'

More wine was drunk, more cheese eaten, and the conversation returned, in some speculative detail, to Leon and Lyn's relationship. Jack produced a bottle of port and poured two large measures into sherry glasses. She accepted one with a slight raising of one eyebrow.

'A toast to Leon and Lyn?' Jack suggested.

'To Lyn and Leon,' Sarah corrected the sequence. 'You're not trying to get me tipsy, are you, Mr Sugarman?'

She leaned back in her armchair opposite Jack on the couch and crossed her legs, displaying an attractive expanse of thigh.

'Perish the thought, Miss Blackman, but you better not drive home tonight. I had to counsel Harry about that earlier. Anyway, there's still cheese left. Have another port.'

'I didn't drive or would have been here sooner, but I don't think I could walk in anything approaching a straight line now. Perhaps one more teensy glass. Hey, it's hot in here. Is your air-con misbehaving?'

'Could be, it's temperamental. Take your jumper off if you're too warm,' Jack suggested.

'But I'm not wearing anything under it, as I think you've noticed,' she countered with mock outrage, quickly adding, 'I reckon my place will be empty and cold tonight. Probably won't see Lyn till tomorrow. Can I crash here?'

Jack wondered about those signals he was always getting wrong but decided he was getting it right tonight.

'Certainly, you can crash here. We've had a pleasant evening, and I wouldn't like to ruin it with our separation. There's a guest bedroom or,' he hesitated, but only briefly, 'you could share my bed, and we can do something we might regret in the morning.'

Sarah effected shock, stood up, then sat down again, next to Jack.

'What, play board games? I hate board games.'

'Oh, you won't be bored, I can promise you that.'

'You're a bad man, Mr Sugarman. Come on then, this way, is it?'

She led him to Jack's bedroom. Sarah's apartment, however, remained empty and cold, just as she had predicted and quietly hoped, ever since she left it earlier in the evening.

◆

Chapter 15

Tung Beer

'I'm starving,' Sarah complained, 'any eggs or bacon going?'

'No eggs or bacon,' Jack apologised, 'catering has all gone to pot the last week. We can have breakfast out. You want to go home and change first?'

With a hint of a blush, Sarah said she'd brought a change of essentials stuffed in her handbag.

'Oh, did you now? Very forward-thinking of you. I ought to be offended, but I'm not. OK, get dressed, and we'll hit the Blue Café.'

Angie was serving as usual and suggested to Jack he should get frequent flyer points, as he'd been in so often recently. After introducing Sarah, they selected a table by the window, having first ordered a long black and, for Sarah, an espresso. She perused the menu. There weren't many customers, as the breakfast crowd had come and gone, and the morning tea people were just starting to trickle in.

'Full English looks good, no hash browns though,' she said. Jack thought he was falling in love, then spotted a black Range Rover parked opposite. He quickly assessed it. Two baby seats in the back alleviated his brief concern. It was just an ordinary Range Rover.

Neither had mentioned what had occurred the previous night, but Jack felt obliged to.

'I feel guilty,' he confided. 'We had sex on our first date, but without the date. We should go out. How about dinner?'

Sarah smiled.

'I think I deserve dinner after all the hard work I put into seducing you.'

Jack smiled back.

'Right. Looking back, I… see, I don't read women very well. Usually seeing signals that aren't there and missing ones that are. I'm glad you persisted. There's a new restaurant on the waterfront, Macquarie Wharf, you've probably seen it. I'll see if I can book a table. Is tomorrow night good?'

Sarah reminded him that since her suspension, she had plenty of time on her hands, and tomorrow night would be fine.

Jack took another phone call from Sayer, again listening intently and saying little. Terry had discovered that a senior planning officer from the council had also disappeared, this time without announcing he was going on leave. He'd just not turned up for work and was ignoring phone calls. This was the planning officer, Sayer discovered, who had approved the development application for the Domain Data Centre.

'That's interesting, don't you think,' he suggested.

Jack agreed.

Sarah asked, grinning, if Sayer was going to call every time she was with Jack.

'Don't know, but if he does, I hope he calls often,' Jack said.

'You flirting with me?' Sarah asked.

'Ha, that's rich,' he replied. 'Anyway, I don't flirt. I have a way with the ladies.'

Angie delivered their breakfast.

'Two Full English, *sans pommes de terre rissolées*,' she announced, blending ethnicity. 'Sorry, no bubble and squeak today.' Jack explained the reference to bubble and squeak.

Their meal consumed, the pair parted company with a not-too-short embrace, each returning to their respective apartments. Jack realised he had no plans for the day, and no new developments seemed to have materialised for the Southwood situation. He would order some groceries online and have them delivered. He hadn't set foot in a supermarket for at least two years.

As his day drifted by, Jack speculated when he would hear more from Terry, Steve, Harry, or Leon. How would Southwood intervene in his life again? And when? Since his pleasant night with Sarah, time seemed to have slowed down. Groceries had been ordered and delivered. His attempt to reserve a table at the Shoreside Redemption was problematic. Fully booked the following day and closed for private functions the next two, he left it in abeyance. His dinner date would have to wait.

As a distraction, he went online and searched for likely *Dark History* events during the Maunder Minimum period he'd told Sarah about. After a couple of fruitless hours, he had nothing new to write up, only a few pages of scribbled bullet points.

'Blank, blank and blank, Jack,' he said to himself, adding, 'No, wait, double blank.'

He fell into a period of quiet reflection and found himself, for no apparent reason, remembering the balmy summer days of his childhood when he would play games with young friends in the sunroom of a house long since left behind. Scrabble, Monopoly, Park and Shop – and he suddenly thought of dominoes. A double in dominoes is placed across the chain of already laid tiles. Because of its zero value, it's a strong tile to hold at the end of a hand. It also links to other tiles with blank ends.

Retrieving a scrap of paper, he circled a note headed 'Earthquake Santiago 1647' and another 'Earthquake in Chile novel Anita Adler'.

The earthquake in question hit Chile in 1647, a mere two years into the Maunder Minimum timeframe. It reputedly destroyed almost every building in Santiago and was probably – Jack underlined the word 'probably' – a shallow focus intraplate event, not a regular megathrust occurrence. Jack suspected, from his readings on magma flow theory, that the relatively rare intraplate quakes were likely the result of magma movements at partial fractures of tectonic plates.

Moving to the novel *The Earthquake in Chile,* he located a translated summary, printed it, and settled into an armchair to read. He smiled, thinking of Sarah sitting in it the night before. The author described several familiar preliminaries to the event. Despite being a warm spring Sunday, 13 May, a dark sky seemed to plunge the city into a localised cold spell that lasted several hours. Strong winds preceded the earthquake, which killed over 600 people and made thousands homeless.

Jack grabbed a bright highlighter and marked a single sentence, 'Of course, the black dogs disappeared.' In the original German text, it read 'Natürlich sind die schwarzen Hunde verschwunden.' He made a note to locate a copy of the book. It would need to be a copy, as it was published in 1665.

'Why "natürlich"?' Jack asked himself. What did the Chileans of three and half centuries ago know about dogs, black ones in particular?

Late in the afternoon, he had another call from Terry. His suspension had been lifted, as was Sarah's, thanks to the acting commissioner being a friend – 'It's not what you know, sometimes,' he said – and he'd be back in his office tomorrow. He'd already spoken to Sarah, who was, if not excited, certainly gratified. When asked if any developments had occurred, Jack reported it had fallen very quiet. There was nothing more to go on. He almost let slip about Ric's offer to help with a raid on the Domain facility but stopped in time. There's only so much a detective inspector can turn a blind eye to.

◆

At about the same time as this phone call, an Air New Zealand flight landed at Hobart International Airport. The business class passengers had priority when exiting, and Mr Southwood was the first of that elite group to disembark. Not waiting for his luggage – it would be collected and sent on – he spotted his limousine. The driver, in formal chauffeur uniform, held open the left rear door.

'Dunkley Point Hotel, is it Mr Southwood?' he asked.

'Correct. How far?'

'A little over 20 kilometres. We should be there in 25 minutes at this time of day,' the chauffeur said.

Mr Southwood looked at his watch.

'Very good. Let's go. I prefer not to converse with my driver in transit.' He said this matter of factly, and apart from, 'Understood,

Sir,' the chauffeur said no more until he pulled up at the entrance to the hotel.

'I understand your luggage will be here within half an hour, Sir.'

Mr Southwood knew the fare had been paid but slipped a $50 note into the chauffeur's hand. 'A most satisfactory journey,' he said.

The driver tapped his cap visor in acknowledgment.

'Thank you kindly, Sir. If you need our services further, they call me Diver.'

He'd checked in remotely en route, collected a room key from the concierge, briefly inspected the suite, made a short phone call, and left again. At the 15th-floor lift, he was met by a heavy-set man, who nodded slightly. He was the hired muscle.

'This way, Sir,' he indicated.

Mr Southwood was curious. 'You're not from Melbourne, are you?' he asked.

Satisfied with the news that his minder was 'a Tassie boy, born and raised,' he met his liaison, who welcomed him with cordiality but not friendliness. Both understood there was no room for social niceties in their business. They shook hands.

'Lehmann, Carl Lehmann,' the other man introduced himself, 'and of course, I know who you are. Welcome to Hobart.'

Summoning a bartender, Lehmann ordered a whisky sour for himself while Mr Southwood chose a dry martini. The conversation turned to business, but not before his host described the geography of their view. To the north, across the River Derwent, was Hobart's eastern shore, which was primarily residential. The river's estuary extended south, to their right, and the city to their left.

Their business, so far as it could be discussed, was in a holding pattern pending the launch of the second Auxiliary Satellite 10. Neither man could say when or where the right conditions would present themselves. However, they would determine that within the next few days. Lehmann confidently assured his visitor that those conditions would not occur today, most likely not tomorrow, but possibly the next day. He had his finger on the pulse of the universe.

'We continue to receive and extrapolate data. Our AI algorithms display excellent forecast capabilities, and preliminary conjecture is that the Awatere Valley will be active again soon. Failing that, possibly Dismal Swamp.'

At the raising of an eyebrow, he continued by describing that Dismal Swamp, despite the name, was an agreeable, if little-frequented nature reserve in the north-west of the state. As a launch location, it wasn't favoured due to accessibility issues. Mr Southwood broke his own Deep Sleep rule regarding communication. He immediately sent a message to Merlin in New Zealand, 'Suspend decommissioning Awatere facility. Reply confirmation.'

Within minutes, Merlin had responded, 'Confirmed.' He didn't say that the decommissioning process had barely started.

For another 24 hours, Southwood and its adversaries were frustrated by a lack of activity. Lehmann spent the best part of the following day showing his guest the sights of Hobart, including a ferry trip on the river and a cable car ride to the pinnacle of Mount Wellington. He explained that the aerial railway was new. Having been rejected by the local development authority, the state government had subsequently approved it after a landslide destroyed a long stretch of the only road to the pinnacle. At the lookout, Mr Southwood quietly took in the sweeping vista and, with more emotion than Lehmann had witnessed before, exclaimed, 'Now that's impressive.'

◆

Jack had exhausted his theoretical deliberations and taken a break from anything related to Southwood, Dragonfly and his *Dark History* project. Realising he hadn't collected his mail from the rented G.P.O. private box, he was pleased to find a handful of envelopes waiting for him. A couple contained stamps for his collection, items he'd forgotten he'd ordered a few weeks before. The afternoon, then, was spent at the dining table. Strewn with albums, stock books, catalogues and the inevitable pair of spade-ended tweezers, he was in his element.

For a moment, he thought of his father, who set up his first stamp album. His 'new' father, Jim Walker, was also a collector; they spent many hours at their hobby together. Jack could now indulge his passion for stamps and, by his own admission, spent too much money on the little scraps of paper with no intrinsic value. Today, he added some Great Britain King George V to a stock book, waiting for the time to create a dedicated album page for them.

With no news from Jack, Lyn and Leon spent time together doing nothing unusual. Harry Steve John 'Trousers' was with his cronies trying, unsuccessfully, to locate anything online or over the airwaves from Southwood. D.I. Terry Sayer and P.C. Sarah Blackman were back at work, being brought up to speed on Hobart's minor crime wave of housebreaking and car thefts. They crossed paths only once through the day and briefly, enough time to confirm to each other that they hadn't heard any Southwood-related news from Jack. Sayer confided that he'd been making surreptitious enquiries into the commissioner's whereabouts. No one had any clue. Even Human Resources was in the dark.

Ric Martin enjoyed a quiet day on one of his motorcycles, visiting friends. Derek Asquith had returned to his home, indulging in a different conspiracy theory. Dr Robert and his wife resumed their quiet retirement in the country. Even with his Hague connections, Steve Andrews was frustrated by the apparent evaporation of Southwood intelligence. He would be recalled and assigned to a different case if nothing new appeared soon. But late in the afternoon, Steve took a phone call. He listened intently, planning his next move even before the call ended.

He immediately phoned his new friend and colleague.

'Jack, old son, two things. Number one, the bar in my hotel has the longest Happy Hour I've ever come across. One-B, I owe you a drink, and two, there's some news I need to share. Great, see you in eight and a half minutes.'

Jack appeared at the bar in the eight and a half minutes prescribed to find Steve waiting with two beers.

'Just a starter, I reckon this will be a bit of a session,' Steve said.

They moved to a quiet table, although the bar was quiet anyway.

'I've just had a call from one of our tech guys. They've been monitoring OTD buoys – ocean tsunami detection buoys before you ask. No tsunamis to report from the regular units, but the D types, deep ocean, well, different kettle of dolphins altogether. The American buoys were recently modified to record very deep seismic activity, and they've been getting strange anomalies. Well, I guess most anomalies are strange, eh!

'They've been using AI to create sound recordings from numerical data. I'm told it's mostly like white noise, but sometimes it isn't. There are patterns... patterns that, logically, shouldn't be there. Essentially, they can listen to magma movements, which they thought were always at a consistent speed. Consistent within certain parameters, anyway. The interesting bit is that some magma doesn't move much, if at all...'

Jack interrupted, 'Tung magma?'

'Yeah, how'd you know that? Or heavy magma. This science is all new stuff.'

Jack outlined the theoretical work of Axel Furst and how 250 or more kilometres underground, or under the ocean in this case, the conflict between magma currents and stationary heavy magma caused an enormous mass-into-energy event.

'Want a tung beer then?' Steve asked with a grin.

Jack just nodded, his mind going into overdrive. Two steins of Erdinger wheat beer were ordered and delivered to their table.

'My blokes are having a lot of fun with their AI,' Steve continued. 'Their big computer, Shoelaces, dropped a bombshell today. It decided, all on its own, to monitor harmonics of these recordings. I didn't even know that energy had harmonics. Anyway, in particular places, at particular times, for brief periods, energy signatures are off the chart. It's big, Jack, really big. They say that even gravity can be affected. They've christened those incidents Peak Energy Events. I think they just like the acronym. How's the Erdinger?'

With some degree of truthfulness, Jack told Steve that none of this was a surprise. His research into Furst's suppositions was just being confirmed, though modern science was now providing validation.

'And the beer is great. One of my favourites. Any food in this bar?'

Steve said there had been a large private function the previous night, and one of the bartenders confided there was plenty of food left over. Toasted turkey sandwiches with cranberry sauce would be complimentary for guests. Jack suggested that turkey demanded a suitable wine and that a pinot noir would suit. Steve left that choice to Jack.

'You seem to be getting on well with your bartender. Ask him for a Coal Valley pinot. You won't be disappointed.'

Steve complied.

'Now,' Jack continued, 'I expect you're going to tell me that Shoelaces has given your blokes a forecast of something or other?'

Steve pretended he wasn't impressed with Jack's guess, 'You'll be interested to hear that it's given us a forecast for the next 48 hours. Timing isn't that precise, but it reckons on 42 degrees south and 173 degrees east. I looked it up before we got here. The Awatere Valley, New Zealand. Sound familiar?'

Jack smiled broadly.

'Pardon me if I grin. It's just that it's taken a long time for science to confirm the theories of my favourite Norwegian geologist. Remind me to find you a copy of *Dyp Strøm*. You'll read all about geomagnetic hot spots and gravitational pressure points from an 1895 perspective. Fascinating stuff. Tell your people to check it out. Axel Furst might finally be famous.'

Steve revealed that his team in New Zealand would continue surveillance of the Awatere Valley site. It would be a minimum-personnel exercise. Fixed cameras and drones would do most of the work, though there would be more for this next phase in Southwood's operation.

Finally exhausting their discussion, the pair enjoyed the last of their wine and parted company. Back in his apartment, Jack reflected on Steve's revelation and, with his mind taking sideways steps, moved from deep ocean tsunami buoys to Axel Furst, then to Norway generally. He recalled a frustrating document in his collection. Its frustration was because it was an article about an article, or possibly a longer work, that he had not been able to secure.

He retrieved the paper, made himself comfortable and reread *The Real Reason Hitler Invaded Norway.*

◆

The Norwegian Campaign of the Second World War is well documented. That is, up to a point. The problem with official history is the first word, 'official'. That means it's either incomplete, inaccurate, or both. Norway's part in that war is much more than the 62 days between 9 April and 10 June 1940. Let's consider a brief official history first.

Before the campaign proper, the Royal Navy had already commenced Operation Wilfred, mining Norwegian waters to hamper Germany's transport of iron ore from Sweden through Norwegian territory. Wilfred was overtaken, however, when Germany invaded Norway and Denmark on 9 April.

World domination aside, the German invasion of Norway was mainly for economic reasons. Its heavy reliance on Swedish iron ore, mostly shipped from Narvik, demanded military action to control this supply. The availability of sites for submarine bases was also cited as a reason for the invasion.

On Sunday, 16 February 1940, HMS *Cossack* entered Norwegian territorial waters. The destroyer intercepted a German auxiliary ship, *Altmark,* which had been operating in the Atlantic to support the heavy cruiser *Admiral Graf Spee.* At the time of the intercept, *Altmark* was carrying 299 Allied prisoners of war, captured when their ships were sunk by the *Graf Spee.*

Bergen's naval commander denied *Altmark* access to the port as Norway's neutrality regulations prohibited other countries' naval ships from entering specific ports. However, the naval commander's strictly correct denial of access was overturned. When the German ship was located, six British destroyers were sent to the area. *Altmark* was escorted by three Norwegian ships, but none intervened when HMS *Cossack's* crew boarded the German vessel and freed all 299 prisoners.

Germany lodged a protest with Norway, which, in turn, protested to Great Britain. While Britain's action was a violation of Norway's neutrality, they claimed that the freeing of the POWs meant it was morally justifiable. Plans for the invasion of Norway were approved by Hitler less than two weeks later, on 1 March 1940. The invasion commenced soon after.

Such is a much-abbreviated, official, and widely published story of Norway's entry into the Second World War. While not disputing the events, gaps and inconsistencies in the broader narrative are prevalent. These have been partly rectified by at least one historian who worked under the nom de plume Libelle. Rarely published and barely credible is his (or her) alternative history. *The Real Reason Hitler Invaded Norway* first appeared in 1955 in a low-circulation publication aimed at devotees of the works of Charles Fort. The article's author focussed on identifying and confirming omissions in the approved history, notably anomalies in Germany's and Britain's apparently non-military activities.

In refusing Norway's inspection of his ship, the *Altmark* captain wasn't being obstructive for its own sake. Hidden in the hold were several large crates indicated as containing mining equipment. For purely civilian cargo, the containers were more securely sealed than such contents would ordinarily require, and they were under armed guard 24 hours a day. The guards, curiously, the author suggested, were from a Wehrmacht unit, not Kriegsmarine men. There was no mistaking the importance of the crates, being plastered with warning signs and threatening documents. The documents were stamped Hüter der Stille, German for Keeper of the Silence. Libelle stated in a footnote that this title had been encountered during research into other matters. Also on board *Altmark* were 'a number' of technicians, at least one of whom was not remotely connected with mining.

That the Royal Navy sent no fewer than six destroyers to the area where *Altmark* was located was a curious reaction to the sighting of a single German auxiliary ship. At the time, Britain didn't know how many POWs were on board. The lead ship, HMS *Cossack*, like *Altmark*, also carried non-naval personnel. Eight scientists were housed in specially outfitted quarters and were kept apart from the crew. They even had their own cook and a liaison officer. While they had no contact with the crew or ship's officers, their presence was no secret. Their quarters were referred to as boffin boxes. No one, not even the captain, knew anything about the scientists other than that they were to disembark at Bergen. With the drama of the freeing of nearly 300 prisoners of war, few noticed the scientists' departure.

With the confusion of personnel movements overseas in wartime, how the British and German scientists and their equipment reached their destination is not recorded. Libelle described the frustration of attempting to source German records 10 years after the war. Most of the research material was British, and the venture records appeared to be as much about the German operations as their own. Those records were freely available until 1955 when Libelle's article was published, after which they were mysteriously classified and locked away 'for national security.' Most of the German documents were destroyed in the war, and some reportedly moved to Moscow. Russian archivists deny the existence of any such records.

Libelle suggested that the Germans requisitioned a fleet of local trucks and made their way some distance north. He claims that German and British scientists worked together on a specific project, though it appears to have been non-military. According to Libelle's report, the collaboration was to investigate gravitational anomalies in an unspecified area of Norway. The local indigenous people, the Sámi, supposedly avoided the region and referred to it as morašlaš eana, or sad ground, presided over by Mubpienålmaj, the god of evil.

◆

In the report, more was made of the researchers than what they were researching. Reading between the lines, however, Jack surmised that this was another instance of an organisation – he presumed Southwood – using its incredible influence to investigate a region Axel Furst probably knew about. 'Norway again,' he said aloud as he wondered at the power of this mysterious society. Could an essentially civilian group manipulate the British military, and by inference, the British government, as well as German High Command, at a time of war, to further its own ambitions?

The Real Reason Hitler Invaded Norway is Libelle's only known published work. Jack had already noted that, in the Frisian language, Libelle translates to Dragonfly. He also wondered if the author was actually Axel Furst, though *Dyp Strøm* was published 60 years earlier, so it appeared unlikely. Possibly a grandson.

With a single malt in hand, Jack stood on his balcony. He again watched his part of Hobart slow down and noticed a nearby neighbour apparently doing the same thing. They raised their glasses in salute – probably the closest he would ever get to socialising with this particular woman.

'Here's to tomorrow, whatever it brings,' he said quietly. But he had plans.

◆

Chapter 16

The Domain Facility

'That's a surprise,' Control declared, 'these things usually recur after a much longer Fibonacci period.'

He was speaking to Merlin, both still waiting at the Awatere Valley facility, along with the operations team. The conditions for another launch – they continued to use the word launch – would be in place in two days and again the day after. The Fibonacci delay referenced the time between such conditions, sometimes 34 or 55 days, and often 89 days or longer. Anything less than 34 was unusual, and Merlin was cautious about using harmonic timeframes.

'Risky,' he warned, 'harmonics can be unstable. But it's not my call. Have we heard from Mr Southwood yet?'

Their boss was still in Hobart, relying on his liaison, Lehmann, to coordinate data extrapolation and forecasting. The Domain facility had been allocated that technical function for the next launch. Mr Southwood, still smarting from the failure of Auxiliary Satellite 10, was impatient and eager to have the system finalised. He was satisfied with the speed at which a new one had been prepared. It would be delivered to the Awatere Valley within hours.

After several lengthy phone calls, he briefed Lehmann.

'Tell Merlin the new satellite will be with them imminently. I want the earliest possible launch time. Keep me informed of progress. And get me a car, ask for Diver. I need to see this Domain facility we spent so much money on. What do we call it, Vilin IV?'

Lehmann was surprised to hear the facility referred to by its formal classification. He knew that some staff called it Viv, as in 'I have a date with Viv,' meaning a work shift. He had to tell Mr Southwood that there was no longer any vehicular access. Part of the development approval process was reducing the service road to a combined cycleway and footpath.

'Perhaps the light rail would suit,' he tentatively suggested, 'There's a station next to your hotel.'

Southwood frowned.

'Public transport isn't to my taste, and I haven't been on a bike since I was 12. It will have to be the light,' he conceded, adding, 'I'll want a briefing on Black Knight too.'

Only a few brief stops interrupted the three-kilometre run into the city, where the train stopped a little longer. Elizabeth Street Pier was the most utilised station, as it was close to the shuttle bus that took visitors to the cable car station at Strickland Park. From here, there was a stop at the Royal Tasmanian Botanical Gardens, then a short run to the King's Domain station. Mr Southwood and Carl Lehmann were the only passengers to alight there, and no one got on.

'It's virtually a private station,' Lehmann said. 'Though the public can use it, few do.'

'That's what we hoped for,' Southwood replied.

The entrance to Vilin IV was uninviting, appearing stark and utilitarian, an intentional design strategy. Lehmann entered a six-digit number onto the keypad that appeared and placed his right thumb on a pad. A metallic voice demanded, 'Status?'

'Lehmann, Carl, and Mr Southwood. Scheduled.'

Immediately, a sliding door opened with a low-pitched hum, and the two visitors entered a reception area, though there was no reception desk nor any staff. The atmosphere was clinical, and the metal walls and ceiling were slightly blue. The air was perceptibly cooler. There was no signage. Only a fire extinguisher interrupted the featureless presentation. Even Southwood couldn't avoid all building regulations. The door behind them closed, and another opened. Lehmann relieved any potential concern, revealing that the system wouldn't allow both doors to be open simultaneously.

They were met by a man who was obviously a security officer. His uniform of jacket and trousers was what Jack, the stamp collector, might call 70% grey. Heavy black boots afforded the man more height than nature provided, though he was already six-feet tall. Several pockets and a utility belt contained the instruments of his profession.

'Gentlemen,' he said without emotion, 'I'm instructed to escort you to Control. You can call me Andersen.' A discrete name badge said as much. He clearly didn't like using his given name, Mads.

'Very good, Andersen,' Mr Southwood said. 'Tell your superior to get rid of that VIV sign at your entrance. It's not approved.'

Taken aback slightly, Andersen muttered 'Sir' and led them along an open and somewhat elevated gantry. On either side of them were 12 workers in white lab coats, each seated at a spacious semi-open workstation. In front of each, three curved computer monitors captured their professional attention. These were the data centre operators.

Beyond the workers, on the same level, sat banks of computers with masses of cables and a myriad of blinking or static lights. On the gantry level, beyond the data centre, another thumbprint-activated sliding door opened.

The three were met by a man in a suit.

'That will be all Andersen,' he said. 'Mr Southwood, Lehmann, delighted to have you visit us. It's an interesting time. I'm Control.'

He wore no name badge. To his staff, he was just Control. This man in charge of the facility was a long-standing Southwood man, aged about 60 but looked younger. Leading his visitors through one of the other three doors revealed another 12 workers, again in white lab coats. These were what Control called 'the others.'

Through another door, Control welcomed Southwood and Lehmann to his 'office' though it looked unlike any other office. With no windows, the monotony of wall space was alleviated by a massive monitor displaying what would be the view – over Cornelian Bay and the River Derwent – had a window been installed. He explained.

'Closed circuit TV. We have several such screens for the mental health benefits of staff. Seems to work. Now, you wanted a briefing on Black Knight. But where are my manners?'

He pressed a button behind his lapel. 'Coffee for three. And something to eat.'

Control continued with a few comments about the facility and its operations, and a young man entered with a trolley. It offered a large plunger of coffee, obviously strong, a metal jug of hot water, and an assortment of biscuits. Two smaller jugs were labelled Light Milk and Proper Milk, respectively. It was the only lighthearted element in the facility.

'Ah, excellent. I hope you like Pfeffernüsse, Florentines or whatever these things are.'

Southwood was becoming impatient. He poured a black coffee and selected a macaroon, signifying he wouldn't be influenced by his host's culinary prejudices. Control then spent some time outlining the situation with Black Knight.

'Some of our people call it Dragonfly. Pet name. It's been moved from its polar orbit to a geostationary position over the equator at 180 degrees east. Over the Pacific Ocean, even when stationary, it's unlikely to be noticed. Our stealth material is better than anything the Americans have, and they like to have the best. To be safer, though, we adjust its altitude periodically. Telecom satellites are usually at about 35,000 kilometres altitude. Black Knight is 40,000 minimum. Anyway, we leave it in hibernation most of the time.'

'Hibernation?' Lehmann asked.

'Very useful. AKA Silent Running. Some of our guys call it Life Support. It's like the sleep mode regular computers have. Minimal power consumption, close to zero electromagnetic emanations, but still with functioning fail-safe protocols. Can be woken up and fully functional in seconds.'

Control took another 30 minutes to fully outline Black Knight's operational parameters, most of which Southwood knew. On the other hand, Lehmann heard plenty he hadn't known about. In particular, he learned he liked Pfeffernüsse.

'I may be asking out of turn here,' Lehmann apologised in advance, 'but I'm mostly administration and management. The science has me baffled. How does this system work?'

Control looked to Mr Southwood for permission to explain. He nodded. Control topped up his coffee.

'OK. Earth has a naturally occurring energy grid at its surface, though it's generated at great depths. There are hundreds of energy areas; 14 major ones, both poles and the other 12 roughly equidistant around both hemispheres. They're relatively stable, particularly at the poles. The minor areas come and go, but there are always hundreds at any given time. The primaries are usually low-energy – that's illogical and counterintuitive. You get used to that sort of thing with science, but we're not dealing with regular science here.

'It's the connecting lines between these areas that actually emit most of the energy. We're mapping all that in real-time, or will be when the tenth satellite is up. The vital part of the energy grid isn't the areas themselves, but those connecting lines. Initially, we thought they ran only north-south and east-west. That's mostly the case, but they seem to have no respect for directional regularity. The strongest energy emanations occur at line intersections. It's erratic in output and sometimes position. The system is dynamic and delicate, and its character changes according to sunspot activity, magma movement, and planetary alignment. I won't go into all that.

'It's odd that older civilisations knew about this centuries ago, or something of it anyway. They called them ley lines. In more recent times, Nikola Tesla recognised the phenomenon.

'Now, at this point, the planet teaches us a bit about energy, or tries to. The movement of magma, lots and lots of the stuff, is kinetic energy, which we can't use. We theorise that there's a process by which it's converted to electrical energy, which we can use. Interaction with gravity probably holds the key there. That's the theory part of the explanation.

'Practical application. Difficult. There are two effects. Number one is optimised electromagnetic and electrostatic levitation. As a catch-all name, we call it gravitic propulsion. These are byproducts of the process, and we've used it to launch our satellites. There's a lot of mathematics in mapping and much more in forecasting. Fortunately, our quantum computers can deal with that.

'Number two, ah, does anyone want more coffee?'

His audience declined.

'Number two, of course, is the capture, storage and transmission of the electrical energy generated by the battery we call Earth. Our satellites constantly collect massive amounts of data. That data is downloaded to ground stations where forecasting software does its magic. Often, there is no time to take advantage of energy bursts, sorry, emanations. But the strongest ones are a long time developing, and we have time to move Black Knight to the appropriate position.'

Control poured what was left of the coffee into his cup and Lehmann helped himself to the last Pfeffernüsse.

'I'll go back a bit. It was called Dragonfly because of its appearance. The elongated body holds the batteries and is separate from the comms and computer section. Four long reciprocal curve receptor panels from that segment extend, two on either side. They are fitted with solar panels and energy receivers. Another 12 retractable panels swing out from behind these for significant events, forming a dish. We call it an isosceles circle. I'm not sure that's a real thing, but it's what we call it.

Once in position, Dragonfly captures between 20 and 40 per cent of the electricity that would otherwise be lost in space. It can store four petawatts almost indefinitely but in practice, would transmit that by a focussed, very-far-field radiative technique to any suitable storage facility on the planet. That's another technology we've mastered, a development of your microwave oven. Any questions?'

There were no questions, but Mr Southwood thanked Control for concisely describing the Dragonfly program. Lehmann added his own thanks.

'Oh, yes,' Control added, 'I forgot to say we called the whole shebang Dragonfly.'

Southwood flinched at Control's frivolous language but let it go. There were more important considerations to deal with. The organisation had arrangements with several cities worldwide, initially no more than one in each country. A city in the English midlands had modified some of its electricity infrastructure to receive transmitted energy. It was a small city, which suited Southwood's test parameters. Council members insisted it was a city, not a large town because it boasted a cathedral. Such was England's historical legacy of granting city status. Modern thinking has different ideas. However, Southwood wasn't concerned about Bridsal-on-Slade's status, only its council's willingness to be part of the Dragonfly trial.

Control invited Mr Southwood and Lehmann to examine the rest of the facility, though they had already seen most of it. Agreeing, they spent another half hour viewing the technical aspects of the data centre and what Control called the 'real' operational and management zones. He was relieved that his boss seemed satisfied with his inspection. He asked again if there were any questions, Mr Southwood asked how supplies were received, given there was no adequate roadway.

'Good question. If you look at that monitor,' he indicated a screen on an otherwise featureless wall, 'that's the scene outside. Bottom-left, you'll see a floating jetty with access to our main entrance, though we usually use the loading dock 120-metres to the west. We had some issues with people fishing from it, but we've dealt with that. No fish in the bay now and no fishermen. It was a brutal solution, but it worked.'

Lehman suggested that adequate is good enough sometimes, then had an idea. He knew Control was previously in security and asked if he knew Sugarman. Control thought for a moment.

'You're going back a bit. Yes, I remember Roger Sugarman. In the nineties, I think. He was interfering in local programs and getting uncomfortably close. We considered buying him off, but he was one of those dedicated types. In the end, we put him in the Degree Absolute category. That's what we called it in those days. Something else now, I suppose. I haven't been in security for years. Turns out we could have saved the cost of the effort. He drove into a tree and killed himself. Wife too. Can't remember her name. Left a son behind, I think.'

Mr Southwood intervened.

'Jan. His wife was Jan, collateral damage. Unavoidable. I've read the file. It's his son that Lehmann was asking about. Jack Sugarman. He and his contacts have been a thorn in our side for a week or more. I've put a watch and report alert on him,' he looked at Lehmann, who nodded, 'but he's been quiet the last 24 hours. The closer we get to system implementation, the less danger he can be. But he might have caused a great deal of inconvenience.'

Mr Southwood decided against asking Control what he knew of The Hague but asked if Keeper was still in New Zealand. He was. The local security people would have to deal with Jack. As the meeting was concluding, Control spotted a small boat approaching the jetty.

'It looks like we have a delivery a little earlier than expected. There's efficiency for you. If you want to wait 15 minutes, I'll have the boys take you back to your hotel.'

Carl looked at his watch.

'There's a train in three minutes,' he said.

Southwood promptly chose the train option.

'I have another meeting in 20 minutes. Thank you, Control, for your time. Excellent work. We'll probably not meet again.'

On departure, he turned to see the doors closing with their low-pitched hum and was pleased to see a workman in a white lab coat, probably one of the technicians, about to remove the VIV signage.

'Anderson's on the ball,' he said to Lehmann.

Had he elected to return by boat, Mr Southwood may have recognised one of the crew as Diver, his limo driver. Their train ride was uneventful and quiet, with only a few other passengers, and the 'meeting in 20 minutes' was attended punctually.

Mr Southwood disliked meetings with the organisation's accountants. They always appeared to be defensive and lacked imagination. When asked, yet again, about potential markets and pricing, he reeled off his much-rehearsed speech.

'You ask who will pay our price for electricity? Everyone. Look at Australia, and New South Wales specifically. The average price there is nearly 34 cents per kilowatt hour. We'll sell ours at eight cents. The energy providers can charge what they like, but it means they'll very quickly shut down coal-fired and gas-turbine power stations to the tune of over 100 GW per day. That will make the environmentalists happy, anyway. Eventually, solar, hydro and wind generators will cost more to maintain than they're worth. That's another 15 GW, roughly. I'm sure you've crunched those numbers already. We anticipate two years, maximum, to saturation. Probably less. By then, householders with solar panels will be the only people not using our electricity.'

That spiel assuaged the accountants' concerns, and Mr Southwood decided they were only attempting to validate decisions already made. The meeting was brief, and when it was over, he sat alone on his presidential suite balcony. With a scotch on the table in front of him, he admired the view. It was race day for one of the local yacht clubs, and the river was replete with sailing vessels. Raising his glass, he took a sip and thought, 'Pretty soon, no more world to conquer.'

He made a mental note of the next steps:

- Launch Auxiliary Satellite 10
- Compliance testing
- Test transmission to Bridsal-on-Slade
- Full implementation
- Phase two.

He also considered Jack Sugarman, but he would be dealt with separately. The list remained mental but Mr Southwood had long ago learned not to write down such lists. No one was ready for Phase two, not even the hotel's cleaners.

After a room-service dinner, Mr Southwood sent an encrypted message to Supervisor in the Awatere Valley, 'Deep Sleep rescinded 2400h your time.'

◆

In his apartment, Jack spent a quiet evening listening to a random selection of 1950s rock and roll music and perusing a recently received stamp auction catalogue. He had no idea that his archnemesis was so close, nor that his name had been singled out to be 'dealt with'. Debating whether to bid on a 'splendid John Ash imprint block of the 1938 10-shilling Coronation Robes' stamp, his deliberations were interrupted.

A Jimmy Dorsey recording sounded familiar. It was one of his father's favourite pieces, and Jack realised he'd been thinking about his parents more often recently. He also realised he hadn't contacted Sarah since their recent liaison. Never knowing how long to leave before making the 'call after the night before', he didn't want to appear too eager or, on the other hand, disinterested. A phone call saved him from making a decision.

'Sarah, hi, I was just about to call.'

'Big fibber,' she joked, 'I've just finished my shift. Walking by your place, thought I'd drop in, unless you're out or have company.'

'Yes, I'm here. I'm usually here, and when I'm here, apart from the past week, I'm usually alone. No company tonight. Not yet, drop in,' Jack replied.

On arrival, Jack put on his hospitality mode, 'Drink? Anything to eat?'

'Thanks, it's been a long day. I ate in our canteen, but is anything open,' she asked, then spotted a bottle of red on a sideboard. 'That looks good.'

Jack poured two glasses, though he'd been planning an alcohol-free day – 'Doesn't happen very often,' he quipped.

Sarah then noticed the music, saying she didn't think Jack would have been a big band music fan. He explained that his father loved Jimmy Dorsey, Benny Goodman, Glen Miller, and Harry James and that it influenced his own preferences, which were many and varied.

They talked about her and D.I. Sayer's reinstatement and their first day back on the job. Sarah admitted there was no word on Dragonfly, Southwood, The Hague, or any mention of their activities.

'It's like they just vanished,' she confessed.

'Same here,' Jack replied. 'Zilch. I'd expected something, anything, but Harry is strangely quiet, and as for Steve, it's like our engagement is off. Not a word. I plan to call everyone tomorrow and get the lowdown. Something's got to be happening somewhere.'

As their unplanned evening progressed, activity at Southwood's Awatere Valley facility also advanced. At midnight in New Zealand, 10:00 p.m. in Hobart, the Deep Sleep constraint was lifted.

Chapter 17

Heavy Water

The next morning, off the west coast of New Zealand, mariners on the Tasman Sea were stunned to find their expected speed diminished. The first mate on board a cruise ship heading to Milford Sound jokingly asked if they were sailing uphill. Having checked the wind and the ship's engine output, he was at a loss as to why the expected 18 knots was noticeably less.

He was younger than the captain, who had experienced the phenomenon before. The older man nodded knowingly and said they were, indeed, sailing uphill.

'It's raining phones in a graveyard. Unexpected. This is bigger than we usually encounter but we're coming out of a depression, and I don't mean the atmospheric type. If you check your weather instruments, you'll see the ocean is much colder than it should be. I expected six to eight degrees. What is it?'

The first mate looked at his met display.

'Bloody hell, three and a bit.'

The captain nodded again and said they were probably sailing over something called a negative energy vortex.

'Now, when something is identified as "something called" whatever, it's either a government conspiracy or a trade secret. Or complete bullshit. In this case, it's none of those. It's not the devil, it's the deep blue sea. They don't last long, these things, usually only hours, sometimes a few days, but they're caused by gravitational pressure points or geomagnetic hot spots. Maybe both.

'It creates depressions on the ocean surface, sometimes miles across, and the water becomes heavier and denser. That's why we've slowed. You see, we talk about sea level, but it's never level. Not really. Our science people explained it to me. You've heard of heavy water used in nuclear reactors. Did you know it's naturally occurring?'

The first mate shook his head.

'It's called deuterium oxide and is water with more than the usual hydrogen isotope deuterium. But here's the interesting thing. Heavy water freezes at 3.82 degrees. What's the water temperature now?'

'3.7, no, 3.6 and falling.'

The captain continued.

'Right, we might see some ice out there, but it's not likely because heavy ice will sink in seawater. Anyway, it probably won't last long, and we can make up the time dreckly, we're not dead in the water. Our grockles will never notice. If it was dark, they'd see plenty of bioluminescence, though. Plain sailing soon, mark my words.'

The captain was a Cornishman and always called his passengers grockles, a term usually limited to tourists visiting Cornwall and Devon from 'up north', meaning anywhere else in England. He made a final observation that there would soon probably be other weird phenomena associated with what his ship was sailing through now. Neither the captain nor his first mate would know how accurate that observation would be.

As predicted, the ship's speed later increased to its programmed rate. Neither the captain nor the mate knew whether it was because the phenomenon had run its course or they had left it behind. Another crew member, the communications officer, joined the conversation.

'Should I draft this into your log?' he asked the captain.

'Better. Might be important,' the captain instructed, then had a thought.

'Have you ever heard of the plane that went missing near here in '62? It was a 1930s de Havilland, a pretty little biplane. Flight path was Christchurch to Milford Sound, where we're heading, but they never made it. Never found the plane either. It's supposedly New Zealand's greatest aviation mystery. The flight had been delayed by a few days because of crappy weather. It's thought that conditions deteriorated during the flight; the pilot had been told the weather was "a bit unusual this morning." But there's something else.'

He paused, not sure whether to share what he had in mind.

'This area is sometimes called New Zealand's Bermuda Triangle. I don't really go much for that stuff, but you never know, I suppose, not after what we've just sailed through. At least four other planes have vanished since 1962. Um, don't log that bit, eh.'

The aircraft in question was a de Havilland DH.90 Dragonfly.

◆

At Southwood's Awatere Valley facility, the Deep Sleep protocol was no longer in place. Suspended activities were resumed, online overlay networks reactivated, and routine communications recommenced. Southwood's equipment was receiving transmissions from its satellites, which was a large backlog of data. The organisation may have been quiet, but their computers never slept. Within a few minutes, an alert had been sent to Supervisor and Merlin that their next window of opportunity for a launch was late the following day.

Supervisor had learned that the replacement satellite was being delivered in the afternoon. That would give them only a short time for inspection, programming and compliance testing.

'It'll be a long night,' he told Merlin, 'but we can do it. The guys won't like working late, but there's no choice. I'll clear it with Mr Southwood first, though.'

His request was answered almost immediately with the single all-caps word 'PROCEED', which meant urgency rather than the usual discourteous shouting. Having briefed the team of technicians, a flurry of activity quickly readied the site for another launch. The same Bell 429 helicopter easily lifted the 700kg satellite and delivered it to the site. After placing it gently on a well-cushioned landing pad, itself fixed to a motorised trolley, Auxiliary Satellite 10 was soon in the care of its technicians.

Supervisor watched as his team partially disassembled the device, permanently removing shipping components, testing individual modules, and reinstalling them. He understood some of the work but admitted to Merlin that much of it was a mystery. Eventually, the replacement ASatX – as the technicians still insisted on calling it – was back in one piece, thoroughly checked and issued an imaginary certificate of compliance. Only one element bothered one of the team.

'The self-regulating stabilising software seems to have some odd coding in it that I can't identify. A few ghost lines, probably left over from a previous version. Shouldn't be a problem. There's plenty of built-in failsafe protocols to counter any issues. I'd work on it more, but I gather there's a deadline?'

Merlin studied the data on a monitor, glanced at his watch, and decided his team member was right. It shouldn't be a problem. He leaned back in his chair, looked at the satellite sitting quietly on its platform and realised the entire team was watching him, waiting for a decision. Some only wanted their late evening meal and to get to bed.

'Get yourselves ready for launch,' he finally said, still wondering about launching at a harmonic timeframe.

Shortly before midnight, ASatX was prepared. It and the launch crew were now waiting only for the right conditions.

◆

Jack didn't like early morning calls but forgave his eager caller this time. It was Harry.

'Jack, mate, sorry for the timing, but this is important. It's all going crazy here,' he blurted out.

Jack yawned and clambered out of bed.

'Hang on, I'm not awake yet. Let me put my dressing gown on, at least. OK, you're on speaker. I'm listening. Making coffee, but listening. What are you on about?'

'Yeah, yeah, dressing gown, coffee, you have all the luck.' Harry continued, 'Listen, we've been monitoring all channels for Southwood, Dragonfly, the works. Nothing for ages, then, bang, it all started again. 10 o'clock last night, data like you wouldn't believe. Most of it's just numbers – coordinates, we think – but their dark website is yielding some fascinating stuff.'

'Yielding, is it?' Jack asked.

'My clever word for the day. I promise not to say it again. We keep seeing references to ASATX, which we think might be a plural shorthand for satellites.

'Or Satellite 10,' Jack suggested.

Harry agreed that made more sense and described the data they were getting. It seemed to be about energy outputs, specifically about timing, duration and magnitude.

'But that's only part of the story. We've been getting plain text material as well. I say plain text; it's encrypted but not too hard to read. We have our Genesis paper and dealt with it pretty quickly. It confirms what we already know, or suspect at least. Southwood will soon have 10 satellites in orbit and operational, five on either side of the equator. These things are loaded with sensors that look for your pet things, gravity pressure points, and magma movements. Before you ask, no, I didn't remember that. It's all in this document.

'The data is transmitted contemporaneously – another clever word in the document – to ground stations. There are loads of those around the world. Don't know how many. They analyse the data. As I said, it's timing, duration and magnitude of energy outputs. But get this. They forecast not only when, where, and for how long energy is generated but also exactly where it's focussed. Those forecasts are transmitted to another satellite, the big one called Dragonfly or Black Knight. That one is self-regulating, to a degree, and – I'm reading this – can relocate to a geostationary position to capture some of the energy. Most of it wanders off into the cosmos. I didn't read that bit. It just stands to reason.

'I should say this isn't actually working yet, but it's almost ready. When it is, Dragonfly will be able to transmit energy by microwave to any electricity storage facility on the planet. How's that grab you? One more thing. That document was signed.'

Jack took all this in, saying nothing. What Harry just told him did confirm a lot of conjecture. As to the last challenge, he made no guess.

'Go on, I give up.'

'Brother Ringo,' Harry said. 'This bloke's an enigma. Seen his name quite a bit recently. Sometimes I think he's a Southwood man, but then I think he could be working for The Hague.'

Jack offered profuse thanks to Harry and asked him to pass on his gratitude to the team. He topped up his coffee and tried to put everything together in his mind. By now, Hobart was coming to life, and the hoi polloi were sharing roads with the upper crust and everyone in between. On buses and light rail trains, everyone was equal.

Something that seemed not to have occurred to Harry was to ask why Brother Ringo had authored this revealing document. Also, how was it transmitted from one of Southwood's satellites at this time? Jack made another guess. Maybe the benevolent author was also the programmer for Southwood and had inserted the exposé to reveal the organisation's processes to the world, or a small part of it anyway. That just presented another question. Simply, why do that? Jack tried changing places with BR – he wanted a shorthand name – and wondered if it was an allegiance reversal. Again, why would BR have considered that necessary or at least desirable? It must be a question of trust. Southwood was, after all, a criminal organisation. Perhaps Brother Ringo's past strategy no longer aligned with Southwood's dream of his future.

Jack decided it was too early in the morning for this sort of deliberation and thought instead of breakfast. In the kitchen, with a bowl ready to receive whatever cereal he would select, another phone call left this decision in abeyance. It was The Hague's man, Steve.

'G'day Steve, thought you must have abandoned us. You've been quiet.'

'Yeah, sorry about that. Essentially, I had to whoosh off to Melbourne for a high-level meeting with high-level bosses in a high-level building. You know how it is. Anyway, it's been quiet for a while. Not now, though. Our people in New Zealand are still monitoring that Awatere facility. Some of the Southwood people left, then came back. No idea why, but they're buzzing about like blue-arsed flies now, getting ready for something. Then they had a delivery by chopper. In a pretty solid-looking crate. Must have weighed half a tonne, at least. We reckon it's another satellite.'

Jack then spent some time outlining his previous call from Harry. The cereal bowl remained empty. They discussed the latest developments and decided that something big was about to happen. Leaving Jack to his breakfast, Steve promised to keep him in the loop, then dropped his bombshell.

'This is off the record, Jack, very much off any record. I reported our conversation about raiding that Domain facility, just as a thought bubble kind of thing. My bosses surprised me; sometimes they do that, and gave me a green light, but basically, it's only an observation exercise. We need to know precisely what their so-called data facility is. We're going to need your mate Harry, and if Ric's offer still stands, his little band of cutthroats. No offence. What do you reckon?'

Jack had filled his bowl with Crunchy Nut Corn Flakes and was about to add milk when he pushed it away.

'I've had two surprises today. Not sure if my heart can handle it, but leave it with me, and I'll get back to you. This needs some planning.'

'Plan away, mate,' Steve said. 'Can you plan to pick me up from the airport tomorrow? I'll text you the flight details but it'll be late-morning.'

'Sure, I'll bring the Commodore.'

Jack ate his cereal and two slices of toast with marmalade, his adopted mother's favourite, and wondered how many times Steve would say 'essentially' and 'basically' each day. When in planning mode, serious thinking, as he sometimes called it, Jack liked to be dressed and wear lace-up shoes. It was something his father told him was a good psychological benefit. Showered and dressed, he sat at his dining table and planned. Several sheets of pad paper were discarded until an hour later, he had the bones of an approach.

With the day, time and team selected, it might just work. The rest of the morning was spent on the phone. He was surprised and pleased that each name on his list was followed by a bold tick. Everyone was available. Everyone wanted to help. Later in the day, Ric called to say he'd recruited three ex-soldiers ready for a bit of excitement. 'Retired soldiers need a "fix" from time to time,' he'd said. Jack told him they might need small arms but nothing heavy. This was all going down virtually in the middle of a residential area. A map showed that the suburbs of North Hobart, New Town and Lutana were only minutes away. He hoped there would be no noisy confrontation. Apart from public safety, this action was highly illegal.

Jack called his locks and security expert, Sam, a second time. He was eager to assist but said there was a problem. He was familiar with the setup at the Domain facility.

'I hate to put a dampener on things. To get in this joint, you'll need a six-digit PIN, a thumbprint and the right voice. It's state-of-the-art security. Let me make a call.'

On the list, the tick after Sam's name was crossed out and replaced by a question mark. Would this whole plan be scuttled before it started? On the basis that sometimes you can know too much, Jack proceeded to make more calls and left the access question alone.

'Keith, it's Jack, I'm going to need you and your boat again. Tomorrow night. A quick ferry service to Cornelian Bay and back. Four passengers. Possible?'

Hearing a positive response, Jack told Keith what he needed to know and a little of what he didn't. There was a degree of precision required, timing-wise.

'I'm at your service, mate. The tide will be OK at that time. As to the other, I'll get Diver. He's always up for a bit of shenanigans.'

'Diver, eh? Friend?' Jack asked.

'Well, he's never tried to kill me, so yes, that makes him a friend. He has a boat like mine. Not as fast. See, here's the thing, he makes deliveries to that place. Has access to the loading bay. Security isn't as tight there, he says. Bit of a design cock-up if you ask me. I don't know about internal security. Diver might have some clues. I'll call him and get back to you.'

Jack started to think his scheme might work. Just might. He considered the three surprises, thinking such things happen in threes. At the bottom of his list of names, a little distant from the rest, Sayer appeared. Several biro dots indicated 'no decision.' Perhaps four surprises were going to be one too many. He crossed out Sayer's name.

Keith did call back later that day and said that Diver would be 'only too happy' to help. His relationship with whoever ran the Domain facility was not one of goodwill. The boat owners would be at a ship chandler shop the following morning. It was close to Jack's apartment, and Keith suggested they meet.

Jack leaned back in his chair, somewhat uncomfortably as he'd been sitting for hours. He now knew, rather than suspected, that he should on no account involve D.I. Sayer. In real terms, his plan was an illegal entry to a private facility with armed men to engage in what the victims would regard as industrial espionage, if not terrorism. Despite a verbal go-ahead from The Hague, that body had no official jurisdiction in Tasmania. He wondered what else they could be charged with if it all went horribly wrong. Ric knew what else but decided not to let Jack into that little secret until it was too late to turn back.

◆

Chapter 18

Ignoring Harmonics

Dawn in the Awatere Valley produced a sublime, picture-postcard scene. Those Southwood personnel who struggled from their bunks early enough were treated briefly to a serene picture worthy of the area's national park status. Several decided to have their breakfast al fresco, though they had to improvise chairs and a table. The outdoor activity, innocent as it was, alerted The Hague observers in the nearby hills. One onlooker suggested the early start might indicate imminent activity of a more significant nature. Neither he nor the diners knew just how correct that suggestion would be.

Inside Southwood's facility, the satellite sat ominously at its prescribed location, silently waiting for its launch. Supervisor and Merlin were satisfied that their hardware was ready and took a minute to admire its stealth matte black finish. They were also happy with the programming, although both harboured a niggling doubt about the ghost coding lurking somewhere in its software. Merlin had already decided it shouldn't be a problem, but he didn't like it.

Since the lifting of Deep Sleep, the latest data had been meticulously evaluated. The next launch timeframe forecast was a 90-minute window that night. New data was being continuously received, and the window narrowed progressively. Merlin took the centre of the range and told his crew to prepare for a launch at '11:24 pm, plus or minus.'

'Another late one,' someone grumbled. Merlin ignored the complaint.

All personnel were confident that the launch hardware and all fixed facilities were ready. The lateral convergence issue had been dealt with and no wave interference was anticipated. The excitement of the timeframe announcement stimulated the launch crew, eager to see their tenth satellite off the ground. That eagerness lessened as the day proceeded with little activity. By midday, the window had decreased to 65 minutes, and one crew member started a 'book', with almost everyone betting on the launch time.

As with previous launches, primary line movement was as anticipated, with the computer forecasting no divergence. Secondary line movement fluctuated along standard deviations. The technician monitoring this told Supervisor and Merlin that, unexpectedly, tertiary lines were pulsing beyond regular phase activity. Merlin suggested that minor movement in geomagnetic field polarity may impact those lines. He was concerned that there may be a cumulative impact but kept his anxiety to himself.

One of the crew was tasked with keeping an eye on the weather. He called himself 'the meteorologist' but had no qualifications. Without asking, he provided a near-term forecast.

'Temperature tonight looks like 10 to 12 degrees, a moderate breeze from the west. No rain. Haven't had rain for a fortnight.'

Merlin didn't respond, but Supervisor nodded to the meteorologist, acknowledging his report. The weather shouldn't impact the team's efforts tonight, but they were all experienced enough to know that sometimes things happen that shouldn't.

The last 12 hours before a launch were usually quiet. The hard work had been done, emergencies were rare, and system monitoring was the only job on hand. By mid-afternoon, the launch window had narrowed to 25 minutes. Some of the crew had already lost their bets. A couple put in another $20 and a revised guess. No one anticipated problems, none that couldn't be dealt with anyway, but even the most experienced were about to be met with an issue never encountered before.

◆

While the Southwood team in New Zealand were planning the launch of Satellite 10, Jack was finalising his own scheme. By the time some launch crew gamblers revised their betting, the Domain facility raid had been organised. Jack called it Operation Derek in recognition of Derek Asquith, who started the whole thing and might have lost his life because of it.

The meeting with Keith and Diver – Jack thought it couldn't be his real name – was brief. Diver told them he was contracted to deliver goods to the Domain facility but was never paid on time, and then often with incongruous 'deductions'. There was no love lost between him and the organisation. Being undervalued, unappreciated and underpaid, he would enjoy any opportunity to get back at his ungrateful employer.

Steve's flight was arriving in 20 minutes and Jack knew it took 15 to drive there once out of his car park. Traffic was light, and he relished the clear run. There was a theoretical five-minute limit at the passenger pick-up point, and Jack spotted a stern parking attendant looking at his watch, then towards his Commodore. The attendant walked towards his car but turned back, looking for other prospective offenders, when its flashing blue lights in the rear window dissuaded him. Steve arrived at the same time, carrying a modest-sized case.

'Now there's a useful little accessory,' he said. The pair shook hands.

'One day, someone will realise the police don't use Commodores anymore, then I'll be in trouble,' Jack replied.

On the drive back to the city, Steve outlined his position. The Hague was determined to find out what Southwood's supposed data centre really was. His managers had given him carte blanche, something they always did with covert operations.

'I'm to give you every assistance, but I don't know what that will look like. I've told my people this is your gig. They seem happy with that as it gives them someone to blame if it all goes tits up.'

Jack described, in detail, how Operation Derek would pan out. Everyone was ready, knew the timetable and what was expected. His only concern was that they were amateurs playing a dangerous game. He called the group his friends in low places or the Informals, in recognition of Sherlock Holmes' Irregulars.

'There's a shift change at 20:00. I've had it watched, and there's never been any deviation. The train stops for two minutes exactly. 12 blokes get off, sometimes a few women amongst them, they go in, and 30 seconds later, the replaced crew leaves. It's always by train. I don't know what they'd do if the rail system was down for any reason. They'd have a backup plan, but the infrastructure is very efficient.

'That's our time. They won't be confused, but they won't be ready. The element of surprise. We won't go in the front door, though. My bloke said it's as good as impossible.'

Jack asked if Steve had booked a room in the same hotel. He had.

'Cancel it. I have a guest bedroom, and my place is central. Probably better we stay close for 24 hours at least.'

By the time the pair reached the city, accommodation arrangements were finalised, and Steve confessed he was ready for a decent coffee.

'Airline coffee just doesn't cut it,' he complained.

'I'll ask Angie to rectify that,' Jack replied. 'Blue Café, near my place.'

Steve surprised Jack first by ordering a double-shot almond mocha, then again by commenting on the stylish runners Angie was wearing. Jack grinned, remembering his shoe-related exchange with Leon days before. So much had happened since then, it seemed ages ago.

'My brother works in the fashion industry and thinks everyone else is fascinated by it,' Steve explained, 'so I pick up a few insights.'

The conversation returned to the real matter at hand, and by the time their late morning coffee had turned into an impromptu lunch, both had refined that evening's little soiree – as Steve called it – to the nth degree. Names, functions, equipment and times were decided. A flurry of text messages from Jack confirmed, in his mind, that the arrangements were finalised.

'These friends of yours in low places. Who are they exactly?' Steve asked.

Jack pondered for a moment. 'If you don't mind, I'll keep that list to myself. This whole thing is getting bigger than a superhero movie franchise. On the other hand, you'll meet some of them tonight anyway. But now we have some time to kill. If you want, I'll show you some of the sights.'

Unknown to either of them, Jack's Informals were making their own meticulous plans.

◆

So it was that Jack Sugarman and Steve Andrews spent a pleasant few hours visiting Hobart's popular tourist spots. The visitor was particularly taken by the view from Mount Nelson, an easy 15-minute drive from the city. A little over 350 metres above sea level, the Signal Station lookout provided spectacular views over Hobart and the River Derwent.

'You can see the King's Domain from here,' Jack pointed out. 'We'll be working on the other side, though, the river side. Might be the best night's work we ever did.'

Steve was thoughtful and said nothing for a while, then added, 'Or the worst mistake of our lives.'

'I wasn't going to suggest that, but so long as we both understand.'

The pair agreed that the afternoon seemed like the calm before a storm but turned their conversation to other matters. Each gave the other a potted biography of their lives. They had at least one thing in common, the loss of their parents while very young. Steve became an orphan aged four and had only vague memories of the two people he should have known all his life. His knowledge of them was little more than what uncles and aunts had told him and newspaper reports of the plane crash that took their lives.

As to their professional experiences, both were constrained by various secrecy and non-disclosure limitations. Such was part of their career choices, though Steve confessed he 'kind of fell into The Hague' after a brief secondment in Paris.

'I shouldn't even have mentioned Paris,' Steve said with little regret.

'Paris? What Paris? You never mentioned Paris,' Jack reassured him.

Their afternoon finished with a ferry ride to the Museum of Old and New Art, though there was no time for a visit. Having decided not to indulge in alcohol before the big event, they returned to Jack's apartment for coffee.

Jack was feeling a little uneasy about the raid. He was relying on people with more enthusiasm than expertise, and of Ric's friends, he knew nothing.

'Three hours to go. I'll text everyone and make sure everything's OK. Don't want it to fall in a heap at this stage,' Jack confessed.

That job done, and with positive replies coming in, he felt better and suggested they have an early dinner before preparing for their role.

'Crayfish?' he asked Steve.

'If that's the same as lobster, yes,' he replied with relish.

Then came a strange text from Leon, 'Lyn says watch out for the tall man.' Jack shared the warning with Steve, then forgot about it in preparation for their meal.

◆

In New Zealand, Supervisor watched a monitor and fell back in his chair. The 11:24 pm launch time was falling back. The variation allowance of 25 minutes was expanding. He alerted Merlin, but Southwood's technical expert had already spotted the anomaly, who attacked a keyboard, sending instructions to the control computer. It responded immediately. Merlin turned to his number two.

'You can scrap our launch time. It will be earlier, much earlier. Those damned tertiary lines are phasing. Big time. We're seeing geomagnetic field polarity movements and that means,' he tapped his computer monitor with a forefinger, 'that means our timetable is now very fluid. I'm not a happy man right now.'

Supervisor asked for a recommendation.

'Get someone to check for any unusual shipping reports, you know the kind of thing. And contact the Wildlife Service people. Ask about whale strandings on the west coast. That's a sure sign. Whales get confused about directions when this happens. I'm surprised no one has picked up on that yet.

'But here, I want everyone at their stations now. Launch could be anytime. Our readings now look like… well, I don't know what they look like. They keep changing, but to have a target time, take 10:30 p.m. That's rubbery, though.'

Supervisor immediately let his team know that 10:30 p.m., plus or minus, was the new launch time. He delegated the shipping reports task to the nearest team member but decided to call about whale strandings himself. It was a short call.

'The wildlife people want to know how we knew about the latest stranding event. They only heard about it five minutes ago. About 60 pilot whales stranded themselves at some place called Haast Beach. It's happened before. The last time was 2022. I told them we found it on social media. You can blame a lot on social media.'

Recent unusual shipping events produced several reports, mainly on New Zealand's west coast, all around 44 degrees south.

Merlin asked for the latitude of Haast Beach.

'43.88 south,' someone replied. 'That tells us something about, um, something.'

Merlin let the vagueness pass. Supervisor still wanted a recommendation and was told that everyone was to stay alert and at their stations. The two senior men would monitor the changing parameters presented to them. A wall-mounted monitor was set to display 22:30 with the current time beneath, both in a bold, stark typeface. Between the two, in a larger, red font, was the countdown figure to the second. The whole team watched as it changed to 40.00 – in theory, 40 minutes to go.

Someone complained, 'There goes my 20 bucks then.'

◆

Jack and Steve enjoyed their evening meal mainly in silence. They had exhausted the conversational possibilities of the mission and what they were permitted to reveal about their work. Declining the offer of dessert, in case it induced, as Jack called it, a 'post-prandial lethargy', the pair returned to his apartment to change into heavier, darker clothing. A final check of texts revealed no untoward messages.

At Battery Point, Keith's boat sat serenely beside a jetty, its owner going through his usual pre-sail check. Two vehicles pulled up at the same time. Jack and Steve arrived first, in time to greet Ric and his team, all dressed in near-military outfits. Each retrieved a small bag from the back of their SUV. Preliminaries took little time, and Ric decided that the identities of his friends should not be revealed. Jack agreed and said he wouldn't probe, and in the privacy of the boat shed, he instructed his small team.

'Anonymity is a good idea, but you need to know that this is my gig. If anything goes wrong, you can blame me. This is a brown-water campaign only for the approach. Ric has already briefed you on the on-land element. I see you're well-equipped. Planning is complete, ops are underway – you're part of that – and control is down to me and Steve here. He's my 2IC. You can take instructions from him as if they were my words. Any questions?'

Only to reassure his friends, Ric asked about the escape plan. Keith outlined his role, to deliver them all to the Cornelian Bay access jetty and to wait for their extraction. He used the word 'extraction' with a degree of pride as if he'd done this kind of thing before. He hadn't.

A voice behind a ski mask asked, simply, 'Timeframe?'

Jack described the 20:00 shift change process and that Keith would have them on the jetty precisely at 20:02. He confessed that he couldn't tell how long the raid would take. It would depend on what they found and how difficult negotiating the facility would be. As to equipment, 'Ric?'

Ric patted his black bag, 'In hand, Jack, all in hand.'

Keith butted in. 'OK, guys. This trip at 10 knots will take 13 minutes. I did the run yesterday to check. If you'd care to make yourselves comfortable as far forward as possible, we'll take you on a pleasant trip to Cornelian Bay. I'll skip the safety talk unless anyone insists.'

No one insisted. Under a cloudless night sky, the near-full moon provided a serene view of the river, with countless lights on both shores defining the river banks. On any other boat, at any other time, the passengers of *Cirrhosis of the River* might be enjoying just such a pleasant river cruise with a glass of wine and finger food. Ric's friends spent a few minutes each checking the contents of their bags, something they'd already done several times.

There was almost no traffic on the water – 'There never is, this time of night,' Keith said – and the short journey took the 13 minutes anticipated.

At 20:00, the scheduled light rail service arrived at Norton Halt. As always, 12 passengers alighted and quickly entered Vilin IV. A minute later, 12 others exited, all clad in their blue-grey uniforms, boarded the train, and it left the station. By 20:02, the shift change was complete, efficiently and effectively. At the same time, Keith tied up his boat and discharged the small band of passengers to begin their precarious mission.

Jack led the group up a gently sloping concrete pathway towards the facility's main entrance. Upon crossing the rail line, the dimly lit station looked utilitarian and uninviting. He guessed that was intentional to dissuade casual visits; most stations boasted neatly tended gardens.

Ric, alarmed, pointed out the security camera above the entrance.

'Well spotted. What you haven't spotted is a drone, about 20 metres up, over the water.'

Ric looked to where Jack pointed. 'I can't see… oh yeah, there it is. Pretty quiet. What gives?'

Jack explained. 'My mate Frank is a drone aficionado. He's around somewhere doing his remote pilot thing. That drone is fitted with a laser and effectively blinds the camera. And a sonic beam is playing havoc with the microphone. One of his mates is doing the same to the camera over the loading dock entrance. And I expect some poor security bloke is wondering what the hell is going on. It gives us time. Let's go.'

The group made short work of the 120-metre trip to the loading area after leaving the main entrance. Here, they were met by Harry and Diver, both relieved to see their colleagues. Jack made the briefest of introductions.

'Guys, Harry here is my tech expert. Diver is our means of entry, a disgruntled… I suppose you'd say, contractor for this crowd. Thanks for being here, you two. It'd be a short party without you. Time for your contribution, Diver.'

Diver stepped forward, entered a six-digit number on the control panel, and presented his thumbprint to the panel that revealed itself.

A featureless voice demanded 'Status?'

'Mutton, Denis, unscheduled delivery,' Diver replied. Harry looked at him as the door slid open.

'Denis Mutton?' he asked.

'A proud Cornish name,' he said.

Jack thanked Diver and suggested, 'You better disappear for a week or so.'

'Yeah, I'm off. You have 40 seconds to get in. Press and hold the green button when you want to leave. It takes three seconds to activate. Good luck. I'm on a flight tomorrow heading for…'

'No, stop,' Jack interrupted, 'it's better we don't know.'

Diver left, his effort providing revenge for his poor treatment by Southwood. He would be enjoying the sun and surfing Queensland's Gold Coast tomorrow.

Steve had studied the site plans thoroughly and led the way.

'These two doors are to storage areas. We need the third one. Ric, your area, I think.'

Ric nodded and led his three friends to the door, but not before handing Jack, Steve and Harry a gas mask.

'You'll want these,' he said before pressing and holding the door's green button.

It opened obediently, and Ric's colleagues threw three small cylinders into the large room. They instantly discharged a thick, white vapour, which quickly cleared. The security man was on his way to the door but didn't make it, slumping to the floor.

'Don't ask me about those. It's classified,' Ric said.

Jack was curious.

'Classified by who?'

'That's classified too. But it's a pretty efficient concoction, near immediate effect, and becomes inert in three minutes, some reaction to oxygen they say. Anyone in that room will be unconscious now. Air conditioning will take care of anyone else pretty quickly. We can take these off in two minutes.'

Harry asked if the people now slumped at their workstations would be OK. Ric assured him they'd be out for a few hours and wake up with a severe thirst and a slight headache. 'No more than that.' Harry located and disabled the internal security cameras for 90 minutes. Two minutes later, the team removed their gas masks.

With no personnel to impede any investigation, Harry moved to what he decided was the master control computer. It was still active. With Steve's help, he relocated the previous operator and took over the keyboard.

A minute later, he made reassuring noises. 'This looks familiar,' he said, 'pretty standard stuff. I hate to say it, but it looks like ordinary data control software. Let me look at...' he didn't finish the sentence but made fewer reassuring noises. 'Sorry guys, this is all very garden-variety data. It's a legit data centre. Oh, and I've deactivated the cameras.'

Jack and Steve looked disappointed until Harry stood up suddenly, exclaiming, 'There must be another part to this. Look around. We saw 12 guys change shifts, and there are only six here, seven if you count the security dude.'

Steve consulted his floor plan and pointed to a blank section of the wall towards the back of the room on the gantry level. On it in seconds, he determined that, far from being part of the wall, it was a door. Clever design and intentionally dim lighting made it unrecognisable at a casual glance. Another thumbprint panel, well hidden, resumed Jack's disappointment, and he regretted sending Diver away so soon. His thumb might be needed again. Steve had other ideas.

'We need that bloke's thumb,' he said, pointing to the figure now slumped near the workstation Harry had taken over.

'Why him?' Jack asked.

'He's senior.'

'How do you know that?'

'I know that because, one, he was at this particular terminal, and two, he's wearing expensive shoes. I told you I picked up a few insights into the fashion industry, didn't I?'

Ric and one of his friends manhandled the unconscious man, somewhat indelicately and scuffing his expensive shoes in the process, to the thumbprint panel. Luckily, no 'Status?' voice confirmation was demanded, and the door slid open. Here, the remaining personnel were as asleep as their colleagues who copped the initial gassing.

Harry immediately sat at one of the workstations. Its operator was conveniently away from his station when Ric's gas found its way through the air conditioning ducts. He was slumped by a wall in a puddle of coffee, a mug still in his hand.

'This is more like it,' Harry said, 'Much better. Look, Jack, this is satellite tracking data. Real-time, by the looks of it. And an energy reading, well, several. Some odd sequencing here. Oh, this is really cool stuff. Geomagnetic measurements; don't know what that's for. Give me a few minutes, and I'll suss it out.'

While Harry investigated the centre's darker operations, Ric and his friends checked their victims for injuries. There were none, and, surprisingly to Jack, they made each one as comfortable as they could lying on the hard floor. They would wake up uninjured, at least. Steve was busy photographing the entire layout, careful not to include any of his team in shots. With these and a technical briefing from Harry, The Hague finally would have an insight into Southwood's capabilities.

Harry looked for a connection to the computer. There were no USB ports.

'This one's been modified. No obvious access. On the other hand, this headphone jack might not be a headphone jack. There has to be a diagnostic or maintenance port somewhere.'

He rummaged in his bag, retrieved a cable and connected it to an electronic device, which in turn was cabled to a small hard drive. After a flurry of keystrokes and more reassuring noises, Harry had access and started downloading files.

'This will take a while, he said, 'but help me with this, will you?'

He was looking at radio transmission equipment. No one noticed the supposedly unconscious tall man crawling across the floor.

'Not my field, but I'm guessing this mob doesn't rely on online technology alone. Anyone here know radio stuff? I don't recognise some of it.'

One of Ric's team members revealed he was a communications man with the army – he didn't say whose army – and sauntered over.

Steve stood by and asked for a rundown on the gear.

'Bog standard, mostly. Mundane but top quality. This though, this is different.' He gently stroked one of the sets with an approving hand.

'SINGCARS. Definitely. Single Channel Ground and Airborne Radio System. It uses frequencies reserved for military use, but there's plenty of spectrum chaos around these days. No respect.'

'Yes, but what's it for?' Harry asked.

'Comms for ground and air platforms; voice and data. But hang on.'

He removed the unit's casing with a practised hand and examined the interior.

'There it is. Thought so. Modified. See that?'

Harry said yes but had no idea what he was supposed to see.

'You don't see many of these. That's a Petrikas booster, that is. They could reach satellites with this. We used three of these in – oh, never mind where – three of these to triangulate satellite positions. Part of the relocation gear. Top stuff. Can I keep it?'

Ric said nothing was to leave the premises. His friend said 'Shame' and replaced the casing. Harry returned to his downloading task and told Jack he had everything he needed, though he would happily spend hours there.

The tall man had reached a desk and was groggily trying to retrieve a phone.

'Your baby now,' Ric's colleague said, handing the hard drive to Steve. 'I can tell you they have a centralised computer system. This isn't it, but it's linked. Anyway, who doesn't have a CCS these days? I expect they have system protection and continuous backup, but making it centralised, well, a single point of control can also mean a single point of failure. We, or perhaps you, need to find where that is.'

He was looking at Jack, who, in turn, looked at Steve.

'Are we done? The less time we spend here, the better.'

Steve agreed and, looking at the newly acquired hard drive, said, 'Yes, let's went. Better leave the way we came in, just in case. Wait. Ric. There.'

Ric spotted the tall man and rushed over, knocked the phone from his hand, and applied a Jiu-Jitsu chokehold. The restriction of blood to the brain rendered him unconscious. Ric again laid his victim comfortably on the floor and looked at the phone.

'That was close. No call made. One in 10,000 aren't affected by this gas. Just our luck to find a freak on their payroll. Let's get the flock out of here, as the shepherd said.'

Jack silently thanked Leon and Lyn for the warning and wished he'd paid more attention.

The disparate group's departure was considerably more straightforward than its arrival. The three-second press of the green button opened the loading dock door, and in less than a minute, they were back on the jetty. Keith was waiting with his boat's engine idling. Jack was last aboard as he waited to send a text message to Frank. In three minutes, his drone pilot would switch off the laser and sonic beam and hit a 'return to base' button. The pilot's associate would do the same with the second drone. In four minutes, both would be gone, their job done.

The return boat ride was enjoyed by all aboard, everyone satisfied with their evening's work. Jack and Steve thanked them all. Ric's men had removed their ski masks, each now confident that their new-found colleagues would preserve their anonymity. They were, after all, now partners in crime.

As they separated, Ric and his team headed for a bar.

'It's an old-fashioned pub,' he said, 'You can walk in and just order "a beer". No size, no style, no fancy craft stuff. You just get a 10-ounce draught.'

It was 21:12. The raid had taken little more than an hour. Harry made a confession.

'I was checking some of the coding, but back end. Found something interesting. Some software writers like to sign their work. It's harmless and pointless, but I was looking for something in particular.'

'And?' Jack demanded.

'And I found a chunk of ghost coding. Always well hidden unless you know how to look for it. I know what it does, but not what it's for. But it was signed.'

This time, Steve jumped in.

'Signed?'

'Signed "Peace and love, Brother Ringo."'

Steve smiled.

◆

Southwood's Awatere Valley team were on edge. They were used to precision, and there was nothing precise about Satellite 10's launch timing. The building's roof was open, and focussing equipment was humming in standby mode. Everyone had already triple-checked their control units. The wall display read 22:30, their rubbery launch time. The red countdown changed to green, and the count started up rather than down. There was a murmur across the floor.

'Settle down, team,' Supervisor said. 'We anticipated this possibility.'

At that moment, his monitor revealed a new forecast from the AI computer. With millions of measurements at its disposal, it deduced that a magma movement had been blocked and doubled back on itself, creating a diamagnetic vortex fluctuation. That fluctuation would cause a pulse providing the lift for ASatX. It wasn't the energy source expected, but it would do the job.

Merlin was reading the same message and reset the launch clock reading to 22:39, seven minutes away.

'Stay alert, everyone,' he ordered. 'Supervisor, advise Mr Southwood. He's still in Hobart. And contact Vilin IV. I want them to monitor this.'

Supervisor sent a brief message to their boss in Hobart and opened a line to Vilin IV. There was no response. It was 20:40 in Hobart, and Jack's raid was still in progress, with all Southwood personnel sleeping uncomfortably on the floor. There would be no reply from them for at least two hours. Supervisor followed protocol and tried to contact the centre's security man. He was as unresponsive as the others. A detailed message to Vilin V in Victoria advised that unit should take over the monitoring function.

Merlin tapped into the Domain facility's internal closed-circuit camera system. With every part of the complex visible, he counted 13 bodies scattered on various floors. He couldn't tell if they were dead or unconscious, and the three small canisters he saw could deliver a tranquilliser or a more deadly nerve agent. That could wait, though, and wasn't his concern anyway. The issue at hand was the imminent launch.

A technician observed, aloud for Merlin's benefit, that data migration was slowing. Supervisor suggested it would be class two data only, non-essential to the present operation, but indicated it was 'a programmed buffering deceleration to allow priority analysis computing.'

Merlin was impressed.

'I concur. Trace it. Might be something else entirely. But don't lose sight of our priority here.'

At 22:43, an emotionless computer-generated androgynous voice announced, 'Optimal conditions imminent.' It repeated the declaration twice. Technicians rearranged themselves in their chairs, ready for any and all activity.

Merlin proclaimed, 'We're in the lap of the gods now, not that I believe… you know, figure of speech. Release launch locks.'

The same artificial voice spoke again, 'Launch in progress.' A delicate tone was repeated at half-second intervals.

Everyone knew this meant the satellite would leave the premises within seconds. There would be no exhaust or noise, only a curious vertical light reaching no one knew how high. Merlin thought this was caused by molecular excitation of the atmosphere. Around the satellite, the light appeared red but faded to white above the roofline. It would dissipate quickly.

Satellite 10 left its launch platform as expected. There were a few half-hearted cheers from the technicians, but they knew it wasn't over yet. Supervisor frowned at two seated men high-fiving each other but made no protest.

The half-second tones stopped, replaced by a continuous sound of the same frequency. This indicated the ground station's launch activity had concluded. It stopped after 30 seconds.

From their vantage point, still undiscovered by Southwood, The Hague recorded the event with multiple video cameras and took technical readings. The launch speed was phenomenal, and, as before, the visual record produced only a few seconds of useful footage. From previous experience, The Hague's technicians had learned to observe the course by detecting the satellite's wake. High-level clouds conveniently provided an image of where the craft had been, if not of the device itself. For these ground observers, the vertical beam of light protruding through the clouds was the only evidence that anything unusual had occurred.

Neither The Hague nor Southwood knew that deep beneath the Earth's surface, the strange circumstances that produced launch conditions were throwing that launch into chaos. A secondary but simultaneous energy grid event was disrupting the plans of even Southwood's AI computations. Immediately after launch, the satellite's vertical trajectory was corrupted. It would not park itself in the projected orbit. That would take some time to rectify. The Awatere Valley technicians' day was not over yet.

Annoyed at ignoring the harmonics element, Merlin contacted Mr Southwood in Hobart and briefed him on the launch. They discussed the ramifications dispassionately. It was only business, after all, although an expensive one.

Ten minutes later, Mr Southwood called his local security man.

'What's the latest assessment of Sugarman?'

The security analyser was ready for his question.

'We're still watching, but my resources have been reduced recently. Up till two hours ago, there's been virtually no activity. Deep Sleep worked its magic there, I think. He has proven unexpectedly competent, but we still rate his threat level as "potential," with only low impact. More a nuisance than anything. He knows almost nothing and probably understands even less. His team is too small to be dangerous but too big to be ignored. The closer we get to Dragonfly implementation, the less of a danger he can be. It's a watching brief, unless you want something done.'

'No. No action yet. We don't want any unnecessary attention at this stage.'

He dialled another number, his liaison Carl Lehmann.

'Lehmann? Southwood. I want you to get to the Domain facility tomorrow, 0400 hours. Yes, I know it's early. That's when the morning shift gets there. Take a couple of security people with you. There's been an incident. I want a full report. Be here at 0600. I'll buy you breakfast.'

He rang off without the usual courtesy.

◆

Jack and Steve were mentally tired after the evening's exertions, slight as they had been physically. A restorative cocktail at a waterfront restaurant's bar partially revived the pair, but they decided not to follow Ric's teams' lead with a night out. Steve needed to upload the hard drive to his masters in Melbourne, which could be done from Jack's apartment. That data, at least, was something he didn't need to evaluate. He'd be briefed in due course.

'You'll need a glass of red to do that properly,' Jack suggested. 'I have a decent Rhone I've been saving for a data uploading evening.

The wine is just as impressive as the label, something that doesn't always happen.'

'Of course you have. I always have a Rhone red on hand for such occasions,' Steve quipped, adding that if there was a satisfactory pizza outlet nearby, that might speed up the process. Jack made the catering arrangements, and Steve set about his task, monitoring progress between slices of meat-lovers pizza and sips of Domaine Richaud.

While his new friend was occupied, Jack phoned Sarah. He felt guilty for not calling earlier but realised she hadn't called him either. The old times when only men took such initiatives were very much old times. His guilt was dismissed.

Sarah was chatty and seemed happy. Her work, particularly D.I. Sayer, was still keeping her busy. There was talk of a promotion, working with ISCU, the Incorrectly Solved Crimes Unit.

Jack steered the conversation to their relationship, at which point Steve considerately moved to the guest bedroom, taking a topped-up glass of wine with him.

'Any regrets,' Jack asked, trying to sound nonchalant.

'Not a one, you?'

'Same, when this Southwood thing is over, I hope we can spend more time together.'

Sarah was silent for a moment.

'You remind me of an old boyfriend,' she said.

'Is that a good thing?'

'Yes and no. I lost him years ago. I've avoided relationships since then. I don't want to lose you too.'

It was Jack's turn to hesitate.

'You don't remind me of anyone,' he admitted.

'Bad thing?' she asked.

'No. You're rare, and I don't want to lose you either.'

'Well, we better not get lost then, huh?'

Their conversation was a pleasant distraction and continued for several more minutes. Eventually, Steve opened the door of his guest room and peered out.

Jack took the hint and ended his call with a promise not to leave the next one for so long.

'Data uploaded,' Steve said. 'I've been on the blower, and our tech guys are as excited as tech guys get. Shiny started blathering on about stuff way over my head. I left them to it.'

'Shiny? One of your assets?' Jack asked.

'Shiny Springfield. The opposite of Dusty. I guess he can't sing. He's new. And we don't call our people assets; that's a Hollywood thing. But now, I'm going to call it a day. It's been a doozy.'

Jack insisted on a nightcap, a 'rather fine Rutherglen muscat.'

◆

Chapter 19

Ghost Coding Activated

Carl Lehmann presented himself to Mr Southwood's hotel reception promptly at 6:00 a.m. the next day, having inspected the Domain facility at 4:00 a.m., as instructed. Told he was expected, Lehmann took the lift and, with some reluctance, knocked on the ornate door. Southwood opened it quickly and beckoned in his guest. He was on a call, speaking fluent German. The call terminated, and Southwood appeared annoyed and frustrated.

'That was Berlin. I was briefing them on what I know, which is whatever Vilin V could determine from tapping into IV's CCTV. Sit down. I'll make a few statements. You confirm or deny. One, the security cameras appear to be working, correct?' he asked.

'Correct, they're operating fine,' Lehmann confirmed.

'Two, all personnel were knocked out by some nerve agent.'

'Yes, they're OK now, though.'

'Not important. Three, no hardware was removed.'

'Correct. No damage or modifications either.'

'Four, apart from our 13 people, there is no evidence of anyone having entered the facility.'

'Well, yes, but absence of evidence isn't...'

'Isn't evidence of absence, yes, I've read the book. What can you add? Be concise.'

Lehmann suspected where this was leading.

'The timing of whatever happened seems to have been pretty precise. At 8:00, the new shift was in; at 8:02, the old shift was out and gone. And that's when the cameras went down. Audio too. None of the entrance security was tampered with. My conclusion is that it was an inside job, but it's curious.'

Lehmann paused, and Southwood pounced.

'I said be concise, not dramatic. What's curious?'

'We found no evidence of data transmission after 8:02, nothing. No radio activity either. And there were no additional laptops, hard drives or memory sticks found. Bottom line is we don't know what the plan was. Possibly, it was something that all went wrong.'

'Or was just abandoned,' Southwood suggested.

He revealed that he had ordered an urgent HR review of the 8:00 p.m. shift personnel, including the security man. In the organisation, such reviews often ended badly for the individuals concerned.

Lehmann didn't comment, but after more discussion about filling any vacancies at the Domain facility, he changed the subject to the breakfast he'd been offered. Mr Southwood slid a spare pass key across the table.

'The dining room on level 9 is for guests only. This will give you access. I won't join you. Leave the key at reception when you leave.'

That was all the 'goodbye and thanks' Lehmann was to get. As he left, determined to select the most expensive breakfast possible, he heard his boss make another call. Once again, he was speaking German.

It was a long morning for Mr Southwood. One phone call immediately followed another until, eventually, he contacted Merlin in New Zealand . With the 10 satellites launched, he and his upper echelon in the organisation wanted a demonstration. What's more, they wanted it immediately.

Merlin was stunned.

'I wouldn't advise it, Sir. Repositioning and calibration are still underway. Auxiliary Satellite 10 is yet to be parked in its correct orbit. The AI refined some programming, too. We're looking at that for efficiency compliance. Then we want to do some beta testing to...'

'Just do it, Merlin, let me know when it's in place,' he insisted.

Supervisor was listening and just shook his head. Both knew it wasn't done to say no to a direct order from Mr Southwood, indeed any Mr Southwood. Merlin also knew they now needed to accelerate the satellite's orbit placement and analyse the revised AI programming.

'AI is all well and good,' he told his colleague, 'but I'd rather have a handle on it. I can delay the "immediate" by 15 minutes. Tops. Even our esteemed leaders know these things aren't as simple as pressing a button,' he said.

The pair discussed the issue at length, instructed staff on what they needed to do and, with the desperation that drives individuals, made themselves strong black coffee. After some deep thought, Merlin asked about their second AI computer. This was an off-grid experiment that had been shelved a few weeks before. With some hurried preparation, it could be fed the data the first AI computer was processing without being connected to the primary unit. It might give them an alternative strategy.

The first AI computer was called Brian for no reason anyone could remember. The second was Sophia, from a Greek name meaning wisdom, but also a tribute to its programmer. Merlin decided the fastest way to get Sophia up to speed was to link it, or 'her', to Brian. Merlin spoke and worked at the same time, partly for Supervisor's benefit but mostly his own. It was a case of working it out as he went along. Finally, he explained his logic.

'When the data is shared, both computers will analyse it separately. If I've got this right, they would then communicate to identify and evaluate options to achieve optimal configuration of commands to SatX. We can then upload commands to Dragonfly. It's an interesting exercise: two AIs working on the same problem. I don't know anyone who's done it before.

'The danger, or perhaps the genius, is that they were programmed differently. Brian is a solid, logical, data-grounded thinking machine, pretty well immovable once a result is in. Sophia is different. If her programming is anything like the programmer – I met her a few times – she'll use data for sure but will "think up the left", whatever that means, and be an irresistible force. I'm watching this with as much hope as expectation.'

Supervisor remained silent. Merlin was the expert on these matters, but he had one thought.

'You know what happens when an irresistible force meets an immovable object, don't you?' he asked.

'Hmm, what?'

'Oh, the woman always wins.'

Merlin laughed out loud at his own joke. Almost as an afterthought, he asked Supervisor when and where the next energy grid event would likely occur.

'I've been monitoring that. It won't be near us. Vilin XII will be the nearest station. We've hacked into the American tsunami detection submersibles, and there's some curious activity near Japan. Our sound recordings indicate a shallow focus intraplate event building. Not a strong one, but enough energy for Dragonfly to capture if we can relocate in time. Maybe tomorrow.'

'That might give us time,' Merlin conceded, 'but only just. I'm still not convinced Auxiliary Satellite 10 will be in place correctly. I'll alert Mr Southwood. He'll have to be happy with that. It's the price on the box.'

They decided against warning that the demonstration, whenever it might occur, should be regarded as experimental, not tactical. Both men then relaxed a little. Their crisis was not over, but it was more or less under control.

◆

While the two senior men in the Awatere Valley were dealing with their demonstration crisis, Jack had a crisis of his own. D.I. Sayer, with a sombre-looking police constable in tow, called at his apartment, none too pleased with having to be 'let in' to the building. He wasn't used to barriers.

Jack offered him coffee.

'This isn't a social call,' Sayer replied, 'this is more serious. There was a raid at the Domain Data Centre last night. Very expertly done, so I don't think you had anything to do with it.'

'Thanks very much,' Jack retorts with mock outrage. 'Why the visit then?'

'My superiors think I should pull you in straight away. They seem to think you had a hand in it somewhere, something about motive. Convince me we shouldn't have this conversation at the station,' Sayer demanded.

Jack sighed. He suspected their previous professional relationship, one of mutual tolerance at best, was reasserting itself. The budding comradeship seemed to have been abandoned by the detective inspector, with his official duties retaking centre stage. He tried to remember if he'd mentioned the raid to Sarah the previous evening. He hadn't.

'Well, I confess I heard a little about it. I hear a little about many things and a lot about a few things. But what I don't know is a longer list than what I do know. This event, sorry, I can't help you. It wasn't my party, and I wasn't invited. I was here all night with Steve. I can show you the pizza boxes and wine bottles. You know Steve from The Hague? He's investigating the disappearance of your commissioner. Any news there? Some things I hear nothing about.'

Deftly deflecting the subject at hand, Sayer confessed the commissioner's whereabouts was being dealt with 'upstairs', but he was entirely in the dark. Steve was out at this time, and Jack considered it prudent not to mention that he was a house guest.

'But never mind him,' Sayer continued, 'this raid thing has landed on my desk, and you're a person of interest. Yes, we use that expression. I can't place you at the scene, and I'm not saying you've lied to me, but I think you've denied me the truth.'

Jack asked who had nominated him for the person of interest moniker and with what evidence.

'Information received, you needn't concern yourself with that.'

'Look, of course, I'd cooperate if I could, but there's not much I can tell you. I'll give you one name, though. Southwood. That's an organisation and an individual. Well, individuals, plural. You already know about them. My information received, please don't ask from whence it came,' – again he effected his thumb and forefinger gesture – 'is that Southwood is about to launch something on the world which may be benevolent and may be not. I'm pretty sure it's not. Your people 'upstairs', if they don't know about it, bloody well should. Ask them, not me, I'm only trying to help, but without the resources your lot can muster, shit, I can only do so much.'

Jack was surprised at his rising anger and realised it wasn't helping his case. On the other hand, self-righteous resentment might have the opposite effect. The detective inspector seemed to be placated.

'All right, Jack, settle down. I have no solid evidence that you had anything to do with this raid. Just following orders. You know how it works. The data centre's cameras were knocked out for the duration, don't know how yet, so we have no vision. No sound either. It was a professional job, beyond your expertise, no offence. If you hear anything, you let me know.'

Jack promised to do that and, as an afterthought, asked about the well-being of the centre personnel. Sayer reported, in a disinterested manner, that they were OK, aside from slight headaches.

'One curious thing, the security man has disappeared. No lead on him.'

Jack suggested he may have joined the commissioner, wherever he was. Sayer grimaced.

'You sure you don't want coffee before you go?' Jack asked, making no effort to look like he wanted his visitors' stay to continue.

The police constable looked disappointed as Sayer declined, and they both left. A few minutes later, Steve returned , saying he'd spotted the police car nearby, presumed 'it was a sign', and waited till it was driven away. He'd been meeting with yet another Hague agent and discussing the data on the hard drive that Harry had provided.

'I think your Harry deserves a medal of some kind. The stuff he scored is priceless. We now have more than an inkling of what Southwood is up to. We have a conflict of opinions, internally that is. On the face of it, this organisation intends to be a legitimate, almost benign energy provider to the world. But underneath all that, it's a criminal organisation with a very rotten history.

'Oh, one small advancement. The Bureau now accepts that Mr Southwood can refer to any of a couple of dozen senior operatives worldwide. With all our precautions, I've been thinking that Diver is the only one who can be identified. We used his thumbprint and his voice. Is he OK where he is?'

'I'd considered that,' Jack answered. 'We don't know where he is, and I reckon he's savvy enough not to travel under his real name. Anyway, hopefully, this whole thing will be over in a week. Maybe less.'

The pair discussed what their next steps would be. After The Hague had completed analysing its newly-acquired data, it would liaise with the local police and what Steve vaguely called 'other authorities'. Their input was on pause, though. Jack thought his personal contribution might be coming to an end.

◆

In the Sea of Japan , two ships of the Chinese Navy were monitoring exercises being carried out by the navies of Japan, South Korea and the USA. The manoeuvres were interrupted by intermittent onboard electrical malfunctions. There was a flurry of radio messages between the Chinese and US captains, each accusing the other of sabotage. No one knew they were in the middle of a wide area experiencing an anomalous energy grid event. A handful of cooks wondered why their microwave ovens stopped working.

On the west coast of Japan, the Vilin XII staff, led by Mahoutsukai (Wizard) and Kantoku (Director), carefully scrutinised the energy readings. The interior of their facility, near Murakami, was meticulous, embracing the Japanese '5S' principle – sort, set in order, shine, standardise, and sustain. Staff were clad in uniforms, almost military in appearance and functionality. If Southwood was inclined to appreciate and recognise such inconsequential matters, Vilin XII would take a 'neatest facility' award.

The Japanese equivalents of Merlin and Supervisor observed the data being downloaded from the nearest Southwood satellite. With polished procedures and advanced technology at their disposal, efficiency was assured. Having been briefed by Vilin V in Victoria, they were pleased to see the system working as planned. Fortuitously, the enormous Dragonfly satellite, referred to locally as Kuro Kishi, or Black Knight, didn't need to modify its orbit much and would soon be in optimal position.

'Tonbo esayari,' Kantoku said soon after. The expression was translated to 'Dragonfly feeding' and transmitted to Vilin V and the Awatere Valley facility.

No one outside Southwood knew that the Sea of Japan was experiencing an unusual occurrence. Magma movements and the expected shallow focus intraplate movement produced gravitational pressure points deep below the crust. By a process little understood, that kinetic energy became electrical energy. Most of it, impervious to gravity, dissipated into space, lost forever. But for three hours , Southwood's satellite, with its 300-metre 'wings' expanded to the so-called isosceles circle, harvested the planet's gift. The giant array of receptors did its job in that short time, even at 40,000 kilometres above the Earth's surface.

When the event had run its course, Dragonfly's energy banks held enough electricity to power a sizable city for a year. All Vilin centres had access to the data. The tenth satellite's positioning appeared to have been corrected in time. By agreement with Mr Southwood in Hobart, Merlin and Supervisor at the Awatere Valley facility had assumed control of this exercise and were congratulated.

The Japanese, South Korean and US navies resumed their program on the Sea of Japan, and China continued to shadow. Its flagship received a message from the USS *Nixon*, 'We didn't do anything wrong and promise not to do it again.' A few minutes later, the *Nixon* captain received an unexpected and humorous response in English, 'It seems our dragons got a bit excited. Have a nice day.'

'We might get a bonus,' the New Zealand Supervisor suggested.

Merlin shook his head.

'Not likely,' he said, 'the next part of this demonstration is a power transmission to one of our test receivers. There's only one ready in the northern hemisphere, in England.'

He consulted a report.

'Bridsal-on-Slade. Ha, didn't even have to buy anyone there. Socialist council. Mugs.'

It would take several hours for Dragonfly to be repositioned. That suited Merlin as he wanted a more detailed analysis of the recent activity from Japan. He also instructed Supervisor to review the relationship between Brian and Sophia, the AI computers. Their interaction seemed to be digital cooperation, but each had delegated or adopted specific tasks, not something their handlers had anticipated.

◆

Steve spent an instructive hour on another video call with management and technical people of the International Co-operative Strategic Defence and Security Alliance Bureau, The Hague. He briefed Jack.

'It seems there's some activity in Japan. Sea of Japan, to be precise. That's an hour behind us. There are some naval exercises happening, some of our allies with China rattling sabres in the background. We're monitoring some strange goings on in the ocean, and note I said "in", not "on". A deep ocean tsunami detector sent up what the boffins call anomalous readings. There was no quake as such, but something moved under the crust.

'There's a Southwood facility on Honshu, but we couldn't figure out what they were doing, if anything. Anyway, that's incidental. Our people have been scanning the obvious spots for this Dragonfly satellite, even using other satellites. That took some doing.

'We found nothing. Their stealth technology is good, very good. But one of our blokes had an idea. If we can't find something we know is there, we'll look for the absence of something else we know *is* there. Noise. Well, what would be noise if anyone could hear it in space. There's a lot of clatter hitting us from other stars, other galaxies, and the space in between.

'We have every available radio telescope on the planet – that took some doing too, I can tell you – scanning the heavens. The trouble is, we have to work fast when we find it. It's probably nomadic, you know, not in a fixed orbit. Anyway, that's in the hands of others. My orders are to find something a little easier. Mr Southwood. He's right under our noses, according to, well, never mind who. But here in Hobart. My people are contacting hotels and whatnot, but he might be in private accommodation.'

Jack listened intently and let Steve deliver his news.

'And here's me thinking we might have a day off in *Zurich* tomorrow,' he said.

Steve raised an eyebrow.

'My weekender. It's not far away. Maybe the day after.'

Steve's eyebrow was still raised when a text message came through. The eyebrow maintained its upward attitude and appeared to attain even more height. One of his colleagues had located their target at the Dunkley Point Hotel. He had checked in as Mr Southwood. Two agents were assigned to follow their target and report activity, particularly if he left the hotel premises.

The pair discussed the ramifications of this bombshell. They had a Southwood facility's vital data, they'd located the organisation's resident superior, and they would soon, hopefully, know where the Dragonfly satellite was. They did have two problems, though. First, The Hague had no jurisdiction in Tasmania, so an arrest was out of the question, and Jack had no jurisdiction anywhere. Second, they had no evidence that the local Mr Southwood was responsible for the kidnapping of Derek and Lyn.

They would soon have a third problem.

◆

The mighty Dragonfly satellite was soon in a geostationary orbit over England's midlands. Bridsal-on-Slade's energy provider had been alerted. Its technicians were preparing their receiving equipment and establishing a safety zone. Only personnel with dedicated functions were permitted within 500 metres of the site.

At the prescribed time, remote access was granted to Southwood, and the local technicians sat back and waited. They had little time to wait. Within seconds, Southwood's far-field radiative wireless energy transmission technology brought Bridsal's power banks to life. It started slowly as the equipment self-calibrated for optimal transfer. As the rate increased, some technicians were alarmed by the loud humming and rising temperatures indicated on their gauges.

'Do we have a kill switch?' one asked.

The senior man shook his head.

'It's in Southwood's control now,' then a few seconds later reassured his colleagues, 'there you go.'

The transfer rate slowed. The noise decreased, and temperatures retreated from the gauges' redlines.

With the process satisfactorily underway, Merlin, in the Awatere Valley, smiled broadly.

'Perhaps we'll get a bonus after all. Allow all Vilin centres access to telemetry.'

Supervisor complied with a few keystrokes.

This is what Brother Ringo was waiting for. Those few keystrokes activated his ghost coding in Satellite 10. The concealed software was immediately replicated in the other nine satellites and Dragonfly, and telemetry was now accessible to The Hague. Its technicians overcame their initial astonishment at this digital windfall and began analysing. One wondered what other surprises their tame hacker would present.

At midday, in the English midlands, a local council approved their energy provider's request to lower its electricity prices by 60% for 12 months.

'There'll be votes in that,' one councillor suggested.

Another, with a more altruistic attitude, said it might attract new industry to the area.

In Hobart and the Awatere Valley, the players in this operation separately agreed it had been a 'full-on' day. The New Zealand Southwood team was advised that the demonstration had been well received, but a second was necessary. It took little time for Supervisor to identify another suitable energy grid event, but suggested it should be managed by Vilin XX in Argentina. Mr Southwood accepted the suggestion and instructed Merlin to brief the Purmamarca team and then dismantle the Awatere Valley facility. Their work was done.

A long-prepared statement from Southwood was sent to the British Prime Minister, the Minister for the Armed Forces, MI5 and 6, GCHQ, and other security organisations. It was also sent to The Hague and the world's news agencies. With some blanks recently filled in, the statement outlined what had just happened to benefit the Bridsal-on-Slade energy provider and the community it served. Southwood was at pains to point out this was done solely at its own expense. It was, the organisation claimed, a wholly philanthropic exercise that would be replicated worldwide, courtesy of several anonymous billionaire benefactors. There was no return address.

Steve received a lengthy text, which he shared with Jack.

'Another universal remote situation,' he said. 'Changes everything.'

In his apartment, Jack looked at his watch.

'It's gone beer o'clock,' he proclaimed, retrieving two Weihenstephaner wheat beers from his fridge and a pair of Erdinger glasses from a cupboard.

'Sorry about the mismatch, but it makes no difference to the beer. What is different now is this power thing. Free electricity sounds nice but there's no such thing as a free lunch, is there?'

Steve agreed. He received another text message.

'Shit, our local Mr Southwood has left the state. Gave our blokes the slip, somehow. That's a problem. As to a free lunch, how about dinner, my shout? I'm on expenses, after all. Then you better call Sarah, or you'll be in big trouble, my friend.'

◆

Chapter 20

Free Electricity

With the Hobart Mr Southwood having left the state, an equivalent would oversee the second demonstration event and chose to do this from anywhere in the same time zone as Argentina. The Southwood team at their facility near Purmamarca was basking in their new role and started preparations. The crew had no experience with energy grid events at the nearby Salinas Grandes, a 5,000 square-kilometre salt flat, but they knew it had a history. The resident Qulla people regarded the salt pan as *un lugar de extrañeza*, a place of strangeness. Much to the annoyance of at least two Southwood technicians, the locals would not clarify that strangeness. They were about to experience it for themselves.

As if timetabled, Southwood's AI computer forecast a gravitational pressure point anomaly for the next day, precisely at 9:00 a.m., Argentina time . The two-AI computer configuration had been shared with all sites and had just been implemented in Argentina. The local Merlin was sceptical about the new system's necessity but accepted that orders were orders. All Vilin centres had identical equipment, and technicians enjoyed the same training. There should be no mistakes, except for the ongoing situation of The Hague now receiving all Dragonfly transmissions.

In Hobart, Steve was alerted to the Argentine activity scheduled for 9:00 a.m. the next day, 10:00 p.m. locally.

'We can only watch and wait, Jack,' he said. 'My people will keep me updated.'

The next day was a respite from the recent excitement. Steve was sporadically occupied with phone calls and video meetings, and Jack spent hours with his stamp collection. An afternoon stroll to the post office resulted in more stamps from various online sellers. Coffee and meals broke the day at the appropriate times.

'We're like an old retired couple,' Steve joked, 'relaxing in our remaining years and doing bugger all. Pleasant as this is, I've got a feeling it's all going to change pretty soon.'

Southwood dispatched several drones to the designated area of the salt flats where *el evento*, the event, was expected to take place. The technicians were eager to see how the ground surface would react. The 9:00 a.m. scheduled time was almost perfect. Instruments detected underground anomalies a few minutes beforehand. From 09:03, Dragonfly, which had reached its self-programmed position an hour before, began *alimentación*, feeding.

The drones produced footage of a remarkable occurrence on the flat surface of salt. Only a few centimetres thick and formed into a tessellated pattern, over several hundred square metres, each segment began vibrating, the edges breaking off. Roughly disk-shaped, they started rotating and gradually disintegrated. The separated salt crystals formed a pulsating mist, clearing occasionally to reveal the super-salted turquoise groundwater. When *el evento* concluded, after just 60 minutes, the suspended salt crystals fell back to their watery home. In a day, there would be no evidence that anything unusual had occurred. When reviewed later, the video also showed a group of Qulla people observing from a distance. Two black dogs appeared to run away.

The Southwood technicians celebrated their contribution to the occasion, and Dragonfly changed its 40,000-kilometre orbit. It was soon over a gas turbine power plant in Maravilla Province. As with England's Bridsal-on-Slade installation, the authorities willingly accepted Southwood's offer of free electricity. However, the smooth energy harvesting from Salinas Grandes was not replicated with a faultless transfer to the nearby power station.

Southwood's AI computers, called Brián and Sofía locally, had failed to calculate the impact of a secondary energy grid event during Dragonfly's transmission to the ground. Its target was missed by a fraction of a degree and only briefly. The incorrect calibration was rectified, but not before hundreds of sheep and several horses were killed. The radiative wireless energy transmission technique was not immune to interruption.

Argentina's news services also reported an unexplained shutdown of TV and radio transmissions in parts of the country. Thousands of households and businesses suffered safety switches being tripped for no apparent reason. Its technicians concluded this was due to variations in Earth's magnetic field, a partial geomagnetic field polarity movement. Senior Southwood scientists confessed they 'weren't expecting this till next year.' Despite the power station otherwise successfully receiving its electricity, this time, Southwood sent no glowing statement to anyone.

The Argentine Mr Southwood demanded an explanation of the AI computer malfunction. His Merlin, *Esmerejón*, was ready for that demand. His analysis was that both computers had allocated the role of monitoring synchronous energy grid events to the other. Neither had accepted the role and, in Merlin's words, were sulking and refused to discuss the matter.

Mr Southwood was silent for 30 seconds before saying he would recommend that each Vilin facility restore the previous AI system and use only one AI computer. He neglected to say which one.

In the UK and Argentina, a handful of investors started selling shares in energy companies. Southwood was buying put options and warrants, betting on share prices falling further. The organisation's finance people anticipated spectacular profits as the program was rolled out. A video meeting of Southwood's senior people, having seen the result of two demonstrations, approved unanimously to proceed with full implementation. The Argentine calibration issue was glossed over and identified, vaguely, as 'a technical issue since resolved.' The conference concluded with a bizarre statement from the most senior man: 'The illusion is almost complete.'

◆

Jack was at a loss. He had nothing to do after the Domain facility raid and Mr Southwood's departure. Steve had effectively taken over the local role, though both were glad to have the other as a sounding board, discussing possibilities and theories. A late email to Steve from his Melbourne counterpart gave them plenty to discuss. He summarised the English and Argentine events for Jack's benefit.

'This whole Southwood thing has moved on. Basically, the cost of that free lunch just went up, big time. Southwood's technology can be weaponised. Maybe already has been. We're still reading their Dragonfly transmissions. No evidence yet, but the writing's on the wall. We're liaising with MI40, and the thinking is that there's a weapon out there.'

'Wait, MI40, remind me,' Jack interrupted.

'Right, not many people know about it. First World War. Originally housed in Admiralty Room 40. They don't work with MI5 or 6 but are friendly with the armed forces. That might come in useful for us. They didn't want to play nicely at first, but we've been sharing the Dragonfly data, and they're very chummy now.

'While we're on the subject, my people have brought in the Americans. A bit late, but they couldn't decide which organisation had jurisdiction. Turns out no one really, but the NSA – that's their National Security Agency – is working with the DHS – Department of Homeland Security. Probably formed some kind of committee, you know what these organisations are like. NASA's in the mix, too, I reckon. Everyone's getting the same info we're sending the Brits. By the way, have you heard from your mate Leon recently?'

As if on cue, within seconds Jack took a call from Leon, who seemed to have left the game.

'G'day, Jack, sorry I've been away, did you miss me?'

'Not a bit, you never were very useful anyway,' Jack joked. 'But I'm glad you called. It's good to hear from you. Tell Lyn her warning about the tall man was spot on. Our latest exploit could have come a cropper.'

He neglected to tell Leon that it was a 'just in the nick of time' situation, and briefed him on the raid.

'I'll tell her,' Leon said. 'And here's something else, are you planning to fly anywhere soon? Well, don't. Lyn says there's going to be a problem with a plane. No details, it's all up in the air, if you'll pardon the pun.'

◆

For four days, Southwood took advantage of opportunities and introduced its version of free electricity to three countries in Southeast Asia, the Middle East, and North Africa. The value of traditional power generation facilities declined, as did the share prices of publicly owned companies. The future of the global fossil fuel industry seemed precarious. The trickle-down consequences were being evaluated closely. Those who benefited from free electricity were delighted, and environmentalists were thrilled. Investors and employees were less impressed.

Southwood's substantial investment in the Dragonfly program was paying off. Returns from shorting investments on the world's share markets reaped massive profits. At another worldwide video meeting of the organisation, its leaders were informed of the millions made daily. There was no reason to think their profits wouldn't continue for many months.

Most of the meeting participants were nodding appreciatively. That nodding stopped with the next statement.

'We are a business, just like any other commercial enterprise. Where we differ is our methodology and our vision of the future. We've seen living standards decline. The world has watched but done nothing. The degradation of agriculture is the key marker. The world's population is too big. It's as simple as that. We will rectify that. We can no longer produce enough food for the number of people on our planet. We can't make Earth bigger, but we can redress the other end of the equation. If you can't solve a problem, eliminate it.

'To that end, we conducted a small test in North Africa. As far as the world is concerned, it was a tragic accident. Losses are estimated to have been 80,000 people, but the media put it higher. More newsworthy if it's six figures. It'll be forgotten in a few days. These people were some of the world's poorest. They won't be missed.'

A few people shifted in their chairs, uncomfortable with what they were hearing. Over its history, Southwood periodically changed its views of society depending on prevailing attitudes and sensibilities. The members present, for the most part, acknowledged the organisation's priority. Financial gain was the number one element of its corporate policy statement, unwritten as it was. No one knew anyone in North Africa anyway.

'To save society,' the chairman continued, 'a percentage of that society must be sacrificed. Population reduction by attrition would be too slow. Faster means have been devised. Development of it has been our most secretive project, and the few deemed worthy of knowing have been told only half the story. The energy control element is genuine and will allow Southwood to dominate the world's energy production.'

Clumsily named but frightening, reducing the world's population was called Thinning the Herd, a more palatable reference than genocide. Southwood would gradually reveal the program to a broader audience. Management thought most of that audience would accept it as necessary. They could assuage any sense of guilt with whatever level of noisy reluctance they decided to present. Ultimately, knowing their own lives were safe would be a significant factor. Zero-risk bias was alive and well in Southwood. Value need only be perceived to be accepted.

The world would be a better place with the organisation's efforts, and it would be one of the wealthiest organisations in that world. Already, a few of the 'less important' governments had been sounded out and, in general terms, were briefed on Southwood's intentions. It was suggested that if you supported Thinning the Herd, something was wrong with your heart; if you opposed it, something was wrong with your head. The Chairman concluded his delivery with a curiously ambiguous statement: 'We've come a long way since the Club of Berlin days.'

The video conference was held in the same room as the one hacked into by, they thought, Brother Ringo nearly a fortnight before. The security man overseeing today's assembly, Keeper of the Silence, assured his superior that hacking was no longer possible. He explained to Mr Southwood that logins were now subject to encrypted two-step verification, and both steps were processed through Dragonfly. The meeting's sound and vision were also transmitted from space, the 10 satellites acting as repeaters.

'As safe as you can get,' he claimed, little knowing that Brother Ringo's efforts with Dragonfly's software made the conference as private as a public broadcaster. The Hague was listening and watching.

Despite Keeper's assurance, Brother Ringo was also watching and had to restrain himself from posting embarrassing questions on Lisbon's monitor.

◆

The Southwood revelation stimulated frenzied action in the ranks of all Jack's allies, as he now saw them: MI40, the NSA, the DHS, NASA, and their equivalent agencies in other countries. Lesser staff were stunned and amused to see high-ranking officials running between offices when they couldn't contact someone by phone. The situation was firmly in quadrant one of everyone's Urgent-Important Matrix, and the more OCD operatives put it in their own sub-quadrant one of that square as a measure of its status.

Steve was kept informed with regular communications from his Melbourne office. When asked whether he should 'return to base', he was told 'stay put.'

'Looks like I'm here for a while longer,' he told Jack. 'I can move back to my hotel if you…'

'No, no. I can tolerate your company if you can put up with mine,' Jack retorted. 'Besides, I've just been sent a spectacular 25-year-old single malt. Needs to be shared, and I know you appreciate these things.'

'25 years? All right, if you insist. I'll stay. That stuff'll give you superpowers.'

Jack grinned. 'I don't need superpowers; I've got two library cards.'

'Is that it?'

'I can moonwalk forwards, understand the offside rule, and do origami with pastry. Oh, and squirrels trust me,'

Steve threw a curve ball, 'You ever been married, Jack?'

'I was engaged once, years ago. Sandy. She died.'

'Sorry to hear that, mate.'

'Electrocuted by a karaoke machine. She was singing *I Will Survive*.'

Jack's grin gave the joke away.

He continued, 'No, never married, never engaged, never interested in all that settling down raising a family stuff. The way I see it, without kids, no mess, no stress. Most children are hideous little creatures. I've always been one of life's outsiders, a non-participating observer. You see more when you're not involved. What about you?'

Steve confessed he held much the same view, but his career didn't fit the family lifestyle anyway. Changing the subject, the two friends commiserated that they seemed to be doing nothing to assist the now worldwide threat from Southwood, in particular, bringing someone to justice for the killing of 80,000 people. Jack pondered his role in bringing Southwood into the open. That role had now been taken over by bigger players. His personal ambition was now to avenge the death of his parents all those years ago. The individuals responsible were probably impossible to identify now, let alone locate. As much as he hated the expression, he wanted 'closure'. How that would be achieved was a burning question.

Steve's phone played a standard call theme. It was one of his local colleagues who had been shadowing Mr Southwood when he vanished.

'Hang on, I'm with Jack. I'll put you on speaker. Go on.'

'Your Mr Southwood, who we thought left the state under the radar. Well, he hadn't. Seems he was hiding out with one of his liaison people. You'll catch some of this on the news, but only some. Seems he chartered a light plane at a private airfield on the east coast. He used another name, but he has a licence. There were no passengers. Flight plan listed an arrival point near Geelong.

'Here's the thing though. His route was over the water, not direct, so we think he intended to land further north in Tassie. He'd only been in the air for 10 minutes when there was a mayday call. He crashed into the sea a minute later, close to the coast. Some fishermen saw it all happen, and they were on the scene pretty quick, but the plane sank before they got to it. No survivor. Our Mr Southwood is a goner, for sure. That was early this morning. There ought to be more information by now. Check out the TV news.'

That evening, the 7:00 p.m. news did provide more detail. In summary, an interstate visitor, Greg Fischer, had paid a 'sum of money' to the local owner of a Cessna to hire his single-engined plane for three days. A flight plan to Geelong was logged correctly, but Fischer took a curious route up the east coast of Tasmania, where the aircraft struck trouble. The pilot's mayday call didn't specify his problem, only that he would attempt an emergency landing on a beach. According to nearby fishermen, the plane briefly changed direction towards land but spiralled into the sea, hitting the surface at about 45 degrees. By the time they reached the location, nothing was to be seen except a few pieces of wreckage. It was thought unlikely that the pilot could have survived. Search and Rescue divers would scour the sea floor tomorrow. The plane was at a depth of between 100 and 150 feet. There was no mention of the name Southwood.

'That must be the end of that particular Mr Southwood,' Steve suggested. 'Fischer with a "C", that's a German spelling, isn't it? Handy to have subtitles on your news.'

Jack rather sombrely revealed that he would consider Fischer's demise as vengeance for his parents' deaths in 1996, although he would rather have had a closer role in it. The pair discussed the possibility of a replacement being sent to Hobart, but they decided it was unlikely. Whatever Mr Southwood's function was locally, his departure suggested it had concluded. However, the Domain facility remained and was still operational. Higher authorities would have to deal with that.

'Cause of death: gravity? Basically.' Steve asked, trying to lighten the mood but sounding macabre rather than humorous.

Jack returned from his introspection. 'That's right, Steve, that is correct, ain't no use saying it isn't. I'd like to know what went wrong with the plane. Now then, hands up if you're hungry. A man's death is no reason to celebrate, but needs must as the devil farts, or whatever the saying is. What day is it? I've lost track. OK, the Blue Café has Cameron in the kitchen tonight. He's better with bacon butties than soufflés. Does a decent steak, though, and they're BYO. For me anyway.'

Steve corrected the expression to 'devil drives' and agreed that a steak sounded good. The café was sparsely populated, and their custom was more appreciated for that.

'A table for two and four Bordeaux glasses, please, Angie. No need for the menu. Two scotch fillet steaks, one medium-rare, pepper sauce, chips and salad, the other…'

'Same for me,' Steve completed the order.

Angie took the order to the kitchen and returned with four glasses. She expertly opened the bottle with her waiter's friend corkscrew, then admired the label of Jack's chosen wine, a 2015 third-growth Margaux. He asked about her legal studies as he poured four glasses and gently manoeuvred two towards the waitress.

'One for you and one for Cameron,' Jack explained.

Angie returned to the kitchen, where the chef promptly selected two larger steaks. He appeared at the door and raised his glass to Jack and Steve, who returned the salute. There would be no corkage on their bill tonight.

'Better than a tip, usually,' Jack said to Steve.

As the pair enjoyed their meal, events unfolded that they would not hear about for hours.

The Hague's efforts coordinating the largest-ever array of radio telescopes had resulted in the Dragonfly satellite being located. It was being tracked by the most sophisticated international cooperation achieved in space exploration. What was now regarded as Southwood's weapon was no longer invisible. All that remained was to destroy it. One military strategist suggested that might only happen when a donkey climbs a tree. No missiles could reach it, and everyone denied the existence of 'Star Wars weaponry'. A minor technician in one of the world's smaller space agencies asked if anyone had a 'disposable' satellite they could use to crash into Dragonfly.

Initially, no one came forward, but Britain conceded it had a mapping satellite nearing its end of life. They suggested, however, that Dragonfly might have anti-collision mechanisms in place, so a direct impact would be difficult to achieve. By chance, the satellite they had in mind had a self-destruct mechanism on board which, if detonated nearby, would damage, if not destroy the target.

The Hague accepted Britain's offer. Within an hour, its satellite's trajectory had been recalibrated, and the self-destruct module reprogrammed to DOC, detonation on command. In the silence of space, one small satellite boldly emblazoned with a Union Jack started its final mission. Satellite MS9 had enough power and propulsion fuel for only one attempt. Computer calculation indicated interception would take four hours, and then only if Dragonfly stayed in its current position.

When MS9 left its familiar orbit, Jack and Steve were enjoying dessert, sticky date pudding with butterscotch sauce. Having shared their bottle of wine, there was nothing to be done now but return to the host's apartment and open another. Steve was briefed on Britain's plan with MS9.

'I wish we could watch it on TV,' Jack said.

The exercise was coordinated from London. A Hague operator programmed what she called an enhanced progressive virtual image from radio telescopes as they moved into scanning positions. Dozens of radio signals, only seconds apart, revealed Dragonfly's location by the absence of space noise. The combined sound files were converted to a single visual representation.

'Well, as it happens, you can watch it on TV,' Steve said, 'Hand me the remote. I can cast this feed to your set.'

A few minutes later, Jack's 75-inch TV displayed an eerie black shape on a background of visual static. The black shape was simply the entire scene with the background noise blocked. This was Dragonfly, the first time anyone outside Southwood had seen it, although it was only a virtual representation. The elongated body and four giant wings made its name appropriate. A running commentary by technicians appeared along the bottom of the screen.

Jack and Steve sat engrossed in this strange entertainment, glasses of wine at hand. The commentary was only intermittent but was supplemented by scrolling data, primarily technical. A distance-to-target figure revealed 2,000 miles and was reducing rapidly.

'Trust the Brits to use miles,' Jack said, 'This might be a two-bottle wait.'

A metallic voice announced, '1,500 miles.'

Jack pondered his contented circumstances and considered what might happen if this experiment failed.

'900 miles.'

'What if this doesn't work?' he asked.

Steve didn't answer. They sat in silence, watching the changing graphic.

'200 miles. Self-destruct activated.'

'100 miles.'

At a Southwood facility, an alarm sounded. It was Dragonfly's proximity alert warning. Supervisor announced that on-board monitoring would initiate avoidance measures if required.

The scrolling commentary resumed. 'Optimal distance to detonation is 400 yards at approach.'

'20 miles. Self-destruct available on command.' Someone had the unenviable job of deciding when to press the red button.

At one mile, the distance displayed changed to 1,760 yards and counted down in five-yard intervals.

Dragonfly's altitude changed slightly.

'800 yards, 700 yards, 600 yards.'

'Farewell MS9,' a technician said, flipping the perspex cover from his red button.

'500 yards.'

His finger hovered.

'400 yards.'

The red button went down with a satisfying click.

The commentary recommenced. 'Detonation successful. Reviewing imagery.'

From 40,000 kilometres, Dragonfly had reduced altitude slightly, but enough to avoid all of MS9's shrapnel. The plan had failed.

It took a few minutes for observers to conclude that the target remained undamaged. The danger remained. Those same observers were still reading Southwood's communications from Dragonfly. Brother Ringo's little trick was still in place and undiscovered. The proximity alert had terminated, and a message from an unknown technician read, 'Collision avoided, seemed to be a rogue satellite. Returning to standard altitude.' Southwood seemed to be unaware of MS9's explosive sacrifice. Another message appeared, 'Altitude control malfunction. No response to command. Initiating remedial measures. Stand by.'

Jack's television continued its display of space noise with the black stencil of Dragonfly. Steve leaned forward, pointing at the screen.

'Altitude. Look at the altitude. It was a steady 40,000. Now, look, 39,800 and falling. What are they up to now?'

In a Southwood facility, technicians frantically transmitted commands to their satellite which steadfastly refused to respond. The local Supervisor took over and sent a reboot override directive. That would take a minute to process. In the meantime, the altitude reading maintained its steady decline. Around the world, Southwood and Hague personnel watched their monitors, mostly in silence. Somewhere, the man known as Brother Ringo also watched. It was the second part of his ghost-coding doing the damage. He knew, though no one else did, that Southwood had lost control of Dragonfly.

Brother Ringo's confidence in Southwood's intentions had been shaky, and the North Africa test, with so much loss of life, was Southwood's undoing. The Dragonfly satellite was now in a slow freefall. It would start to burn up in the mesosphere, about 80 kilometres above the Earth's surface. Eventually, it would crash into the Pacific Ocean, dismembered into a thousand fragments. The display would be spectacular.

Southwood and The Hague received a statement: 'Black Knight is dead. R.I.P. – Brother Ringo.'

Jack opened his 25-year-old single malt and poured 'two fingers of sippin' whisky' into crystal tumblers. While he and Steve enjoyed their celebratory drink, Southwood desperately, though ultimately futilely, attempted to regain control. It would take two days, but the organisation would stoically admit defeat and dismantle its Dragonfly infrastructure. Their VIV centres would become 100 per cent whatever each cover operation was. It had, inadvertently, endowed considerable benefit to several countries, if only briefly.

But Southwood remained, now quiet, invisible and unassailable.

Steve raised his glass and toasted, 'Peace in our time,' but more as a question than statement.

Jack responded, 'As my mother used to say when I was probably wrong, "I'm sure you're right."'

◆

Epilogue

'You won't like it.'

A week later, Dragonfly's re-entry created a 'meteor shower' unsurpassed in recent years. Residents and visitors of the Hawaiian Islands were treated to a magnificent display, little knowing the avoided danger it represented.

On one restful day, Jack managed to track down Stan Wright, the police officer who provided the documents his father had produced. Stan had long since retired and was living comfortably, with his wife and two cats, in a country town in Victoria. He was soon to receive a long letter from Jack.

Jack put on a party in his apartment. Sarah helped with the organisation, booking catering and hiring a bartender. She arrived with D.I. Sayer – again 'Terry' to Jack, their friendship resumed – soon followed by Leon and Lyn, hand in hand. Harry Steve John 'Trousers' arrived with a laptop at hand. Ric, Keith, Jimi, Sam and Frank trickled in through the evening. Steve flew back from Melbourne, not wanting to miss the full stop at the end of this adventure.

Jack gave a brief speech thanking and congratulating everyone for their contribution in bringing Southwood to heel.

He concluded with: 'The organisation, Steve tells me, has retreated into obscurity and now exists only vaguely, *obscurum per obscurius,* you might say, obscured by something more obscure. Now eat and drink. This is a celebration. And don't talk to me about Southwood or Dragonfly tonight. I'm as deaf as a post office. Starting tomorrow, I'll be busy with the first draft of *Dark History*. Or maybe I'll republish *Dyp Strøm* first.'

The post office reference reminded Terry of something. 'I got mail from Canada today. Your stuff, I reckon. Do you need it?'

Jack smiled, 'Ah yes, I posted a memory card with my *Dark History* drafts and other stuff on it. To a friend in England, who posted it to someone in Singapore, then to Canada, then to a certain Detective Inspector Sayer. But no thanks. My records survived this business, much expanded as it happens. I've got more work to do on my book now.'

Harry's phone pinged, and he read a lengthy email.

'Jack, remember that Dragonfly blog?'

'As if I could forget.'

'Looks like someone's revived it. Active too. Run by the same bloke judging by the style.'

Jack was intrigued.

'OK, anything I should know about?'

'Two words keep cropping up. Dragonfly is the first, but no surprise there.'

'And the other?' Jack asked.

'Cerberus. That's a Navy ship. Or a base somewhere?'

'Both. But it's also the name of the guard dog to the underworld. There's your mythology again. It had three heads. I hope it's not some obscure allusion to three parts of this Southwood crowd. Anything else?'

'Yep. You won't like it,' Harry said.

'Go on.'

'Several references to Northwood.'

'Bugger.'

◆　◆

Acknowledgements

My thanks for their invaluable assistance in the publication of *Dragonfly Illusion* go to...

- Di Bond – beta reader, tea and sympathy
- Evy Richardson – beta reader
- Kat Richardson (www.peskyploverstudio.com) – editor
- Graham Himmelhoch-Mutton – support and encouragement.

... and especially heartfelt gratitude to my wife, Di, for her remarkable patience and unwavering support through my countless hours of writing, rewriting, editing, and all the hazy in-between moments of bringing this book into the light.

◆

Jack Sugarman will return in

Dragonfly Shadow

2026

The Author

Born in Essex, England, in 1955, Peter Bond joined a family already shaped by hardship and resilience. His family's early years were marked by tragedies, including the devastating North Sea flood of 1953, a disaster that influenced his family to seek a new beginning on distant shores. After some delays, they emigrated to Australia in 1958, settling in tranquil Tasmania.

Throughout his adult life, Peter navigated the changing landscapes of city and suburban life, living at 21 addresses in and around Hobart. Now retired, he shares a peaceful existence with his wife, Dianne (Di), in a serene semi-rural setting, embracing the quietude he has long cherished.

Peter's literary journey began early. A capable student in English subjects, he ventured into writing and publishing in 1973. Inspired by the dissolution of the official Beatles Fan Club, he established the (Australian) Beatles Appreciation Society, publishing a bimonthly newsletter/magazine. This endeavour lasted until 1976, marking a later dedication to writing and publishing.

Born Peter Mutton, he changed his name to Peter Bond in 1996, having briefly revelled in the name Lord Peter St John Gordon-Bennett.

His love for stamp collecting, an interest that took root at age six, eventually intertwined with his writing. Over the years, Peter's expertise in philately saw his work appear in many stamp collecting magazines, including *Australian Stamps Professional*.

Serious publishing took on a new dimension in 2012 with the release of *The Spice of Life*, a paperback edition of his father's memoirs. This marked the inception of Scribbled Lines Publishing, his own imprint. After 46 years of service in the Australian Commonwealth and Tasmanian state public sectors, he retired in 2018, turning his attention fully to his literary pursuits. He now publishes under his full name, Peter James Bond.

9 780648 771388